INHERITOR OF THE STARS

When James P. Hogan's first novel was published in 1977, Isaac Asimov heralded the debut of a new star: "*Inherit the Stars* is pure science fiction...Arthur Clarke move over!"

Now with the publication of Hogan's big new novel, Arthur C. Clarke concedes: "Much though it hurts me to say so, Isaac, you are right. Welcome, Jim Hogan, to the hardcore science-fiction club."

IN THIS EXTRAORDINARY NOVEL OF SCIENCE, POLITICS, AND RELIGION, JAMES P. HOGAN ENTERTAININGLY TAKES ON THE AGE-OLD QUESTIONS OF PHILOSOPHY—SUCH AS WHAT IS MAN? WHERE DOES HE COME FROM? AND TO WHOM DOES HE OWE ALLEGIANCE? THEN HE TURNS THEM ON END AND COMES UP WITH SOME SURPRISING CONCLUSIONS.

By James P. Hogan
Published by Ballantine Books:

THE GIANTS' TRILOGY
Book One: Inherit the Stars
Book Two: The Gentle Giants of Ganymede
Book Three: Giants' Star

THE GENESIS MACHINE
THRICE UPON A TIME
THE TWO FACES OF TOMORROW
VOYAGE FROM YESTERYEAR
CODE OF THE LIFEMAKER

CODE OF THE LIFE MAKER

a novel by

James P. Hogan

A Del Rey Book

BALLANTINE BOOKS • NEW YORK

A Del Rey Book
Published by Ballantine Books

Library of Congress Catalog Card Number: 82-22676

ISBN 0-345-30549-3

Manufactured in the United States of America

First Hardcover Edition: June 1983
First Paperback Edition: June 1984

Cover art by David B. Mattingly

To IRIS, and long overdue

Prologue

THE SEARCHER

1.1 MILLION YEARS B.C.; 1,000 LIGHT-YEARS FROM THE SOLAR SYSTEM

HAD ENGLISH-SPEAKING HUMANS EXISTED, THEY would probably have translated the spacecraft's designation as "searcher." Unmanned, it was almost a mile long, streamlined for descent through planetary atmospheres, and it operated fully under the control of computers. The alien civilization was an advanced one, and the computers were very sophisticated.

The planet at which the searcher arrived after a voyage of many years was the fourth in the system of a star named after the king of a mythical race of alien gods, and could appropriately be called Zeus IV. It wasn't much to look at—an airless, lifeless ball of eroded rock formations, a lot of boulders and debris from ancient meteorite impacts, and vast areas of volcanic ash and dust—but the searcher's orbital probes and surface landers found a crust rich in titanium, chromium, cobalt, copper, manganese, uranium, and many other valuable elements concentrated by thermal-fluidic processes operating early in the planet's history. Such a natural abundance of metals could support large-scale production without extensive dependence on bulk nuclear transmutation processes—in other words, very economically—and that was precisely the kind of thing that the searcher had been designed to search for. After completing their analysis of the preliminary data, the control computers selected a landing site, composed and transmitted a message home to report their findings and announce their intentions, and then activated the vessel's descent routine.

Shortly after the landing, a menagerie of surveyor robots, equipped with imagers, spectrometers, analyzers, chemical sensors, rock samplers, radiation monitors, and various manipulator appendages, emerged from the ship and dispersed across the surrounding terrain to investigate surface features selected from orbit. Their findings were transmitted back to the ship and processed, and shortly afterward follow-up teams of tracked, legged, and wheeled mining, drilling, and transportation robots went out to begin feeding ores and other materials back to where more machines had begun to build a fusion-powered pilot extraction plant. A parts-making facility was constructed next, followed by a parts-assembly facility, and step by step the pilot plant grew itself into a fully equipped, general-purpose factory, complete with its own control computers. The master programs from the ship's computers were copied into the factory's computers, which thereupon became self-sufficient and assumed control of surface operations. The factory then began making more robots.

Sometimes, of course, things failed to work exactly as intended, but the alien engineers had created their own counterpart of Murphy and allowed for his law in their plans. Maintenance robots took care of breakdowns and routine wear and tear in the factory; troubleshooting programs tracked down causes of production rejects and adjusted the machines for drifting tolerances; breakdown teams brought in malfunctioning machines for repair; and specialized scavenging robots roamed the surface in search of wrecks, write-offs, discarded components, and any other likely sources of parts suitable for recycling.

Time passed, the factory hummed, and the robot population grew in number and variety. When the population had attained a critical size, a mixed workforce detached itself from the main center of activity and migrated a few miles away to build a second factory, a replica of the first, using materials supplied initially from Factory One. When

Factory Two became self-sustaining, Factory One, its primary task accomplished, switched to mass-production mode, producing goods and materials for eventual shipment to the alien home planet.

While Factory Two was repeating the process by commencing work on Factory Three, the labor detail from Factory One picked up its tools and moved on to begin Factory Four. By the time Factory Four was up and running, Factories Five through Eight were already taking shape, Factory Two was in mass-production mode, and Factory Three was building the first of a fleet of cargo vessels to carry home the products being stockpiled. This self-replicating pattern would spread rapidly to transform the entire surface of Zeus IV into a totally automated manufacturing complex dedicated to supplying the distant alien civilization from local resources.

From within the searcher's control computers, the Supervisor program gazed out at the scene through its data input channels and saw that its work was good. After a thorough overhaul and systems checkout, the searcher ship reembarked its primary workforce and launched itself into space to seek more worlds on which to repeat the cycle.

FIFTY YEARS LATER

Not far—as galactic distances go—from Zeus was another star, a hot, bluish white star with a mass of over fifteen times that of the Sun. It had formed rapidly, and its life span—the temporary halt of its collapse under self-gravitation by thermonuclear radiation pressure—had demanded such a prodigious output of energy as to be a brief one. In only ten million years the star, which had converted all the hydrogen in its outer shell to helium, resumed its collapse until the core temperature was high enough to burn the helium into carbon, and then, when the helium was exhausted, repeated the process to begin burning carbon. The ignition of carbon raised the core temperature higher still, which induced a higher rate of carbon burning, which in turn heated the core even more, and a thermonuclear runaway set in which in terms of stellar timescales was instantaneous. In mere days the star erupted into a supernova—radiating with a billion times the brightness of the Sun, exploding outward until its photosphere enclosed a radius greater than that of Uranus' orbit, and devouring its tiny flock of planets in the process.

Those planets had been next on the searcher's list to investigate, and it happened that the ship was heading into its final approach when the star exploded. The radiation blast hit it head-on at three billion miles out.

The searcher's hull survived more-or-less intact, but secondary x-rays and high-energy subnuclear particles—things distinctly unhealthy for computers—flooded its interior. With most of its primary sensors burned out, its navigation system disrupted, and many of its programs obliterated or altered, the searcher veered away and disappeared back into the depths of interstellar space.

One of the faint specks lying in the direction now ahead of the ship was a yellow-white dwarf star, a thousand light-years away. It too possessed a family of planets, and on the third of those planets the descendants of a species of semi-intelligent ape had tamed fire and were beginning to experiment with tools chipped laboriously from thin flakes of stone.

Supernovas are comparatively rare events, occurring with a frequency of perhaps two or three per year in the average galaxy. But as with most generalizations, this has occasional exceptions. The supernova that almost enveloped the searcher turned out to be the first of a small chain that rippled through a localized cluster of massive stars formed at roughly the same time. Located in the middle of the cluster was a normal, longer-lived star which happened to be the home star of the aliens. The aliens had never gotten round to extending their civilization much beyond the limits of their own planetary system, which was unfortunate because that was the end of them.

Everybody has a bad day sometimes.

ONE MILLION YEARS B.C.

One hundred thousand years after being scorched by the supernova, the searcher drifted into the outer regions of a planetary system. With its high-altitude surveillance instruments only partly functioning and its probes unable to deploy at all, the ship went directly into its descent routine over the first sizeable body that it encountered, a frozen ball of ice-encrusted rock about three thousand miles in diameter, with seas of liquid methane and an atmosphere of nitrogen, hydrogen, and methane vapor. The world came nowhere near meeting the criteria for worthwhile exploitation, but that was of no consequence since the computer programs responsible for surface analysis and evaluation weren't working.

The programs to initiate surface activity did work, however, more or less, and Factory One, with all of its essential functions up and running to at least some degree, was duly built on a rocky shelf above an ice beach flanking an inlet of a shallow methane sea. The ship's master programs were copied across into the newly installed factory computers, which identified the commencement of work on Factory Two as their first assignment. Accordingly Factory One's Supervisor program signaled the ship's databank for a copy of the "How to Make a Factory" file, which included a set of subfiles on "How to Make the Machines Needed to Make a Factory," i.e., robots. And that was where everything really started to go wrong.

The robots contained small internal processors that could be reprogramed via radiolink from the factory computers for each new task to be accomplished. This allowed the robots to proceed with their various jobs under autonomous local control and freed up the central computers for other work while they were waiting for the next "Done that—what do I do now?" signal. Hence many software mechanisms existed for initiating data transfers between the factory computers and the remote processors inside the robots.

When the copying of the "How to Make a Factory" file from the ship to Factory One was attempted, the wrong software linkages were activated; instead of finding their way into the factory's central system, the subfiles containing the manufacturing information for the various robots were merely relayed through the factory and beamed out into the local memories of the respective robot types to which they pertained. No copies at all were retained in the factory databank. And even worse, the originals inside the ship managed to self-destruct in the process and were irretrievably erased. The only copies of the "How to Make a Fred-type Robot" subfile were the ones contained inside the Fred-types out on the surface. And the same was true for all the other types as well.

So when the factory's Supervisor program ordered the Scheduler program to schedule more robots for manufacture, and the Scheduler lodged a request with the Databank Manager for the relevant subfiles, the Databank Manager found that it couldn't deliver. Neither could it obtain a recopy from the ship. The Databank Manager reported the problem to the Scheduler; the Scheduler complained to the Supervisor; the Supervisor blamed the Communications Manager; the Communications Manager demanded an explanation from the Message Handler; and after a lot of mutual electronic recriminations and accusations, the system logging and diagnostic programs determined that the missing subfiles had last been tracked streaming out through the transmission buffers on their way to the robots outside. Under a stern directive from the Supervisor, the Communications Manager selected a Fred from the first category of robots called for on the Scheduler's list, and beamed it a message telling it to send its subfile back again.

But the Fred didn't have a complete copy of the subfile; its local memory simply hadn't been big enough to hold all of it. And for the same reason, none of the other Freds could return a full copy either. They had been sprayed in succession with the datastream like buckets being filled from a fire-hose, and all had ended up with different portions of the subfile; but they appeared to have preserved the whole subfile among them. So the Supervisor had to retrieve different pieces from different Freds to fit them together again in a way that made sense. And that was how it arrived at the version it eventually handed to the Scheduler for manufacture.

Unfortunately, the instruction to store the information for future reference got lost somewhere, and for each batch of Freds the relevant "How to Make" subfile was promptly erased as soon as the Manufacturing Manager had finished with it. Hence when Factory One had spent some time producing parts for Factory Two and needed to expand its robot workforce to begin surveying sites for Factory Three, the Supervisor had to go through the whole rigmarole again. And the same process was necessary whenever a new run was scheduled to provide replacements for robots that had broken down or were wearing out.

All of this took up excessive amounts of processor time, loaded up the communications channels, and was generally inefficient in the ways that cost accountants worry about. The alien programers had been suitably indoctrinated by the alien cost accountants who ran the business—as always—and had written the Supervisor as a flexible, self-modifying learning program that would detect such inefficiencies, grow unhappy about them, and seek ways to improve things. After a few trials, the Supervisor found that some of the Freds contained about half their respective subfiles, which meant that a complete copy could be obtained by interrogating just two individuals instead of many. Accordingly it made a note of such "matching pairs" and began selecting them as its source for repeat requests from the Scheduler, ignoring the others.

Lost along with the original "How to Make a Fred" subfiles were the subsubfiles on "Programs to Write into a Fred to Start It Up after You've Made It." To make up for the deficiency, the Supervisor copied through to the

Scheduler the full set of programs that it found already existing in the Freds selected to provide reproduction information, and these programs, of course, included the ones on how to make Freds. Thus the robots began coming off the line with one-half of their "genetic" information automatically built in, and a cycle asserted itself whereby they in turn became the source of information to be recombined later for producing more Freds. The method worked, and the Supervisor never figured out that it could have saved itself a lot of trouble by storing the blueprints away once and for all in the factory databank.

The program segments being recombined in this way frequently failed to copy faithfully, and the "genomes" formed from them were seldom identical, some having portions of code omitted while others had portions duplicated. Consequently Freds started taking on strange shapes and behaving in strange ways.

Some didn't exhibit any behavior at all but simply fell over or failed during test, to be broken down into parts again and recycled. A lot were like that.

Some, from the earlier phase, were genetically incomplete—"sterile"—and never called upon by the Supervisor to furnish reproductive data. They lasted until they broke down or wore out, and then became extinct.

Some reproduced passively, i.e., by transmitting their half-subfiles to the factory when the Scheduler asked for them.

A few, however, had inherited from the ship's software the program modules whose function was to lodge requests with the Scheduler to schedule more models of their own kind—program modules, moreover, which embodied a self-modifying priority structure capable of raising the urgency of their requests within the system until they were serviced. The robots in this category sought to reproduce actively: They behaved as if they experienced a compulsion to ensure that their half-subfiles were always included in the Scheduler's schedule of "Things to Make Next."

So when Factory One switched over to mass-production mode, the robots competing for slots in its product list soon grabbed all of the available memory space and caused the factory to become dedicated to churning out nothing else. When Factory Two went into operation under control of programs copied from Factory One, the same thing happened there. And the same cycle would be propagated to Factory Three, construction of which had by that time begun.

More factories appeared in a pattern spreading inland from the rocky coastal shelf. The instability inherent in the original parent software continued to manifest itself in the copies of copies of copies passed on to later generations, and the new factories, along with their mixed populations of robot progeny, diverged further in form and function.

Material resources were scarce almost everywhere, which resulted in the emergence of competitive pressures that the alien system designers had never intended. The factory-robot communities that happened to include a balanced mix of surveyor, procurement, and scavenger robots with "appetites" appropriate to their factories' needs, and which enjoyed favorable sites on the surface, usually managed to survive if not flourish. Factory Ten, for example, occupied the center of an ancient meteorite crater twelve miles across, where the heat and shock of the impact had exposed metal-bearing bedrock from below the ice; Factory Thirteen established itself inside a deep fissure where the ice beneath was relatively thin, and was able to melt a shaft down to the denser core material; and Factory Fifteen resorted to nuclear transmutation processes to build heavier nuclei from lighter ones frozen in solution in the ice crust. But many were like Factory Nineteen, which began to take shape on an ill-chosen spot far out on a bleak ice field, and ground to a halt when its deep-drilling robots and transmutation reactors failed to function, and its supply of vital materials ran out.

The scavenger and parts-salvaging robots assumed a crucial role in shaping the strange metabolism that was coming into being. Regardless of what the Schedulers in the various factories would have liked to see made, the only things that could be assembled readily were the ones for which parts were available, and that depended to a large degree on the ability of the scavengers to locate them, or alternatively to locate assemblies suitable for breaking down—"digesting"—and rebuilding into something useful. Factory Twenty-four was an extreme case. Unable to "metabolize" parts directly from any source of raw materials because of the complete failure of its materials-procurement workforce, it relied totally on its scavengers. Factory Thirty-two, on the other hand, could acquire raw materials but couldn't use them since it had been built without a processing facility at all. Its robots delivered instead to Forty-seven, which happened to produce parts for some of the scavengers being manufactured by Thirty-two, and the two factory-robot organisms managed to coexist happily in their bizarre form of symbiosis.

The piles of assorted junk, which shouldn't have accumulated from the earlier phases of the process but had, were eaten up; the machines that broke down were eaten up; and the carcasses of defunct factories were eaten up. When those sources of materials had been exhausted, some of the machines began to eat each other.

The scavengers had been designed, as they had to be, to discriminate between properly functioning machines and desirable products on the one hand and rejects in need of recycling on the other. However, as with everything else in the whole, messed-up project, this function worked well in some cases, not so well in others, and often not at all. Some of the models turned out to be as likely to attempt the dismantling of a live, walking-around Fred as of a dead, flat-on-its-back one. Many of the victims were indifferent to this kind of treatment and soon died out, but others succeeded in developing effective fight-or-flee responses to preserve themselves, thus marking the beginnings of specialized prey and predators in the form of "lithovores" and "artifactovores."

This development was not always an advantage, especially when the loss of discrimination was total. Factory

Fifty was consumed by its own offspring, who began dismantling it at its output end as soon as they came off the assembly line, and then proceeded proudly to deliver the pieces back to its input end. Its internal repair robots were unable to undo the undoings fast enough, and it ground to a halt to become plunder for marauders from Thirty-six and Fifty-three. The most successful factory-robot organisms protected themselves by evolving aggressive armies of "antibody" defenders, which would recognize their own factory and its "kind" and leave them alone, but attack and attempt to destroy any "foreign" models that ventured too close. This gradually became the dominant form of organism, usually associated with a distinct territory which its members cooperated in protecting collectively.

By this time only a few holes in the ground remained at opposite ends of the rocky shelf to mark where Factories One and Two had once stood. They had failed to keep up with the times, and the area had become the domain of Factory Sixty-five. The only trace left of the searcher spacecraft was a long, rounded depression in the ice beach below, on the shore of the liquid methane sea.

The alien engineers had designed the system to enjoy full planetary communications coverage by means of satellites and surface relays, but the idea hadn't worked too well since nothing had been put into orbit and surface relays tended not to last very long. This enabled some of the organisms without strong defenses to remain protected, for a while, from the more metal-hungry empires by sheer distance. But, to allow for communications blackouts and interference, the aliens had also provided a backup method of program and data exchange between robots and factories, which took the form of direct, physical, electrical interconnection. This was a much slower process than using radiolinks, naturally, since it required that the robots travel physically to the factories for reprograming and reporting, but in a self-sustaining operation far from home the method was a lot better than nothing. And it kept the accountants happy by protecting the return on the investment.

With defects and deficiencies of every description appearing somewhere or other, it was inevitable that some of the organisms would exhibit partial or total communications breakdowns. Factory Seventy-three, built without radio facilities, was started up by programs carried overland from Sixty-six. None of its robots ever used anything but backup mode, and the factories that it spawned continued the tradition. But this very fact meant that their operating ranges were extended dramatically.

So the "defect" turned out to be not so much of a defect after all. Foraging parties were able to roam farther afield, greatly enlarging their catchment areas, and they frequently picked up as prizes one or more of the territories previously protected by geographical remoteness. Furthermore, selective pressures steadily improved the autonomy of the robots that operated in this fashion. The autodirected types, relying on their comparatively small, local processors, tended to apply simple solutions to the problems they encountered, but their close-coupled mode of interaction with their environment meant that the solutions were applied quickly: They evolved efficient "reflexes." The teledirected types, by contrast, tied to the larger but remote central computers, were inclined to attempt more comprehensive and sophisticated solutions, but—as often as not—too late to do any good. Autodirection thus conferred a behavioral superiority and gradually asserted itself as the norm, while teledirection declined and survived only in a few isolated areas.

The periodic instinct to communicate genetic half-subfiles back to their factories had long become a universal trait among the robots—there could be descendants only of ancestors who left descendants—and they responded to the decline of radio as a means of communication by evolving a compulsion to journey at intervals back to the places whence they had come, to return, as it were, to their "spawning grounds." But this method of reproduction had its problems and posed new challenges to the evolutionary process.

The main problem was that an individual could deliver only half its genome to the factory, after which the Supervisor would have to store the information away until another robot of the same type as the first happened to show up with a matching half; only then could the Supervisor pass a complete copy to its Scheduler. If, as frequently happened, the Supervisor found itself saturated by a peak workload during the intervening period, it was quite likely to delete the half-subfile and allocate the memory space to other, more urgent things—bad news for the Fred that the data had come from, who would thus have enacted the whole reproductive ritual for nothing. The successful response to this problem came with the appearance of a new mode of genetic recombination, which, quite coincidentally, also provided the solution to an "information crisis" that had begun to restrict the pool of genetic variation available for competitive selection to draw on for further improvement.

Some mutant forms of robot knew they were supposed to output their half-subfiles somewhere, but weren't all that sure, or perhaps weren't too particular, about what they were supposed to output it into. Anything with the right electrical connections and compatible internal software was good enough, which usually meant other robots of the same basic type. And since a robot that had completed its assigned tasks was in a receptive state to external reprograming, i.e., ready for fresh input that would normally come from the factory system, an aspiring donor had little trouble in finding a cooperative acceptor, provided the approach was made at the right time. So to begin with, the roles adopted were largely a matter of circumstance and accidental temperament.

Although the robots' local memories were becoming larger than those contained in their earlier ancestors, the operating programs were growing in size and complexity too, with the result that an acceptor still didn't possess enough free space to hold an entire "How to Make a Fred" subfile. The donor's half, therefore, could be accommodated only by overwriting some of the code already residing in the acceptor. How this was accomplished depended on the responses of the programs carried inside the various robot types.

In some cases the incoming code from the donor was allowed to overwrite entire program modules inside the acceptor, with the total loss to the acceptor of the functions which those modules controlled. This was usually fatal, and no descendants came into being to repeat such mistakes. The successful alternative was to create space by trimming nonessential code from many modules, which tended to leave the acceptor robot with some degradation in performance—usually manifesting itself as a reduction in agility, dexterity, and defensive abilities—but at least still functioning. The sacrifice was only temporary since the acceptor robot would be reprogramed with replacement modules when it delivered its genetic package at the factory.

But in return for these complications and superficial penalties came the immense benefit that the subfiles presented at the factories were complete ones—suitable for dispatch to the Schedulers without delay and the attendant risk of being deleted by overworked Supervisors. The new method thus solved the reliability problem that had plagued the formerly universal "asexual" mode of reproduction.

The information crisis that it also solved had developed through the "inbreeding" caused by the various Supervisors having only the gene pools of their respective "tribes" available to work with, which made recombination difficult because of the restrictive rules imposed by the alien programers. But the robots swapping genes out on the surface were not always averse to adventuring beyond the tribal limits, knew nothing and cared less about programers' rules, since nothing approaching intelligence or awareness was operative yet in what was unfolding, and proceeded to bring half-subfiles together haphazardly in ways that the aliens' rules didn't permit and which the Supervisors would never have imagined. Most of the offspring resulting from these experiments didn't work and were scrapped before leaving the factories; but the ones that did radiated functionally outward in all directions to launch a whole new, qualitatively distinct phase of the evolutionary process.

The demands of the two sexual roles reinforced minor initial physical differences and brought about a gradual polarization of behavioral traits. Since a female in a "pregnant" condition suffered the loss of some measure of self-sufficiency for the duration, her chances of delivering (literally!) were improved considerably if her mate happened to be of a disposition to stay around for a while and provide for the two of them generally, thus helping to protect their joint genetic investment. Selection tended, therefore, to favor the genes of this kind of male, and by the same token those of the females who mated preferentially with them. As a consequence a female trait emerged of being "choosy" in this respect, and in response the males evolved various repertoires of rituals, displays, and demonstrations to improve their eligibility.

The population had thus come to exhibit genetic variability and recombination, competition, selection, and adaptation—all the essentials for continuing evolution. The form of life—for it was, wasn't it?—was admittedly somewhat strange by terrestrial standards, with the individuals that it comprised sharing common, external reproductive, digestive, and immune systems instead of separate, internal ones... and of course there were no chains of complicated carbon chemistry figuring anywhere in the scheme of things.... But then, after all, what is there apart from chauvinism to say it shouldn't have been so?

1

KARL ZAMBENDORF STOOD GAZING DOWN OVER SEVenth avenue from the window of his penthouse suite in the New York Hilton. He was a tall man in his early fifties, a little on the portly side but with an erect and imposing bearing, graying hair worn collar-length and flowing, bright, piercing eyes, and hawklike features rendered biblically patriarchal by a pointed beard that he bleached white for effect. Although the time was late in the morning, Zambendorf's breakfast tray on the side table beside the window had only recently been discarded, and he was still in his shirt-sleeves from sleeping in after his team's late-night return from its just completed Argentina tour.

A prominent Argentine news magazine had featured him as THE AUSTRIAN MIRACLE-WORKER on its cover for the previous week's issue, and the hostess of one of the major talk shows on Buenos Aires TV had introduced him as "Perhaps one of the most baffling men of the twenty-first century, the scientifically authenticated super-psychic . . ." Thus had Latin America greeted the man who was already a media sensation across the northern continent and Western Europe, and whose ability to read minds, foretell the future, influence distant events, and divine information inaccessible to the human senses had been proved, the public was assured, by repeated tests to be beyond the power of science to explain.

"Karl, I don't like it," Otto Abaquaan said from behind him. Zambendorf pursed his lips and whistled silently to himself while he waited for Abaquaan to continue. The exchange had become a ritual over the years they had worked together. Abaquaan would voice all the reasons why they shouldn't get involved and couldn't afford the risks, and Zambendorf would explain all the reasons why they didn't have any choice. Abaquaan would then reconsider, and eventually, grudgingly, he would concede. Having disposed of the academic issues, they would then proceed somehow to resolve the crisis. It happened that way about once a week. Abaquaan went on, "We'd be out of our minds to get mixed up in it. The whole situation would involve too much of the wrong kind of exposure. We don't need risks like that."

Zambendorf turned away from the window and thrust out his chin. "It was reported as if it were our idea in the first place, and it received a lot of news coverage," he said. "We can't afford to be seen to back down now. On top of that, it would destroy our credibility not only with a lot of the public, but with GSEC... and GSEC can do us a lot of good, Otto. So the situation didn't work out as we expected. What's new? We're stuck with it, but we can handle it."

Otto Abaquaan, a handsomely lean and swarthy Armenian with black hair, a droopy mustache, and deep brown, liquid eyes, rubbed his nose with a knuckle while he considered the statement, then shook his head and sighed. "Why the hell did you have to get us into it, Karl? You said the GSEC Board would never take any notice of a turkey like Hendridge. That was why the rest of us agreed to go along with the crazy idea—because there would be all kinds of good publicity opportunities when GSEC turned it down... you said." He threw out his hands and sent an exasperated look up to the ceiling. "But now what have we got? Mars!... as if we didn't have better things to do than go fooling around on Mars for six months. Is there really no way we can get ourselves out of this?"

Zambendorf shrugged unconcernedly and showed his empty palms. "Certainly—we can call the whole thing off and admit to the world that we never really expected anybody to take us seriously . . . because that's how they'll see it. And as for better things to do, well, maybe we could spend the time in better ways and then, maybe not. Who knows? When was the last time a psychic operated from Mars? The situation might turn out to have opportunities we never thought of."

"Very philosophical," Abaquaan commented, with less than wild enthusiasm. It was all very well for Zambendorf to talk about grandiose schemes and opportunities; it would be Abaquaan and the rest of the team who did the legwork.

"'Philosophical,' my dear Otto, is the state of mind one reverts to when unable to change anything anyway. And that's the situation we are in. In short, we don't have a choice."

GSEC, General Space Enterprises Corporation, and NASO—the European-American military and civilian North Atlantic Space Organization that had grown from a merger of many of the former interests of NASA, ESA, and NATO—were funding expansion of one of the pilot bases on Mars to test ideas on the organization of extraterrestrial communities as a prelude to the construction of full-scale colonies. A GSEC director by the name of Baines Hendridge—a long-standing true believer in ESP and the "paranormal," and a recent convert to the Zambendorf cult—had proposed sending Zambendorf with the mission in order to perform the first-ever tests of clairvoyance and psychic communication over interplanetary distances, and to conduct ESP experiments in conditions free from terrestrial "interference." Zambendorf, confident that the GSEC Board would never go along with the idea, had reacted with a show of enthusiasm, partly because anything else would have failed the expectations of the faithful and partly to set the stage in advance for exploiting another "Scientists Back Off Zambendorf Challenge" story when the proposal was turned down. Baines Hendridge's influence had turned out to be greater than he had calculated, however, and the Board's acceptance of the proposal had left Zambendorf in a position that he could retreat from only at the cost of more public ignominy than his image could afford.

"I guess you're right," Abaquaan conceded after a short silence. "But I still don't like the idea of getting mixed up with a NASO space mission." He shook his head again, dubiously. "It's not like dealing with the public. There are some good scientists in that outfit... in a different league from the assholes we're used to handling. It's risky."

"Scientists are the easiest to fool." That was one of Zambendorf's favorite lines. "They think in straight, predictable, directable, and therefore misdirectable, lines. The only world they know is the one where everything has a logical explanation and things are what they appear to be. Children and conjurors—they terrify me. Scientists are no problem; against them I feel quite confident."

Abaquaan smiled humorlessly. "Confidence is what you feel when you don't really understand the situation." He raised his arm to glance at his wristset.

Zambendorf was about to reply when the call tone sounded from the room's comnet terminal. Abaquaan walked across to answer it. The screen came to life to show the smooth, clean-cut features of Drew West, Zambendorf's business manager, calling from another suite farther along the hallway. "Those NBC people should be arriving downstairs anytime now," West said. "You'd better be getting on down to the lobby." Clarissa Eidstadt, who handled the team's publicity affairs, had arranged for a short television interview to be taped that morning, for screening later in the day to mark Zambendorf's return to New York.

"I was just about on my way," Abaquaan said.

"Has Karl finished breakfast yet?" West asked. "Time's getting on. We've got a full schedule this afternoon."

"Yes," Abaquaan said. "He's right here. You want to talk to him?"

"Good morning, Drew," Zambendorf said cheerfully, stepping into the viewing angle as Abaquaan moved away.

"Yes, I'm almost ready. How did you sleep?" He nodded across the room as Abaquaan let himself out the door.

"Hi, Karl. Fine, thanks," Drew West acknowledged. West had accepted the Mars situation matter-of-factly. Taking the team to the Andromeda galaxy would have been fine by him as long as there was money in it. "The NBC team's due here in about fifteen minutes, and there are a couple of things we need to go over before they show up. If you're through with breakfast, we'll come on down."

"Yes, why don't you do that," Zambendorf said. "We can talk while I finish dressing."

"See you in a couple of minutes, Karl."

Downstairs, at the hotel's side foyer in front of the ramp leading down to the parking levels, Otto Abaquaan pretended to study a New York street map while he memorized the details and registration number of the car that had arrived with the NBC van from which two men were unloading TV cameras and recording equipment. The smartly dressed, fair-haired woman who had driven the car was standing nearby, holding a briefcase and a sheaf of papers and talking with two colleagues—another woman and a man—who had come with her. Abaquaan guessed her to be the owner of the car and also the reporter who would be interviewing Zambendorf; but he needed to be sure.

NBC had neglected to advise them of the name of their reporter in advance, which was unusual and meant, possibly, that Zambendorf was being set up for something. An enquiry from Clarissa Eidstadt or from Drew West could no doubt have answered the question easily enough, but that would have wasted an opportunity of exactly the kind that Zambendorf and his team excelled at seizing. A gamble was involved, of course—Abaquaan might turn up nothing in the short time available—but one of the advantages enjoyed by psychics was that negative results were always soon forgotten.

A hotel valet drove the car away toward the ramp, and

the woman and her two companions walked through into the main lobby with Abaquaan following them inconspicuously at a short distance. One of the clerks at the front desk raised his eyebrows enquiringly. "Can I help you, ma'am?"

"Yes. My name is Marion Kearson, from NBC. I arranged with the assistant manager, Mr. Graves, to tape an interview in the lobby with Karl Zambendorf. Is Mr. Graves available, please?"

"One moment. I'll call his office."

That answered one question. Time was now crucial if the gamble was going to pay off. Abaquaan turned and walked quickly to the line of comnet terminals at the rear of the lobby, sat in one of the booths, closed the door, and called a number in the Vehicles Registration Department of the State of New Jersey. Seconds later a man with pink, fleshy features and a balding head appeared on the screen. "Hello, Frank. Long time no see. How're things?" Abaquaan spoke quietly but urgently.

The face frowned for a moment, then recognized the caller. "Say, Harry! Things are good. How's the private-eye business?" Abaquaan never made public appearances and hence could command a long list of aliases.

"It's a living. Look, I need some information fast. The usual deal and terms. Any problem?"

Frank glanced about him with an instinctively furtive look. "Can I ask what it's to do with?"

"Nothing to lose any sleep over—a domestic thing. I need to find out who owns a car that's been seen in a couple of places. The usual suspicious husband routine."

Frank licked his lips, then nodded. "Okay. Got the number?"

"New Jersey registration KGY27–86753."

"Hang on a minute." Frank looked away and began operating another terminal offscreen. Abaquaan produced a pen and notebook, and then sat drumming his fingers on the side of the terminal while he waited. "Well?" he asked as Frank at last turned back to look out of the screen.

"It's registered under the name of a Mrs. Marion Kearson, 2578 Maple Drive, Orangeton," Frank said. "You want details of the car?"

"I've got a description. Has it been reregistered at the same address for very long, and is there any accident record?"

"Renewed successively for the last three years. No accidents."

"Any other vehicles registered at the same address? What information do you have on the drivers? . . ."

"Very well, we'll be down in a few minutes," Drew West said to the screen of the terminal in the living room of Zambendorf's suite. He cut the call, turned, and announced, "That was Graves, the assistant manager. He's with Clarissa downstairs. The NBC people are all set up and ready when we are."

Dr. Osmond Periera, middle-aged, wispy haired, wearing a bow tie with a maroon jacket and smoking a Turkish cigarette through an ornate silver holder, resumed talking from the point where the call had interrupted. The introductions and author profiles in his best-selling pseudoscience books described him as Zambendorf's discoverer and mentor; certainly he was among the staunchest of the disciples. "One of the most intriguing possibilities on Mars will be the opportunity to verify that extrasensory information does indeed propagate in a mode not constrained by any form of inverse-square law. Although experiments on Earth seem to suggest that the field strength does not diminish with distance at all, my feeling is that until now the scale has simply been too small to reveal significant differences. After all, even though we are venturing into a completely new phenomenological realm, we mustn't allow ourselves to lose our sense of realism and scientific plausibility, must we?"

Zambendorf blinked and rubbed his nose with the back of his hand. Periera's ability to invent the most outrageous explanations for Zambendorf's feats and, moreover, to believe them himself totally uncritically and without reservation, constantly amazed even Zambendorf. "It's an interesting thought," he agreed. "Another possibility is that the remoteness of negative influences might well have a beneficial effect on repeatability."

Periera brought a hand up to toy unconsciously with his bow while he considered the suggestion. It was intriguing—certainly something that hadn't occurred to him before. "I could design tests to be conducted through the voyage for investigating any correlations with distance," he mused. "That might be very informative."

"Yes, why don't you do that," Zambendorf agreed.

Periera turned to Baines Hendridge, a dark-haired, clean-shaven man with a collegiate look about him, who was wearing his usual intense expression. Hendridge had come to the Hilton early that morning to convey personally the news of the GSEC Board's decision concerning the Mars project, and to invite Zambendorf and colleagues to lunch with some of the other directors. "It is a well-established fact that manifestations of paranormal phenomena differ from observables at the more mundane, material level of existence in that their repeatability is affected by the presence of negative or critical influences," Periera explained. "The effect is predictable from elementary quantum mechanics, which proves the interdependence between the observer and the observed." Hendridge nodded as he absorbed the revelation, and looked even more intense.

The call tone sounded from the room's terminal. Drew West answered, and a second later Otto Abaquaan's face appeared on the screen. "Is Thelma there?" Abaquaan enquired, signaling with an eyebrow that he had information to impart. "I need to talk to her." He meant that he couldn't talk openly with Periera and Hendridge there in the room.

Zambendorf looked across at Thelma, the team's blonde, shapely, long-legged secretary, who was listening from the couch by the far wall. "Oh, it's probably about some places I told him he ought to see while we're in New York," Thelma said. "He's planning to spend the afternoon touring the city."

"Yes, well, can you talk to him on the extension next door?" Zambendorf said. Thelma nodded, unfolded herself from the couch, and disappeared into the suite's bedroom. Drew West switched the call and cleared the screen in the living room. Periera and Hendridge could be tedious at times, but their wealthy and influential social acquaintances made them worth putting up with.

"Where are we due to have lunch?" Zambendorf asked, looking at West.

"At that Austrian place you liked last time—Hoffmann's on East Eighty-third," West answered. "We can go straight on after the interview. I'll have a cab waiting."

"Is Osmond joining us?" Zambendorf asked.

Periera shook his head. "I have to attend a meeting this afternoon, thanks all the same. Next time, hopefully."

"A pity," Zambendorf murmured, and went on to talk for a minute or two about the food at Hoffman's. Then, judging that they had given Abaquaan and Thelma enough time, he gave West a barely perceptible nod.

West glanced at his watch. "We'd better be moving."

Joe Fellburg, the huge, six foot three, black ex-fighter and former military-intelligence agent who functioned as Zambendorf's bodyguard and the team's security man, straightened up from the wall just inside the doorway, opened the closet next to him, and took out Zambendorf's overcoat.

Zambendorf shook his head as he put on his jacket. "No, I don't think the weather's quite cool enough for that, Joe. Perhaps my blue cape . . . " He looked around the room. "Oh yes, I left it next door. Excuse me for a moment." He went through into the bedroom where Thelma was waiting and allowed the door to swing shut behind. "What have you got?" he asked in a low voice.

"We're in luck," Thelma said, speaking quickly. "The reporter is a woman called Marion Kearson. She drives a 2018 Buick six-seat limo compact, hydrogen-burning, silver-gray, black trim, white wheels; small dent on driver's side, front; registration is New Jersey, KGY27–86753. Kearson's address is 2578 Maple Drive, Orangeton." Zambendorf nodded rapidly as he concentrated on memorizing. Thelma went on, "Two other drivers with cars are registered at the same address: William Kearson, born August 4, 1978, five ten in height, brown hair, green eyes, one hundred eighty pounds—has to be her husband; drives a USM Gazelle, new this year; speeding fine last April, minor accident the previous fall; also a Thomas Kearson, born January 14, 2001, also five ten, fair hair, gray eyes, one twenty pounds; drives a 2013 Datsun—sounds like the son."

Zambendorf repeated the information, and Thelma confirmed it. "Good," Zambendorf said. "Will you and Otto be able to get anything on those GSEC people we're having lunch with?"

"Maybe. Otto's following up a couple of leads."

"Call Drew or me at Hoffman's after twelve-thirty with whatever you come up with."

"Hoffmann's, East Eighty-third, after twelve-thirty," Thelma confirmed. "Okay. You'd better get moving."

Ten minutes later, Zambendorf, his sky-blue silk cape flowing grandly over his black velvet jacket, swept into the lobby with Drew West, Joe Fellburg, Osmond Periera, and Baines Hendridge bringing up the rear. Clarissa Eidstadt, the team's publicity matron, her short black hair cut off in a fringe across her forehead, her eyes framed by heavy-rimmed butterfly glasses, and her mouth accentuated by lipstick that was too heavy and too red, was waiting. She escorted Zambendorf over to Marion Kearson and the NBC crew while curious hotel guests began to gather in the background. "Who's the reporter?" Zambendorf murmured. "The blonde in the pink coat?"

"Yes."

"Do you know her name?"

"They didn't tell me, and I didn't ask them," Clarissa muttered from the corner of her mouth.

Zambendorf nodded and smiled to himself. "Even better."

And then a rapturous Marion Kearson was pushing a microphone close to Zambendorf's face. "Well, here in the New York Hilton after getting back from South America only last night is Karl Zambendorf, who I'm sure needs no further introduction. Welcome home."

"Thank you."

"And how was your tour?"

"Most enjoyable and extremely successful."

"I'm glad to hear that. In fact I'd like to come back to that subject in a moment. But first, before I do any more talking that might give things away, I wonder if I could persuade you to accept a small challenge for the benefit of the viewers." Kearson smiled impishly for a second. "Now, I can certainly vouch that we've never set eyes on one another before, and it might interest the viewers to know that back at NBC this morning, we didn't even know ourselves which reporter was coming on this assignment until five of us drew lots less than an hour ago." She paused to allow that to register, and then said, "Now, I wonder, Herr Zambendorf, what you can make of me, a complete stranger... apart from that I'm blonde, medium in height, and have a few freckles." She smiled into the camera at the joke, then turned back toward Zambendorf and waited curiously.

Zambendorf looked at her for a few seconds, then closed his eyes and appeared to concentrate his powers. The people watching around the lobby fell quiet. An expression of calm and serenity spread over his face, and he smiled faintly. When he opened his eyes again, his features remained tranquil but his gaze was piercing. "You are not from the city," he said slowly, still searching her face with his eyes. "I see water. Your home is across water, but not very far from here... to the west. It must be across the river, probably in New Jersey. Somewhere in the Newark area seems to suggest itself... with a name that suggests a fruit or a color... lemon, maybe, or orange..."

Kearson's eyes widened incredulously; the cameramen and engineers exchanged glances that said they were impressed. "This—this is absolutely amazing!" she stammered at the camera. "I swear this man and I have never met before this moment."

"There are two men very close to you," Zambendorf went on. "One of them is called William, William or Bill. He is the older of the two . . . your husband, unless I am mistaken. You do have a husband?" Kearson nodded numbly. "Mmm," Zambendorf said knowingly. "I am beginning to see him a little more clearly now—tallish, with brown hair . . . No, don't say anything, please. Just continue to concentrate, if you will, on the image of your husband. . . ."

2

"HMPH!" WALTER CONLON, DIRECTOR OF THE NORTH Atlantics Space Organization's Planetary Exploration Program, scowled down at the sheet of paper lying on the desk in front of him, took in the objections and deletions copiously scattered in heavy red ink along with the initials of various people from the top levels of NASO's management hierarchy, and raised his face defiantly. It was a florid pink face with untamable bushy eyebrows, and made all the more vivid and pugnacious by his white, inch-cropped hair, short, stocky build, and somewhat bulbous nose. The senior scientists in PEP called him the GNASO Gnome. "I still don't see what's wrong with it," he repeated. "It says what needs to be said and it's factual. You wanted my input. Well, that's it. I'm not in the political cosmetics and don't-upset-the-freaks business. What else can I say?"

Allan Brady, the NASO North American Division's recently appointed broad-shouldered, fair-haired, and stylishly dressed public relations director, managed to suppress his exasperation with an effort as he sat in the chair opposite. He had been warned to expect problems in dealing with Conlon, and had thought that in going out of his way to solicit Conlon's opinion on the Korning UFO-flap press release, due out the next day, he would at least be making a start in the right direction. But the draft that had come back over the wire from Conlon's desk terminal within fifteen minutes of Brady's request had come close to causing heart attacks in the PR department. "But we can't go putting out things like this, Walt," Brady protested. "It's saying in effect that a U.S. senator is either a simpleton or a fraud. And the—"

"He is," Conlon retorted. "Both. Scientifically he's an illiterate, and if the truth were known, he's got about as much interest in New Gospel Scientific Solidarity as I have in medieval Turkish poetry. It's pure politics—bankrolling, bandwagoning, ballyhoo, and baloney. You can quote me on that."

Brady bunched his mouth for a second, and then raised his hand briefly in a conciliatory gesture. "Okay. That's as may be, but we can't make allegations like this in an official NASO statement. Ethics apart, we're a government-driven operation, and we can't afford to make enemies of people like Korning. And programs like PEP that are still primarily public funded—" He broke off and shook his head, giving Conlon a puzzled look. "But I don't have to spell things like that out to you, Walt. You know how the system works. We just need something milder in tone and worded more tactfully. It doesn't really even have to say anything."

Conlon shook his head. "Not from me. The precedent has gone too far already and should never have been set in the first place. We can't afford to let ourselves be seen acquiescing to things like this. If it goes on the way it is, we'll end up with every kook and nut-cult in the country parading crusaders around Washington to decide what NASO's business ought to be. I don't want to get mixed up with them. I've got enough already with this Zambendorf nonsense on Mars. I don't have the time; I don't have the budget; I don't have the people."

The New Gospel Scientific Solidarity Church of Oregon had combined a complete retranslation of the Bible with the latest pseudoscientific writings on ancient astronauts to produce a new, "rationalized" doctrine in which all the revelations and mystical happenings of old were explained by visitations of benevolent aliens with supernatural powers, who had access to secrets that mankind would be privileged to share on completion of its "graduation." The Second Coming was really a symbolic reference to the time when the Powers would be divulged, and contemporary UFO lore had been woven into the theme as tangible evidence that the Day of Return was imminent. The church claimed a following of millions, certainly commanded a monthly income of such, and had been campaigning vigorously for recognition of scientific legitimacy, which—the skeptics quickly noted—would qualify the movement for federal research funding. Orthodox scientists challenged to refute the sect's claims found themselves in the usual no-win bind: If they responded at all they were proclaimed as having "acknowledged the importance" of the assertions, and if they didn't they had "no answers." The church supported an ardent lobby that was demanding, among other things, specific allocations of NASO resources and funds for investigating UFO phenomena, and which had ostensibly succeeded in recruiting Senator Korning of Oregon as a spokesman and champion. And Korning had made the headlines often enough to ensure a response of some kind from NASO.

Brady sought to avoid leaving the meeting empty-handed. "Well, I guess PR can handle the Korning side of it, but there's another part of this draft that ridicules the whole UFO phenomenon and doesn't mince any words about it." He sat back and showed his palms imploringly. "Why go out of your way to upset lots of people who don't care about Korning and aren't interested in any religion, but who tend to be enthusiastic about the space program? NASO has some strong supporters among UFO buffs. Why antagonize them?"

"I'm in the science business, not the business of making myself popular by propping up popular myths," Conlon replied. "That means looking for explanations of facts. In that area there aren't any facts that need explaining. Period."

Brady looked across the desk in surprise. He wasn't a scientist, but he thought he did a pretty good job of keeping abreast by reading the popular literature. Something was going on in the skies that scientists couldn't account for, surely. And, Senator Korning's demands aside, Brady rather liked the idea of NASO's committing some serious effort to investigating the subject. It would be an exciting activity to be associated with and something interesting to tell his friends about. "But there has to be something out there," he objected. "I mean, I know ninety-five percent, or whatever, of what's reported is rubbish, but what about the other five? How can you explain that?"

Conlon snorted and massaged his forehead. How many times had he heard this before? "I can't, and neither can anyone else," he replied. "That's why they're what they call unidentified. That's what the word means. It's no more mysterious than car accidents. If you analyze the statistics, you'll find that some percent are due to drunks, some to carelessness, some to vehicle defects, and so on until you end up with five percent that nobody can pin down to any specific cause, and nobody ever will. The causes are unidentified—but that's no reason to say they have anything to do with aliens. It's the same with UFOs."

"That doesn't prove they don't have something to do with aliens though," Brady pointed out.

"I never said it did," Conlon replied. "I can't prove Santa Claus doesn't exist either. You can't prove a negative. Philosophically it's impossible."

"So, what are you saying?" Brady asked him.

Conlon tossed his hands up and shrugged. "I told you, I'm a scientist. Science doesn't have anything to say about it. It's not a scientific matter."

"How can you say that, Walt?" Brady sounded incredulous. "It's connected with space and spacecraft, alien life . . . How can you say it's not scientific?"

"The way a theory is constructed logically is what makes it scientific. Not its content. To be scientific, one of the conditions a theory has to meet is that it must be falsifiable—there must be some way you can test it to see if it's wrong. You can never prove, absolutely, that any theory is right. If you've got a theory that says Some

UFOs might be alien spacecraft, then I agree with you—some might. There's no way I could prove it false. That's all I could say, and that's all science says. It isn't a falsifiable theory. See what I mean?"

Brady was shaking his head reluctantly. "I can't buy that. There has to be some way for science to evaluate the subject, some way to test some part of it at least."

"There is. You invert the logic and put forward the theory that I do: No UFOs are alien spacecraft. Now, that theory can be falsified conclusively and very simply, but not by anything that's been offered as evidence so far."

"But what about the astronomers who've endorsed it publicly?" Brady persisted.

"What astronomers?"

"Oh, I can't recall their names offhand, but the ones you read about."

"Pah!" Conlon pulled a face. "You mean people like Jannitsky?"

"Well, he's one, yes."

"He used to be a scientist—shut up in a lab all day with nobody ever having heard of him. Now he's a celebrity. Some people will do anything for recognition. How many more like him can you find? You can count 'em on one hand, and in a country this size that's the least you'd expect. It doesn't mean a damn thing, Al. Less than two percent of professional American astronomers consider the subject even worth showing an interest in. That *does* mean something." After a few seconds of silence Conlon added, "Anyhow, asking astronomers for opinions on something like that is ridiculous. It's not a subject they're competent to comment on."

"What!" Brady exclaimed.

"What does an astronomer know about UFOs?" Conlon asked him.

Brady threw up his hands helplessly. "Well, how do I answer that? They're things in the sky, right? So, astronomers are supposed to know about things in the sky."

"What things in the sky?"

"What things? . . . The ones people say they see."

"Exactly!" Conlon sat back and spread his hands in a show of satisfaction. "The things people *say they see*—All of the evidence boils down to eyewitness testimony. What does an astronomer know about evaluating testimony? How many times in his whole career does he have to try to learn whether a witness believes his own story, or decide whether the witness saw what he thought he saw, and whether it meant what he thought it meant? See my point? An astronomer's the wrong guy. What you need is a good lawyer or police detective, except they've all got other things to do than worry about investigating UFOs."

"But at least you know an astronomer's not just any dummy," Brady said.

"If that's all you need, why not ask a heart surgeon or a poker player?" Conlon shook his head. "Being an expert in one field doesn't make somebody's opinions on subjects they're not qualified to talk about worth more than anybody else's. But all too often they think they're infallible about anything and everything, and people believe them. You can see it everywhere—political economists who think they know more about fusion than nuclear engineers do; lawyers trying to define what's alive and what isn't; Nobel Prize-winning physicists being taken with simple conjuring tricks by so-called psychics. What does a physicist know about trickery and deception? Quarks and photons don't tell lies. We have stage magicians and conjurors who are experts on deception and the art of fooling people—it's their business. But who ever thinks of asking them in?"

Conlon's tone had mellowed somewhat while he was talking, and Brady began to sense the message that he was trying to communicate: Whether Brady agreed with him or not about UFOs, Conlon and the people in the Planetary Exploration Program had better things to do than get involved in public relations concerning the likes of Senator Korning. That was Brady's department. And the way Conlon was beginning to fidget in his chair said that he was getting near the end of the time he was prepared to spend trying to communicate it.

Brady spread his hands for a moment, then acknowledged with a nod and picked the paper up from Conlon's desk as he rose to his feet. "Well, sorry to have taken your time," he said. "We'll take care of this. I just thought... maybe you'd appreciate the opportunity to contribute something." He turned and walked over to the door.

"Al," Conlon called out gruffly as Brady was about to leave the room. Brady stopped and looked back. "I realize that you meant it for the best. Don't think you goofed. You've got your job to do—I know that. I guess from now on we understand each other, huh?"

Brady returned a faint smile. "I guess so," he replied. "I'll talk to you more about UFOs sometime."

"Do that."

"Take care." With that, Brady left.

Conlon sighed and sat staring down at the desk for a while with his chin propped on his knuckles. He wondered where it would all lead—pendulum-wavers being hired by oil companies to locate deposits; degrees in the "paranormal" being awarded by universities that should have known better; kook papers appearing in what used to be reputable scientific publications; politicians calling for a phase-down of the fusion program because they were convinced of the imminence of unlimited "cosmic energy" forever from pyramids, this at a time when the U.S. was having to import up-to-date tokamak reactors from Japan.

It was becoming all but impossible to find good engineers and technicians. Science, engineering, the true arts, and the professions—in fact just about anything that demanded hard work, patience, and diligence—were coming increasingly, it seemed, to be regarded among younger people as out of style, strictly for nurds. And as fast as they were trained and gained some experience, the ones who did manage to turn themselves into something worthwhile tended to leave for more lucrative and challenging opportunities overseas. The peoples of such places as Japan, China, India, and Africa had lived too close to reality for too long to be deluded by notions of "finding themselves," whatever that meant, or searches for mystical bliss. Having "found" the twenty-first century, they were rapidly abandoning their trust in the magic and superstitions that had solved nothing, and were busy erecting in their place the solid foundations of advanced, industrialized, high-technology civilization.

Conlon wasn't really sure where the degeneration had started either—in the latter half of the twentieth century, he suspected from what he had read. In earlier times, it appeared, the American system had worked fine as a means of stimulating productivity and creativity, and of raising the living standards of a whole nation for the first time in history. But habits of thought had failed to change as quickly as technology. When the spread of automation made it possible for virtually all of life's basic needs to be met with a fraction of the available capacity, new, artificial needs had to be created to keep the machines and the workforce busy.

With the Third World looking after its own, a major portion of the West's ingenuity and effort came to be expended on manufacturing new appetites for trivia and consumer junk in its own domestic markets. Unfortunately, left to themselves, rational, educated, and discerning people tended not to make very good consumers; therefore no great attempt had been made to create a rational, educated, and discerning population. The mass media that could have been an instrument of genuine mass education had become instead an instrument of mass manipulation which delivered uncritical audiences to advertisers, and the school system had degenerated to little more than a preprocessing which cultivated the kind of banality that moved products. Nevertheless, despite the plethora of conspiracy theories in vogue among intellectuals, academics, and political activists, Conlon didn't believe that cabals of tycoons plotting secretly in boardrooms had planned it all; things had simply evolved, a little at a time, through the selective reinforcement of whatever happened to be good for profits.

The call tone from his desk terminal interrupted his thoughts, and Conlon tapped the unit's touchpad to accept. The face that appeared on the screen was of a man approaching fifty or so, with a high forehead left by a receding hairline, rugged features setting off a full beard that was starting to show streaks of gray, and bright, penetrating eyes that held an elusive, mirthful twinkle. It was Gerold Massey, a professor of cognitive psychology at the University of Maryland and one of Conlon's longstanding friends. Massey was also an accomplished stage magician who took a special interest in exposing fraudulent claims of paranormal powers. It was Conlon's familiarity with Massey's work that had prompted him to mention the subject to Allan Brady earlier.

"Hello, Walter," Massey said. "My computer tells me you've been calling. What gives?"

"Hi, Gerry. Yes, since yesterday. Where've you been?"

"Florida—Tallahassee."

"Oh? What's happening there?"

"Some research that Vernon and I are working on." Vernon Price was Massey's assistant, magical understudy, and general partner in crime. "We're presenting Vernon in an ESP routine to classes of students around the country. Some are told beforehand that it's just a conjuring act, and some are told it's the real thing. The object is to get a measure of how strong preconceived beliefs are in influencing people's interpretations of what they see, and how much difference what they're told at the rational level makes." Massey's specialty was the study of why people believed what they believed.

"Sounds interesting."

"It is, but I doubt if you were calling to ask me about it," Massey replied.

"True. Look, I'd like to get together with you and talk sometime soon. It's about a NASO project we've got coming up, but I really don't want to go into the details right now. How are you fixed?"

"Sounds like you might be trying to offer me a job," Massey commented. While he spoke he looked down to operate the terminal, and then back up again but slightly to the side, apparently reading something in an inset area of his screen. "Pretty busy just about every day for a while," he murmured. "Any reason why we couldn't make it an evening? How would you like to come round here again? We could make it a dinner, and maybe go to that Italian place you like."

"Sounds good," Conlon said.

"How about tomorrow?"

"Even better. Oh—and I'll be bringing Pat Whittaker with me. He's involved with it too."

"Why not? I haven't seen him for a while." Patrick Whittaker was a production executive with Global Communications Networking, a major provider of TV and dataservices. Massey's features contorted into a bemused frown. "Say, what the hell is this all about, Walt? Are you sure you don't want to give me a clue even?"

Conlon grinned crookedly. "Get Vernon to tell you via ESP. No, really, I'd rather leave that side until tomorrow. We'll see you at about what, six-thirty?"

"That'll do fine. Okay, we'll see you then."

Conlon returned his attention to his desk and allowed his eyes to stray over it while he reviewed what he planned to do next. His gaze came to rest on the folder from the Project Executive Review Committee containing the final appraisal, specification of goals, and departmental assignments for the Mars project. Lying next to it was a copy of that day's *Washington Post*, folded by someone in the department and marked at an item reporting Karl Zambendorf's return to the U.S.A. The hue of Conlon's face deepened, and his mouth compressed itself into a tight downturn.

"Psychics!" he muttered to himself sourly.

3

"LOOK, WE HAVE TO DO A TV SHOW THAT'S GOING OUT live at seven-thirty," Drew West shouted through the partition at the cab driver. "There's an extra twenty if we make it on time."

Grumbling under his breath, the cabbie backed up to within inches of the car behind, U-turned across the oncoming traffic stream amid blares of horns and squeals of brakes, and exited off Varick into an alley to negotiate a way round the perpetual traffic snarl at the Manhattan end of the Holland Tunnel. On one side the streets were blacked out for seven blocks beneath the immense, ugly canopy of aluminum panels and steel-lattice supports that made up the ill-fated Lower West Side Solar Power Demonstration Project, which was supposed to have proved the feasibility of supplying city electricity from solar. Before the harebrained scheme was abandoned, it had cost the city $200 million to teach politicians what power engineers had known all along. But it kept the streets dry in rainy weather and a thriving antique, art, and flea market had come into being in the covered arcades created below.

"I'm certain there's more to it, Drew," Zambendorf resumed as West sat back in his seat. "Lang and Snell were only being polite to avoid embarrassing Hendridge. They were classical corporation men—hard-nosed, pragmatic, no-nonsense—and not a grain of imagination between the two of them. They weren't at lunch because of interest in paranormal powers. They were there on GSEC business."

West nodded. "I agree. And what's more my gut-feel tells me they're representative of official thinking inside GSEC's Board, which says that GSEC isn't interested in psychic experiments on Mars. That's just for public consumption. But if that's so, what's the real reason they want to send us along, Karl?"

The cab slowed to a halt at the intersection with Broadway. From the seat on Zambendorf's other side, Joe Fellburg kept a watchful eye on a group of unkempt youths lounging outside a corner store smoking something that was being passed round. "Maybe someone in the corporation somewhere decided it's time that space arrived for the people," he offered.

Zambendorf frowned and looked at West. West shrugged. "What do you mean?" Zambendorf asked, looking at Fellburg.

Fellburg relaxed as the cab began moving again, turned his head from the window, and opened a pair of black ham-fists. "Well, things like space and space bases have always been for astronauts, scientists, NASO people—people like that. They've never been for just anybody. Now, if GSEC is making plans to put up space colonies someday, somebody somewhere is gonna have to do some work to get that image changed. So maybe they figure that getting someone like Karl in on this Mars thing might do them a lotta good."

"Mmm... you mean by sending along a popular figure that everyone can relate to..." Drew West nodded and looked intrigued. "It makes sense... Yes, if you could establish that kind of connection in people's minds... And that could also explain why Lang, and Snell, and probably most of the other GSEC directors might go along with Hendridge even if they think the guy's crazy."

"That's just what I'm telling you," Fellburg said. "What would they care whether Karl's for real or not?"

Zambendorf stroked his beard thoughtfully while he

considered the suggestion. Then he nodded, slowly at first, and then more rapidly. Finally he laughed. "In that case we have nothing to worry about. If GSEC has no serious interest in experiments, then nobody will be trying very hard to expose anything. In fact, when you think about it, good publicity for us would be in their interests too. So the whole thing could turn out to be to our advantage after all. I told you that Otto worries too much. The whole thing will be a piece of cake, you'll see—a piece of cake."

Hymn-singing evangelists with placards warning against meddling in DARK POWERS and denouncing Zambendorf as a CONSORT OF SATAN occupied a section of the sidewalk opposite NBC's television studio by the Trade Center when the cab rounded the corner into Fulton Street. Drew West spotted Clarissa Eidstadt waiting at the curb in front of the crowd outside the entrance, and directed the cabbie to stop next to her. She climbed in by the driver and waved for him to keep moving. "The freaks are out in force tonight," she said, turning her head to speak through the partition. "The stage door's under siege, but I've got another one opened for us round the side." Then to the driver, "Make a right here . . . Drop us off by those guys talking to the two cops."

The cab halted, and they climbed out. While West was paying the driver, Clarissa slipped Zambendorf a folded piece of paper, which he tucked into his inside pocket. Written on the paper were notes of things that Otto Abaquaan and Thelma had observed and overheard during the last hour or so, such as oddments glimpsed inside a purse opened in the course of purchasing tickets at the box office, or snatches of conversation overheard in the ladies' room and the cocktail lounge. Upon such seeming trivia were many wondrous miracles built.

The party was whisked inside, and Zambendorf excused himself to visit the washroom in order to study the notes Clarissa had given him. He rejoined the others in a staff lounge five minutes later and was introduced to

Ed Jackson, the genial host of the popular "Ed Jackson Show," on which Zambendorf would be appearing as the principal guest. Jackson exuberated and enthused for a while in the standard manner of a media-synthesized Mr. Personality, and then left to begin the show with the first of the evening's warm-up guests. Zambendorf and his companions drank coffee, talked with the production staff, and watched the show on the green-room monitor. A makeup girl came in and banished a couple of shiny spots on Zambendorf's nose and forehead. Zambendorf checked with the stage manager that a couple of props would be available on the set as previously requested.

At last it was time to descend backstage, and Zambendorf found himself waiting in the wings with an assistant while Ed Jackson went through a verbal buildup with the audience to fill an advertising break on air-time. Then Jackson was half turning and extending an arm expectantly while the orchestra's theme crescendoed to a trumpet fanfare; the director's finger stabbed its cue from the control booth, and Zambendorf was walking forward into the glare of spotlights to be greeted by thunderous applause and a wave of excitement.

Jackson beamed as Zambendorf turned from side to side to acknowledge the applause before sitting down behind the low, glass-topped table, and then took his own seat and assumed a casual posture. "Karl, welcome to the show. I guess we're all wondering what kinds of surprises you might have in store for us tonight." Jackson paused to allow the audience and viewers a moment to attune themselves to his approach. "Were you, ah . . . were you surprised at the small demonstration outside in the street here when you arrived earlier?"

"Oh, I'm never surprised by anything." Zambendorf grinned and looked out at the audience expectantly. After a second or two he was rewarded with laughter.

Jackson smiled in a way that said he ought to have known better. "Seriously though, Karl, we hear some rather scary warnings from certain sections of the religious community from time to time concerning your abilities and the ways in which you make use of them—that you're dabbling in realms that no good can come out of, tapping into powers that we were never meant to know about, and that kind of thing.... What's your answer to fears like these? Are they groundless? Or is there something to them that people ought to know about?"

Zambendorf frowned for a second. This was always a delicate question. Anything that sounded like a concession or an admission would not serve his interests, but nothing was to be gained by being offensive. "I suspect it's a case of our not seeing the same thing when we look at the subject," he replied. "Their perceptions result from interpreting reality from a religious perspective, obviously, and must necessarily be influenced by traditional religious notions and preconceptions... not all of which, I have to say, are reconcilable with today's views of the universe and our role in it." He made a half-apologetic shrug and spread his hands briefly. "My interpretation is from the scientific perspective. In other words, what I see is simply a new domain of phenomena that lie beyond the present horizons of scientific inquiry. But that doesn't make them 'forbidden,' or 'unknowable,' any more than electricity or radio were in the Middle Ages. They are simply 'mysterious'—mysteries which cannot adequately be explained within the contemporary framework of knowledge, but which are explainable nevertheless in principle, and will be explained in the fullness of time."

"Something we should treat with respect, then, possibly, but not something we need be frightened of," Jackson concluded in an appropriately sober tone.

"The things that frighten people are mostly products of their own minds," Zambendorf replied. "What we are dealing with here opens up entirely new insights to the mind. With improved understanding of themselves, people will be able to comprehend and control the processes by which they manufacture their own fears. The ultimate fear of most people is the fear of being afraid."

"Maybe there isn't any real conflict at all," Jackson commented. "Isn't it possible that religious mystics through the ages have experienced intuitively the same processes that people like you are learning to apply at the conscious level, scientifically . . . in the same way, for example, that magnetism was applied to making compasses long before anyone knew what it was? At the bottom line, you could all be saying the same thing."

"That is exactly how I see it," Zambendorf agreed. "The medieval Church persecuted Galileo, but religion today has come to terms with the more orthodox sciences. We can learn a lot from that precedent." Zambendorf was being quite sincere; the implication was ambiguous, and what he meant was the exact opposite of what most people chose to assume.

Jackson sensed that the audience had had its fill of profound thoughts and heavy philosophy for the evening, and decided to move on. "I understand you're just back from a long trip, Karl—to Argentina. How was it? Is there as much activity and enthusiasm in Latin America as here?"

"Oh, the visit was a success. We all enjoyed it a lot and met some very interesting people. Yes, they are starting to get involved in some serious work there now, especially at one of the universities we visited—But speaking of long trips, have you heard about our latest one, which has just been confirmed?"

"No, tell us."

Zambendorf glanced out at the audience and then across at the live camera. "We're going to Mars as part of an official NASO mission. Not many people know how much research NASO has been doing in the field of the paranormal, especially in connection with remote perception and information transfer." That was true. Not many people did know; and the ones who did knew that NASO hadn't been doing any. "We've been talking with NASO for some time now via one of the larger space-engineering corporations, and the decision has been made to conduct comprehensive experiments to assess the effects of the extraterrestrial environment on parapsychological phenomena. . . ."

Zambendorf went on to outline the Mars project, at the same time managing to imply a somewhat exaggerated role for the team without actually saying anything too specific. Jackson listened intently, nodded at the right times, and injected appropriate responses, but he kept his eye on the auditorium for the first signs of restlessness. "It sounds fascinating, Karl," he said when he judged the strain to have increased to just short of breaking point. "We wish you all the success in the world, or maybe I should say out of the world—this one, anyhow—and hope to see you back here on the show again, maybe, after it's all over."

"Thank you. I hope so," Zambendorf replied.

Jackson swiveled to face Zambendorf directly, leaned back to cross one foot over the opposite knee, and allowed his hands to fall from his chin to the armrests of his chair, his change of posture signaling the change of mood and subject. He grinned mischievously, in a way that said this was the part everyone knew had to come eventually. Zambendorf maintained a composed expression. "I have an object in my pocket," Jackson confided. "It's an item of lost property that was handed in at the theater office earlier this evening, probably belonging to somebody in the audience here. Somebody thought Zambendorf might be able to tell us something about it." He turned away for a second and made a palms-up gesture of candor toward the cameras and the audience. "Honestly, folks, this is absolutely genuine. I swear it wasn't set up or anything like that." He turned back to resume talking to Zambendorf. "Well, we thought it was a good idea, and as I said, I have the object with me right here in my pocket. Can you say anything about it . . . or maybe about the owner? . . . I have to say I don't know a lot about this kind of thing, whether this would be considered too tough an assignment, or what, but—" He broke off as he saw the distant look creeping over Zambendorf's face. The auditorium became very still.

"It's vague," Zambendorf murmured after a pause. "But I think I might be able to connect to it. . . ." His voice became sharper for a moment. "If anyone here has lost something, please don't say anything. We'll see what we can do." He fell silent again, and then said to Jackson, "You can help me, Ed. Put your hand inside your pocket, if you would, and touch the object with your fingers." Jackson complied. Zambendorf went on, "Trace its outline and visualize its image... Concentrate harder... Yes, that's better... Ah! I'm getting something clearer now... It's something made of leather, brown leather... A man's wallet, I think. Yes, I'm sure of it. Am I right?"

Jackson shook his head in amazement, drew a light tan wallet from his pocket, and held it high for view. "If the owner is here, don't say anything, remember," he reminded the audience, raising his voice to be heard above the gasps of amazement and the burst of applause that greeted the performance. "There might be more yet." He looked back at Zambendorf with a new respect. When he spoke again, he kept his voice low and solemn, presumably to avoid disturbing the psychic atmosphere. "How about the owner, Karl? Do you see anything there?"

Zambendorf dabbed his forehead and returned his handkerchief to his pocket. Then he took the wallet, held it between the palms of his hands, and stared down at it. "Yes, the owner is here," he announced. He looked out to address the anonymous owner in the audience. "Concentrate hard, please, and try to project an image of yourself into my mind. When contact is established, you will feel a mild tingling sensation in your skull, but that's normal." A hush fell once more. People closed their eyes and reached out with their minds to grasp the tenuous currents of strange forces flowing around them. Then Zambendorf said, "I see you... dark, lean in build, and wearing light blue. You are not alone here. Two people very close to you are with you... family members. And you are far from home... visiting this city, I think. You are from a long way south of here." He looked back at Jackson. "That should do."

Jackson swiveled to speak to the audience. "You can reveal yourself now if you're here, Mr. Dark, Lean, and

Blue," he called out. "Is the owner of this wallet here? If so, would he kindly stand up and identify himself, please?"

Everywhere, heads swung this way and that, and turned to scan the back of the theater. Then, slowly and self-consciously, a man rose to his feet about halfway back near one of the aisles. He was lean in build, Hispanic in appearance, with jet-black hair and a clipped mustache, and was wearing a light-blue suit. He seemed bewildered and stood rubbing the top of his head with his fingers, looking unsure of what he was supposed to do. A boy in the seat beside him tugged at his sleeve, and a dark-skinned woman in the next seat beyond was saying something and gesticulating in the direction of the stage. "Would you come forward and identify your property, please, sir," Jackson said. The man nodded numbly and began picking his way along the row toward the aisle while applause erupted all around, lasting until he had made his way to the front of the auditorium. The noise abated as Jackson came forward to the edge of the stage and inspected the wallet's contents. "This is yours?" he said, looking down. The man nodded. "What's the name inside here?" Jackson enquired.

"The name is Miguel," Zambendorf supplied from where he was still sitting.

"He's right!" Jackson made an appealing gesture as if inviting the audience to share his awe, looked back at Zambendorf, and then stooped to hand the wallet to Miguel. "Where are you from, Miguel?" he asked.

Miguel found his voice at last. "From Mexico... on vacation with my wife and son... Yes, this is mine, Mr. Jackson. Thank you." He cast a final nervous glance at Zambendorf and began walking hastily back up the aisle.

"Happy birthday, Miguel," Zambendorf called after him.

Miguel stopped, turned round, and looked puzzled.

"Isn't it your birthday?" Jackson asked. Miguel shook his head.

"Next week," Zambendorf explained. Miguel gulped

visibly and fled the remaining distance back to his seat.

"Well, how about that!" Jackson exclaimed, and stood with his arms outstretched in appeal while the house responded with sustained applause and shouts of approval. Behind Jackson, Zambendorf sipped from his water glass and allowed the atmosphere to reinforce itself. He could also have revealed that the unknown benefactor who had turned the wallet in after picking Miguel's pocket, and whose suggestion it had been to make a challenge out of it, had also been of swarthy complexion—Armenian, in fact—but somehow that would have spoiled things.

Now the mood of the audience was right. Its appetite had been whetted, and it wanted more. Zambendorf rose and moved forward as if to get closer to them, and Jackson moved away instinctively to become a spectator; it had become Zambendorf's show. Zambendorf raised his arms; the audience became quiet again, but this time tense and expectant. "I have said many times that what I do is not some kind of magic," he told them, his voice rich and resonant in the hall. "It is anyone's to possess. I will show you... At this moment I am sending the impression of a color out into your minds—all of you—a common color. Open your minds... Can you see it?" He looked up at the camera that was live at that moment. "Distance is no barrier. You people watching from your homes, you can join us in this. Focus on the concept of color. Exclude everything else from your thoughts. What do you see?" He turned his head from side to side, waited, and then exclaimed, "Yellow! It was yellow! How many of you got it?" At once a quarter or more of the people in the audience raised their hands.

"Now a number!" Zambendorf told them. His face was radiating excitement. "A number between one and fifty, with its digits both odd but different, such as fifteen... but eleven wouldn't do because both its digits are the same. Yes? Now... think! Feel it!" He closed his eyes, brought his fists up to his temples, held the pose for perhaps five seconds, then looked around once more and announced, "Thirty-seven!" About a third of the hands went up this time, which from the chorus of "ooh"s and "ah"s was enough to impress significantly more people than before. "Possibly I confused some of you there," Zambendorf said. "I was going to try for thirty-five, but at the last moment I changed my mind and decided on—" He stopped as over half the remaining hands went up to add to the others, but it looked as if every hand in the house was waving eagerly. "Oh, some of you did get that, apparently. I should try to be more precise."

But nobody seemed to care very much about his having been sloppy as the conviction strengthened itself in more and more of those present that what they were taking part in was an extremely unusual and immensely significant event. Suddenly all of life's problems and frustrations could be resolved effortlessly by the simple formula of wishing them away. Anyone could comprehend the secret; anyone could command the power. The inescapable became more palatable; the unattainable became trivial. There was no need to feel alone or defenseless. The Master would guide them. They belonged.

"Who is Alice?" Zambendorf demanded. Several Alices responded. "From a city far to the west . . . on the coast," he specified. One of the Alices was from Los Angeles. Zambendorf saw a wedding imminent, involving somebody in her immediate family—her daughter. Alice confirmed that her daughter was due to be married the following month. "You've been thinking about her a lot," Zambendorf said. "That's why you came through so easily. Her name's Nancy, isn't it?"

"Yes . . . Yes, it is." Gasps of astonishment.

"I see the ocean. Is her fiancé a sailor?"

"In the navy . . . on submarines."

"Involved with engineering?"

"No, navigation . . . but yes, I guess that does involve a lot of engineering these days."

"Exactly. Thank you." Loud applause.

Zambendorf went on to supply details of a successful business deal closed that morning by a clothing salesman from Brooklyn, to divine after some hesitation the phone number and occupation of a redheaded young woman from Boston, and to supply correctly the score of a football game in which two boys in the second row had played the previous Tuesday. "You can do it too!" he insisted in a voice that boomed to the rear of the house without aid of a microphone. "I'll show you."

He advanced to the edge of the stage and stared straight ahead while behind him Jackson wrote numbers on a flip-chart. "Concentrate on the first one," Zambendorf told everybody. "All together. Now try and send it... Think it... That's better... A three! I see three. Now the next..." He got seven right out of eight. "You see!" he shouted exultantly. "You're good—very good. Let's try something more difficult."

He picked up the black velvet bag provided by prior arrangement and had Jackson and a couple of people near the front verify that it was opaque and without holes. Then he turned his back and allowed Jackson to secure the bag over his head as a blindfold. Then, following Zambendorf's instructions, Jackson pointed silently to select a woman in the audience, and the woman chose an item from among the things she had with her and held it high for everyone to see. It happened to be a green pen. She then pointed to another member of the audience—a man sitting a half dozen or so rows farther back—to repeat the procedure. The man held up a watch with a silver bracelet, and so it went. Jackson noted the objects on the flip-chart. When he had listed five, he covered the chart, turned the stand around to face the wall for good measure, and told Zambendorf he was free to remove the blindfold.

"Remember, I'm relying on every one of you," Zambendorf said. "You must all help if we're going to make this a success. Now, the first of the objects—recall it and picture it in your minds. Now send it to me...." He frowned, concentrated, and pounded his brow. The audience redoubled its efforts. Viewers at home joined in. "Writing... something to do with writing," Zambendorf said at last. "A pen! Now the color. The color is . . . green! I get green. Were you sending green?" By the time he got the fifth item correctly, the audience was wild.

For his finale Zambendorf produced his other prop—a solid-looking metal rod about two feet long and well over an inch thick. Jackson couldn't bend it when challenged, and neither could three men from near the front of the audience. "But the power of the mind overcomes matter," Zambendorf declared. He gave Jackson the rod to hold, and touched it lightly in the center with his fingers. "This will require all of us," Zambendorf called out. "All of us here, and everybody at home. I want you all to help me concentrate on bending. Think it—bending. Say it—bending! *Bending!*" He looked at Jackson and nodded in time with the rhythm as he repeated the word.

Jackson caught on quickly and began motioning with a hand like a conductor urging an orchestra. "Bending! Bending! Bending! Bending! . . ." he recited, his voice growing louder and more insistent.

Gradually, the audience took up the chant. "Bending! Bending! *Bending! Bending!*" Zambendorf turned fully toward them and threw his arms wide in exhortation. His eyes gleamed in the spotlights; his teeth shone white. "*Bending! Bending! Bending!*" He laid a hand on the rod. Jackson gasped and stared down wide-eyed as the metal bowed. Some of the audience were staring ashen-faced. Zambendorf took the rod and held it high over his head in one hand, gazing up at it triumphantly while it continued to bend in full view while a thousand voices in unison raised themselves to a frenzy. Women had started screaming. A number of people fled along the aisles toward the exits. A bearded, hawk-faced man with an open Bible in one hand climbed onto the stage, pointed an accusing finger at Zambendorf, and began reading something unintelligible amid the pandemonium before security guards grabbed him and hustled him away.

A frantic viewer in Delaware was trying to get past a jammed NBC switchboard to report that her aluminum chair had buckled at the precise moment that Zambendorf commanded the rod to bend. Another's lighting circuits all blew at the same instant. A hen coop in Wyoming was struck by lightning. A washing machine caught fire in Alabama. Eight people had heart attacks. A clock began running backward in California. Two expectant mothers had had spontaneous abortions. A nuclear reactor shut itself down in Tennessee.

In the control room on a higher level behind the stage area, one of the video engineers on duty stared incredulously at the scenes on the main panel monitor screens. "My God!" he muttered to the technician munching a tuna sandwich in the chair next to him. "If he told them to give him all their money, rip off their clothes, and follow him to China, you know something, Chet—they'd do it."

Chet continued eating and considered the statement. "Or to Mars, maybe," he replied after a long, thoughtful silence.

4

EARLY THE FOLLOWING EVENING, CONLON AND WHITtaker arrived at Gerold Massey's house, situated at the end of a leafy cul-de-sac on the north side of Georgetown. Although lofty, spacious, and solidly built, it was an untidy and in some ways inelegant heap of a house—a composition of after-thoughts, with walls and gables projecting in all directions, roofs meeting at strange angles, and a preposterous chateau-style turret adorning the upper part of one corner. The interior was a warren of interconnecting rooms and passages, with cubbyholes and stairways in unexpected places, old-fashioned sash windows, and lots of wood carving and paneling. The part of the cellars not dedicated to storing the junk that Massey had been accumulating through life contained a workshop-lab which he used mainly for developing psychological testing equipment and perfecting new magic props, while the floors above included, in addition to the usual living space, an overflowing library, a computer room, and accommodations for his regular flow of short-term guests, who varied from students temporarily out on the street to fellow magicians and visiting professors from abroad.

Contrary to widespread belief, including that prevalent among many scientists, scientific qualifications were largely irrelevant to assessing reliably the claims of alleged miracle-workers, mind readers, psychics, and the like. Scientists could be fooled by deliberate trickery or unconscious self-deception as easily as the average layman and, sometimes, more easily if competence and prestige earned in other fields were allowed to produce delusions of infallibility. The world of natural phenomena that was properly the object of the scientist's expertise could be baffling at times, but it never resorted to outright dishonesty and always yielded rational answers in the end. Theorems were provable; calculations, checkable; observations, repeatable; and assumptions, verifiable. Things in the natural world meant what they said. But that was seldom the case in the world of human affairs, where illogic operated freely and deception was the norm. To catch a thief one should set a thief; the adage tells; and to catch a conjuror, set a conjuror. If the skills of the physicist and the neurochemist were of little help in comprehending the deviousness of human irrationality and the art of the professional deceiver, those of the psychologist and the magician were; Gerold Massey happened to be both, and he was engaged regularly by government and private organizations as a consultant on and investigator of matters allegedly supernatural and paranormal.

That was how Massey and Walter Conlon had come to know each other. In 2015 a "psychic" had claimed to travel over vast distances through the "astral plane" and described the surface features of Uranus and Neptune in vivid detail. When French probes finally arrived and sent back pictures contradicting his accounts, his excuse had been that he had perhaps underestimated his powers and projected himself to planets in some entirely different star system! The year 2017 had seen another flap about bodies from a crashed alien spacecraft—this time hidden in a secret base in Nevada. A year later some officials in Washington were giving serious consideration to an offer from a California-based management recruiting firm to screen NASO flight-crew applicants on the basis of a crank numerology system involving computerized personal "psychometric aptitudinal configurator charts." And, inevitably, there was always someone pushing for NASO to involve itself in the perennial UFO controversy. In fact Massey supposed that Conlon wanted to talk about Senator Korning and the whatever-it-was Church of Oregon. But Massey was wrong. Conlon had involved him in some strange situations over the years and occasionally sent him off to some out-of-the-way places. But never anything like this. Conlon had never before wanted him to leave Earth itself, and travel with a NASO mission across interplanetary space.

"The idea is to expand the pilot base at Meridiani Sinus into a mixed, experimental community of about five hundred people to provide data on extraterrestrial living for future space-colony design," Conlon explained from a leather armchair standing before a grandfather clock built to look like an Egyptian sarcophagus. "One area that needs a lot more study is how such conditions will affect the behavior and emotions of sizeable groups of people, what kinds of stress are likely to be experienced, and so on, which means there'll be a number of psychologists going along. Officially you'd be filling one of those slots, with Vernon there to assist. Unofficially some of us in NASO want somebody knowledgeable to get the real story on this Zambendorf stunt... and maybe even blow the whole thing out of the water if the opportunity presents itself. It's gone too far, Gerry. We've got better things to do. If we don't put a stop to this nonsense now, the next thing will be astrologers being hired to fix launch dates."

Massey returned a puzzled frown from across the room, where he was sitting sprawled untidily across a couch with one foot propped on a piece of a partly dismantled trick-cabinet that he had been meaning to move for weeks. "You have to do something," he agreed. "But what I don't understand is why it's happening at all. What on earth possessed NASO to go along with this Zambendorf thing in the first place?"

Conlon sighed and threw up his hands. "That was how it came down the line to me... there's been a lot of high-level politics between GSEC and NASO that I'm not in on. Anyhow, most of the funding's coming from GSEC.

Defense takes first place for government money; social experiments on Mars don't even get on the list. With lawyers and accountants taking over the government, we've had to depend more on the private sector to keep a planetary program going at all. Naturally, that gives outfits like GSEC a say in the planning and policymaking."

"Maybe the best thing would be for you to opt out," Vernon Price said from an elaborately ornamented stool, his back to the church organ that Massey had picked up in a yard-sale six years previously while driving through Mississippi. He was in his late twenties, lithe, with dark, wavy hair and alert, bright brown eyes. "I mean, if the mission's being turned into a circus, the wisest thing might be to keep PEP out of it."

Conlon shook his head. "I hear what you're saying, Vernon, but we can't do that. The scientific opportunities are too valuable to miss. And besides that, the mission will involve the first operational use of the *Orion*, which we have to retain our interest in for the sake of planetary projects now on the drawing boards. If we dropped out, it would leave the Pentagon as the only government department with an interest in further development of the *Orion*. We can't afford to let that happen."

The European-American scientific base near the Martian equator at Meridiani Sinus had begun as a purely American attempt to rival the Soviet plan for establishing a permanently manned facility at Solis Lacus. However, the U.S. program had bogged down over problems with the development of the inertial fusion drive considered essential to supporting human life reliably over interplanetary distances. A crash program conducted cooperatively with the European NATO nations and Japan had eventually provided a prototype system that did work, and Meridiani Sinus had followed as a joint U.S.-European venture two years behind both the original American schedule and the Soviets; shortly afterward, the space agencies on both sides of the Atlantic were merged to form NASO. Intensified work from then on had made up for some of the lost time and produced a series of test designs for thermonuclear-propelled space-vehicles, culminating in the *Orion*—the first vessel built specifically for carrying heavy payloads and large numbers of passengers between planets. Completed in orbit in 2019, the *Orion* had been shuttling back and forth on trials between Earth and Moon for over half a year, six months to a year ahead of a similar project which the Japanese were pursuing independently. The Soviets, who were concentrating on large platforms in Earth orbit, had nothing to compare with either of the large interplanetary ships, so at least the U.S. had some compensation for the embarrassment incurred by its earlier fiasco.

Massey turned his head to look across at Whittaker, tall and tanned, with dark, crinkly hair just beginning to show gray at the temples, who was sitting in the armchair opposite Conlon. With the comfortable income that he commanded independent of his position at Global Communications Networking, he seemed to regard his job as much as an intellectual exercise and a challenge in problem-solving as anything else, and had always struck Massey as something of an enigma. "So how do you fit into this, Pat?" Massey asked. "Is this where you get your chance to give us some real news for a change?"

Whittaker's eyes twinkled briefly as he nodded. "It sounds as if it could be, doesn't it."

Things that were different were supposed to constitute news, Whittaker had often said. But miracle-workers, disaster-imminent scares, nonexistent Soviet superweapons, economic ruin always just around the corner, and all the other media-manufactured myths that kept millions glued to screens in order to sell products were no longer different. Therefore they weren't news. But turning a contrived sensation round and boomeranging it by reporting the intended deception straight for once—*that* could be very different.

"Well, if Pat did manage to pull something spectacular out of it, it might persuade other GSECs to stay out of NASO's business in future," Vernon remarked.

"That's what I want," Conlon said, nodding emphatically.

Whittaker spread his hands and made a face. "Well, I mean...using a NASO mission to try and legitimatize this kind of nonsense? Do you think the directors at GSEC believe in it?"

Massey shrugged. "How do I know? Nothing would surprise me these days, Pat. I hope you guys at GCN don't rely too much on them for advertising revenues though."

"Aw, what the hell?" Whittaker said. "Someone's got to do something to put a stop to this nonsense before it goes any further."

There wasn't a lot more to be said. Conlon looked from Vernon to Massey and asked simply, "Well?"

They looked at each other, but neither of them had pressing questions. "What do you think?" Massey asked at last. Vernon raised his eyebrows, hunched his shoulders, and opened his arms in a way that said there could be only one answer. Massey nodded slowly, tugged at his beard and thought to himself for a few moments longer, and then looked back at Conlon. "I guess we'll buy it, Walt. You've just got yourself a deal."

Conlon looked pleased. "Good. The *Orion*'s scheduled for liftout from Earth orbit three months from now. I'll have NASO's confirmation of the offer, including remuneration, wired through within forty-eight hours. We'll have the other details and specifics worked out for you both in about a week. There'll be a training and familiarization course at the NASO Personnel Development Center in North Carolina for all the non-NASO people going on the mission, so leave the last three weeks or so clear when you make your arrangements for leave of absence from the university, et cetera."

Whittaker sat up in his chair, rubbed his hands together, and picked up his empty wineglass from the side table next to him. "I think this calls for a refill," he said. "Same again for everyone?"

"I'll get them," Massey said.

Whittaker watched as Massey collected the glasses and took them over to the open liquor cabinet. "Did you see Zambendorf on the Ed Jackson Show last night?"

"Uh-huh," Massey grunted over his shoulder.

"Quite a performance," Whittaker said.

"Oh, Zambendorf's a good showman—let's not make any mistake about that," Massey answered. "And if he'd only be content to come up with a straight act, he'd make a first-rate stage magician. But I can't go along with this business about claiming to be genuine. A lot of people are taken in by it and spend too much of their time and money looking for fairyland when they could be getting something worthwhile out of life. It's a tragic squandering of human potential and talent."

"The thing with the color and the number was pretty straightforward, I thought," Whittaker said.

"Simple probability matches, weren't they?" Conlon said, looking at Vernon. Vernon nodded. Whittaker looked at him inquiringly.

"With an audience that size, enough people would think of yellow to make the demonstration look impressive—or any other color you care to name, come to that," Vernon explained. "Zambendorf didn't have to be thinking of anything. The audience only assumed he was because he said he was."

"How about the number?" Whittaker asked. "That couldn't have worked the same way, surely. Thirty-something . . . thirty-seven, wasn't it? I'd have thought the odds would be much worse there."

"So would most people," Vernon said. "But think back to what Zambendorf said—a number below fifty with both digits odd but different. If you work it out, there aren't really that many possibilities. And do you remember him giving fifteen and eleven as examples? That narrows it down further because for some reason hardly anyone will pick them after they've been mentioned. Of the numbers that are left, about thirty-five percent of a crowd will go for thirty-seven every time. No one knows why. It's just a predictable behavior pattern among people. Psychologists call it a 'population stereotype.' And it also happens to be a fact that around twenty-three percent will choose thirty-five. So all that business about changing his mind at the last moment was baloney to widen his total catch to over half. And it worked—it looked as if every hand in the place were up."

"Mmm . . . interesting," Whittaker said.

"Do you remember Zambendorf telling the woman about her daughter's being about to get married to a navigation officer, in the navy, on submarines?" Massey asked, turning away from the cabinet and coming back with two refilled glasses.

"Yes," Whittaker said. "That was impressive. Now how could he have known all that?"

"He didn't," Massey replied simply. Whittaker looked puzzled. Massey handed the drinks to Whittaker and Conlon, then returned to the cabinet to pour his own and Vernon's. "Your memory's playing tricks, Pat. We've got a recording of the whole show that I'll replay if you like. Zambendorf only said Alice's daughter was about to get married to a sailor. He never said navy, he never said submarines, and he never mentioned navigation. Alice did—but people don't remember it that way. In fact Zambendorf guessed that the guy was in engineering, which was reasonable but wrong as it happened, and Alice corrected him. But not only that—she turned the miss into a semihit by manufacturing an excuse for him. Did you notice? I'd bet that practically everyone who saw it has forgotten that failure; but if he'd guessed right, they'd all have remembered. People see and remember what they want to see and remember. The Zambendorfs in the world get a lot of mileage out of that fact."

Vernon nodded. "So the only information he actually originated himself was that the daughter was marrying a sailor."

"So how could he have known even that much?" Whittaker asked.

Massey shrugged. "There are all kinds of ways he might have done it. For instance, anyone hanging around the box office before the show could have overheard plenty of that kind of talk."

Whittaker looked astonished. "What, seriously? You're kidding! I mean, it's too—too simple. A child could have thought of that."

"Easily," Massey agreed. "But most adults wouldn't. Believe me, Pat, that one's been worked for years. The simpler the answer, the less obvious it is to most people. They always look for the most complicated explanations imaginable." Massey handed a glass to Vernon and began moving past Whittaker to return to the couch.

"Was the wallet planted?" Conlon asked. "Martha says it had to be, but I'm not so sure. Somehow I don't think Ed Jackson would have gone out of his way to lie so brazenly."

Massey was about to reply when his arm knocked against the side table beside Whittaker, causing a drop of wine to spill from the glass that Massey was carrying. "Oh, I'm sorry, Pat! Here, I'll take care of it," he exclaimed, setting down the glass and dabbing lightly at the collar of Whittaker's jacket. "Only a spot—it won't show." Then Massey picked up his drink again, sat down on the couch, and looked over at Conlon. "Sorry, Walt. What were you saying?"

"I said I wasn't convinced the wallet was planted."

"Oh yes, I think I agree with you," Massey said. "The Mexican guy looked genuine enough to me. That part didn't come across as an act at all."

Whittaker looked from Massey to Vernon, who was grinning oddly, and back at Massey. "So . . . how did he know it was a wallet, and how did he know who owned it?" he asked.

"You really want to know?" Massey asked lightly.

"Well, sure." Whittaker looked puzzled. "What's so funny? Am I missing the obvious or something? If I am, all I can say is that a hell of a lot of other people must have missed it too."

There was silence for a few seconds. Then Vernon said, "Remember, we're pretty sure that Zambendorf had a confederate or two around the place. The information he came up with was all the kind of stuff you'd expect to find inside a wallet, plus he knew what the owner of the wallet looked like. Now think about that."

Whittaker thought hard for a while, then looked over at Conlon. Conlon shrugged. Whittaker looked back at Massey, shook his head, and showed his empty palms. "Okay, I give in. How'd he know?"

Massey laughed, produced Whittaker's wallet from his armpit, and tossed it back to him. "That tell you enough? And there wasn't anything on your jacket, by the way, so don't worry about it."

"You're kidding!" Whittaker protested. "You mean somebody stole it and then turned it in?"

"See what I mean, Pat—too simple to think of, isn't it?"

"And the things the people showed while he had the bag over his head?"

Massey brushed an imaginary speck of dust from his eyebrow, rubbed the tip of his nose with a thumb, drew a finger lightly from left to right along his upper lip, and then pinched the lobe of his right ear. "A confederate giving coded signals from somewhere in the front rows . . . probably an Armenian character called Abaquaan, who's always close by Zambendorf somewhere, but you never see him."

"And the metal bar?"

"Standard magician's equipment. If you saw it done at a school variety show without all the hype, you'd applaud politely and say it was a clever trick. In fact that's one aspect of some research that Vernon and I are into at the moment. It's amazing—if people have made their minds up that what they're seeing is genuine paranormal power in action, they'll stick to their conviction even after they've agreed that any good stage magician can produce exactly the same effect. No amount of appealing to reason will change them. In fact—"

At that moment the organ behind Vernon blasted out a series of rising and falling notes, and a hollow, synthetic computer voice announced, "Visitor at the portals."

Massey glanced at the sarcophagus clock. "That'll be the cab. Drink up. We can have a couple more at the bar before we sit down to eat."

They left the house five minutes later and stopped for a moment below the porch to pick out the pinpoint of Mars in the evening sky. "It makes you think," Conlon said absently. "Sometime back in the eighteen hundreds, they thought it was miraculous when the first clipper ship made it from Boston round the Horn to San Francisco in under a hundred days. And here we are a century and a half later, going to Mars and back in the same time."

"*Limits to Growth*," Vernon murmured.

"Huh?" Whittaker said.

"Oh, it's the title of some dumb book I read from the seventies," Vernon replied.

"I see no limits," Conlon said, scanning the stars. "Where do I look?"

"In people's minds," Massey answered.

A thoughtful look came over Vernon's face as he followed Conlon's gaze upward. "I guess there have to be other intelligences out there somewhere," he mused. "Do you think they have kooks too, or is it a uniquely human thing?"

Massey snorted as they resumed walking toward the waiting cab. "Nothing out there could be dumber than some people," he said.

5

FRENNELECH, PRESIDING EMINENCE OF THE HIGH Council of Priests at Pergassos, the principal city in the land of the Kroaxians, stared down from his raised, central seat behind the Council bench and waited for the accused to begin his explanation. His tall headdress of fine-grown, reflective organic scales and his imposing robes of woven wire, heavily embroidered with carbon fibers and plastic thread, enhanced his stature and made all the more intimidating the stern expression formed by the setting of the coolant outlet vanes above his chin and the thermal patterns radiating from his metal facial surfaces. An acolyte standing behind the chair held the organic-grown rod of yellow and red spiral stripes, topped by an ornamented ball, that was Frennelech's emblem of office, while to the left and right, the lesser priests sat in solemn dignity, holding their own, lesser emblems in their steel fingers.

Heavy chains rattled as the accused, Lofbayel, Maker-of-Maps, rose nervously to his feet in the center of the Council Chamber. The guards standing on either side of him remained impassive while for a few seconds he stared, cowed and bewildered. Then Horazzorgio, the sadistic-looking captain of the Royal Guard who had been in command at the time of Lofbayel's arrest, jabbed him roughly in the back with the handle of a carbide-tipped lance. "Speak when the Illustrious One commands!" he ordered.

Lofbayel staggered, and caught the bar before him to

steady himself. "My words were not spoken with any intent to contradict the Holy Scribings," he stammered hastily. "Indeed, they were not spoken with thought of the Scribings at all. For—"

"Aha!" Rekashoba, Prosecuter for the High Council, wheeled round abruptly and pointed an accusing finger. "Already he confesses. Is it not written: 'In all thy words and deeds, be thou mindful of the Holy Scribings'? He stands condemned by his own words."

"The impiety has been noted," Frennelech said coldly from the bench. And to Lofbayel, "Continue."

The mapmaker's imaging matrixes flickered despondently. "It has long been my practice to collect writings and drawings of travelers, navigators, explorers, soldiers, and scholars from both this and other lands," he explained, and added, "...for the purpose of further improving the quality of the services that I render to His Supreme Majesty, the King."

"May the Lifemaker protect the King!" Horazzorgio shouted from behind.

"Let it be so," the bench of priests chanted in response, with the exception of Frennelech, whose rank excused him from the obligation.

Lofbayel continued, "In amassing many such records originated over a time of many twelves of twelve-brights, I found impressing itself upon me a strange but persistent recurrence: that beyond any place that lies as far to the east as one may choose to name, there are always reported more places that lie yet farther to the east... until they become places that other travelers have encountered to the west. And the same is found to be true of north and south, for either becomes the other. I have evidence which suggests the same is true for all directions, and for a journey commenced at any place." Lofbayel looked along the line of stony-faced priests. "Consideration of these facts—if they are facts, of course—led me to the supposition that any journey, if protracted long enough without hindrance or deviation, must eventually close a path back to its beginning."

"And therefore you conclude the entire world to be round in form?" Frennelech sounded incredulous and at the same time appalled. "Through idle daydreaming, you believe that you can acquire knowledge . . . spurning the Scribings, which are the sole source of all true knowledge? What arrogance is this?"

"I . . . It was intended merely as a conundrum concocted for the amusement of students who seek my instruction in the methods of calculation and the graphic arts," Lofbayel replied. "We asked: 'What form has no center, yet has centers everywhere, and is limited in size but unlimited in extent?' Further contemplation and experiment revealed that the sphere alone possesses properties consistent with the conditions which the riddle specified, and this prompted the further question: 'Given that the world shares properties in common with the sphere, must it not follow that it shares the sphere's form also?'"

Rekashoba, the Prosecutor, snorted and turned away contemptuously, indicating that he had heard as much as his patience would withstand. He straightened and raised his head to address the bench. "First, to dispose of the possibility of there being any factual basis to this allegation, I will present three independent proofs that the world cannot be round. And second, I will show that this is no mere innocent exercise in riddles as has been claimed, but a pernicious attempt to challenge the authority of the Lifemaker's worldly representatives by poisoning the minds of the young and casting doubts upon the teachings of the divinely inspired Scribings. Therefore the strictest of penalties is not only in order, but mandatory."

Rekashoba paused, appealed to the chamber with a flourish, and then picked up a cellulose ball and a goblet of methane. "My first proof is based on no more than the sense that is common to all robeings, and will delay us for but a short while." He poured a small quantity of liquid onto the top of the ball and watched as it trickled down to the underside and finally fell away in a thin stream to the floor. "A body of liquid cannot sustain itself upon the surface of a sphere," he observed. "It follows that the surface of a world formed as a sphere could not contain oceans of methane. But the oceans exist, do they not? Or am I misinformed? Or do thousands of navigators and voyagers delude themselves?" He looked penetratingly at Lofbayel. "What reply do you have, Denier-of-Oceans?"

"I have none," Lofbayel murmured unhappily.

Rekashoba put down the goblet and tossed the ball aside as unworthy of consuming more of the Council's time. "But were the sphere vast enough, the oceans might be constrained just to its upper regions, one might suppose," he said airily. "However, that brings us to my second proof—that what has been claimed contradicts itself logically." Rekashoba half turned to point to one of Lofbayel's charts, which was being displayed on one side of the chamber as evidence. "This chart, we are told, represents the entire world in extent, although much of it remains blank and devoid of any detail," he said. "Now observe—do not the oceans compose the major portion of it? But were this indeed the entire world, and were that world indeed a sphere, the oceans, being constrained by necessity as shown in my first proof to occupying only its upper regions, would compose the minor portion. Therefore either the world cannot be a sphere, or the chart does not depict the entire world. If the world is not a sphere, then the proof rests. If the chart is not of the entire world, then the accused's own words stand in contradiction to the fact, and since his conclusion follows from an assertion thereby shown to be erroneous, the conclusion is disproved. Hence, by the second alternative also, the world is not a sphere. Since there was no third alternative, the proposition is proved by rigorous logic."

Rekashoba surveyed the faces of the Council members solemnly. "My third proof follows from sacred doctrine." His voice had taken on an ominous note, and he paused for a moment to allow the more serious mood to take effect. "If this matter had no further implications, I could dismiss it as a consequence of nothing more than foolishness and ignorance. But it transcends far beyond such limits by denying one of the fundamental teachings given to us in the Holy Scribings: the Doctrine of Temporal Representation and Succession." He paused again, turned to address the whole chamber, and raised a hand in front of him.

"The world was created in a form designed by the Lifemaker to provide a constant reminder that the Church and State function as the divinely ordained instruments of His authority, and that their organizational hierarchies constitute visible embodiments of His will. Thus the solid canopy of the sky, beyond which the mortal world is not permitted ever to look, symbolizes the Supreme Archprelate"—the Prosecutor turned and inclined his head deferentially in Frennelech's direction—"who sits at the highest position attainable by mere robeings. The sky is supported by the unscalable mountains of the Peripheral Barrier that bounds world, just as the Supreme Archprelate is supported by the spiritual and secular leaders of the civilized world, who are chosen to command heights unclimbable by ordinary robeings, one of whom, of course, is His Supreme Majesty."

"May the Lifemaker protect the King!" Horazzorgio shouted.

"Let it be so," the bench responded.

Rekashoba continued, "The lesser mountains support the higher, and the foothills support the lesser, just as the lower clerics and officials of the State support higher edifices above them. And below, the plains and deserts must reconcile themselves to their rightful place in the scheme, as must the masses." He extended a warning finger. "But the masses must not make the mistake of imagining from these considerations that their lot is a harsh or an unjust one. Indeed, quite the opposite! For, just as the lowlands are sheltered from the storms that rage in the mountains and nourished by the streams flowing down to them from above, so the common masses are protected and receive spiritual nourishment from the Lifemaker through the succession of higher agencies that He has appointed."

Rekashoba's voice took on a harder note as he looked

back at Lofbayel. "But a round world would be incompatible with the sacred translations of the Scribings. Since the Scribings cannot be questioned, a round world cannot exist." He waited a second for his argument to register, and then continued in a louder voice, "But, more than that, any claim to the contrary must therefore constitute a denial of the Scribings. And such a denial amounts, in a word, to . . . heresy!" A murmur ran round the chamber. Lofbayel clutched weakly at the bar and for a moment looked as if he was about to collapse. The full penalty in the event of a charge of heresy being upheld was the burning out of both eyes, followed by slow dissolution in an acid vat. Horazzorgio's eyes glinted in gloating anticipation; the arresting officer had first option to command the execution in the event of a death sentence. The Council members leaned forward to confer among themselves in low voices.

Seated behind the officials and scribes, to one side of the chamber, was a rustic-looking figure, simply attired in a brown tunic of coarse-woven copper, secured by a heavy, black, braided belt, and a dull red cloak assembled from interlocking ceramic platelets. Thirg, Asker-of-Forbidden-Questions, drew in a long stream of nitrogen to cool his overworked emotive circuits and took a moment to prepare himself. As a longtime friend of Lofbayel, a fellow inquirer after truth, and one who had enjoyed the hospitality of Lofbayel's house on many occasions during visits from his solitary abode in the forest below the mountains, Thirg had promised Lofbayel's wife that he would plead her husband's case if the trial went badly. Thirg was far from optimistic about his ability to achieve anything useful, and what he had seen of Rekashoba's zealousness led him to fear that the mere act of speaking out in his friend's defense might well be enough to make him a marked person in future, subject to constant scrutiny, questioning, and harassment. But a promise was a promise. Besides, the very idea of not trying was unthinkable. Thirg braced himself and gripped the edges of his seat.

Frennelech looked back out over the chamber. "Does

the accused have anything to say before the Council's verdict is announced?"

Lofbayel attempted to speak, but fear made him incoherent. Frennelech shifted his gaze to the Court Warden. "One is present who is willing to speak for the accused," the Warden said. Thirg took off his cap of aluminum mail, and clutching it before him, rose slowly.

"Who speaks for the accused?" Frennelech demanded.

"Thirg, a recluse dweller of the forest, who describes himself as a friend of the accused," the Warden replied.

"Speak, Thirg," Frennelech ordered.

The court and the priests of the Council waited. After a slight hesitation, to find his words, Thirg began speaking cautiously. "Illustrious members of the High Council and officers of the Court, it cannot be denied that words have been uttered rashly, which a moment of prudence and wisdom would have left unsaid. Since truth and justice are the business of the Court, whatever consequences must lawfully follow, it is not my desire to dispute. But the suggestion of heresy, I would respectfully submit, warrants further examination if the possibility of a hasty decision unbecoming of the elders and wisest of Kroaxia is to be avoided." He paused to look along the line of faces, and found a modicum of reassurance that he was being heeded.

"For by its very definition, a heresy, we are told, is a denial of the truths set forth in the Holy Scribings. But does not a denial require a statement of that which is denied? We have heard no such statement uttered, and neither has anyone attributed any such statement to the accused. Instead we are assured, by accused and accuser alike, merely of a question's being asked. Since a question cannot of itself presume its own answer, nothing that may rightfully be judged as heresy can have been stated."

Some of the Council priests were looking at each other questioningly while others were muttering among themselves. It sounded as if at least some of them were seeing the issue in a new perspective. Encouraged and feeling a spark of genuine hope for the first time, Thirg set down his cap, made a brief gesture of appeal, and went on, "Further, I would, with the Court's approval, offer not a third alternative to the two presented in the learned Prosecutor's proof by logic—for he has assured us that no third possibility exists—but rather the suggestion that the second alternative may be seen, upon closer inspection, to divide itself into two subtler variations, namely: Either the world is round, or the anecdotes of travelers cannot be relied upon. Thus, by offering a manifest absurdity as one of the possible answers for his students to choose, the teacher's question is revealed as a cryptic lesson on the reliability of faith as a guide to truth as opposed to the evidence of the senses, when the two are found to be in conflict."

Some of the priests were looking impressed, and even Frennelech's expression seemed to have softened a fraction. Thirg concluded, "My final observation is that in his capacity as an assistant to the Royal Surveyor, the accused renders valuable service to His Sup—" Thirg caught a pained look from Frennelech and emended, "to the nation of Kroaxia, which is of especial importance at a time such as this, when we are threatened by foreign enemies. If the Lifemaker in His wisdom has seen fit to send us a competent maker of maps and charts, we would be well advised, in my humble submission, to think carefully before dispatching His gift back to Him unused."

With that, Thirg sat down and found that he was shaking. The Council went into further deliberation, and after much murmuring and head-wagging, Frennelech quieted the chamber and announced, "The verdict of the Council is that the accused stands guilty of irresponsibility, irreverence, and impiety to a degree inexcusable of a common citizen, and criminally indictable for a teacher." He paused. "The charge of heresy, however, is not substantiated." Lofbayel swayed on his feet and cried out aloud with relief. Excited murmurs rippled round the chamber, while Rekashoba turned angrily away and Horazzorgio looked at Thirg venomously. Frennelech continued, "The Council has accepted a motion for leniency, and the sentence of this Court is that the accused be fined to the amount of one-quarter of his possessions; that the accused shall serve two brights of penance and recantation in a public place; and that the accused be banned permanently from all practice of teaching, writing of materials for public distribution, all other means of disseminating ideas, thoughts, or opinions in public, and all forms of activity associated therewith. The session is now ended."

"The Court will rise," the Warden ordered. Everyone stood while Frennelech rose from his seat, turned, and swept from the chamber, followed by two attendants and the acolyte. After a respectful pause the other Council members filed out in silent dignity. Lofbayel nodded numbly but managed to send the ghost of a grateful smile in Thirg's direction as he was led away. Voices and murmurs broke out all around, and the remaining attendees broke up and began to drift toward the doors individually or in small groups.

On one side of the chamber Horazzorgio moved closer to Rekashoba, who was gathering up his documents while he watched Thirg disappear among the figures crowded outside the doorway. "Who is he?" Rekashoba asked in a low, menacing voice. "What do you know of him?"

"But little, I fear," Horazzorgio answered. "He lives well away from the city, at the upper edge of the forest below the mountains. But I have heard talk of his proclivity for dabbling in Black Arts and sorcery. I will make inquiries."

"Do so," Rekashoba growled. "And have him watched. Get every shred of evidence you can find against him. We must make certain that all the eloquence in the world will not save *him* from the vats when he stands accused before the Council."

6

KARL ZAMBENDORF HAD BEEN BORN IN THE NORTH Austrian city of Werfen in 1967 as Karl Zammerschnigg, the third of a family of three brothers and two sisters whose father was a hard-working bookkeeper and whose mother, a teacher. At a comparatively early age he had made the disturbing discovery that his parents, though honest, intelligent, industrious, and exemplary in the various other virtues that were supposed to earn just reward, would never be as wealthy as he thought they deserved, nor would their labors earn any public recognition or acclaim. He gradually came to perceive this anomaly as simply a part of the larger conspiracy of systematic self-deception practiced by society in general, which while dutifully praising knowledge and learning, lavished riches and fame not on its thinkers, creators, and producers, but on those who helped it to defend its prejudices and sustain its fantasies. Knowledge, if the truth were admitted—which was rarely the case—was in fact the enemy; it threatened to explode the myths upon which the prejudices and the fantasies were based.

He left home at the age of nineteen and teamed up with a Russian defector who was causing a small stir in Europe by claiming to have been a subject of top-secret Soviet military experiments in psychic perception. Over the following few years, which proved educational as well as profitable, young Zammerschnigg came to recognize fully his own innate talents, and in the process discovered an irresistible way to thumb his nose at the whole system of stylized rules and artificial standards by which the drab, the dreary, the gullible, and the conforming would have had him be like them. The Russian, however, was not attuned to exploiting the opportunities afforded by commercialized Western mass-media culture. So Zammerschnigg changed his name and embarked on his own career with the aid of an influential West German magazine publisher. Within five years Karl Zambendorf had become a celebrity.

His road to worldwide fame and fortune opened up in Hamburg when he was introduced to Dr.—of what, was obscure—Osmond Periera from Arizona, a researcher of the paranormal and a convinced UFOlogist who had written a number of best-sellers claiming among other things that the roughly circular North Polar Sea was in fact a gigantic crater caused by the crash of an antimatter-powered alien spacecraft; that the area had once been a continent harboring an advanced human culture ("Polantis," not Atlantis—the legend had been distorted); and that a polar shift and the climatic upheavals caused by the impact were at the root of all kinds of ancient myths and legends. Ridicule from the scientific community had merely reinforced Periera's lifelong ambition to go down in history as the Sigmund Freud of parapsychology; and after his "discovery" of Zambendorf, he displayed the fervor and ecstasy of a wandering ascetic who had at last found his guru. Whatever else his peculiarities, Periera's books had made money, which meant he possessed the connections necessary to boost Zambendorf to even higher orbits; accordingly, Zambendorf accepted an invitation to accompany Periera back to the U.S.A.

The U.S. scientific community remained largely aloof and disinterested, and the "experts" that Periera produced to vindicate his claims turned out to be from its more credulous fringes. Zambendorf proceeded to divine information from tamper-proof sealed envelopes, influence delicate electrical measuring instruments by pure mind power, alter the decay rates of radioisotopes, read thoughts, prophesy events, and perform many other wondrous feats which America's professional dream merchants built into a world sensation. Zambendorf's confidence grew with every new guffaw as "experts" tumbled in their tumbril-loads.

He owed his success in no small degree to the loyalty of the odd collection of individuals who had attached themselves to him over the years. He especially depended on them for information-gathering, and a characteristic shared by all the members of his team, despite their various differences, was an instinct for information likely to be of value in Zambendorf's business and an ability to acquire it, legally, ethically, and honestly . . . or otherwise. Anticipating future information needs was one of the team's never-ending activities.

The atmosphere by the pool outside Zambendorf's villa overlooking the Pacific from the hills above Malibu was businesslike despite the setting as he, Abaquaan, and Thelma discussed the latest status update forwarded from GSEC, which among other things listed the people nominated so far to accompany the Mars mission. "We'll need background histories and profiles on as many of those names as we can get," Zambendorf said, propped on a sun-lounge by a table of iced drinks and fruits. Thelma, wearing a beach-wrap over a bikini, sat taking notes beneath a sunshade at another table littered with some of the books on Mars, the history of planetary exploration, and NASO that she had been immersing herself in for days. "Make a separate list of the scientists. Clarissa has some useful contacts at most of the professional institutions—she can take care of those."

"Okay . . . Okay . . . That's okay . . . And Clarissa to take care of the scientists. I'll talk to her about it when she gets back tomorrow," Thelma murmured, checking off the items on her pad. "What about the Europeans?"

"Umm . . ." Zambendorf thought for a few seconds. "You'd better leave them to Otto and me." He turned his head to look inquiringly at Abaquaan, who was sitting sideways on another lounge and sipping from a can of beer while he listened. Abaquaan nodded curtly in reply, seemingly preoccupied with something else. "Yes, we'll make some calls to Europe," Zambendorf confirmed. "But get Drew to talk to his newspaper friends about those political people who might be going. We shouldn't ignore sources like that." He looked at Abaquaan again. "Does that cover the main points, Otto?"

"Except Massey," Abaquaan replied.

"Ah, yes," Zambendorf agreed breezily. "A fine mess you've got us into, Otto." Abaquaan rolled his eyes upward in a silent plea for patience and ignored the gibe. He had first expressed concern when the name Gerold J. Massey, nominated by NASO as an "Observational Psychologist," appeared on the schedule. It implied that somebody at NASO had decided things had gone too far and was wheeling up the siege howitzers. Zambendorf went on, "However, you've got us into similar fixes before, and we have always pulled through. The first thing we need to do is make sure he's really there for the reasons you think he is."

Abaquaan threw up his hands. "To make sure? . . . Karl, we know why Massey's there all right! One, he's a stage conjuror. Two, he's a debunker who takes contracts against psi-operators. Three, he's worked for NASO before—remember the headhunters from Long Beach who thought they could sell NASO that psychometric testing crap? Four, Vernon Price is on the list too, and he works as Massey's partner—I mean, hell, Karl, how much more do you want? He's going there to plant a bomb with your name written across it in big letters."

"It sounds highly probable. But let's not make the mistake of overreacting to speculation as if it were fact. In addition you have to admit: Five, the main purpose of the mission has to do with psychological research. Six, he is a psychologist. And seven, NASO has commissioned him to conduct purely scientific studies before. So the nomination could be perfectly legitimate."

Abaquaan got up and paced over to the poolside to stand staring down at the water. "What difference does it make?" he asked, turning back after a short pause. "If you're there and he's there, he's not gonna miss out on the opportunity anyhow. Whether NASO is officially sending him as a nut-watcher or unofficially as something else is beside the point—if he can make trouble, he'll make trouble."

"True, but how much will he be in a position to make?" Zambendorf replied, waving his cigar. "Will he be acting individually, or will he be actively aided by people inside NASO and the resources at their disposal? If it's just him and Price, we could probably afford to take our chances; but if it's them plus NASO, we'd be well advised to use as much help from GSEC as we can get. You see my point—we have to know what to prepare for."

Abaquaan crushed the can he was holding and tossed it into a wastebasket. Thelma leaned back in her chair and looked across at Zambendorf. "True," she agreed. "But how are we supposed to find that out? NASO's hardly likely to make a public statement about it."

Zambendorf didn't reply at once, but drew on his cigar and gazed distantly across the pool. After a while, Abaquaan mused, half to himself, "Do the NASO people just want to send a psychologist, or are they determined to send Massey? If we knew the answer to that, it would tell us something. . . . In fact it would tell us a hell of a lot."

Another short silence ensued. Then Thelma said, "Suppose somebody came up with some good reasons why Massey should be dropped from the mission and replaced by someone else. . . ."

"What reasons?" Abaquaan asked.

Thelma shrugged. "I don't know offhand, but that's a technicality. Since we couldn't afford to be seen originating a demand like that, it would have to come from GSEC—they've got enough lawyers and corporate politicians to think of something."

"Even if they did, can you see NASO dropping Massey if that is what he's there for?" Abaquaan sounded dubious.

"No, but that's the whole point," Thelma replied. "The way they react might tell us what we want to know."

Abaquaan looked at Thelma curiously, seemed about to object for a moment, and then turned his head away again to consider the idea further. A mischievous twinkle had crept into Zambendorf's eyes as he lay back and savored the thought. "Yes, why not, indeed?" he murmured. "Instead of being passive, we can lob a little bomb of our own right into the middle of them, maybe . . . As Thelma says, it probably won't blow Massey overboard, but it might singe his beard a bit. So we have to get the message across to GSEC somehow." Zambendorf took off his sunglasses and began wiping them while he thought about ways of achieving that.

Thelma stretched out a leg and studied her toes. "One way might be through Osmond," she suggested after a few seconds. "We could tell him, oh . . . that in a first-time situation like this, it would be advisable to keep disruptive influences and other unknowns to a minimum until Karl's gained more experience in the extraterrestrial environment . . . something like that?"

"And he'd persuade Hendridge, who'd take it to the GSEC Board," Abaquaan completed. He sounded dubious. Zambendorf looked at him, and then over at Thelma. They all shook their heads. None of them liked it. If the team wanted its relationship with GSEC to be a partnership and not a dependency, it needed to dissociate from Hendridge, not shelter behind him.

"Oh, for heaven's sake, it's obvious!" Zambendorf sat up and leaned across to stub his cigar butt in the ashtray on the table. "We talk to Caspar Lang and tell him that we both have a problem with Massey, and why. We've already agreed that Lang's under no delusions concerning the true situation anyway. And if he's going to Mars as GSEC's senior representative on the mission, then the sooner he and we can start talking frankly and get to know each other, the better."

Two weeks passed before Walter Conlon received an internal notification through NASO that GSEC had expressed concern over Massey's nomination for the Meridiani Sinus mission. Specifically, GSEC was calling attention to Massey's record as a skeptic and debunker of claims concerning paranormal phenomena, and to the fact that Karl Zambendorf was accompanying the mission to test abilities of precisely that nature. Although Massey's capacity was described as that of psychologist, appointing someone with his known predispositions, GSEC suggested, would be inviting the risk of his allowing personal interests to take precedence over official duties, with detrimental consequences to the job he was being sent to do. In view of these observations, therefore, would NASO like to reconsider its choice?

Conlon dashed off a terse reply stating that Massey's function was to assess and report objectively the behavior, attitudes, emotional stresses, and other psychological effects observed among the experimental community. If Zambendorf was going, then Zambendorf would constitute a valid part of the test environment, thus warranting objective reporting as much as anything else. Objective reporting demanded qualified observers, and Massey's unique background fitted him ideally to the total situation. No, NASO would not like to reconsider its choice.

A few days after that, Warren Taylor, the director of the North American Division of NASO, told Conlon that he wanted the decision reversed, making little effort to hide the fact that words had been exchanged among the higher levels of NASO and GSEC management. Conlon could hardly defy a direct instruction from his superior, and accepted the directive with a disinclination to further argument that his colleagues inside NASO found surprising.

That same afternoon, Conlon gave Allan Brady a draft of a press bulletin for immediate release, stating that Massey was to be dropped from the Mars mission and spelling out the reasons why: The proposed inclusion of a competent stage magician was considered threatening to a psychic superman being sponsored by a multibillion dollar corporation. Brady balked; Conlon demanded to sign the release note himself, and Brady retreated to seek higher counsel. Eventually the decision came back down the line that clearance was denied. At that point Conlon went back to Taylor to protest the unconstitutional and illegal suppression of information not relating to national security, and threatened to resign with full public disclosure.

And, suddenly, the heat was off. The order to drop Massey was rescinded, Conlon tore up his press bulletin, and everybody stopped talking about the law, the Constitution, and threats of resignation.

Not long afterward, Massey received an invitation to give a private performance "...for the further entertainment of our guests..." at a banquet to be held in the residence of Mr. and Mrs. Burton Ramelson in Delaware. All expenses would be paid, naturally, and the fee was left open, effectively giving Massey a blank check. It just so happened that the Ramelson family were controlling stockholders in a diversity of mutually enriching industrial enterprises, which, among other things, included General Space Enterprises Corporation and the majority of its bondholding banks.

7

"AMAZING!" ONE OF THE LADIES IN THE ENTHUSIASTIC throng crowding around Massey at the end of the dining hall in the Ramelsons' mansion exclaimed. "Truly amazing! Are you sure you're not deceiving us just a little when you insist that you don't possess genuine psychic powers, Mr. Massey?"

Massey, resplendent, his full beard flowing above tuxedo and black tie, shook his head firmly. "I did all the deceiving earlier. I'm here purely to entertain. I don't pretend to be anything I'm not."

"Could I have an autograph, possibly?" a buxom woman, festooned with jewels and wearing a lilac evening dress, asked. "Here on this menu card would be fine."

"Certainly." Massey took the card and seemed about to open it when another voice caused him to turn away.

"I'm not sure I believe it," a tall, distinguished-looking man with thinning hair and a clipped mustache declared. "You're genuine all right, Massey, but you haven't realized it yourself yet. It's happened before, you know—plenty of reliable, authenticated stories."

In an apparently absentminded way, Massey handed what looked like the same menu card back to the woman in the lilac dress. It was always a safe bet that someone would want a menu card autographed at an occasion like that, and Massey made a point of beginning such evenings with a few prepared cards concealed about his person. "I would be most surprised," he told the distinguished-looking man sincerely.

"I simply must know how you did that thing with the envelope," an attractive girl somewhere in her twenties said. "Can't you give us just a hint, even? I mean . . . it was so impossible."

"Oh, you should know better than to ask things like that," Massey said reproachfully.

"But you never touched it."

"Didn't I?"

"Well, no. We all know what we saw."

"No—you just know what you think you saw."

"Is Karl Zambendorf genuine?" a tubby man with a ruddy face asked. He was swaying slightly and looked a little the worse for drink.

"How could I know?" Massey replied. "But I do know that I can duplicate everything he's done so far."

"But that doesn't prove anything, does it," the tubby man said. "You're all the same, you fellows . . . If Zambendorf walked across the Chesapeake Bay from here to Washington, you'd just say, 'Oh yes—that's the old walking-on-the-water trick.' Just because you can imitate something, it doesn't mean it had to be done the same way first time, does it?"

"When he walks across the bay, I'll give you my comment," Massey promised.

"Er, Mr. Massey, you did say you'd autograph my menu card," the woman in the lilac evening dress reminded him hesitantly.

"That's right. I did."

"I still have it here, and—"

"No, you misunderstood me. I have."

"I don't think I quite—"

"Look inside it."

"What? Oh, but . . . Oh, my God, look at this! How did that get in here?"

At that moment Burton Ramelson appeared behind Massey, smiling and holding a brandy glass. He was small in stature, almost bald, and even his exquisitely cut dinner jacket failed to hide completely the sparseness of his frame; but his sharp eyes and tight, determined jaw instilled enough instant respect to open a small circle in the guests before him. "A splendid exhibition!" he declared. "My compliments, Mr. Massey, and I'm sure I speak for everyone when I add—my thanks for turning our evening into a sparkling occasion." Murmurs and applause endorsed his words. He turned his head to address the guests. "I know you would all like to talk to Mr. Massey forever, but after his exertions I think we owe him the courtesy of a few minutes' rest in relative peace and quiet. I promise I'll do my best to persuade him to rejoin you later." Turning once more toward Massey, he said, "Perhaps you'd care to join a few friends and myself for a brandy in the library."

As they proceeded out of the dining room and across a hall of paneled walls, gilt-framed portraits, and heavy drapes, Ramelson chatted about the house and its grounds, which had been built for a railroad magnate in the 1920s and acquired by Ramelson's father toward the end of the twentieth century. The Ramelson family, Massey had learned from Conlon, commanded hundreds of millions spread among its many members, heirs, foundations, and trusts in such a way as to avoid excessively conspicuous concentrations of assets. Most of their wealth had come from the energy hoax and coal boom following the antinuclear propaganda campaign and political sabotage of high-technology innovation in the seventies and eighties, which while achieving its immediate objective of maximizing the returns on existing capital investments, had contributed to the formulation of U.S. policies appropriate to the nineteenth century while the developing nations were thrusting vigorously forward into the twenty-first. The subsequent decline in competitiveness of American industries and their increasing dependence on selling to their own domestic market to maintain solvency was partly the result of it.

The group waiting in the library comprised a half dozen or so people, and Ramelson introduced the ones whom

Massey had not met already. They included Robert Fairley, a nephew of Ramelson, who sat on the board of a New York merchant bank affiliated to GSEC; Sylvia Fenton, in charge of corporate media relations; Gregory Buhl, GSEC's chief executive; and Caspar Lang, Buhl's second-in-command.

Ramelson filled a glass at an open cabinet near the fireplace, added a dash of soda, and passed the glass to Massey. He proffered a cigar box; Massey declined. "I'm so glad you were able to come," Ramelson said. "You possess some extraordinary skills. I particularly admire the insight into human thinking that your profession must cultivate. That's a rare, and very valuable, talent." After the briefest of hesitations he added, "I do hope you find it adequately rewarded in this world of ours."

"It was a good act," Buhl said, clapping Massey on the shoulder. "I've always been about as cynical as a man can get, but I don't mind saying it straight—you came close to converting me."

Massey grinned faintly and sipped his drink. "I don't believe that, but it's nice to hear you say it all the same." Somebody laughed; everyone smiled.

"But it's only your hobby, isn't that right?" Robert Fairley said. "Most of the time you're a professor of human behavior or something . . ."

"Cognitive psychology," Massey supplied. "I study what kinds of things people believe, and why they believe them. Deception and delusion play a big part in it. So, you see, the hobby is really an extension of my job, but in disguise."

"It sounds a fascinating field to be associated with," Sylvia Fenton commented.

"Burton's right—it's valuable," Buhl said. "Not enough people know how to begin telling sense from nonsense. Most of our managers don't know where to start . . . nobody to show 'em how. Financial mechanics are all you get from the business schools these days."

"An interesting point," Ramelson said. He went through the motions of thinking to himself for a few seconds.

"Have you, er...have you ever wondered what your knowledge might be worth to you outside of the academic community, Mr. Massey?" Massey made no immediate response, and after a pause Ramelson went on, "I'm sure I don't have to spell out at great length what it might mean to have the resources of an organization like GSEC at your disposal. And as we all know, such an organization is able, if it so chooses, to reward the services that it considers particularly valuable with . . . well, shall we say, extreme generosity."

The rest of the company had fallen quiet. Massey walked slowly away toward the center of the room, stopped to sip some more of his drink, and then turned back to face them. "Let's come right to the point," he suggested. "You want to buy me off of the Mars mission."

Ramelson seemed to have been half expecting the sudden directness, and remained affable. "If you wish to put it that way," he agreed. "We all have our price—it's a worn and tired phrase, but I believe it nevertheless. So what's yours, Massey? Name it—research facilities and equipment? Staff? Effectively unlimited funding? Publicity? . . . Someone like you doesn't need the details elaborated. But everything is negotiable."

Massey frowned at the glass in his hand, and, perplexed, exhaled a long breath, then answered obliquely. "I don't understand all this. I know that you know Zambendorf is a fake. Okay, so the stunt on Mars could be good for business—but I can't see what makes it so essential. The logical thing would be to drop Zambendorf now since it looks like more trouble than it's worth. But that's not what's happening. What do people in your positions care whether he keeps his image clean or not? So what's the real story?"

"You just said it," Buhl replied, shrugging and following Ramelson's candid lead. "It's good for business. The more the idea of colonies is popularized, the sooner they'll become financially viable and potentially profitable. Yes, we like making money. Who doesn't?"

The answer sounded more like a rationalization than

a reason and left Massey feeling dissatisfied. But his instincts told him that any attempt at delving deeper would be futile. "I've nothing against trying to popularize the colonies," he said. "But if you're going to do it, why can't you do it through rational education and reason? Why resort to spreading miseducation and unreason?"

"Because it works," Sylvia Fenton said simply. "It's the only thing that has ever worked. We have to be realistic, not idealistic. We didn't make people the way they are. What benefit has rational education ever had, except on a small minority of any population, anytime in history? Nobody wants to hear it."

"Some people do," Massey replied. "There are a lot of people on this planet who used to starve by the millions, and while their children withered away and died like flies, they prayed to cows that wandered the streets. Now they're building their own fusion plants and launching moonships. I'd say they got quite a bit out of it."

"But that kind of thing takes centuries to trickle down," Fairley pointed out. "We don't have centuries. No popular mass movement was ever started in a laboratory or a lecture theater. Thinking things through takes too much time for most people. Sylvia made a valid point—look at anybody from Jesus Christ to Karl Marx who got results fast, and see how they did it."

"And what were the results worth?" Massey asked. "Generations of people wasting their lives away buying crutches because they'd been brainwashed into thinking they were cripples."

Buhl studied his glass for a moment, then looked up. "That's a noble sentiment, Mr. Massey, but who's to blame for people being conditionable in the first place?"

"A society that fails to teach them to think for themselves, trust in their own judgment, and rely on their own abilities," Massey said.

"But that's not what most people want," Sylvia Fenton insisted. "They want to believe that something smarter and stronger than they are knows all the answers and will take care of them—a God, the government, a cult leader, or some magic power . . . anything. If they're going to change, they'll change in their own time. All you can do until then is take the world as you find it and make the most of your opportunities."

"Opportunities for what?" Massey said. "To persuade ordinary people that wanting a better living is really a trivial distraction from the higher things that really matter, and fob them off with superstitions that tell them they'll get theirs later, in some hereafter, some other dimension, or whatever—if they'll only believe, and work harder. Is that what I'm supposed to do?"

"Why do you owe them anything else?" Buhl asked. He shrugged. "The ones who can make it will make it anyway. Are the rest worth the effort?"

"From the way a lot of them end up, no," Massey agreed frankly. "But the potential they start out with is something else. The most squandered resource on this planet is the potential of human minds—especially the minds of young people. Yes, I believe the effort to realize some of that potential is worth it."

The conversation continued for a while longer, but the positions remained essentially unaltered. Each side had heard the other's viewpoint before, and neither was about to be converted. Eventually Mrs. Ramelson appeared with a request from the guests for a further, impromptu, performance, and after a few closing pleasantries Massey left with her to return to the dining room.

Silence descended for a while after their departure. At last Ramelson commented genially, "Well, at least we know where we stand: If we fly our flag on the good ship Zambendorf, Massey will be out to torpedo it. I can't say I'm entirely surprised, but we all agreed it had to be tried. . . ." He looked across at the saturnine figure of Caspar Lang, the deputy chief executive of GSEC, who had said little since Massey's arrival and was brooding in one of the leather armchairs opposite the door. Lang raised his ruggedly chiseled, crew-cut head and returned a hard-eyed inquiring look as he caught the motion. "So if we're sending our ship into hostile waters, we'd better make sure it has a strong escort squadron," Ramelson went on. He closed his eyes and brought a hand to his brow. "You could find yourself with a tough job on your hands at the end of your voyage, my powers tell me, Caspar. . . . We'd better make sure you take plenty of ammunition along."

"Don't give me any of that crap, you little tramp!"

"Who the hell do you think you are to call me a tramp? You—you of all people!"

"Just stop screaming for two seconds and listen to yourself for chrissakes! What sort of a woman screams like that? What do you—"

"Me? *Me? I am not screaming!*"

"Goddamit!"

The exchange ended with a shout and the crash of breaking china as Joe Fellburg flipped a switch to cut off the sound. He sat back and cocked an inquiring eye at Zambendorf. "What do you think?" he asked.

Zambendorf nodded and looked impressed as he ran his eye once more over the compact assembly of electronics and optical gadgetry that Fellburg had set up on a small table in an upper room in Zambendorf's villa. The equipment had "fallen off" a CIA truck and found its way to Fellburg via a devious route that involved one of his former military-intelligence buddies and a communications technician with a gambling problem. It contained a miniature infrared laser whose needle-fine beam was at that moment trained on the windowpane of a house almost a mile away. Soundwaves in the room caused the window glass of the distant house to vibrate; the vibrations of the glass were impressed upon the reflected laser light; and a demodulator system extracted the audio frequencies from the returned signal and fed them to a loudspeaker which reproduced the original sound. The device had all kinds of uses.

"It's astonishing," Zambendorf said. "Do you know, Joe, this world will never cease to amaze me. There are silly people everywhere running around in circles looking for miracles, and all the time they're blind to the miracles right under their noses." He motioned with a hand. "I could never produce something like that in a hundred years."

Fellburg shrugged and tipped his chair back to rest a heel on the window sill. "I was talking to Drew about this the other day. He had an idea that maybe the moisture variations that cause skin resistance to change might alter the way the beam's reflected off a person. If they do, then maybe you could detect it with this thing."

Zambendorf looked at him for a few seconds. "What are you getting at—you mean it could monitor skin resistance changes remotely?"

"I don't know, but maybe . . . kinda like a remote-acting polygraph. It might be possible to pick out the stress reaction of, say, one person in a group from across the street or wherever. It could have all kinds of potential."

Zambendorf was looking intrigued. "It certainly could . . . When do you think you'll know something definite?"

"Oh, give me, say, a couple of weeks to fool around with it some more. I oughta be—"

The call tone from the comnet terminal across the room interrupted him. Zambendorf sauntered across to take the call. It was Thelma, speaking from downstairs. "I've got Caspar Lang from GSEC on the line. He wants to talk to you," she told him.

"Put him through, Thelma." Zambendorf turned and sent Fellburg a satisfied grin. "Do you think it's what I think it is?" he asked.

Fellburg raised his eyebrows. "I'd guess so. Anyhow, we'll soon find out."

The flap inside NASO a few weeks previously had told Zambendorf and his team all they wanted to know about why Gerold Massey was being sent to Mars and NASO's determination to send him. It was strange, therefore, that after the dust had settled, Burton Ramelson should invite Massey to the banquet at his home in Delaware. The only reason Zambendorf or any of the others could think of for this was that GSEC had decided upon a last-ditch bid to buy Massey off although it seemed as obvious as anything could be that any such attempt would be a waste of time and effort. Zambendorf had guessed that, predictably and true to form, the GSEC executives would plod unwaveringly along their predetermined course nevertheless, and he had laid a bet with Otto Abaquaan that Lang would call within two days of the banquet to inform Zambendorf of the meeting with Massey that Zambendorf wasn't supposed to know about already.

"Caspar, good evening," Zambendorf greeted as the screen came to life. "What time is it back East for goodness' sake—don't you people ever sleep? And what can I do for you?"

"Hello, Karl," Lang acknowledged. As always he remained serious and came straight to the point. "Look, there's been a further development concerning Massey that you ought to know about."

Zambendorf looked pained. "Oh dear, Caspar, sometimes I really do think you don't believe in me. Do you imagine that I don't know already?"

Lang's face twitched in momentary irritation. "Karl, please, this is business. Let's be serious about it."

"But I'm being perfectly serious. You and your colleagues tried to buy Massey off the mission with offers of plenty of funding for his research and all that kind of thing, and he wasn't interested. Is that about it, or did you have something else to add?" The guesses were the kind that Zambendorf felt comfortable with. For just an instant Lang seemed genuinely taken aback. "But my impressions can be vague at times," Zambendorf went on, smiling. "So yes, please, Caspar, do go ahead and tell me what happened."

As Lang summarized the conversation with Massey, Zambendorf's eyes narrowed, and he listened more intently. He remained quiet, absorbed in his own thoughts for several minutes after Lang had cleared down. Fellburg said nothing and occupied himself with jotting down notes concerning the bugging device, eventually looking up and cocking an eyebrow when he sensed that Zambendorf was ready to say something.

"Joe, are we that important on this mission... I mean as far as GSEC is concerned?" Zambendorf asked.

Fellburg frowned down over his hand while he stroked his mouth with the side of a finger. "Well, I guess it's still the way we talked about before—if lots of people get hyped up on space, it has to be good for business."

"Yes, but isn't the main purpose of the mission to accumulate data for the future design of colonies?" Zambendorf asked.

Fellburg nodded. "Yeah... I guess so."

"And nobody could argue that our being there is vital to that purpose, could they... or even really that important?"

"Nope... I guess not."

Zambendorf nodded, frowned to himself, and paced away to face the far wall. Silence fell again for a while. Then Zambendorf wheeled back. "It doesn't add up, Joe. Why would people like Burton Ramelson and Gregory Buhl involve themselves personally in something like this? It should have been left to the regular GSEC management minions. And if NASO wouldn't back down and the regular management couldn't handle it, then the whole idea should have been dropped. In fact that's probably what NASO expected. But it didn't work out that way. What do you make of it?"

Fellburg stared hard at the table, but in the end shook his head with a heavy sigh. "Got me beat," he conceded.

"It's this mission," Zambendorf said, moving slowly back toward the window. "There's something very strange about the whole situation... You know, I'm beginning to suspect there's a lot more behind it than anybody's been talking about. In fact, it's more than just a suspicion, Joe—it's a dead certainty."

Fellburg pursed his lips while he considered the proposition. "Any ideas?" he asked at last.

Zambendorf frowned. "Not at this stage. But if something's being hushed up and it concerns the purpose of the mission, it has to be something pretty big. Just think what a bonanza it could be for us if we called it before the public or anyone else knew anything." Zambendorf's eyes gleamed as he pictured it. "My nose tells me there's something to be found out that we could turn to our advantage somehow. I want to get the whole team working on it right away."

8

IN COMPARING THE EFFECTIVENESS OF VARIOUS WAYS OF imparting momentum to a projectile, physicists employ the concept of "impulse," which is given by the product of the force acting on the projectile and the time for which it acts. In the case of a spacecraft, a key indicator of performance is the impulse per unit vehicle mass, or "specific impulse," which is measured in units of time and usually expressed as seconds. High specific impulses arise from propulsion systems that generate high-velocity exhaust products. The exhaust molecules from a hydrogen-oxygen rocket are ejected with velocities of the order of three kilometers per second, corresponding to a specific impulse of 450 seconds at best, with the result that interplanetary travel based on chemical propulsion is reckoned in years. A fusion reaction, by contrast, ejects plasma products over three hundred times faster and makes attainable specific impulses as high as 100,000 seconds. That was why a fusion drive had been considered essential to maintaining a base on Mars, and why the *Orion*'s projected flight-time was only fifty days.

The *Orion* was built in two major parts—a forward section and an aft section—connected by a quarter-mile-long structural boom. Its tail end was open to space, and consisted of a framework of girders, struts, and tiebars forming four unenclosed, cylindrical thrust-chambers strapped together in a cluster like a bundle of squirrel cages. Frozen pellets of a deuterium–tritium mix were fired into the chambers in pairs twice every second and imploded on the fly by focused beams of accelerated ions to produce a succession of fusion microexplosions—miniature H-bombs. The electrically charged, high-velocity particles released in the process generated forward thrust by reacting on a configuration of concave magnetic fields, while the uncharged neutrons and x-rays, to which the magnetic mirrors were transparent, could escape harmlessly into space. Magnetohydrodynamic windings at the stern converted part of the outgoing exhaust energy into electrical power for driving the ion accelerators and the superconducting field-generators. The remainder of the aft section, forward of the radiation shield screening the drive chambers, contained the rest of the propulsion system, berthing facilities for the *Orion*'s complement of reconnaissance craft and surface landers, and storage compartments for ground vehicles, construction materials, and heavy equipment.

The forward end of the connecting boom terminated in a large, vaguely spherical housing, referred to in typically colorless NASO parlance as the Service Module, which contained the main air-generating plant and other systems essential to supporting life, plus an independent chemical motor and associated fuel tanks; in the event of an emergency the ship's entire tail could be ditched and the backup propulsion system used to get the mission home again.

Accommodation for the vessel's occupants was distributed among four smaller spheres—Globes I through IV—located ahead of the Service Module and offset symmetrically from the centerline to form a square lying in a plane perpendicular to the main axis. Rotation of the entire ship about this axis, coupled with an arrangement for pivoting the spheres, enabled centrifugal and linear components of force to be combined into a resultant simulation of unit gravity normal to the floors, irrespective of the ship's acceleration. A fifth sphere—the Command Globe, containing the control and communications center—formed the *Orion*'s nose, and was interconnected with the others and with the main structure by a web of supporting booms and communications tubes.

"The god-awful ugliest thing I've ever seen in my life!" Clarissa Eidstadt said as the NASO European Division's shuttle closed in upon the *Orion* ten thousand miles above Earth. "What did they do—copy an eggbeater?" The team had been scheduled to shuttle up from El Paso, Texas, but was flown to Kourou, Guiana, at the last moment, because NASO officials had decided not to antagonize a protest rally that was besieging the El Paso facility. A chemical present in rocket exhaust had been found to cause cancer in mice when administered for six months in ten thousand times the concentration measured at the pad immediately after a launch.

"Oh, I'm not so sure, Clarissa," Thelma said, leaning back in her seat and tilting her head to one side as she contemplated the image being shown on the cabin view-screen. "In a way, I think it's quite beautiful."

"You do? Then I'll know never to buy you an eggbeater as a present. You might frame it and hang it on the wall."

"I'm not talking about how it looks," Thelma said. "I'm talking about what it represents.... One day people will probably go to the stars in something evolved from it."

"How wonderful." Clarissa stared fish-eyed again at the screen through her butterfly spectacles. "Say, know what—my kitchen will never look the same again now you've said that."

Osmond Periera, who was sitting a row ahead of them, turned his head. "I wonder if, when that happens, we'll have learned how to imitate the alien star travelers who visited Earth during the mid-Holocene period. It appears extremely likely that they navigated by means of reactive, psychosympathetic beacons tuned to their mental energy spectra. The geometric spacings of numerous ancient monoliths can be interpreted as yielding a mathematical series that reflects the corresponding psychic resonances."

"Now I can sleep," Clarissa murmured dryly in Thelma's ear. "I've always wondered about those geometric monolith spacings."

"That's really fascinating," Thelma said to Periera in a louder voice. "Is that why pyramids everywhere are the same shape?"

Before Periera could answer, Joe Fellburg sat forward in the row behind, where he was sitting with Zambendorf and Otto Abaquaan, and frowned at the view of the *Orion* as it continued to enlarge on the screen. "What is it, Joe?" Drew West asked from his seat next to Thelma.

Fellburg stared for a few seconds longer at the huge ship, surrounded by shuttles, service craft, and supply ships, and the loose cloud of containers, pipes, tubes, tanks, and assorted engineering that would gradually be absorbed inside during the remaining three days before liftout from Earth orbit. "See those three shuttles docked at the stern cargo section . . . and the other one standing off, waiting to move in?" he said at last.

"What about them?" Thelma asked.

"Those aren't standard NASO models. Two of them are military transports out of Vandenberg or Travis, and one of the others looks like a British air force troop carrier. What the hell are they doing here?"

In the seat beside him, Zambendorf turned his head and gave Abaquaan an inquiring look. Abaquaan raised his eyebrows ominously. The anomaly of Ramelson and his colleagues' getting more involved in the mission than seemed reasonable had been followed by that of the training course at the NASO center at Charlotte, North Carolina, intended to provide the basic skills and knowledge needed by anyone flying with a space mission—how to put on and operate a spacesuit, the safety regulations enforced aboard spacecraft and in extraterrestrial habitats, emergency procedures, and so on. But the mission personnel whom they had met there had been of relatively junior status, such as engineers, scientists, maintenance technicians, medics, and administrators. The mission's senior management, officer corps, or whoever would constitute the upper levels of the organizational tree, had been conspicuous not only by their absence but by their not even having been mentioned. And as Drew West had observed, the mix of people encountered at the course and reflected in the personnel lists had seemed unrepresentative of the populations envisaged for space colonies. There were too many scientists and academic specialists: bacteriologists, virologists, biologists, physicists, chemists, sociologists, and psychologists . . . even some linguists and a criminologist. Obviously the mission offered many opportunities for diverse studies that the academic community couldn't be expected to miss—buses didn't leave for Mars every day of the week—but so many? And where were the agricultural technicians, the industrial workers, the clerks, and the service people who would be expected to make up a large percentage of any projected colony? Hardly any had been met. That seemed strange too.

And now, apparently, a previously unannounced, and by all the signs not insignificant, military force would be coming too. It was in keeping with everything else he had been able to ascertain, Zambendorf reflected as he sat gazing at the screen. Although he was still not in a position to fit the pieces into a coherent pattern, there hadn't really been any doubt in his mind for a long time now: Something very unusual indeed was behind it all.

As the last in a series of prototypes, the *Orion* was intended primarily to prove the feasibility of its scaled-up fusion drive and to test various engineering concepts relating to long-range, large-capacity space missions; like the experimental Victorian steamships that had preceded the gracious ocean liners of later years, its design took little account of luxuries or spaciousness of accommodation for its occupants. Its warren of cabins, cramped day rooms, machinery compartments, stairwells, and labyrinthine passageways reminded him more of a submarine than anything else, Massey thought as he lounged on his bunk and contemplated the view of Earth's disk being presented on the screen built into the cabin's end bulkhead. He and Vernon would share the cabin with two others, both of whom they knew from the training course: Graham Spearman, an evolutionary biologist from the University of California at Los Angeles, and Malcom Wade, a Canadian psychologist. Spearman and Vernon had left to explore the ship and Wade hadn't arrived yet; Massey, therefore, was making the most of the opportunity to relax for a few minutes after arriving on board, checking in, and unpacking his gear.

From his perspective in Globe II, the entire planetary surface of Earth—continents, oceans, and atmosphere—revealed itself as a single, self-sustaining biological organism in which the arbitrary boundaries and differences of shading that divided the maps of men were no more meaningful than they were visible. It was a truth that astronauts and other venturers into space had affirmed repeatedly for over half a century, but it had to be experienced to be understood, Massey realized. Only two days earlier he had paid a final visit to Walter Conlon in Washington, where on every side the world of human affairs scurried and bustled about its urgent business and consumed the output from thousands of lives. But already the whole of it had shrunk to a speck of no particular significance, barely discernible against the background that had remained essentially unchanged since before Washington had existed, and which might persist for long after Washington was forgotten.

The sound of the door being opened interrupted Massey's thoughts, and a moment later Malcom Wade pushed his way in, holding two bags and a briefcase in his hands and using a foot to shove a suitcase along on the floor. "Well, I guess I must have found the right place," he said as he closed the door with his back. "Hi, Gerry. I gather the other two are already here."

"Hello, Malcom. Yes—they've gone exploring. That top bunk's yours. How was the flight?"

Wade took off his topcoat and hung it in the closet space by the door. "Oh, fine—apart from taking half a day longer than it was supposed to. We had to divert to the European base in Guiana." He sank down with a grateful sigh on the bunk opposite Massey. He was a tall, thin-bodied man, with lank hair and pale eyes that always seemed to be glinting with some inner fervor.

"I heard about it," Massey said. "Hey, I think Graham's got a bottle of something stowed away over there. Could you use a drink while you're getting your breath back?"

"Mmm . . . later maybe, thanks all the same."

"Okay. So who else was on the shuttle?"

"Let me see . . . Susan Coulter, the geologist, and that electronics guy from Denver that we had breakfast with one morning at Charlotte . . . Dave Crookes."

"Uh-huh."

"Karl Zambendorf and his people were on it too." Wade cocked an eyebrow at Massey in a way that was partly expectant, partly curious.

"Oh." Massey did his best to keep his voice neutral. He didn't want to get into a long debate just then. Although he hadn't advertised his prime interest in the mission, the question of Zambendorf's being included had been a regular conversation topic at the training center, and Massey had found himself obliged on occasion to express his opinions. Wade described himself as a scientist and was apparently an advisor of some kind to a number of government committees, but he took Zambendorf quite seriously. Massey wondered exactly what he advised the government on.

"I think I know why he's here," Wade said after a short silence. He paused to wait for Massey to ask him why Zambendorf was there. Massey didn't. Wade went on anyway, "It's well known that the Soviets have been conducting extensive research into paranormal phenomena for years—and getting successful results too." Massey swallowed hard but said nothing. There were always anecdotes of anecdotes about things that people were supposed to have done, but never anything verifiable. Wade took a pipe from his jacket pocket and gestured with the stem. "It's been suspected for a while now that they've achieved some kind of significant breakthrough, and a lot of experts have been saying that the main Soviet center for that kind of work is their Mars Base at Solis Lacus—well away from terrestrial interference, you see." Wade paused and began packing tobacco into his pipe from a pouch.

"Well, I guess you know how I feel about all that," Massey said vaguely, while wondering uncomfortably to himself if the conversation was an indication of what to expect for the next fifty days.

"But it all fits," Wade said. "I know you're a bit of a skeptic and so on, Massey, but I believe in being scientific about things, which means being open-minded—in other words, willing to accept that there are things we can't explain. Whether we can explain it or not, we have to accept that Zambendorf is gifted with some abnormal abilities." He eyed Massey for a moment as if the rest should have been too obvious to require spelling out. "Well, I think Zambendorf is part of a classified Western research program to match the Soviets in harnessing paranormal phenomena... or maybe even to counter the Soviets. That could be why they're sending Zambendorf to Mars." Massey stared at him glassy-eyed, but before he could say anything, Wade added triumphantly, "And that would explain why the military is here—to secure the project from possible interference from the Soviets at Solis Lacus. Have you heard about that yet?"

Massey nodded. "We were told they're coming with us to do some training under extraterrestrial conditions... that the Pentagon bought some places on the ship at the last moment or something."

Wade shook his head. "Cover story. Do you know how many there are of them? There were three shuttle-loads disembarking when I came aboard—U.S. Special Forces, a British commando unit, French paratroopers. That's not a few seats bought at the last minute. That was scheduled a long time ago... And they're docked at the stern, which means they're unloading heavy equipment." He produced a lighter and watched Massey over his pipe while he puffed it into life. "In fact it wouldn't surprise me if the idea was to provoke a confrontation with the Soviets at Lacus in order to take their base out. Maybe our people are onto things that you and I haven't even dreamed about."

Massey slumped back and looked away numbly. Surely nobody at the Pentagon or wherever was taking the nonsense about the Soviets that seriously . . . But then again, large sectors of the government and private bureaucracies were dominated by political and economic ideologists incapable of distinguishing sound scientific reasoning from pseudoscientific twaddle, yet commanding authority out of all proportion to their competence. If they listened to kooks like Wade, they could end up believing anything. Surely the insane rivalry that had paralyzed meaningful progress over much of Earth for generations wasn't about to be exported to another world over something as ridiculous as the "paranormal."

Massey stared again at the blue-green image of Earth with its stirred curdling of clouds. Somehow the human race had to get it into its collective head that it couldn't rely on magical forces or omnipotent guardians to protect it from its own stupidity. Man would have to trust in his own intelligence, reason, and ability to look after himself. The decision was in his own hands. If he chose to eradicate himself, the rest of Earth's biosphere—far more resilient than popular mythology acknowledged—would hardly notice the difference, and then not for very long. And as for the rest of the cosmos, stretching away for billions of light-years behind Earth's rim, the event of man's extinction would be no more newsworthy than the demise of a community of microbes caused by the drying up of a puddle somewhere in Outer Mongolia.

9

"AH, LET ME SEE NOW . . . WHEN I WAS A BOY OF ABOUT sixteen, it must have been. 'Pat,' me father says to himself. 'With them Americans walking around on the Moon itself and flying them hotels up in the sky, that's the place you should be for your sons to grow up in.' So we ups and moves the whole family to Brooklyn where me uncle Seamus and all was already living, and that's where the rest of them still are today." Sgt. Michael O'Flynn of the NASO Surface Vehicle Maintenance Unit reversed his feet, which were propped up on the littered metal desk in his cubbyhole at the rear of a cavernous cargo bay, and raised his paper cup for another sip of the brandy that Zambendorf had produced from a hip flask. He had a solid, stocky body that seemed as broad as it was long beneath the stained NASO fatigues, and his face was fiery pink and beefy, with clear blue eyes half-hidden beneath wiry, unruly eyebrows, and a shock of rebellious hair in which yellow and red struggled for dominance, each managing to get the better of the other in different places. O'Flynn spoke through pearly white teeth clamped around a wooden toothpick, in a husky whisper that had retained more than a hint of its original brogue for what must have been thirty or so years.

"What part of Ireland did you move from?" Zambendorf inquired from his cramped perch on a metal seat that folded out from the wall between a tool rack and an equipment cabinet—more comfortable than it looked since his weight near the ship's axis was barely sufficient to keep him in place.

"County Cork, in the south, not far from a little place called Glanmire."

Zambendorf rubbed his beard and looked thoughtful for a few seconds. "That would be roughly over in the direction of Watergrasshill, wouldn't it, if I remember rightly?" he said.

O'Flynn looked surprised. "You know it?"

"I was there a few years ago. We toured all around that area for a few days . . . and up to Limerick, back down around Killarney and the lakes." Zambendorf laughed as the memories flooded back. "We had a wonderful time."

"Well I'll be damned," O'Flynn said. "And you like the place, eh?"

"The villages are as pretty and as friendly as any you'll find in Austria, and I found Guinness remarkably good once I'd gotten used to it. Those mountains, though, what do you call them? Macgilly-something . . ."

"Macgillycuddy's Reeks."

"Yes—how is anybody supposed to remember something like that? Well they're not really mountains at all, are they? You really could use a genuine Alp or two, you know. But apart from that . . ." Zambendorf shrugged and sipped his own drink.

"What are your Alps but more of the same?" O'Flynn said. "Ours have everything a mountain needs to be called a mountain, except a man doesn't have to waste more of the breath he could be using for better things getting to the top."

"The higher a man rises, the farther he sees," Zambendorf said, throwing out a remark that was open for O'Flynn to take any way he pleased. "It's as true of life as it is of mountains, wouldn't you agree?"

O'Flynn's eyes narrowed a fraction further for a moment, and he chewed on his toothpick. "Yes, and the farther away he gets, the less he sees, until he can make out no part of any of it," he replied. "The world's full of people parading their high-and-mightiness, who think they can see everything, but they know nothing." It sounded like a general observation and not a veiled reference to Zambendorf.

"I take it that the noble and the worthy don't exactly inspire you to any great feelings of awe and reverence."

"Ah, and who else would they be but those who make it their affair to mind the rest of the world's business when the rest of the world is quite able to look after itself? It's people whose own business isn't worth minding who mind other people's business, I'm after thinking. A man has work enough in one lifetime trying to improve himself without thinking that he's fit to be out improving the world."

A strange garb to find a philosopher in, Zambendorf thought to himself. "Well, that's certainly been the old way," he said, stretching and looking around, as if for a way of changing the subject. "Who knows? Perhaps Mars will be the beginning of something different."

O'Flynn remained silent for a few seconds and rubbed his nose with a pink, meaty knuckle, as if weighing something in his mind. "So, it's convinced you are that it's Mars we're going to, is it?" he said at last.

Although nothing changed on Zambendorf's face, he was instantly alert. "Of course," he said, keeping his voice nonchalant. "What are you saying, Mike? Where else could we be going?"

"Well now, aren't you the great clairvoyant who sees into the future?" O'Flynn's smile twinkled mockingly for just an instant. "I was hoping that maybe you were going to tell me."

Zambendorf had ridden out worse in his time. "What are you saying?" he asked again. "What makes you think we might be going anywhere else?"

O'Flynn chewed on his toothpick and watched Zambendorf curiously for a second or two, then crumpled the cup and dropped it into a trash disposal inlet. He stood and inclined his head to indicate the doorway. "Come on. I'll show you something." He cleared the distance to the bay area outside in one of the long, slow-motion bounds that was the most economical way to move around in almost zero-gravity surroundings. Zambendorf unfolded himself from his seat and followed.

O'Flynn led between rows of packing cases and halted at a larger area where three surface vehicles were stacked one above the other in their stowage frames to just below the ceiling. At the bottom of the next stack, a couple of NASO mechanics working at the open hatch of a tracked vehicle, and another who was inspecting something from a movable work platform higher up, carried on without paying much attention. O'Flynn gestured toward the lowermost vehicle in front of them—a personal carrier about fifteen feet high, painted mainly yellow, with six huge wheels. An enclosed cabin with lots of antennas and protrusions made up its forward two-thirds, and a clutter of girderwork, pipes, and tanks formed its rear.

"See them wheels," O'Flynn said, pointing. "Them's high-traction, low-friction treads—not what you'd need if you wanted to go joy-riding off across a place like Mars." He ducked forward and indicated a pair of short, fat nozzles projecting from below the vehicle's front end. "Know what they are? Plasma torches and blowers—not the best thing in the world if you get bogged down in a sand drift now, is it?"

"What would things like that be better for?" Zambendorf asked, peering more closely.

"Ice," O'Flynn told him. "Lots of ice." He jerked his thumb sternward. "And the equipment holds back there are full of things like steam hoses and superheated suction tubes, which are also the kinds of things you'd want to take along with you if you expected to be bothered by ice. Now, where would all that ice be on a place like Mars?" He straightened out from under the vehicle and rapped his knuckle on the outside wall of the cab. "Them walls will withstand four atmospheres—outside, not inside. Mars has a low-pressure atmosphere."

Zambendorf searched O'Flynn's face for a second or two and then looked back at the personnel carrier. O'Flynn stepped back a pace and pointed up at the fuselage of a low-altitude, fifteen-man airbus secured in the top frame of the stack. "And do you see that flyer up there? It's wings are detached so you can't see them for now, but they're too short and small to be any use at all in thin air. Now Mars must have changed quite a bit since I last read anything about it, unless I'm very much mistaken."

"But . . . this is incredible!" Zambendorf injected an appropriate note of astonishment into his voice while his mind raced through possible explanations. "Have you asked anyone in authority about it?"

O'Flynn shrugged. "What business is it of mine to be asking people about something they'd already have told me if they wanted me to know?" He hooked his thumbs in his belt and stood back. "Anyhow, we've almost got everyone aboard now. Soon they'll all be talking, and then the questions will start getting asked. I'm not much of a clairvoyant meself, you understand, but I've a sneaky feeling it won't be much longer before we get the answers too."

"Wow! Two hydrogen bombs every second? You're really not joking?" Thelma stared wide-eyed across the table at the young NASO captain smartly attired in his flight-officer's uniform. Around them, with only two days to go before the *Orion*'s departure, the atmosphere in the crowded bar on the Recreation Deck of Globe IV was getting quite partylike.

Larry Campbell, proud of his recent promotion to the staff of General Vantz, commander of the *Orion*, sipped his gin and tonic and grinned reassuringly. "Well, they're really only small ones, and completely under control. There's nothing to be concerned about. We'll take good care of you."

"But it sounds so scary. I mean, how can anybody understand how to control something like that? You must be very clever. What sign were you born under?" Beneath the table, Thelma had pushed Campbell's briefcase back along the wall and within reach of the fingertips of one arm, which was draped casually over the chair next to her. She shifted slightly and lifted her glass to taste her martini while surreptitiously nudging the briefcase under the back of the booth behind her.

Campbell frowned at his glass for a second, then sighed and smiled condescendingly. "Well, let's put it this way—my training in understanding the physics of thermonuclear processes doesn't have anything to do with when I was born, I'm afraid. You don't get these—" he gestured at the captain's tracks on his epaulets "—for knowing about birth-signs, you know."

"You don't?" Thelma said wonderingly. "But you have to know which way to steer the ship. How can you do that without knowing all about stars and planets?" At the booth behind, Drew West finished his drink, got up, and sauntered out of the bar, carrying his jacket loosely over his arm to conceal the briefcase he was holding.

Campbell bit his lip awkwardly. "Look, I, er . . . I don't want to sound like a schoolteacher or anything, but astrology and astronomy aren't really the same thing."

"No, of course they're not—everyone knows that," Thelma agreed brightly. "Astronomy is restricted to what you can see through telescopes, but astrology covers a lot more because it's revealed directly to the mind, right? I read all about it in *Thinking Woman's Monthly Digest*."

"Er, not quite . . . If you want, I'll tell you what the differences really are. But I should warn you, you may find you have to change some ideas you might have grown pretty fond of."

"Oh, would you, Larry! Just imagine—a real starship officer taking all this trouble just for me! My sister will be so mad when I tell her."

In the men's room outside the bar, Drew West had picked the lock of the briefcase and begun selecting interesting papers which he passed over the partition for Joe Fellburg to photograph in the next cubicle. Five minutes later, when Fellburg entered the bar carrying Campbell's briefcase inside a false-bottomed leather portmanteau, the booth at which West had been sitting was taken. So Fellburg edged his way through the throng and stopped partway to the bar to count change from his pocket for the cigarette machine, in the process putting down the portmanteau next to Thelma's seat. The briefcase stayed behind as Fellburg moved on, but the movement of his foot to slide it behind the chair toward Thelma's waiting hand was so smooth that Campbell, on the far side of the table, didn't even register anyone's being nearby as he extolled the wonders of the heavens and expounded on their mysteries.

Clarissa Eidstadt rapped the end of her pen sharply on the top of Herman Thoring's desk in the administrative section of Globe I to emphasize her point. "Look, mister, I've got my job to do too. I'm the team's publicity manager, okay? That means I need to get information to the public. How am I supposed to get information out without proper communications? So do something about it."

Thoring held up his hands protectively. "Okay, Clarissa, I hear what you're telling me, and I'll do what I can. But you have to understand I've got a lot of other responsibilities and obligations to think about. This mission is important to all kinds of other people too." Thoring looked like a person born to carry responsibilities and bear obligations. The tanned dome of his head reflected the light inside a semicircle of black, frizzy hair, and his eyes looked like poached eggs behind thick, heavy-rimmed spectacles wedged above his fleshy nose. He was in shirtsleeves with cuffs rolled back, vest unbuttoned, and tie-knot slipped a couple of inches below his opened collar.

Clarissa tossed up a hand in a curt gesture of finality. "Well, if you don't have the authority to change anything, I'm wasting my time. I thought you were in charge around her. Who do I talk to?"

As it was supposed to, the remark hit a sensitive spot. Thoring's knuckles whitened and a vein stood out on his temple. "You're already in the right office," he managed indignantly. "I'm the Senior Program Director from Global Communications Networking and have *full* responsibility for media liaison. It's a very important position, and I've told you I'll do everything I can."

"Yeah? Phooey. Important? Who says so? What's 'media liaison' anyway? I wanna talk to the captain."

"What captain?"

"Vent? Vant? . . . whatever. What's the driver called?"

"You mean General Vantz?" Thoring looked appalled.

"That's him. Where do I go?"

Thoring shook his head and moaned despairingly. "Look, Clarissa, believe me—you can't go raising something like this with General Vantz. He wouldn't know anything about it anyway. This would come under the mission's Communications Director, and I report directly to him. Okay?"

"Then I wanna talk to the Communications Director."

Thoring raised a hand to his brow, closed his eyes and fiddled with the bridge of his spectacles for a few seconds, then shook his head again and looked back at Clarissa. Before he could say anything, one of the women from the secretarial pool in the outer office called, "I'm through to New York, Mr. Thoring. They're sorry, but Hepperstein is in conference at the moment. Can he call you tomorrow?"

Thoring sighed, stood, and walked round the desk to the open doorway. "No, it can't wait until tomorrow," he said, sounding agitated. "He has to get back to me today. Make sure they get a message to him, and that he knows it's from me personally."

"Okay."

"Who are you trying to kid?" Clarissa asked as Thoring came back to his desk and sat down. At the same time she allowed a hint of doubt into her voice, and marshaled an expression that was a shade more respectful. "I bet you don't even know who the Communications Director is. Why would your job involve dealing with someone like that?"

Thoring lifted his chin and allowed himself a quick smirk of satisfaction. "Well, you'd be surprised, lady. For your information, my level of responsibility on this mission requires a working familiarity with all kinds of confidential material that you don't know about. That's why you have to trust me when I say I'll do as much to help your interests as I can. But that's all I can say. Just accept for now that I have a lot more to worry about than you think."

Clarissa's belligerence evaporated. She leaned forward, glanced furtively across at the open doorway, and hissed in a conspiratorial whisper. "What?"

Thoring's voice lowered itself instinctively. "Come on, Clarissa—you know better than that," he muttered, tapping the side of his nose.

"But I wanna know," Clarissa insisted, her eyes wide with excitement. "Is it gonna be a group-sex experiment in space? Or maybe we're going into another dimension. You can tell me. Do I look like somebody who'd go spreading things around—especially something said in confidence by a Media Liaison Director."

Thoring frowned, bunched his lips perplexedly for a second, and then whispered, "I can't do that... but if I told you it's big, would you stay off my back and let me get on with my job?"

"But of course. I wouldn't wanna interfere with something that might endanger the national interests or something."

"Well, you're pretty close to the mark," Thoring said, nodding somberly. "That's just what it is. You could help us a lot by backing off a little."

"How big is it?" Clarissa asked, covering the side of her face with a hand and murmuring out of the corner of her mouth. "Have they found cosmic energy pyramids on Mars? Are we gonna fight the KGB for them?"

"Nothing like that. But I'll tell you this—the Mission Director is Daniel Leaherney, deputy head of the U.S. National Security Council. His second-in-command will be Charles Giraud, who's connected with the French government. They and their senior staff are on board now, shuttled up yesterday without any publicity. That should tell you enough."

"Never heard of them, but they sound important," Clarissa said. "This is exciting. What else?"

Thoring sat back in his chair suddenly and shook his head. "That's more than I should have mentioned. I can't say any more, Clarissa . . . but will you stay outta my hair from now on, please?"

"I never realized . . . You must have a lot on your mind."

"That's what I'm trying to tell you."

"Okay, I get it. Don't worry—the secret is safe. You can count on me. You know, I always wanted to be an espionage agent with the CIA or something. I figure I'd be good at it. Do you, er . . . do you have people like that working for you?" Clarissa looked at Thoring hopefully.

"Uh? Oh no, I'm afraid not."

"Too bad. Oh well, maybe if you want a secret message taken to the Communications Director, or something like that, you could let me know."

"What? Oh yes, sure. If anything like that comes up, I'll give you a call."

"Okay, well, I guess I'd better let you get on." Clarissa got up and crept furtively over to the door. She opened it a fraction, peered out, and then looked back over her shoulder at Thoring. "I'm sorry I bothered you over something so trivial."

"Oh, think nothing of it. We get it all the time . . . but we have to keep up our cover, you understand."

"That's what I thought." Clarissa nodded a final, solemn reassurance, made an *O* in the air with her thumb and forefinger, and disappeared. Thoring stared disbelievingly at the door for a long time after she had gone. Then he blinked himself back to reality, shook his head, and returned his attention to the papers on his desk.

"The figures for on-board fuel-pellet manufacturing capacity, emergency reserves of chemical propellants, and the range corrections factored into the radar calibration procedures all point to a distance much greater than that of Mars," Thelma said to the rest of the team, who were holding a cramped afterdinner conference in the cabin that

Zambendorf shared with Abaquaan, West, and Fellburg. She gestured at the photo prints lying among other papers on the bunk beside her. "And the flight-profile from Campbell's duty roster gives a voyage of something nearer three months than fifty days."

"I still think the Asteroids is a possibility," Drew West said, lounging on one of the upper bunks. "There's been a lot of talk in recent years about our vulnerability in strategic minerals—in fact, right back to the last century. There's no end of just about everything out there."

Silence reigned for a few seconds. Joe Fellburg made a face. "Too many things don't fit," he said. "Why all the secrecy? Why the military?"

"Protecting our eternal interests," Abaquaan answered, sitting on the floor with his back to the door.

"Who from?"

"Well, it could only be the Soviets," West said.

"Out at the Asteroids?" Clarissa looked inquiringly at Thelma and Fellburg. "Do they have anything that could match the *Orion* at that range?"

Fellburg shook his head. "Not yet. They've been concentrating on near-Earth applications. The Japanese are more interested in Venus and Mercury."

"The Soviets did develop a series of fusion drives as part of their Mars-base program," Thelma said. "But if they'd gone a long way in scaling them up to anything like the *Orion*, we'd know about it."

Clarissa nodded as if that confirmed what she already thought. "And besides, Leaherney and Giraud don't fit into that either," she said. Leaherney used to be chairman of the House Committee on Foreign Economic Affairs and is a onetime U.S. ambassador in Brussels; Giraud was a member of the French cabinet. You wouldn't pick guys like that to head up a prospecting expedition."

The cabin fell quiet again for a while. Everybody looked at everybody else. There were no new suggestions. At last Zambendorf stood up, stepped over Abaquaan's legs to get to the coffee pot by the washbasin, and poured himself a fresh cup. He stirred in a spoon of sugar and turned to face the others again. "Then it has to be as I've been saying," he told them. "No other hypothesis explains all of the facts nearly as well. A low-gravity, low-temperature, icy environment . . . It has to be a moon of the outer planets."

"With not only an atmosphere, but a high-pressure one at that," Thelma agreed, nodding."

Fellburg rubbed his nose between thumb and forefinger for a few seconds, and at last nodded slowly. "I can't fault it . . . And you know something?—the European probe that arrived there two years ago and sent down those surface landers that were all supposed to have failed soon after they reached the surface—that story has always sounded strange to me too."

Abaquaan looked up and turned his head from side to side. "So what are we saying, then—it has to be Titan? We're agreed?"

"It appears extremely probable at least," Zambendorf said. "But the more interesting question, by far, is why."

Why would the Western powers equip an elaborate mission, heavy with scientists from every discipline and experts from many fields, to such a destination, provide it with military protection, and go to great pains to conceal its true purpose from—as in all probability it had to be—the Soviets? Why would they place such a mission in the charge of senior political figures experienced in international negotiation and diplomacy? And why—perhaps most significant of all—were there linguists and so many psychologists among the professionals being taken along, specialists at understanding and communicating with thinking intelligences? In short, just what had the landers from the European probe found under the murky, impenetrable cloud canopy of Titan, Saturn's mysterious moon, equal in size to the planet Mercury?

And, of particular interest to the people gathered in Zambendorf's cabin, why was it considered highly desirable for someone like Zambendorf to be there?

10

IN THE HEART OF THE *ORION*'S COMMAND GLOBE OVER-looking the Central Control Deck—the ship's control and operational nerve center—Don Connel, the senior reporter on the GCN news team assigned to accompany the mission, watched on his monitor the view being transmitted live into Earth's communications net from camera 1. The camera panned slowly across the activity at the crew stations, the colors and formats of the data displays changing and flashing to report condition changes and status updates, and the computers silently marching regiments of bits through their registers, and then came to rest on the image of Earth being presented on the main display screen above the floor. Connel nodded to acknowledge his "ready" cue from the director on the far side of the raised tier of consoles from which General Vantz and a trio of senior officers were monitoring the final-phase countdown operations, and turned to face camera 2. A moment later its light came on to indicate that he was on the air again.

"Well, you've just been looking at the view of Earth that we're getting here on the *Orion*, and seeing what you look like from ten thousand miles up, right at this moment," he resumed. "You know, even I have to admit it's a real problem finding the right words to tell you folks just what it feels like to be up here at a moment like this. Personally I'm still having trouble convincing myself that the image you just saw is real this time—really out there. I'm not looking at something being relayed from a remote space operation that involves other people thousands of miles away, or a recording slipped into a space-fiction movie. If the walls and structures around me here were made of glass and I could look out right through them, I'd be able to see, first-hand with my own eyes, exactly what's on the screen here. You know, it makes those walls and structures seem very flimsy all of a sudden, and the *Orion* very tiny compared to everything else around, which from where I'm seeing it is enough to swallow up even the whole of Earth itself. Well, you can take it from me—I sure hope those NASO engineers and all the other people who designed and built this ship are as good as everyone tells me they are."

From a position just below Vantz's console, a flight engineer motioned to attract Connel's attention and raised five fingers and a thumb, signaling that the countdown was entering its final sixty seconds. Connel's face became serious, and he injected a note of rising tension into his voice. "The countdown is into the last minute now. Back in the tail of this huge ship, the field generators that Captain Matthews talked about are up to power, and those immense accelerators are ready to fire. Here are the final moments now on the Control Deck of the *Orion* as this historic voyage to Mars begins." Connel waited for camera 2's light to go out as transmission switched back to camera 1, then sat back in his seat to follow the proceedings.

"Master Sequencer is Go; Backup Sequencer is Go," the Chief Engineer reported from beside Vantz. "Checkpoint zero-minus-two, positive function. Ground Control acknowledgment checks positive, and GC override veto standing down."

"PSX status?" Vantz queried.

"GCV disconnects one through five confirmed," another voice answered. "PSX integration reads positive function. SSX confirms."

"Tracking two seconds into exit window," another called out.

"Main fields: six-eight, green; seven-seven, green; nine-five on synch."

"Alignment good."

"Focus fields good."

"Injectors primed. Ten-ten, all beams."

"Checkpoint zero-minus-one—holding now."

Stillness descended for a second as General Vantz cast a final eye over the information displays in front of him. He nodded and spoke into his console mike. "Fire for exit phase one."

"Phase one fire sequence activated. Zero-zero at GPZ plus seven point-three seconds."

Connel felt his seat nudge him gently in the back. The *Orion* was moving out of freefall; the journey that would shrink the globe on the screen to a pinpoint and replace it with another world had begun. From the gestures and grins being exchanged among the crew, everything seemed to be going well. Connel relaxed back in his seat and finished his coffee while a sequence of views went out showing Earth, scenes from around the Control Deck, and shots being picked up from the service vessels standing ten miles off in space. He checked the schedule to confirm the next item, which was timed to relieve tenseness after the launch by providing a contrast of subject and mood, then got up and moved down to a space over to one side, where Zambendorf was talking to a production assistant while he waited. With them were Dr. Periera, who Connel privately considered to be crazy, and Zambendorf's middle-aged, equally zany publicity matron, who had bullied Herman Thoring into allocating Zambendorf some valuable air-time at a moment when the world would be watching. In front of them, a couple of technicians were repositioning camera 2.

"All set?" Connel inquired as he joined them. "There are some commercials starting just about now. We'll be going on immediately after."

"Fine," Zambendorf said.

Connel gestured at the sheet of paper in Zambendorf's hand. "Are those questions okay? Are there any you want me to miss?"

"No, these are fine. Were they otherwise, I would have saved you the trouble of typing them by telling you beforehand." Connel wasn't sure whether Zambendorf's expression meant he was joking or not. Connel was skeptical toward claims of paranormal abilities, although he usually had a tough time defending his views with his friends. He grinned and then made a face, leaving Zambendorf free to interpret the response either way. "You are not convinced?" Zambendorf asked, watching him keenly and sounding surprised.

Connel shrugged in an easygoing way. "Well . . . I guess I can't help remembering that the *Orion* is driven by fusion power, not ESP power. I figure that has to say something."

"True," Zambendorf agreed. "And the first ocean vessels were driven by wind power."

"Twenty seconds," a technician advised. The others moved back while Connel and Zambendorf took up their positions; the camera light came on, and they were live.

"Don Connel talking to you again, this time on my way to Mars. Well, before all the excitement of liftout, we talked to General Vantz and a couple of his officers, and to some of the scientists we have with us. Now I'd like to say hello to somebody else also with the mission, who's standing next to me right now—Hello, Karl Zambendorf."

"Hello, Don."

"Karl, this is a first-time experience for you too, I believe. Is that right?"

"Well, in my material body, anyway . . . yes."

"You're supposed to be able to make some uncanny predictions about future events. What about Mars? Do you have anything you'd like to say in advance about the mission, any major happenings in store for us on the Red Planet, big surprises, anything like that?"

"Mars?"

Connel looked surprised. "Well, yes—sure. Is there anything you'd like to predict about events following our arrival there?"

"Mmm . . . If you don't mind, Don, I'd prefer not to make any comment in response to that question . . . for reasons which will become apparent in due course."

"Hey, that sounds kind of sinister. What are you trying to tell us, Karl?"

"Oh, nothing to be alarmed about. Let's just say that I would not wish to lay myself open to charges of indiscretion by the authorities. As I say, the reason will soon become clear. There really is no need for alarm—caution, maybe, but not alarm."

"Now, I wonder what that could mean. I guess we'll just have to wait and see, huh? I hope all you people back there are taking notes of this. Karl, another thing I wanted to ask you concerns all the scientists and other specialists that we've got with us on the ship. Do they worry you at all?"

"Certainly not. Why should they? Aren't we all scientists in some way or another?"

"Well, maybe, but it is a fact that a lot of people from the more, shall we say, orthodox branches of science tend to express skepticism toward your particular branch of—of exploration. Being shut up in a spaceship with so many unbelievers doesn't bother you?"

"Facts are not changed by the intensity of human beliefs or the number of people who hold them," Zambendorf replied. He was about to say something more when the production assistant off-camera nodded to someone behind a door situated to one side, and beckoned. Moments later, Gerold Massey appeared. Zambendorf jerked his head round sharply and gave Connel a puzzled look. Massey and Zambendorf had so far tended to avoid a direct confrontation, confining their acknowledgment of each other's presence to stiff nods exchanged in passing or from a distance.

Connel had set up the surprise on direct instructions from Patrick Whittaker at GCN headquarters. "Karl, people are always trying to spring things on you, aren't they," he said amiably. "I have taken the liberty of asking one of those skeptics to join us because I'm told he has a challenge that he'd like to put to you himself. I'm sure the viewers would all like to hear it too." Before Zambendorf could answer, the assistant ushered Massey forward, and Connel brought him on-camera with a gesture. "Folks, I'd like to introduce Gerry Massey. Now, Gerry is one of the psychologists with us here on the *Orion*, but in addition to that he's also a pretty good stage conjuror, I'm told. Is that right, Gerry?"

"It is an area of interest of mine," Massey replied as he moved forward to join them.

"And you're not a believer in the existence of forces or powers beyond those that are familiar to orthodox science," Connel said. "In particular, you claim you can reproduce any effect by ordinary stage magic, which Karl attributes to paranormal abilities. Is that so, Gerry?"

Massey took a long breath. To say all the things he'd have liked to say would have taken hours. "That is correct. For a long time now I have been attempting to persuade Herr Zambendorf to agree to demonstrate his alleged powers under conditions which I am able to specify and control. That, after all, is no more than would be expected in any other branch of science. But he has persistently evaded giving a direct answer. My suggestion is quite simply that the voyage ahead of us, and the period we will be spending on Mars, offer an ideal opportunity and ample time for this to be settled once and for all. I have a schedule of some initial tests with me right now, but I'm open to further suggestions."

Connel turned and looked at Zambendorf questioningly. Although he maintained his outward calm, inside Zambendorf was thinking frantically. He should have guessed Massey would do something like this, should have watched him more closely. The team had been too busy, with too little time. "Oh, we've heard this kind of thing before," he replied without hesitation. "Just because a stage magician can duplicate an effect, it doesn't prove at all that what's being imitated was achieved in the same way. After all, I'm sure Mr. Massey can produce a rabbit from a hat very convincingly, but he could hardly argue on that basis that all rabbits must therefore come from hats, could he?"

"I never claimed it proved anything," Massey answered. "But if a simple explanation can account for the facts, then there's no need for a more complicated one, or indeed any logical justification for accepting one."

"The simplest explanation for the planets and the stars would be that they revolve above the Earth," Zambendorf pointed out. "But nevertheless we all accept a more complicated one." With luck Massey would allow himself to be diverted into the realms of philosophical logic, totally confusing ninety percent of the viewers, who would then dismiss him as a hair-splitting academic waffler.

"Yes—because it explains more facts," Massey replied. "But all that's irrelevant for now. You said that the presence of competent scientists is of no concern to you. Very well, then what I'm proposing will demonstrate the fact admirably. You said facts aren't altered by beliefs. I agree with you. So let's find out what the facts are."

Clearly Massey was not about to be shaken off. Half the world was watching and waiting for Zambendorf's answer. If he committed himself, Massey would never let him off the hook. "Well, Karl," Connel said after a few seconds of dragging silence. "What do you say? Will you accept Gerry Massey's challenge?"

Zambendorf looked around him desperately. Across the *Orion*'s Control Deck, many of the officers and crew members were watching curiously. If those damn GSEC people had done their jobs, Massey wouldn't have been able to get near him. It was infuriating. Massey had folded his arms and was waiting impassively. Zambendorf hesitated. Then, as their eyes met, he saw the triumph already lighting up Massey's face. That did it.

Zambendorf turned away for a moment, braced his

shoulders and breathed heavily a few times, and then looked up to the ceiling as if summoning strength from above. When he turned back again, his face seemed to have darkened with anger, and his eyes burned with patriarchal indignation. Connel looked suddenly apprehensive. Even Massey seemed taken by surprise. "At a time like this?... At such a moment of historic events about to unfold?... You would have me play games? What childishness is this?" Zambendorf thundered. Dramatic, sure, but it was an all-or-nothing situation. "We, the human race, are about to go forth and meet the destiny for which fate has been shaping us for millions of years, and instead of rising to fulfillment, your minds are distracted by trivia." Connel and Massey looked at each other nonplussed. Zambendorf whirled round upon Massey and pointed a finger accusingly. "I challenge you! Do you see any hint of where this journey will lead us, or what it will reveal? Indeed, do you see anything at all? Or are you like the rest of the blind who believe only in the part of the universe that lies within groping distance of their fingers?"

A bluff to throw him on the defensive, Massey decided. He had to hold the initiative. "Theatricals," he retorted. "Just theatricals. You're not saying anything. Are you supposed to be predicting something? If so, what? Let's have something specific for once, now—not after the event and with hindsight, after we arrive at Mars."

"Mars?" Zambendorf sounded pitying. "You believe we're going to Mars? You live your life in blindness. It is no wonder you cannot believe."

"Of course we're going to Mars," Massey said impatiently.

"Pah, fool!" Zambendorf exploded.

Suddenly Massey was less certain of himself. He could feel the situation starting to slip. It was all wrong. Zambendorf couldn't be turning it around. Massey had had all the aces, surely. Connel was gaping incredulously. "What are you saying, Karl," he demanded. "Are you saying we're not going to Mars? So where do you think we are going? . . . Why? . . . What are you telling us?" Most of the viewers had already forgotten Massey had ever issued a challenge. They wanted to know if Zambendorf had seen something.

Zambendorf was back in his natural element—the showman in control of the show. He extended his arms wide and appealed upward toward the roof. Beside him, Massey and Connel seemed to fade away on a hundred million screens. He brought his fists down to the sides of his head, held the pose for several seconds, and then looked at Connel with a strange, distant light in his eyes. "I have not the names that astronomers use, but I see us traveling over a great distance to a place that is not Mars . . . much farther from Earth than Mars."

"Where?" Connel gasped. "What's it like?"

"A child of the haloed giant who shepherds a flock of seventeen," Zambendorf pronounced in ringing tones. "I know not where I am . . . but it is cold and dark below the unbroken clouds of red and brown that float upon air that is not air. There are mountains made of ice, and vast wildernesses. And . . ." His voice trailed away. His jaw dropped, and his eyes opened wider.

"What?" Connel whispered, awed.

"Living beings! . . . They are not human, but neither are they from any part of Earth. They have minds! I am feeling out to them even now, and . . ."

"Get him off," General Vantz snapped on the far side of the Control Deck.

"Kill it! Get him off!" the Communications Director ordered. An engineer flipped a switch on his console. Voices were jabbering excitedly on every side.

"I don't care! Tell them anything," Herman Thoring yelled over an auxiliary channel to the Production Director in the GCN studio back in New York. "Say we've got a technical hitch. No, I don't know what it's about either, but we've got all hell loose up here."

Back in Globe II, Vernon Price was staring dumbstruck at the cabin wallscreen, which had just switched back to a view of Earth. "Well?" Malcom Wade challenged smugly as he puffed his pipe on the bunk opposite. "So he's a fake, is he? How do you explain that, then, eh?"

In his home in a Washington suburb, Walter Conlon pounded the table by his chair furiously with a fist. "He can't get away with it! He can't! Massey had him, for chrissakes—he had him cold!"

"Warren Taylor is on the line for you," his wife, Martha, said.

Conlon got up and stamped over to the comnet terminal across the room. The face of the NASO, North American Division Director was purple with anger. "What happened?" he demanded. "I thought you were supposed to have an expert up there who could handle that turkey."

In the study of his mansion in Delaware, Burton Ramelson was staring at a screen showing the stunned face of Gregory Buhl, who had just been put through from GSEC's head office. "My God!" Ramelson exclaimed incredulously. "Do you think we might have been wrong about this whole thing? Could there really be something to Zambendorf after all?"

In the Mission Director's executive offices in Globe I of the *Orion*, Caspar Lang was shaking his head at a grim-faced Daniel Leaherney. "Of course it's not genuine," Lang insisted. "We underestimated Zambendorf and his people. We took them for simple tricksters, but they're obviously far more sophisticated. It was a clever piece of espionage—nothing more, and nothing less."

"We'll have to tell the mission," Leaherney said. "It doesn't matter how Zambendorf did it—the result's still the same. We'll have to tell everyone on the ship the real story now."

"But we would have had to tell them before much longer anyway," Lang reminded him. "At least we're on our way, which is the main thing. It's a pity that the Soviets will find out now, instead of later when the *Orion* fails to show up at Mars, I know; but you have to agree, Dan, that with the number of people who've been involved, security has been a hell of a lot better than we dared hope."

Leaherney frowned for a while, but eventually nodded with a heavy sigh. "I guess you're right. Okay, put a clamp on all unofficial communications to Earth, effective immediately, and announce that I'll be addressing all personnel within a few hours. And get that psychic over here right away, would you. I reckon it's about time he and I had a little talk."

In Moscow an official from the Soviet Foreign Ministry, who was aware that the Americans had been conducting top-secret research into paranormal phenomena for many years, protested to the U. S. and European ambassadors that if the *Orion* was being sent to make first contact with an alien intelligence, none of Earth's major powers could be excluded. He demanded that the ship be recalled. The allegation was denied, and in their reply the representatives of the Western states suggested that perhaps the Soviet government was allowing itself to be unduly influenced by rumor and overreacting to sensationalism and unscientific speculation.

That same day aboard the *Orion*, Daniel Leaherney broadcast to the ship's occupants to inform them that, as had been generally concluded already, the ship's destination was indeed Saturn's moon, Titan. Pictures were replayed of the last views transmitted from the European probes that had landed on Titan two years previously, which showed strange machines approaching, and then nothing—the landers having presumably been destroyed. Nothing had been seen of whoever or whatever had built the machines. The orbiter that had launched the landers was still over Titan, but little more had been learned of the surface because of the moon's thick, brownish red clouds of nitrogen compounds and hydrocarbons.

The departments of the U.S. and European governments responsible for initiating the mission had never intended forcing anyone to face such unknowns against their will. Since the first reaction of many people to such a prospect would naturally be fear and nervousness, the original plan had been to announce the true story when the *Orion* was a few weeks out from Earth, which would have given everyone more than a month to discuss the situation and reflect upon its implications. Arrangements had been made for a NASO transporter from Mars to rendezvous with the *Orion* to take off anyone choosing not to stay on after that time. Expectations had been that after due consideration the majority of personnel would elect to continue the voyage and place their services at the disposal of the mission, and Leaherney expressed the hope that this would still be the case. The secrecy had been regrettable but necessary to "...safeguard the interests and security of the North American democracies and their European allies," he said.

Seven weeks later only a few faint souls dropped out when the NASO transporter rendezvoused with the mission ship. The *Orion* then accelerated away once more, its course now set for the outer regions of the Solar System.

11

THIRG, ASKER-OF-FORBIDDEN-QUESTIONS, LIVED IN the higher reaches of the forests south of the city of Pergassos in the land of the Kroaxians, where the foothills rose toward the mountains bounding the Great Meracasine Wilderness.

He lived in something that was more than a hut but less than a house, in keeping with the not quite hermitic but certainly less than sociable life that he preferred to lead. His home was situated in a small clearing amid pleasant forest groves of copper and aluminum wire-drawing machines, injection molders, transfer presses, and stately pylons bearing their canopy of power lines and data cables, among which scurrying sheet riveters, gracefully moving spot welders, and occasional slow-plodding pipe benders supplied a soothing background of chattering, hissing, whirring, and clunking to insulate him from the world of mortals and their mundane affairs and leave him alone and in peace with his thoughts. A low ice cliff stood at the back of the clearing to prop up the hillside rising away toward the mountains beyond, its line broken on one side by the valley of a liquid methane stream which tumbled cheerfully down over cataracts and ice boulders between clear pools where zinc-separating electrolyzers and potassium-precipitating evaporators came to wallow and wade and dip their slender intake nozzles and funnel-shaped scoops at the height of the bright period.

Thirg had grown the actual dwelling himself, having learned the craft from an old friend who was a builder in Pergassos. After laboring to clear the area of dead steel latticeworks and structural frames, the carcass of a transformer that had clung obstinately to its concrete base, and assorted scrap-metal undergrowth, he had prepared an area of the hydrocarbon soil below the cliff with nitrogenous loams collected from the stream bed, and planted the seed culture for the outside wall in a line ten paces out from the cliff base, curving inward at its ends to close off the frontage of a dry cave. Then he had laid out the baselines of the interior walls to provide a living and dining area, a workroom, and a library, and while carefully nurturing with methane solutions gathered from the forest, and pruning and shaping of the windows and doorways while the walls grew upward and merged into a half-dome overhead, he had enlarged the cave at the rear into a second workroom and a storeroom. The doors and window fittings had grown from secondary cultures grafted into the structure when the frames had stabilized at their correct shapes and sizes, and the larger furnishings from premolded miniatures purchased in the city. A conduit of forest piping diverted running methane from the stream, and a power line strung from a nearby distribution mast provided all the comforts of home recharging. To provide the rustic finish that suited his taste, Thirg had lined the walls with polished alloy sheets obtained from the rolling mill a mile farther downstream, and laid the floors with ceramic bricks and lengths of girder from a partly decomposed foundry that he had come across while walking near the stacking meadows just below the cabinet assembly line on the slopes overlooking the north side of the river.

One morning Thirg was sitting outside his house on a stump of steel forging, pondering the mysteries of life while he watched a phosphor-bronze bearing collector buzzing and chattering to itself as it poked and rummaged among a pile of undergrowth on the far side of the clearing. It was a species of a general family of collector animals that a naturalist friend had spent a lifetime cataloguing and classifying—discretely since such inquisitiveness could lead to trouble with the authorities if it was brought to the attention of the priests. Like all its related species, it selected just one type of metal composition by sniffing the emissions from a tiny spot that it vaporized with a needle laser, and then only from samples of a particular size and shape, and delivered its trophies to the nearest conveyor to be carried off to other parts of the forest. Thirg's friend had spent many hours following components through miles of forming, processing, and finishing stations to the assembly places where animals came to life, and observing the furnaces that devoured reject components and excreted pure materials from which new components were manufactured; he had drawn elaborate charts depicting the merging and branching patterns by which components and subassemblies flowed through the forest; and he had dismantled hundreds of dead animals and other machines in an attempt to trace where their organs and constituent parts had come from, via what routes, and where the raw materials had originated. But even with the findings of generations of earlier naturalists to build on, the work was barely begun. The intricate, interlocking, mutually interdependent pathways by which Nature recycled its materials as it constantly renewed the living world were so bewildering that Thirg sometimes suspected that, despite all the effort, hardly a fraction of the whole had been glimpsed yet, let alone comprehended. It was fascinating to think that one of the scraps of metal being sorted by the collector that he was watching now might be found twelve-brights later inside the rotor mounting of a centrifuge located miles away, or perhaps in the wheel bearings of a dead plastics-browser on the other side of Kroaxia.

Although Thirg had never elected to start a family of his own, his natural curiosity had led him at times to the places where subassemblies of robeings—the unique, self-aware species to which he belonged—came together for final assembly. He had watched in awed fascination as the embryos grew to their final forms and shapes while anxious parents scurried back and forth to make sure all the parts were available and all the requirements of the assembly machines satisfied, and he had shared their elation when the new robeing was at last activated and departed trustingly with the proud couple to its new home to begin the process of learning language, behavior, customs, and all the other things that characterized an adult member of society.

The assembly process was essentially identical to the ways in which animals and other life forms grew. Thirg's naturalist friend had assured him that all forms, including robeings, were supplied from the same sources of components, and it seemed remarkable that one species should exhibit thinking abilities sufficient to distinguish it so sharply from all the others. On the face of it, the difference seemed to support the orthodox teaching that robeings were unique in possessing souls which would eventually either return to the Lifemaker after undergoing worldly quality-assurance testing, or else be consigned to the Great Reduction Furnace below, from which the liquid ice volcanoes originated. But the physicians who had carefully dismantled and studied bodies of dead robeings had been able to find nothing more than was found in any other machine: the same kinds of perplexing arrangements of tubes, fibers, brackets, and bearings, and baffling arrays of intricate patterns etched into countless slivers of crystal that descended to levels of detail way beyond the power of the most powerful protein lenses to resolve. So where was the soul? If it existed, why was there no sign of anything different to say that it existed? True, nobody could explain how robeings were able to think, but on the other hand nobody could explain how animals came to act the way they did or to know what they seemed to know either. So did the existence of robeings require anything fundamentally "different" to be explained? Thirg wasn't at all sure that it did. To him the "fact" of the soul sounded suspiciously as if it had been invented to suit the answer; the answer hadn't been deduced from the facts in the way that was required by the system of rules he had constructed for answering questions reliably. And in all of the tests that he had subjected them to, the rules had never failed him.

A sudden grinding sound from the edge of the clearing interrupted his thoughts. Moments later the grinding changed to sharp clacking as Rex began gnashing his cutters and running backward and forward excitedly in front of the trail leading from the forest. Thirg stood up just as a tall figure clad in a woven-wire tunic and a dark cloak of carbon fiber came into view. He was wearing a hat of ice-dozer wheelskin and carrying a stout staff of duralumin tubing. "Down, Rex," Thirg said. "It's only Groork coming to pay us a rare visit. You should know him by now." And then, louder, "Well, hello, brother, Hearer-of-Voices. Have your voices led you up into these parts, or do you bring us tidings from the world?"

Groork came into the clearing and approached between the metallic-salt deposition baths on one side of Thirg's garden and a decorative row of subminiature laser drilling and milling heads busily carving delicate aesthetic patterns in an arrangement of used gas cylinders and old pump housings. His radiator vanes were glowing visibly after his exertions, and he was puffing coolant vapors. "There are many strange voices in the sky of late, the like of which I have never heard before," he replied. He didn't smile in response to Thirg's greeting; but then he was a mystic, and so never smiled at anything. "Surely it is an omen of great things that will soon come to pass. I am called to go out into the Wilderness of Meracasine, and there I will find the Revelation that many have sought. For it is written that—"

"Yes, yes, I know all about that," Thirg said, holding up an arm of silver alloy, jointed by intricately overlapping, sliding scales. "Come in and rest. You look thirsty. A drink of invigorating mountain methane is what you need. I don't know how you stand that polluted muck that they run into the city at all."

Thirg led the way inside, and Groork sat down gratefully on the couch by the wall in the dining area. While Thirg was pouring a cup of coolant, Groork selected one of the array of power sockets sprouting from the transformer unit, each of which designated a particular strength and flavor, drew it out on the end of its extension cord, and connected it to a plug inside a flap below his chin. "Ah, that does feel a lot better," he agreed after a few seconds.

Thirg passed Groork the cup, then glanced at his hands and down at his feet in their wheelskin sandals. He gestured toward the electroplating attachment. "If you're wearing hungry anywhere, help yourself."

"You've eaten already?"

"Yes, I've had a plate. I can recommend a new composition of chromium and vanadium that you ought to try. Delicious—home-regulated, fresh from the garden. Or a top-up of lube, perhaps?"

Groork shook his head, and the fervent glint returned to his imaging matrixes. "My purpose is not to trifle over pleasantries, Thirg. I have a higher calling to answer, and I do indeed bear thee news—grave news, O brother who forsakes his soul for Black Arts. Thy heresy hath betrayed thee! A writ has been issued by the King's Chancellor for you to be brought before the High Council of Priests by the time of the next west-bright, to recant the public utterances in which you have denied the Holy Scribings. Soldiers of the Royal Guard have already departed the city and will arrive hither this bright. Flee now and save thy wretched body while it lives, for its spirit is surely lost already to the Dark Master thou wilt never renounce!"

"Oh . . . And what am I supposed to have said now?" Thirg asked. Despite the tone of Groork's words, the thermal patterns playing on the surfaces of his face painted expressions of a concern that was genuine.

"Does thy memory ail?" Groork said. "Is that not the first symptom of the madness that afflicts all blasphemers and drives them into the deserts to perish seeking covenant with the accursed in the lands of the Unbelievers?"

"I'd have said they did it more to get away from the

priests and avoid being dipped in acid baths," Thirg replied, and asked again, "What am I supposed to have said?"

"Didst thou not, in the hearing of many who were in the marketplace, deny the Sacred Doctrine of the Divine and Unknowable Essence of the Maker of All Life?" Groork whispered, as if fearful of uttering the words too loudly.

"Hardly. What I said was that some of the sacred logic strikes me as precarious. For is not the existence of Life cited as proof that the Lifemaker must have made it . . . a least when one troubles to penetrate the confusing tangles of words?" Thirg shrugged and took a short draught from another cord to be sociable. "But we would never permit such a form of argument in our more mundane world of everyday affairs. For example, if I decided to invent an Unknowable Windowmaker, I could hardly claim that because windows exist the Windowmaker must have made them, could I? It is known that windows grow from cultures that are engineered by builders. Like the first, the argument is circular: It begins by assuming that which it sets out to prove."

Groork, who had raised his hands in an attempt to block his ears, lowered them again with an anguished moan. "Blasphemy!" he exclaimed. "What false creed of faith is this?"

"It's not a creed of faith at all, but a process by which truths can be shown to follow necessarily from simple observations," Thirg told him. "My task has been the reduction of this process to a series of rules which can be written down in a form of language and used by anyone. Truly the results astonish me. Shail I demonstrate some examples?"

Groork looked aghast. "Do you presume to impose rules upon the Lifemaker Himself? You would dare constrain how He might choose to manifest His design? You would confine His works to the understanding of mere mortals? What arrogance has taken possession of thee? What manner of—"

"Oh, shut up," Thirg said wearily. "I impose no rules of my own invention on anyone. I merely observe the world as it is, and attempt to understand the rules that are written into it already. It seems to me that if the Lifemaker saw fit to endow us with intelligence at all, He would have meant us to use it. Well, what use would be better fitting than discovering reliable methods of acquiring knowledge?"

"Know ye of the things that the wise shall not seek after, and the mysteries that the holy shall not question," Groork recited shrilly. "There are some things that we were not meant to know, Thirg."

"Oh, and how do you know?"

"It is written in the Scribings."

"Who wrote them, and how did they know?"

"Those who were inspired to know. Truth cannot be found by following false paths. All of the true knowledge that was meant to be divulged is divulged in the Scribings."

"And who says that?" Thirg challenged. "The Scribings. Again we see an argument that leads itself into a circle."

Groork looked away despairingly and his eyes came to rest on an orb covered with unfamiliar markings and notations, standing at one end of Thirg's worktable. "Thou art bewitched by circles," he said. "The same madness that has damned Lofbayel is afflicting thee. I have heard of the insanity that deranges his mind with belief the world is round."

"I have studied his evidence closely, and it is persuasive," Thirg replied. "Since his trial before the Council, he has entrusted his charts and his records to me for safekeeping." He gestured toward a large map hanging on the wall above the worktable—a map unlike any that Groork had seen before. "Behold, the world upon which you walk. Much remains to be filled in, as you can see, but Lofbayel has convinced me that in its main features it is reasonably accurate. See how tiny the whole of Kroaxia is upon it."

"It has straight edges," Groork objected after staring in mute protest for a while. "It is taught that the world is as a platter, bounded by the unscalable Peripheral Barrier of mountains that support the sky. You talk of rules of reason, but no fool in his wildest ravings would conceive of reason such as this."

"The edges of the sheet upon which the map is drawn can no more influence what the map represents than the edge of a portrait can cause its subject to be beheaded," Thirg pointed out.

"And so the world is beheaded on all four sides," Groork replied. "The Barrier does not appear anywhere. Thus this map cannot represent the entire world. Your words are belied."

"In all his searchings Lofbayel was unable to find a single authenticated account of anyone ever finding the Barrier," Thirg said. "High mountains, yes; immense chains whose very passes are higher than the highest peaks in all Kroaxia, yes; mountains whose summits are sometimes lost from sight in vapors no more substantial than the mists that rise from the stream outside at early bright, yes. But mountains upon which there rests a solid roof of sky? Never. Always there is another side beyond the mountains, and always another shore beyond the ocean."

"Now you would presume to dictate limits to the Lifemaker again," Groork accused. "This time you tell Him how large He is permitted to make His world. The distance to the Barrier is not written. It is unknown and therefore unknowable."

"Another reason for it's being unwritten and unknown might be that it doesn't exist," Thirg commented.

"It is written that it exists!"

"How could it be written about if no one's ever seen it?"

"How could it not exist? The world must be bounded."

"Because your imagination is bounded and unable to conceive of any alternative?" Thirg asked. "Now who is imposing his limits upon the Lifemaker? But this map covers the whole world, and no Barrier appears on it.

Where, then, is the Barrier if it exists?"

"The map cannot cover the whole world," Groork answered.

"But it leaves no direction open for any more of the world to exist in." Thirg picked up the sphere and showed it. "There is the world, Groork! For just one minute forget your dusty texts, written long ago by clerks in their dungeons, who never saw an ocean, let alone crossed one, and who never looked beyond any mountain. This form, and only this form, is consistent with all the facts that have been recorded; no form of platter can be contrived of which the same can be said. Which form, therefore, should we accept as representing more closely the reality that exists?"

Groork unplugged himself from the transformer unit and shook his head in protest. "Your facts are in error, for did you not claim they were amassed from travelers who have seen the farthest limits of north, south, east, and west? But it is obvious that no traveler could venture beyond a small region at the top of that . . ." He pointed at the globe. "Otherwise they would fall off, as indeed would the methanes of the oceans. But the oceans persist. There is a fact, Brother Thirg, which you would appear to have chosen conveniently to ignore."

"That was a source of vexation to me too for a while," Thirg admitted. "But a possible answer suggested itself to me one bright when I was strolling in the forest. I stopped to rest for a while by a glade where spectrometers are assembled, and picked a magnet from one of the storage bins to savor its scent. The iron grains that it attracted from the debris around where I was sitting prompted me to wonder if perhaps the world-sphere might draw all things to itself in the same way that a magnet draws iron grains to itself—from any direction. Just as every line toward the magnet is uniformly 'down' for the grain, so 'down' at every place on the world-sphere would be toward the ground. The methanes of the oceans would thus seek a level nearest to the center and remain in the lowest regions, which is as we know to be true. Hence, you see, the fact is explained."

Thirg paused, but Groork made no response. Thirg held up the sphere to study it for a moment or two, and then continued in a more distant voice, "The fact that nobody has ever found a Barrier holding up a solid sky leads me to wonder if the sky is really solid at all. Could it be nothing more than vapors? And if so, how far do they extend? Forever? If not, what lies beyond them? Could there be other worlds? The question intrigues me. Ever since it occurred to me after I began familiarizing myself with Lofbayel's work, I have been studying the cycles of full-brights and half-brights as they follow one another across the world. On the basis that the world is indeed a sphere and the sky nothing more than vapors, the bright and half-bright periods could be accounted for by two brilliant objects moving beyond the sky in a complicated but repeating motion. Where would you look in your Scribings for the knowledge to answer questions like these, Groork?"

Groork stood up suddenly and dismissed the whole matter with a gesture. "I did not come here to listen to you compounding your folly by adding more heresies to those you are guilty of already," he said. "The High Council will not look leniently upon you one more time. Their patience is exhausted. May the Lifemaker forgive me for my weakness, but I cannot abandon my brother though the madness boils within him. Collect together the possessions you would carry with you, Thirg, and for this bright we can travel together. But on the far side of the mountains I must lead a lone path to the destiny that has been written but which is yet to be revealed. Hurry. There may be little time."

Thirg stared back sadly. "I doubt if you could ever understand, Groork, even if I had all the rest of time to try and explain it. Your beliefs are taught without a question's being tolerated, while mine are learned only after posing every question. What does it say for the worth of beliefs if they cannot survive critical scrutiny and dare not permit a word of dissent to be voiced? Would truth or untruth be the first to tremble in the presence of the other? It seems—"

At that moment the sound of Rex's agitation again came from outside. Groork rushed to the doorway. "Too late!" he moaned, turning a fearful face as Thirg strode across the living area after him. "They're here. The King's soldiers have arrived." Thirg reached the door and looked out past Groork. Mounted figures in single file were approaching on the trail leading to the clearing.

12

THIRG STARED FOR SOME SECONDS, AND THEN THE louver vanes covering his ventilation inlets bristled into a puzzled frown. "Those are not soldiers," he said to Groork as the new arrivals emerged from the trail and came fully into view. He went out and stood before the door; Groork followed warily.

Although the riders carried weapons, they were clad in rough mountain garb, with heavy cloaks of flexible laminate mail, body armor of acid-resistant and heat-absorbing organics, and knee-length boots of heavy polymer. The one who appeared to be the leader, a large, broad-shouldered robeing with rugged, weather-worn features and a heavy black beard of accumulated carbon-impregnated plating about his lower face, crossed the clearing and brought his exhaust-snorting steellion to a halt before Thirg and Groork. The others fanned out into a semicircle behind.

"Outlaws, unless I am much mistaken," Thirg muttered to Groork. He raised his head to look up at the leader and asked in a louder voice, "Am I honored with guests, or merely treated to the rare pleasure of welcoming passersby?"

"Oh, you are indeed honored," the leader replied. His voice was deep and firm, but his tone more jovial than harsh. "I take it you are Thirg, who asks forbidden questions. And do you find many answers?"

"As to the first, I am. And this is my brother Groork—a hearer. As to the second, each new answer comes inseparably joined to a new question of whether or not the answer is true. Thus the number of questions to be answered can never diminish, however many answers may be found." Thirg cast an eye over the company. "But who is it that honors us with his visit, and what would bring such as you to the dwelling of a thinker and a seeker-of-truth? If you have come in search of plunder or of a body that would command a high ransom, I fear you will be disappointed. If, on the other hand, your desire is to rest awhile and conjecture upon the riddles of Nature while engaging in philosophical discourse, then I have more to offer. But I would not advise it; the King's soldiers have departed hither from Pergassos, I am told, and have been riding since early bright."

"We know all about them," the leader said. "The King's generals would better spend the royal funds buying intelligence from us than paying their own officers. But the soldiers will have found the bridge over the cable-spinning ravine blocked, which will slow them down awhile." He paused and looked from one to the other of the two figures standing in front of him. "I am Dornvald, called by many Freer-of-Bondslaves, by others, Subverter-of-Rebels, depending on whether you pay the King's living or he pays yours. We present ourselves here as trusty escorts for your journey through the mountains and across the Wilderness to the city of Menassim in the country of the Carthogians."

"What makes you think that I wish to travel to Carthogia?" Thirg asked.

"I didn't say you did," Dornvald told him. "I just said you were going."

"To preserve the likes of one such as I from priests?"

"If you choose not to preserve yourself."

"Why should that be a matter of concern to outlaws?"

"It isn't. But we enjoy freedom of passage through the borders of Carthogia and other immunities, in return for which we render certain services to Kleippur, the ruler of Carthogia. It appears that Kleippur values your casing more highly than you do yourself. I do not make it my business to question his reasons, but word is that other sorcerers who have fled to his realm have spoken well of your magic, Thirg. Thus it is that we have been entrusted for many six-brights now to watch over you for danger of the kind that now threatens."

Thirg rubbed his power inlet housing thoughtfully while he considered the situation. Carthogia had once been a part of neighboring Serethgin, a larger country than Kroaxia. It was now ruled by a former general called Kleippur, who had led a successful uprising against the incumbent Serethginian prince, ousted the traditional nobility and clergy, and established an oppressive military tyranny. Various alliances between the remainder of Serethgin, Kroaxia, and a number of other kingdoms had waged a series of wars to free the hapless people of Carthogia from their yoke, but so far they had been unable to prevail against the Carthogian army, which though small in numbers fought fanatically because of the ruthless discipline imposed upon its soldiers, and with the advantage of innovative weaponry created by enslaved craftsmen who lived chained to their workbenches.

At least, that was the official story told by the priests and teachers of Kroaxia. But Thirg had heard rumors of a different kind—rumors of a Carthogian society that tolerated inquirers such as himself and permitted them to ask their questions openly; of a slaveless society in which even the serfs were free to own property and keep the major portion of the wealth earned by their labors; and of an army of free robeings who fought to defend themselves against what they saw as a return to the very form of slavery that Kroaxians were conditioned to believe was normal and natural—all of which the priests and teachers insisted were lies spread by Carthogian agents to undermine the faith and trust of the people.

Thirg had never known what to believe. But he did know that many of his friends had departed for Carthogia, and though from time to time he heard scraps of news of them, none had returned; on the other hand, he had never met nor heard tell of a Carthogian who had fled the other way. Did that mean they had found freedom and tolerance as Thirg sometimes suspected? Or had they been kidnapped and forced to remain in captivity as the Kroaxian teachers maintained?

For some reason, running away from the priests of his own volition would have been, in his own mind, a betrayal of all that he felt he stood for. But, if forced to leave by a band of armed brigands . . . well, that wasn't the same thing at all, was it? He looked up again at Dornvald and asked, so as to be able to justify everything to himself later, "Have I a choice, Kidnapper-of-Thinkers?"

"Most certainly, for have I not presented myself as an agent of the Land-That-Gives-Freedom?" Dornvald answered heartily. "You can mount a steed and ride with us freely, or you can be placed on a steed and ride with us bound—a perfectly free choice to decide how you get there."

"In that case I'll come with you," Thirg said.

"Wisest, without a doubt," Dornvald agreed solemnly.

Thirg glanced at Groork for a moment, then looked back at Dornvald. "My brother is passing by on his way to the Wilderness, where he goes in search of his voices," he said. "Our roads will run together for a while. Besides, we could not in good conscience abandon him to the mercies of King's servants unlikely to find the disappearance of their quarry a source of any great amusement."

"We have spare steeds," Dornvald said, looking at Groork. "Would you travel in company as far as the village of Xerxeon, Hearer, though I should warn you I have no ear for holy words?"

"Arghhh!" Groork shrank back into the doorway of the house and covered his imagers protectively with an arm. "Wouldst thou defile me with the stain of thy followers, Henchman-of-Unbelievers? I will travel my road in solitude, for thine leads not upward to the Lifemaker, but downward to the precipice of doom."

Dornvald shrugged his shoulder cowlings. "As you will.

But I doubt that your voices will afford you the same safety on your journey." He looked back at Thirg. "There is one pack-mount for the possessions you would bring with you. Kleippur has given particular instructions for the charts and records belonging to the mapmaker, Lofbayel, to be preserved. If you have a safe hiding place, I suggest you use it for anything else of value. Who can foretell when the strange workings of fate might bring you this way again?"

"Kleippur knows of the charts?" Thirg sounded amazed.

"Kleippur makes it his business to know many things," Dornvald replied.

Thirg spent a short while selecting personal belongings and some of his more highly prized books and journals. While a couple of Dornvald's outlaws were packing these items into bundles with Lofbayel's charts and securing them, Thirg covered the remainder of his books, his study samples, and his finer measuring instruments in oiled wrappings and locked them in chests which two more outlaws carried to a concealed hole, sealed by a boulder, at the base of the cliff a short distance from the house.

Then Thirg stood to take a last look around his garden while the outlaws who had been helping him remounted. Another led forward a sleek, powerful-looking mount with a dark, copper-tinted sheen and titanium-white flashes around its head and neck. Thirg eyed it apprehensively as he stepped closer—riding was not one of his greatest skills—and then cocked an imager-shade curiously as he noticed the royal crest etched into its rear flank. Dornvald followed Thirg's gaze and laughed. "Until recently the swift carrier of one of His Majesty's messengers, who has departed for a place to which that steed could not take him. We must make haste now, Collector-of-Books-and-Objects-That-Mystify-Me, or His Majesty's servants will be here to take his property back for him."

Thirg mounted carefully while one of the outlaws held the animal's harness to steady it. Then the riders formed up with Dornvald at the head, Thirg next with Rex waiting suspiciously but faithfully alongside, and the remaining dozen or so falling into a column behind. Groork crept out from the shadows at the back of the house and watched. They had left behind one steed, which Dornvald had ordered to be tethered to a pillar at the edge of the clearing.

"Which officer is it who leads the soldiers?" Dornvald inquired casually to Geynor, his lieutenant, as the riders moved off. "Do we know of him from encounters past, or by repute, perchance?"

"Oh indeed," Geynor replied, speaking just as loudly. "Captain Horazzorgio, no less, whose rage causes even his own soldiers to tremble, or so I have heard tell."

"Not the Horazzorgio whose inventions of tortures and torments are beyond the ability of even the keepers of the King's dungeons to bring themselves to speak?"

"The same. 'Tis said heretics have been slowly melted, starting at the toes."

"Really? How awful!"

The column filed out of the clearing into the gully of the stream, and began following the narrow trail that led upward toward the High Country. They had covered only a short distance when Fenyig, the rearguard, called to attract Dornvald's attention. A lone mounted figure, holding well back to keep its distance, had come into view lower down the trail. It halted when it saw that the column had stopped to wait. Groork's voice came floating up hollowly from below. "Thy demons have damned thee, Thirg. Even now doest thou go willingly with the servants of Darkness to deliver thy soul into eternal bondage. Heed my words, for surely wilt thou melt in the Great Furnace."

Thirg smiled to himself as he turned back, and Dornvald ordered the column to resume moving. From there on he kept his eyes on the peaks of methane-capped ice looming in the distance ahead. His future lay beyond the mountains now, and that was where he should look.

13

TITAN, SECOND IN SIZE AMONG THE MOONS OF THE solar system only to Jupiter's Ganymede and then by just the barest of margins, had been a constant source of enigmas for astronomers and planetary physicists virtually since its discovery by Christiaan Huyghens in 1655. One of the first questions to be asked was whether it possessed an atmosphere, thus making it unique among the planetary satellites. When that was at last resolved affirmatively in the early 1940s, other questions arose: What did the atmosphere consist of, and what were its physical conditions at various depths? For more than thirty years attempts at measuring the body's optical, infrared, and radio spectra yielded inconsistent and sometimes contradictory results. Then the close flyby of the American *Voyager I* probe in 1980 resolved some of the basic issues: Titan's atmosphere was mostly nitrogen, with significant proportions of argon, methane, and hydrogen, plus trace amounts of numerous hydrocarbons and nitrogenous compounds. Surface pressure was around 1.5 times that of Earth's atmosphere, which at the estimated temperature of minus 179 degrees Celsius and with Titan's surface gravity of 0.14 suggested about ten times as much gas per unit area as on Earth. As had been suspected by many theorists, the dense, reddish clouds blanketing the surface turned out to be an aerosol suspension at an altitude of two hundred kilometers, consisting of molecular fragments formed by ultraviolet dissociation of the gases in the upper atmosphere. According to most models, the aerosol particles would gradually recombine into heavier polymers and precipitate out of the atmosphere to form surface deposits of considerable depth, but this hadn't been verified since the clouds were everywhere opaque. Because of the cloud blanket and Titan's remoteness from the Sun, daylight on the surface would be about as bright, it was estimated, as a moonlit night on Earth.

The returned data were consistent with surface conditions close to the triple-point of the solid, liquid, and gaseous phases of methane, which raised the intriguing possibility that methane could well exist as a gas in the lower atmosphere and a liquid on the surface, thus playing a role similar to that of water on Earth. Conceivably, therefore, the surface of Titan could consist of methane oceans and water-ice continents covered by nitrogenous-hydrocarbon soil, above which methane rain precipitated from methane clouds formed below the aerosol blanket. It was even possible that the release of radioactive heat in the interior might maintain reservoirs of water that could escape to the surface as "ice lava," and perhaps provide a fluid substrate for mountain-building and other tectonic processes. But with the diversion of funding from planetary exploration programs to feed the ongoing insanity of the arms race, little more was learned until the arrival of the European probe at Saturn, less than three years before the *Orion*.

Radar mapping by the *Dauphin* orbiter had indeed revealed the existence of vast oceans, islands, continents, and mountains below Titan's all-obscuring clouds, and details of the natural geography had been published widely. However, as the *Orion*'s occupants had learned only after leaving Earth, the orbiter had also sent back radar images of highly reflective objects suggestive of artificial metallic constructions, which in many places covered huge areas too densely to be resolved individually. All mention of that had been censored from the published information, along with any reference to the machines glimpsed by the

Dauphin's short-lived surface landers and the advanced culture that had originated them. At least, the inferred sizes of the constructions and the areas which they covered on some parts of the surface had seemed indicative of an advanced culture. But in almost three years the orbiter's instruments had failed to observe any activity in space around Titan, or even to detect any sign of aircraft in the lower atmosphere; and except for intermittent transmissions emanating from a few sources pinpointed on the surface, the radio spectrum had been strangely silent.

No more was learned until the *Orion* went into orbit above Titan and began sending reconnaissance drones down through the aerosol layer and the lower-altitude methane clouds to scan the surface. The views sent back had been at first perplexing, then bewildering, and finally staggering as the mission's scientists gradually unraveled what they implied. The views had shown what appeared to be alien towns consisting of unusual buildings that resembled enormous, intricately shaped hollow plants more than anything fabricated according to recognizable methods, which was difficult to explain since there were also plenty of examples of immense and elaborate engineering constructions. If the aliens had the technology to build factories, why didn't they build cities to live in? Perhaps because of their notions of values and aesthetics, somebody had suggested.

Then had come the first indications that maybe the aliens weren't so professional at managing their technology after all. View after view showed chaotic situations where entire industrial complexes seemed to have overflowed their boundaries, spilling plant and machinery out across the surrounding country with outgrowths from different centers invading each other's territories and mixing themselves up in hopeless confusion. In some areas the mess of working and broken-down machinery, all buried amid piles of scrap and assorted parts, stretched for miles, yet much of it managed, somehow, to continue functioning. If the alien engineers were capable of efficient and purposeful design at all—and some of the designs seemed astonishingly advanced—how could they have let things get into such a state? It made no sense.

As the drones were sent lower to obtain telescopic close-ups both in infrared and at normal wavelengths using flares and searchlights, the scientists monitoring the views back in the *Orion* had waited breathlessly for their first glimpse of an alien. But they never found any. There were thousands of ingeniously conceived, freely mobile machines, to be sure, some of them displaying extraordinary degrees of versatility and behavioral adaptability, with all manner of types apparently specialized for just about every task imaginable . . . but never once was there a trace of the aliens whose needs all the activity was presumably intended to serve. Some of the scientists had speculated that the aliens were too tiny to show up on the pictures. But if so, why would they make machines that were so much larger? It didn't add up. Maybe the aliens lived below the surface and never came out, leaving the machines to manage everything on the surface. Maybe they just stayed in their vegetable houses all the time. Maybe . . . but nobody found such suggestions very satisfying.

And then, as the scientists continued to study replays from all over Titan, they began noticing something remarkable about a particular "species" of erect, bipedal, vaguely humanoid robot that seemed to be represented everywhere to a greater or lesser extent: Everything they seemed to do was unremarkably familiar. Their patterns of coming and going in and out of the houses and about the towns, sometimes alone and sometimes in groups, stopping occasionally upon meeting others, were the same as could be seen in communities anywhere; they tended plantations of odd-looking growths that in some ways resembled their peculiar organic houses; they wore what looked like clothes; they herded flocks of mechanical "animals," and—more amazing still—were frequently seen to ride them; they gathered in crowds, and there was an instance of two groups of them fighting each other; and once or twice when the drones went too low, their reactions showed every characteristic of fear, and occasionally, panic. In short, as far as could be ascertained from pictures, they acted exactly as people did.

Which explained, of course, why nobody was having any luck in finding aliens—at least, not the flesh-and-blood or whatever-and-whatever kinds of "conventional" aliens that planetary biologists had speculated about for years.

Titan was inhabited by machines. It possessed an electromechanical biosphere which included, apparently, a dominant species of culturally developed, intelligent, and presumably self-aware robot. The scientists christened them the Taloids, after Talos, the bronze man created by Hephaestus, the blacksmith son of Hera and Zeus. But clearly Titan could never have evolved such a system from nothing. So how had the machines come to be there? They had to be products of an alien civilization that had either brought them to Titan or sent them there. When? What for? Why Titan? Where were the aliens? Nobody had any answers. As always, Titan had thrown up a new batch of mysteries as soon as the earlier ones were resolved. Evidently it would be far from running low on its supply of them for a while to come.

"Not only aliens; not only intelligent aliens; but intelligent, alien machines—plus undreamed-of technology in virtually unlimited abundance, and a whole new, geologically active world!" Gerold Massey turned back from facing a wall of cable-runs and switchboxes in the generator bay inside the *Orion*'s Service Module and spread his hands emphatically. "Probably the most staggering discoveries within a century, and quite possibly within the entire history of science. Now, that's worth some time and effort . . . But Mars never happened. There isn't any place now for psychic paranonsense, surely."

Zambendorf, leaning with arms folded against a stator housing, sent back a scornful look. "You're being presumptuous, Massey. And besides, you're talking about how I make my living, which I happen to find stimulating, entertaining, and amply rewarding. I would say that's worth a considerable amount of time and effort."

"And how about all the people who waste their minds and their lives thinking they're going to become supermen—have you asked them if they think so too?"

"I don't have to," Zambendorf said. "They've already shown what they think—by how they choose to spend their own time and their own money. They're free-acting individuals in a free society. Why do you insist on making their well-being your business?"

"When I have to live surrounded by mass-produced morons, it is my business," Massey retorted. "We've got scientists emigrating in droves. Japanese power plants are driving half of what's left of our industries. This ship wouldn't be here if it weren't for the Europeans... I mean, Christ!—don't you care what you're doing?"

"Why single me out?" Zambendorf demanded, straightening up and sounding angry suddenly. "Do you think I made people the way they are? I merely accept them as I find them, and if they have failed to develop the sense that would serve them better, or if society has failed to educate them in the use of it, why am I supposed to be the one to blame? Why don't you complain at our so-called educators, or the media mind-puppeteers, or the political dummies who read opinion polls like horoscopes instead of doing something to influence them? Protecting fools from their own stupidity will not make them wiser, Massey. It merely spares them any need even to be aware of the fact that they're fools, which is hardly the best way to begin curing anything. When I find I am unable to make a living, that is when people will have learned something. In the meantime, don't expect apologies from me."

"Ah... you're admitting you're a fake at last, are you?" Massey inquired, looking mildly amused.

Zambendorf calmed down at once and sniffed disdainfully. "Don't be absurd. I admit no such thing."

"So why did GSEC send you here? I wonder," Massey said, ignoring the denial. "Because I know, and I know you know, that Ramelson and the other GSEC people who matter aren't interested in any paranormal claptrap. So their real purpose can't have anything to do with your supposed powers, can it?" He waited for a few seconds but Zambendorf made no reply; either Zambendorf wasn't certain of the real answer himself, or he wasn't saying anything. "Want to know what I think?" Massey asked.

"Very well, since you are obviously determined to tell me anyway."

Massey moved a pace forward and made an open-handed gesture. "Under our system of nominal democracy, He Who Would Shape Public Opinion doesn't need to be King. Society can be controlled indirectly through manipulation of the mass vote. So most people are conditioned practically from birth to have their opinions on anything dispensed to them in the same way they get their deodorants and prescription drugs—secondhand from TV role-models and celebrity images that have been carefully engineered to be easy to relate to."

"Hmph . . ." Zambendorf snorted and paced away across the steel floorplates to halt in front of a ladder leading up to a catwalk overhead. What Massey was saying was uncomfortably close to his own reading between the lines of some of the things Caspar Lang had been saying since the *Orion*'s departure from Earth.

Massey went on, "That's what I figure you are—a general-purpose bludgeon to mold a large sector of public thinking, and therefore to help shape official U.S. policies in a direction calculated to best serve GSEC's interests."

"I see. Very interesting," Zambendorf commented.

"Think about it," Massey urged. "They knew from the *Dauphin* pictures that there was an alien civilization here, but nobody knew what kind of civilization. GSEC has a tough competitive situation globally; the West is still stalemated after grappling with the Cold War for decades. . . . Just think what the chance of exclusive access to advanced alien technology must have meant—and very probably still does! In other words, the response of the U.S. and major European governments to what happens here at Titan could turn out to be some of the most important legislation ever passed in history...and we're well on our way to seeing it being decided by a kookocracy."

"You're being neurotic," Zambendorf said impatiently. "Every generation has been convinced that it's seeing the beginning of the end. Tablets dug up in Iraq from 3,000 B.C. say the same thing."

"It's not just me," Massey answered. "A lot of people at NASO feel the same way. Why else do you think they sent me along? They knew enough to arrive at the same conclusions."

Zambendorf turned back again and made a discarding motion. "Ideologists, all of you. All of the world's troubles have been caused by noble and righteous ideas of how other people ought to live. I look after my own interests, and I allow the world to look after its in whatever way it chooses. That's my only ideology, and it serves me well."

Massey looked at him dubiously for a moment. "Really?" he said. "I wonder."

"What is that supposed to mean?" Zambendorf asked.

"Whose interests are you serving here—your own, or GSEC's?"

"Is there any reason why the two shouldn't coincide? In a good business relationship, both parties benefit."

"When they're allowed to enter into it of their own free choice, sure. But you weren't even told what the deal was."

"How do you know what I was or wasn't told?" Zambendorf asked.

Massey snorted. "It was pretty obvious from the reactions to that stunt you pulled just after liftout what you were and weren't supposed to know. They've been keeping you on a pretty tight rein since, I bet. How does it feel to be simply another owned asset on the corporate balance sheet, for use when expedient? So whose interests do you think will count first?"

"I don't know what you're talking about," Zambendorf maintained stiffly.

But Massey had a point, nevertheless, he conceded inwardly. With nothing to gain from alienating GSEC needlessly, and being a strong believer in keeping open the doors of opportunity whenever possible, Zambendorf had generally behaved himself through most of the voyage and avoided further spectaculars. Now that the voyage had ended, perhaps it was time he began reasserting himself, he decided.

"That's not possible—not in the immediate future, anyway," Caspar Lang said across his desk in the executive offices in Globe I. "The personnel schedules have already been worked out. Besides, you wouldn't have any defined function at this stage."

"I want a trip down to the surface," Zambendorf said again, firmly. "Parties have started going down, and I want a slot on one of the shuttles. I didn't come eight hundred million miles to take snapshots through a porthole from up here."

"Small scientific teams are being sent down to remote areas to investigate surface conditions and collect samples," Lang replied. "That's all. You wouldn't fit into something like that."

"There's a larger expedition being organized to go down sometime in the next few days, to attempt a first contact with the Taloids once a suitable site has been selected," Zambendorf replied evenly.

Lang looked shaken. "How do you know about that?"

Zambendorf spread his hands and made a face in a way that said Lang should know better than to ask. "It doesn't matter . . . But the opportunity would be ideal. It would be good publicity for me, and therefore also for GSEC."

Lang emitted a long breath and shook his head. "It's not my prerogative to decide," he said. Inwardly he was still seething at Zambendorf's discovering and revealing the mission's true destination before it left Earth, which Lang felt reflected on him personally.

"Come on, don't give me that, Caspar," Zambendorf said. "Even if that were true, you could go talk to Leaherney. So fix something. I don't care how . . . but just fix it."

Lang shook his head again. "I'm sorry, but there's no way at present. Maybe later . . . I'll keep it in mind."

Zambendorf looked at him for a few seconds longer, and then hoisted himself to his feet with a sigh. "Well, I'm not going to get into an argument over it," he said. "Since it's a publicity matter, I'll leave it with my publicity manager to handle. She'll probably be giving you a call later." With that, he turned for the door.

Lang groaned beneath his breath. "It won't make any difference," he called after Zambendorf. "I've already told you the answer, and it's final—there's no way you're going down there, and nothing that Clarissa Eidstadt says will change it."

14

"IT HAS LONG BEEN MY CUSTOM TO TRUST NO ONE'S ACcount of another's words, and it has served me well," Dornvald said to Thirg, who was riding alongside him. "Whether any Lifemaker speaks to priests and hearers, I know not—that is His affair and theirs. But it seems to me that any services of mine that He would lay claim upon, He would be able enough to make known to me Himself." The party was moving just below the skyline along a ridge that would bring them to a high pass through the mountains. The main column had doubled up on the barren, open terrain, and scouts were riding a short distance ahead and on the flanks. The forests of southern Kroaxia now lay far below and behind.

Thirg had been surprised and impressed. Although for most of the time Dornvald affected a simple and direct manner, his conversation revealed glimpses of an acuity of thinking and a perspicacity of observation that Thirg rarely encountered. The outlaw seemed to display intuitively the same disinclination to take anything for granted that Thirg had taught himself only after extensive labors. Did the outlaw way of life breed suspicion of appearances and assurances as a habit, Thirg wondered, or did outlaws become outlaws because they were doubters already? At any rate the discourse was providing a welcome distraction from the monotony of the ride.

"A proposition which I would not desire to contest,"

Thirg agreed. "So does the possibility not suggest itself that Nature is no more obliged to contrive an explanation of Life that is simply comprehended by the minds of robeings than it is to construct the world in a shape that is simply perceived? Did Lifemaker indeed create robeing, therefore, or, more likely I am beginning to suspect, did robeing create Lifemaker as the more convenient alternative to widening his own powers of comprehension?"

"I have no answer to that," Dornvald said. "But it seems to me that you are substituting a worse unknown for one that is mystery enough already. Round worlds and worlds beyond the sky are strange notions to contemplate, yet not beyond the bounds to which imagination could accommodate itself. But is not the riddle of Life of a different complexity? For is not all Life in the form of machines that were assembled by machines, which in turn were assembled by machines, and so for as far back as we care to permit our imaginations to postulate? But however far that be, must we not arrive inevitably at the bound which requires the first machine to have been assembled by that which was not a machine? Even if your round world of distances dispenses with need of any Barrier, this barrier more surely bounds the world of imagination. Or would you make a circle out of time itself?"

"Again I am unable to quarrel with your reasoning," Thirg replied. "Nor with that of priests, for that matter, for this is their logic also. That that which was not machine assembled the first machine I would not argue, since were it machine, then that which it assembled could not have been the first machine by our own premise. Nor do I take exception to him who would name this nonmachine machine-assembler 'Lifemaker,' since it is as well described by such a name as by any other. But that the one conclusion should compel us also to construct of necessity a realm beyond reach of reason and unknowable to inquiry, I cannot accept. That is the barrier which I would dispute."

The column closed up again to pick its way in single

file along a narrow track crossing an icefall, with a steep drop below on one side and a sheer cliff extending upward to the crestline on the other. Beyond the icefall the ground became open again and resumed its rise; the riders took up open order once more, and Thirg moved alongside Dornvald.

"The question is no more answered than before, Questioner-of-Barriers," Dornvald observed, evidently having turned the matter over in his mind. "For now we must ask what made the Lifemaker and the Maker of Lifemakers. It seems to me that you have merely moved your barrier to another place. It stands as high as ever, but now you must travel farther to cross it. The gain would appear poor compensation for the exertion, for what does it amount to but tired feet?"

"If the barrier has been moved back, then the world of knowledge that it encompasses is so much the greater," Thirg replied. "And if that world does not close back upon itself but extends indefinitely, then the gain can be without limit even though the barrier is never crossed. Therefore does this barrier in the mind have any more effective substance to it than the Barrier which is supposed to enclose the physical world?"

Dornvald considered the proposition for a while. "But what is there in the knowable universe, apart from machines, that could assemble machines?" he asked at last.

"Nothing of which I am aware . . . in this world," Thirg replied. "But if there should indeed exist other worlds beyond the sky, and if they are knowable, then are we not obliged to include them in the total knowable universe of which you speak? And does not the removal of a barrier to distances so vast leave room enough within to harbor an unknown but knowable Life which, though not machine, might create machine?"

"Now your words become the riddle," Dornvald said. "How could Life exist without machine when both are one?"

"Is Life constrained to take no other form than that

familiar to us?" Thirg asked. "If so, by what law? Certainly none that presents itself to me with credentials sufficient to place its authority above all question."

"Well, now you must answer your own riddle," Dornvald said. "For truly we have arrived at my barrier now, and its faces are unscalable. What form is both Life and not Life, for it is not machine, yet machine is Life?"

"I can conceive of none such, Returner-of-Riddles," Thirg answered. "But then I have never claimed that the borders which bound the tiny country of my comprehension, and the barrier which confines the universe of the knowable must coincide. The greater territory contains vast regions outside the smaller, with room enough to accommodate whole nations of answers both to this riddle and others that I know not even how to ask."

They fell silent, and thoughtful patterns came and went slowly across Dornvald's face for a while. At last he looked sideways at Thirg and said, "Perhaps your thoughts are not so strange after all, Wonderer-about-Lifemakers. There have been tales of flying beasts that descended from the sky."

"I have heard them," Thirg replied. Allegedly a mysterious creature had come down from the sky in a remote area of northern Kroaxia about twelve twelve-brights previously and been devoured by swamp-dwelling saber cutters. Rumors told of similar events in more distant places at about the same time too, but always it was a case of somebody who knew somebody who had actually seen them. "But all through the ages there have been myths of wondrous things. One myth among many will not be made any the less a myth by mere conjecturings of mine that would have it be otherwise."

"If it is a myth," Dornvald said.

"I cannot show that it is," Thirg replied. "And neither can I show conclusively that the fairy beings with which children would inhabit the forests are a myth, for both propositions rest equally on negatives. But the impossibility of proving falsity is no more grounds for asserting the truth of one than of the other. Just as no Lifemaker speaks to you, so no flying beast has made itself visible to me. And neither do I know of witnesses whose testimony forces me to discount all possibility of other explanations for their claims."

Another silence ensued. Then Dornvald said, "I have seen one."

Thirg forced a tone that was neither too credulous nor openly disbelieving. "You saw a creature flying? It actually descended from the sky?"

"So I was assured by one who was there before me," Dornvald replied. "But I did see its remains, and it was the likes of no beast that I have ever seen before in all my travels far and wide across this world. That I can vouch."

Thirg sighed. Always it was the same. He had seen that much himself—a partially dismantled subassembly that his naturalist friend had shown him many twelvebrights before, taken, it was said, from such remains as Dornvald had mentioned. It *had* been unlike anything that Thirg had ever seen from the innards of any familiar kind of animal, with tissues of crude, coarse construction, and components clumsy and ungainly. A strange sample of workmanship for a Lifemaker to have sent down from the sky as proof of His existence, Thirg had commented. And of course, the naturalist hadn't actually seen the descent with his own eyes . . . but the traveler that he had obtained the trophy from had bought it from a hunter who had been present. Thirg had never known what to make of the whole business. He still didn't.

By late-bright, weary and hungry, the party had crossed through the pass and descended into the valley on the far side, which after a long trek through barren, hilly terrain brought them to Xerxeon, the last inhabited place before entering the Wilderness. It was a small farming settlement of crude dwellings fabricated from titanium and steel croppings, centered upon a few rudimentary servicing machines and generators which supported a few score families and their animals. The scrubland around the village had been cleared to make room for a few meager fields of domesticated parts and body-fluid manufacturing facilities which the peasants toiled long hours to keep supplied with materials and components.

Dornvald, whom the villagers evidently knew from previous visits, paid for provisions with a "tax refund," and as dark came over the sky the outlaws commenced taking rest and refurbishment in turns while the others stayed awake to keep watch. After seeing to his steed and Rex at a feed shop nearby, Thirg was almost dropping by the time his turn came to lie down in a robeing-service bay and plug himself into the socket that would deactivate his circuits and send him for a while into blissful oblivion. He awoke refreshed and recharged, with new bearing liners, filters, electrical contacts, and fluids; fresh plating gleamed on his abraded surfaces. With feelings of well-being, Thirg was ready to face the new bright that lay ahead. There would be no rest on the next dark, for apart from infrequent top-ups taken from the wild-grown hydride cells which they would carry with them, the riders would not find food again until they reached the far side of the Wilderness.

Before Thirg was even fully awake, Geynor rushed in from the street. "Good, you're up. We have to get out fast. Come on!"

"What? Are the soldiers here?"

"No time to explain."

Thirg followed Geynor outside and found the whole village in panic. Most of the doors and windows were heavily barred. A few fearful faces peered out here and there; in the central square between the houses, the village Headrobeing and a group of elders were haranguing Dornvald and his outlaws, who were loading up their mounts and obviously preparing to move out in a hurry. On the far side of the square more robeings were down on their knees chanting hymns. Groork stood in front of them, his arms spread wide in supplication, gazing up at the sky. Everything was bathed in a radiance of ghostly violet that seemed to be coming from overhead.

Thirg had taken three paces across the square when he stopped dead, his head tilted back and his body frozen into immobility with disbelief. A smooth, slender, elongated creature, with rigid, tapering limbs and plumes of light streaming from its underside, was hovering motionless in the sky to the east, as if watching the village. There was no way to judge its size or distance with any certainty, but Thirg's immediate impression was that it couldn't be all that far away. He stood, and he gaped.

"The Lifemaker has sent His angel of wrath down upon us!" the village Headrobeing moaned, wringing his hands. "Begone from our midst, Dornvald, Bringer-of-Woes and Dealer-with-the-Accursed. See what retribution awaits even now us who accepted your treacherous bribes."

"Take your followers from this place," another cried. "Truly you are but living dead, risen from the dismantling tombs."

"I shall carry no fear of His wrath within me,
Nor shall I tremble at His coming,
Nor harbor terrors of the beasts of darkness,
For my feet have trod the path of righteousness.
I have not strayed..." Groork's voice recited from across the square.

"Mount up!" One of the outlaws reined to a halt with Thirg's steed held stamping and snorting alongside his own.

Thirg shook himself from his trance and mounted hurriedly. "But what of Groork?" he called to Dornvald, who was turning to join the rest of the band as they grouped in the square.

"He hears only his voices and speaks only to the sky-dragon," Dornvald shouted back. "We must leave."

Then a body of villagers brandishing staffs and blades advanced round the corner ahead, following a huge, grim-faced robeing who was carrying a club of lead-weighted pipe. "You shall not escape, Accursed Ones!" the leader shouted. "The angel calls for a sacrifice in atonement. Let it take you who brought it here, not us!"

"Ride!" Dornvald drew his sword and urged his mount

into a gallop, and the others closed in solidly behind with weapons already unsheathed. Thirg had blurred impressions of bodies reeling back in confusion on both sides as the ground raced by below, of shouting coming from all around him for a moment and then falling away behind . . . and then the road out of the village was opening up ahead with the last houses slipping out of view. The riders remained at full gallop while they passed through the outlying fields and slowed their pace only when they had emerged into the wild scrubland beyond.

When they looked back, they saw that the flying beast had moved from its station and was following them—nearer the ground than before, and off to one side. Then it moved forward rapidly to circle ahead of them, still keeping its distance and directing a cone of pale, violet light at the riders as if to study them from all angles. The column slowed to a cautious pace, and the dragon stayed ahead of them for a while. Finally it moved fully round to come behind them once again, then climbed higher once more and disappeared from sight moving back in the direction of the village. Time passed, and it failed to reappear. Gradually the fear that had gripped Thirg and his companions began to abate.

"What have you to say now about myths of sky-creatures, Seeker-of-Answers?" Dornvald asked Thirg when the latter looked as if he had recovered sufficiently to be capable of speech. "Have you an answer to offer for this?"

"I have none," Thirg replied numbly. He thought back to Groork's recent insistence that voices from the sky warned of the imminence of great events. Had he been mistaken about Groork's voices all along? Thirg said little more as the bright lightened. Slowly the hills flanking the mouth of the last valley flattened out and receded away on either side, and the scene ahead opened out into vast wastes of dunes, scattered boulders, and undulating desert as far as the eye could see.

15

BEHIND A SHALLOW RISE AT THE FOOT OF SOME ROCK outcrops near the fringe of one of Titan's deserts, the surface lander stood in an oasis of light cast by its perimeter arc lamps. Smaller lights flashing and moving on the slopes below and to either side of the rise marked the positions of the landing party's U.S. Special Forces and British marine contingents deploying into concealed positions to cover the approaches.

Inside the lander, Zambendorf and Abaquaan, carrying helmets under their arms and moving slowly in their ungainly extravehicular suits, picked their way forward among the similarly attired figures sitting and standing in the cramped confines of the aft mess cabin, and stopped at the doorway that led into the midships control room. Amid the clutter of crew stations and communications consoles ahead, Charles Giraud, Leaherney's deputy, was talking to an image of Leaherney, who was following the proceedings from the *Orion*, while other screens showed the surroundings outside. One display presented the view from a high-flying drone, and showed as a tiny pattern of slowly moving dots on the computer-generated, false-color landscape the group of approaching Taloid riders, now less than two miles away, that had been selected as first contacts—partly because of their small number, and partly because of the isolated surroundings, which it was felt would minimize possible complications.

"Ah, the psychologists are out in force, I see," Zambendorf remarked, looking down at Massey, Vernon Price, and Malcom Wade, who were sitting nearby.

"At least we've got a good reason," Vernon said. "What the hell are you two doing down here?"

Zambendorf shook his head reproachfully. "Just because you have successfully exposed some rather amateurish frauds, you shouldn't make the mistake of concluding that therefore nothing genuine can exist," he cautioned. "Mustn't rely too much on generalizations from one's own experiences. That's not being scientific, you know."

"A good point," Wade commented. "That's just what I've been saying all along."

"Are the Taloids believed to be telepathic?" somebody else asked curiously.

Zambendorf permitted himself the condescending smile of one unable to say as much as he would have liked to. "Shall we just say that I am here at the personal request of the mission's Chief Scientist?" They could say it if they liked; it wasn't true. Massey turned his head away in exasperation.

Meanwhile Abaquaan was following events in the control cabin through the door ahead of them and talking in a low voice with one of the ship's officers who was standing just inside. Zambendorf moved a pace forward and peered past Abaquaan's shoulder just in time to hear Daniel Leaherney ask from the monitor, "Does it change the situation in your estimation, Charles? If you want to reembark your people down there and wait for a more opportune occasion, you have my approval."

Giraud shook his head. "The armed drones will provide ample reserve firepower if there are any hostilities. Let's get on with it now that we're here. Colonel Wallis agrees. We've decided to leave the arc lights on to give some warning of our presence." Reactions observed previously had confirmed that the Taloids possessed at least some sensitivity to ordinary visible wavelengths.

"What's happening?" Zambendorf whispered.

Abaquaan gestured at the screen showing the terrain across which the Taloids were approaching. "A second group of Taloids is following the first group and catching up fast," he said. "About thirty of them . . . and they've some of those crazy walking carts." The Taloids were known to possess, incongruously, legged vehicles that were drawn by machines running on wheels.

"Is the second group chasing the others or trying to join them?"

Abaquaan shook his head. "Nobody knows, Karl. But the ones in front are taking their time. Either they're not bothered, or they don't know that the other guys are there."

"The lead group of Taloids has stopped moving," an operator announced. On the screen, the pattern of dots had reached the far side of a broad, flat-bottomed depression that lay beyond the rise. "They should be able to see our lights from where they are now."

Giraud studied the display for a moment, and then turned to face the ship's captain, who was standing next to him. "Better get the rest of the surface party outside," he murmured.

The captain flipped a switch and spoke into a microphone. "Attention. Remaining personnel for surface, helmet up and assemble at midships lock. All remaining surface personnel to midships lock."

Five minutes later, Zambendorf and Abaquaan emerged onto the platform outside the lock and stood gazing out at the wall of impenetrable gloom beyond the arc lamps. Ignoring the ladder extending downward on one side, Abaquaan stepped off the platform and allowed his twenty-two pounds of weight to float to the ground six feet below. Zambendorf followed as more figures appeared in the lock hatchway behind, and an instant later his feet made contact with the soil of an alien world. For a moment he and Abaquaan looked at each other through the faceplates of their helmets, but neither spoke. Then they turned and moved forward to join the reception party assembling ahead, fifty yards inside the edge of the circle of light.

16

"IN ALL MY JOURNEYS ACROSS THESE DESERTS, I HAVE seen nothing to compare with it," Dornvald said. "It is as unknown as the dragons that have appeared in the sky. What advice have you to offer, Riddle-Seeker, for no experience of mine can guide us now?"

"Nor any of mine," Thirg replied. "But it would seem possible that the dragons and this latest conundrum are related one to another, for have they not chosen to announce themselves in quick succession? And do we not see again the radiance that comes with heat hotter than the heat that melts ice? We have seen the dragons, and now, methinks, we have found the dragons' lair."

The column had halted among rock and ice boulders on the edge of a low scarp, below which the ground fell for a distance into a wide depression and then climbed again toward a shallow saddle-shaped rise flanked on either side by steeper, broken slopes and crags. The obvious way ahead lay over the rise, but a strange violet radiance, similar to the slender cones thrown by the flying creatures earlier but less sharply defined, lit the skyline above and seemed to come from something just out of sight. The welders and laser cutters in the forest produced the same kind of light at their working points, as did some of the forms ejected by furnaces and other beings that lived at great heat.

"What manner of greeting would dragons reserve for

strangers venturing upon their land?" Dornvald asked. "Do they show their light as a beacon of welcome to weary travelers or as a warning of trespass? Are we therefore to ignore their hospitality with disdain or ignore their warning with contempt, for we know not which course risks giving the lesser offense?"

Thirg stared at the strange glow for a while. "My recollections of Xerxeon are that we feared more for our lives from those of our own kind than from any dragons," he said. "And it seems to me that any dragon with power to command the light that melts steel could have rid itself of us all long before now if its inclinations so directed. But words will not suffice to resolve this. I would propose therefore, with your approval, Wisher-Not-to-Offend-Dragons, that I ride on ahead to conduct the examination which alone will set the matter finally to rest."

"Aha!" Dornvald exclaimed. "So does your compulsion to seek answers drive you irresistibly even now, when dismantling at the hands of enraged dragons might well be the price if your judgment is mistaken?"

"I would know simply which path we are to take," Thirg replied. "Might we not all face dismantling anyway as a consequence of choosing blindly? The risk is none the greater and more likely less, for what dragon of any self-respect would deign prey upon one lone rider when it spurns to molest a whole company as unbecoming of its dignity?"

"Hmm." Dornvald thought the proposition over. "Such is not any duty that you owe, Dignifier-of-Dragons, for was it not I who brought you to this place? Any self-respecting leader of outlaws has his dignity too. I will go."

"You would be more needed here than I, if my judgment should indeed prove mistaken," Thirg pointed out. "For what is of more worth to the robeings behind us—the leader they have followed faithfully, or a dabbler-in-riddles who knows not even the direction that would lead them out of the Meracasine? I say I will go."

"A plague of oxidization on the both of you!" Geynor said as he drew up alongside them. "The one is needed to answer riddles, and the other is needed to lead. I will go."

Before they could argue further, the pounding of hooves sounded from behind. Seconds later Fenyig, who had been riding well back from the main body as lookout, came into view and galloped by the waiting riders to come to a halt at the head of the column. "King's soldiers!" he announced. "Flying the pennant of Horazzorgio—two dozen or more, with chariots."

"How far?" Dornvald snapped.

"A mile or less, and closing rapidly. They must have stayed on the move all through dark."

"How are they armed?"

"Heavily—three fireball-throwers at least."

"The villagers of Xerxeon are determined to have their sacrifice, it seems," Dornvald said. "They must have been told of our direction." He looked quickly once more over the terrain ahead. There would be no escape on the flat, open area stretching away to right and left since the wheeled tractors that pulled the chariots and fireball-throwers would outrun mounted robeings, and there was ample space for the King's soldiery to maneuver their superior force freely. The only chance was to make the rugged, broken country beyond the rise, where the going would be slow for vehicles and where riders venturing ahead could be picked off from ambush. "Our choices have become Horazzorgio on the one hand, or dragons on the other," Dornvald declared. "One demon I have met and know well; the other I know not. On what I know, I would have us cast our lot with the latter."

"Methinks we would be well advised," Geynor agreed.

"Then our dispute is resolved," Dornvald said, looking from Geynor to Thirg. "We all shall go." And louder, to the rear, "Forward to yonder rise, and at speed! He who fears light in the sky has no place behind me, but among the groveling farmers of Xerxeon. If dragons would contest our way then so be it, but let it not be us who show their weapons first. Forward!"

* * *

"All units standing by, ready to fire," a British subaltern's voice reported to Colonel Wallis on the radio. "A.P. missiles locked and tracking."

"Status of remote-controlled gunships?" Wallis inquired crisply.

"Standing by for launch, sir," another voice confirmed.

"Defenses ready," Wallis advised Giraud, who was now outside and standing at the center of the waiting reception party.

A moment of silence dragged by. Then the captain's voice came from inside the ship. "Ship One to Surface One. It doesn't seem to be an attack. In fact I'm not convinced they even know we're here at all. They started off fast just after their tail-end-Charlie arrived up front. It looks more like they're trying to lose that other bunch behind them."

"Surface Two to forward observation post. Do you see evidence of weapons or hostile intent?"

"Negative, sir."

"We'll sit tight and see," Giraud's voice said. "Hold it for now."

"All units, hold your fire," Wallis instructed.

On the screen of his wristset, Zambendorf followed the progress of the Taloids coming up the far side of the rise. It was unbelievable—clothed robots sitting astride four-legged, galloping machines, now only a few hundred yards away.

"Do you see them?" Thirg called as Dornvald glanced back. Thirg was having enough trouble clinging to the madly heaving mount beneath him as it tackled the steepening rise, without daring to turn his own head.

"Just coming out onto the flat," Dornvald shouted back. "At least we're off the open ground. We should gain more distance now."

"There are heat lights shining from places above us on both sides," Geynor called from Dornvald's other side.

"I see them."

"What manner of thing shines thus in the desert?"

"Who knows what guards the lair of dragons?"

Dornvald, Thirg, and Geynor reached the top of the rise together with Rex whirring excitedly a few yards behind, and plunged on over its rounded crest. An instant later they had crashed to a stunned halt, their mounts rearing and bucking. The remaining outlaws stopped in confusion behind as they appeared in ones and twos over the hill.

Before them, towering proudly inside a halo of almost brilliant dragon light, was the King of Dragons, attended by servants lined up before it in humble reverence. It was smooth and elongated, and had tapered limbs—much like the dragon that had appeared over Xerxeon, but far larger. Its eyes shone like fires of violet, but it made no move as it stood, watching silently. Thirg could do nothing but stare, dumbfounded, while Dornvald and Geynor gazed at the Dragon King in wonder. Rex was backing away slowly, and behind them several of the outlaws had dismounted and fallen to their knees.

Then Thirg realized that one of the dragon's servants was beckoning with both arms in slow, deliberate movements that seemed to be trying to convey reassurance. The servants were not robeings as he had first thought, he saw now; they were of roughly similar shape, but constructed not of metal but some soft, bendable casing more like artificial organics from artisans' plantations . . . like children's dolls. What manner, then, of artificial beings were these? Had the Dragon King manufactured them to attend its needs? If so, what awesome, unimaginable powers did it command?

The servant beckoned again. For a few seconds longer, Thirg hesitated. Then he realized the futility of even thinking to disobey; who could hope to defy the wishes of one with such powers? Without quite realizing what he was doing, Thirg urged his mount forward once more at a slow walk and entered the circle of violet radiance. Nothing terrible happened, and after exchanging apprehensive glances, Dornvald and Geynor followed him. The others watched from farther back, and one by one found the courage to move forward. Those on the ground rose slowly. Then Fenyig, who was standing with the rearguard on the top of the rise behind and looking back anxiously called, "Pray to the dragon to protect us, Dornvald. The soldiers are below already, and almost upon us."

No sooner had he shouted his warning when the first missile from a fireball-thrower sailed over the ridge and splattered itself across an ice boulder. The second hit one of the pack steeds squarely, and the animal fell screeching with its midbody engulfed in violet flames. On the rise, Fenyig and his companions scattered amid a hail of projectiles hurled from below, one of them slumping forward with a corrosive dart protruding from his shoulder. More balls fell, and one of them ignited something metallic halfway up one of the overlooking slopes.

"Number two searchlight emplacement hit!" a voice shouted over the radio. "No casualties."

"Near miss on Yellow Sector. We've got equipment burning from splashes of incendiary."

Another ball landed just in front of the assembled reception party, which broke ranks and fell back toward the lander in alarm. "That one almost got the ship!" a voice yelled.

"Colonel Wallis, engage with maximum force in the approach zone," Giraud ordered.

"All forward units, fire for effect! Launch gunships and engage enemy below point three-seven hundred!"

Thirg whirled to look behind as a thundering roar erupted suddenly from below the rise, mixed with a hail of chattering, loud swishing sounds, and deafening concussions. More roars came from overhead. He looked up. Two of the small dragons were climbing; then violet-flaming darts streaked down and out of view, and an instant later more concussions from beyond the rise jarred his ears. He had never in his life experienced anything like this. His senses reeled. He sat frozen, his body and his mind paralyzed by terror.

And then all was quiet. He looked around fearfully. Dornvald and Geynor were sitting petrified where they had been before the thunder. Farther back, Fenyig and the rearguard were motionless, staring back down the rise. They seemed bewildered. Thirg looked at Dornvald. Dornvald shook his head uncomprehendingly, and after a few more seconds called back, "What terrifies you so, Fenyig? What has happened?"

At first Thirg thought Fenyig hadn't heard. Then Fenyig turned his head slowly, raised an arm to point back the way they had come, and answered in an unsteady voice, "The King's soldiers have been destroyed, Dornvald... Every one of the soldiers is destroyed—torn to pieces and smitten by dragon fire... in a moment."

"A storm of lightning bolts!" another, just before Fenyig, choked hoarsely. "We saw it. The whole of the King's army would have fared no better, nor even twelve-twelves of armies." He looked at Thirg. "What league have you entered into, Sorcerer?"

The servants who had retreated to the dragon for protection were advancing again, and the stunned outlaws were slowly returning to life. More servants were appearing from concealment on the slopes above—there were more of them than Thirg had realized. Although still shaken, he was beginning to feel that the worst was over, as if they had passed a kind of test. For he had seen the awesome anger of the dragon, and the dragon had spared them. Perhaps, then, only those foolish enough to provoke its anger had reason to fear it, Thirg thought. He looked at it again. Still it stood watching calmly, as if nothing had happened. Had disposing of a whole company of King's soldiers really been so effortless and insignificant as that?

The other outlaws seemed to be arriving at similar conclusions. Dornvald had dismounted and was cautiously leading his mount toward the central group of servants, and Geynor was following suit a few yards behind. The servants seemed to be encouraging them with arm motions and gestures. Thirg noticed a movement just to one side and turned his head with a start to find a servant standing close below, with another watching from nearby. A feeling of revulsion swept over him as he glimpsed the grotesque features glowing softly behind the window-face of the head that was not a head—a deformed parody of a face, molded into a formless mass that writhed and quivered like the jelly in a craftsman's culture vat. Luminous jelly held together by flexible casing! Had the Dragon King made its servants thus as a punishment? Thirg hoped that his thoughts and feelings didn't show.

Zambendorf gazed up incredulously at the silver-gray colossus staring down at him from its incongruous seat. It had two oval matrixes that suggested compound eyes shaded by complicated delicate, extendable metal vanes, a pair of protruding concave surfaces that were probably soundwave collectors, and more openings and louvers about its lower face, possibly inlet/outlet ducts for coolant gas. It had nothing comparable to a mouth, but the region below its head, which was supported by a neck of multiple, sliding, overlapping joints, was recessed and contained an array of flaps and covers. The robot was wearing a brown tunic of coarse material woven from what appeared to be wire, a heavy belt of black metallic braid, boots of what looked like rubberized canvas, and a voluminous dull red riding cloak made up of thousands of interlocked, rigid platelets. Its hands consisted of three fingers and an opposing thumb, all formed from multisegmented concave claws connected by ball joints at the finger-bases and wrists. A smaller machine, suggesting in every way a ridiculous mechanical dog, stayed well back, keeping the steed between itself and the humans.

What kind of brain the creature contained, Zambendorf didn't know, but he felt it had to be something beyond any technology even remotely imaginable on Earth. And yet, paradoxically, the culture of the Taloids showed every appearance of being backward by Earth standards—medieval, in fact. And everything that Zambendorf saw now confirmed that conclusion. So what would a medieval mind have made of the army's recent performance? He examined the robot's face for a hint of bemusement or terror, but saw nothing he could interpret. The face seemed incapable of expression.

"I still don't believe this, Karl," Abaquaan's voice whispered in his helmet, for once sounding genuinely stupefied. "What kind of machines are they? Where could they have come from?"

Still awestruck, Zambendorf moved a pace forward. "It seems to want to say something," he murmured distantly without taking his eyes off the robot. "But it makes no move. Does it fear us, Otto?"

"Wouldn't you, after what just happened to that other bunch?" Abaquaan said, beginning to sound more normal.

To one side, in an attempt to convey reassurance, Charles Giraud and Konrad Seltzman, a linguist, were gesticulating at two robots who had dismounted, but without much apparent success. Maybe the robots hadn't realized that they were safe from their pursuers—some of them kept looking back, as if they still thought they were likely to be attacked. Zambendorf thought he could do something about that. He operated the channel selector on his wristset to display the view from over the rise being picked up by an image-intensifying camera in the army's forward observation post, and raised his arm so that the robot could see the screen. The robot looked at his arm for a second or two, moved its head to glance at his face, and then studied his arm again. Zambendorf pointed to the wristset with his other hand.

Why did the servant wear a small vegetable on his arm, and why was he showing it? Thirg wondered. Perhaps it was an indication of rank or status. No, that wasn't it; the servant wanted him to look at it. He looked. Shapes were visible in the square of violet light, faint and difficult to distinguish in the glare. Thirg adjusted his vision to the nearest he could manage to dragon light and stared for awhile before he realized what he was seeing. It was a view looking out over the open ground they had crossed back beyond the rise. Piles of debris were scattered here and there and lots of buckled and twisted machine parts spread over a wide area, with violet glows and obscuring patches of smoke hanging above . . . And then Thirg gasped as he realized what it meant. Now he understood what devastating powers Fenyig had been trying to describe. In those few brief seconds . . . and there was nothing left. Then it came to Thirg slowly that the servant was trying to show how the dragon had helped them.

But what form of magic vegetable was this, that could see through a hillside? Thirg looked at the servant, and then turned his head several times to look back at the rise, just to be sure he was not mistaken.

Zambendorf felt a surge of elation. Something that they both recognized as having meaning had passed between him and the robot. "It understands!" he said excitedly. "Rudimentary, but it's communication! It's a beginning, Otto!"

"Are you sure?"

"I showed it the scene from over the hill. It understood. It's trying to ask me to confirm that it's seeing what it thinks it's seeing."

Abaquaan motioned for the robot to climb down from its mount, and after a few seconds of hesitation it complied. Then it gestured at Zambendorf's wristset some more, and held up a hand and began pointing at it repeatedly first from the front and then from the back, and in between pointing back at the rise. "It can't make it out," Abaquaan said. "It can't figure how the picture could be coming through solid ground from behind the hill."

The robot was mystified and curious. Suddenly much about it seemed less strange. Zambendorf could feel himself warming toward it already. "I'm sorry, but how could I even begin to explain the technology, my friend?" he said. "For now, I'm afraid, you'll just have to accept it as magic."

"Try getting the idea of a camera across," Abaquaan suggested. "At least it would say we're not actually looking through the hill from here."

"Mmm . . . maybe." Zambendorf switched the wristset to another channel, this time showing a view of the lander and its immediate surroundings from the drone hovering above the landing site.

It took Thirg a while to comprehend that he was looking down on the Dragon King now. Then it came to him with a jolt that the dots to one side of the dragon were the dragon-servants and robeings around him; in fact one of them was himself! He looked at the servant and pointed down at the ground, then up at the sky. The servant confirmed by mimicking him. Thirg tilted his head back to peer upward, and after searching for a few seconds made out a pinpoint of violet light hanging high overhead. Could the servant's magic vegetable see through the eyes of the flying dragons? But that meant that a mere servant who possessed such a vegetable could send his eyes anywhere in the world and see all that happened without moving from one place. If the dragon bestowed such powers upon its servants, what unimaginable abilities did it possess itself?

Zambendorf could sense the robot's awe as it finally made out what the screen was showing. He switched from the drone's telescopic channel to a lower resolution, wide-angle view. The screen now displayed a much broader area of terrain, with the lander barely discernible as a speck in the center. After more pointing and gesticulating, the robot seemed to get the idea. Zambendorf switched to a high-altitude reconnaissance flyer circling just below the aerosol layer, whose cameras covered several hundred miles of the surrounding desert and a large tract of the mountainous region beyond its edge. Then the robot started making excited gestures, pointing upward again with its arm extended as far as it would stretch. "Higher! Higher!" It was important. The robot seemed to be going frantic.

Zambendorf frowned and turned his head inside his helmet to look at Abaquaan. Abaquaan returned a puzzled look and shrugged. Zambendorf stared at the robot, tilted himself back ponderously to follow its pointing finger upward for a few seconds, and then looked at its face again. Then, suddenly, he understood. "Of course!" he exclaimed, and changed bands to connect the wristset through to an image being picked up from orbit by the *Orion* and sent down in the trunk beam to the surface lander via a relay satellite.

Giraud and the others had noticed what was going on and were gathering round to watch curiously. "What's happening with this guy?" one of the group asked.

"What lies beyond the clouds has always been a mystery to its race," Zambendorf replied. "It's asking me if that is where we come from, and whether we can tell it what's out there and what kind of world it lives on. They've never even seen the sky, don't forget, let alone been able to observe the motions of stars and planets."

"You mean you could get all that from just a few gestures?" Konrad Seltzman sounded incredulous.

"Of course not," Zambendorf replied airily. "I have no need of such crude methods."

But beside them, Thirg had almost forgotten for the moment that the dragon-servants existed as he stood staring without moving. For he was seeing his world for the first time as it looked from beyond the sky.

It was a sphere.

And behind it, scattered across distances he had no way of estimating, were more shining worlds than he knew even how to count.

17

DAVE CROOKES PRESSED A KEY ON A CONSOLE IN THE *Orion's* Digital Systems and Image Processing Laboratory, and sat back to watch as the sequence began replaying again on the screen in front of him. It showed one of the Taloids in the view recorded twenty-four hours previously watching a Terran figure make a series of gestures, and then turning its head to look directly at another Taloid standing a few feet behind. A moment later the second Taloid's head jerked round to look quickly at the first Taloid and then at the Terran.

"There!" Leon Keyhoe, one of the mission's signals specialists, said from where he was standing behind Crookes' chair. Crookes touched another key to freeze the image. Keyhoe looked over his shoulder at two other engineers seated at instrumentation panels to one side. "The one in the brown helmet has to be saying something at that point right there. Check the scan one more time."

"Still no change," one of the engineers replied, flipping a series of switches and taking in the data displays in front of him. "There's nothing from VLF and LF, right through to EHF in the millimeter band . . . No correlation on Fourier."

"Positive correlation reconfirmed on acoustic," the other engineer reported. "Short duration ultrasonic pulse bursts, averaging around, ah . . . one hundred ten thousand per second, duration twenty to forty-eight microseconds. Repetition frequency is variable and consistent with modulation at up to thirty-seven kilocycles. Sample profile being analyzed on screen three."

Keyhoe sighed and shook his head. "Well, it seems to be definite," he agreed. "The Taloids communicate via exchanges of high-frequency sound pulses. There's no indication of any use of radio at all. It's surprising—I was certain that those transmission centers down on the surface would turn out to be long-range relay stations or something like that." Readings obtained from the *Orion* had confirmed the *Dauphin* orbiter's findings that several points on the surface of Titan emitted radio signals intermittently and irregularly. Probes sent below the aerosol layer had revealed the sources to lie near some of the heavily built-up centers from which the surrounding industrialization and mechanization appeared to have spread. The patterns of signal activity had correlated with nothing observed on the surface so far.

Joe Fellburg, who was wedged on a stool between Dave Crookes' console and a bulkhead member, rubbed his chin thoughtfully for a second or two. "Do you buy this idea that Anna Voolink came up with about alien factories?" he asked, looking up at Keyhoe.

"Well, we've got to agree it's a possibility, Joe," Keyhoe said. "Why?"

Anna Voolink was a Dutch NASO scientist who had been involved several years before in a study of a proposal to set up a self-replicating manufacturing facility on Mercury for supplying Earth with materials and industrial products. She had speculated that Titan's machine biosphere might have originated from a similar scheme set up by an alien civilization, possibly millions of years previously, which had somehow mutated and started to evolve. What had caused the sytem to mutate, why the aliens should have chosen Titan, and what had happened to them since were questions that nobody had ventured to answer even tentatively.

Fellburg leaned forward to prop an elbow against the side of the console and gestured vaguely at the screens.

"It occurred to me that if everything down there did evolve from some superadvanced version of what NASO was talking about setting up on Mercury, then maybe radio could have been the primary method of communication in the early days. But if the aliens were any kind of engineers at all, you'd expect them to have provided some kind of backup, right?" He looked from Keyhoe to Crookes. Crookes pinched his nose, thought for a second, and nodded.

"Makes sense, I guess," Keyhoe agreed.

Fellburg spread his hands. "So couldn't the answer be that the primary system went out of use—maybe because of a mutation error or something like that—and the secondary became the standard? What we're picking up from those centers could be just a remnant of something that doesn't serve any purpose any more—coming from a few places where it hasn't quite died out yet."

"Mmm . . . it's an interesting thought," Keyhoe said.

"I wonder if the Taloids would still be capable of receiving anything," Crookes murmured after thinking the suggestion over for a second or two.

"I suppose that would depend on where their blueprint information comes from . . . their 'genetics,'" Keyhoe said.

Fellburg rubbed his chin again. "Well, if it's not functionally relevant anymore, and if their evolution is driven selectively the same as ours is, I guess there wouldn't be any strong selection working either one way or the other. So probably some of them can receive radio and some of them can't. Some sensitive ones might still be produced."

Dave Crookes smiled to himself. "If that's true, I wonder what all our radio traffic over the last few weeks might have been doing to them," he said.

"What's your background, Joe?" Crookes inquired casually an hour later in the transit capsule that he and Fellburg were sharing on their way back to Globe II.

"How d'you mean?" Fellburg asked.

"Your technical background . . . I mean, it's pretty obvious you know something about electronics and pulse techniques."

"Why?"

"Oh . . . just curious, I guess."

"Well, Michigan Tech—master's. Six years in industry, mainly computer physics with IBM. Ten years army, finishing up as a technical specialist with intelligence. Good enough?"

The capsule passed a window section of the tube, giving a momentary view of the outside of the *Orion* and of Titan hanging in the background, partly obscuring the magnificent spectacle of Saturn and its rings. Crookes eyed Fellburg uncertainly for a few seconds. "Can I ask you something personal?" he said at last.

"Sure. If I think it's none of your goddam business, I'll say so, okay?"

Crookes hesitated, then said, "Why are you mixed up with this Zambendorf thing?"

"Why not?"

Crookes frowned uncomfortably. Obviously he'd come about as close to being direct as he was prepared to. "Well, it's . . . I mean, isn't it a kind of a wasteful way to use that kind of talent?"

"Is it? Do you know what I'd be getting paid now if I'd gone back into industry after I quit the army?"

"Is that all that matters?" Crookes asked.

Fellburg thrust out his chin. "No, but it's a good measure of how society values its resources. I've already had enough Brownie badges to stitch on my shirt instead of anything that's worth something."

Crookes shook his head. "But when the product is worthless . . ."

"The market decides what a product is worth—through demand, which fixes the price," Fellburg said. "If plastic imitations are selling high today because people are too dumb to tell the difference, who's doing the wasting—me, who accepts the going rate, or the guy who's out on the street in front of his store, giving the real thing away?"

* * *

When Fellburg arrived back at the team's day cabin, Thelma and Drew West were as he had left them, hunched in front of the display console, following developments down on the surface; Clarissa Eidstadt was sitting at a corner table, editing a wad of scripts. "What've you been up to?" Thelma asked as he came in.

"Over in the electronics section with Daves Crookes and a few of the guys, playing back the Taloid shots," Fellburg replied. "Things are getting interesting. It doesn't look as if they use radio to talk after all. They use high-frequency sound pulses. The engineers have started computer-processing the patterns already. Oh, and did you know they're not so poker-faced after all?"

"The engineers?" West said, without looking away from the screen.

"The Taloids, turkey."

"How come?"

"They have facial expressions—surface heat patterns that change like crazy all the time they're talking. Crookes' people have been taping a whole library of them in IR."

"Say, how about that," Thelma said.

"And how long will it be before anyone manages to decode anything from pulse-code patterns collected in the databank?" West asked. He waved an arm at the screen. "Karl and Otto are doing a much better job their own way. They've practically swapped life stories with the Taloids already." Fellburg followed his gaze toward the screen.

Down on the surface a second lander had appeared in the pool of light alongside the first, and the surrounding area was dotted with the lights of ground vehicles and EV-suited figures exploring and poking around in the general vicinity. The first lander's cargo bay had been depressurized and left unheated with its loading doors open to Titan's atmosphere to serve as a shelter for the Taloids. Zambendorf, having snatched a few hours rest inside the ship a short while previously, was now back outside and talking to the Taloids again in his self-appointed role as

Earth's ambassador—which the Taloids seemed to have endorsed by responding to him more readily and freely than to anybody else. Scrawled in white on the hull of the surface lander in the background, and extending back for yard after yard in what looked like a mess of graffiti toward the ship's stern, was a jumble of shapes and symbols, arrows and lines, and dozens of whimsical Taloids interspersed with bulbous, domeheaded representations of spacesuited Terrans. The primary communications medium used in the historic moment of first contact between civilizations from two different worlds had turned out to be chalk and blackboard, and the ship had offered the handiest writing surface available.

"I got Herman Thoring to okay a news flash to Earth to the effect that Karl initiated communications with the aliens," Clarissa said without looking up.

Fellburg laughed and moved closer to take in the view on the screen. "So, what's the latest down there?" he asked.

West turned a knob to lower the voice of the NASO officer who was listening in on the local surface frequencies and keeping up a commentary from inside the lander. "See the Taloid who's waving at Karl now—the one in the red cloak—that's Galileo. He's curious about nearly everything. The one with him is Sir Lancelot. He seems to be the head guy of the bunch."

"Okay," Fellburg said.

"The Taloids have some hand-drawn maps that our people managed to match up with reconnaissance pictures—so now we know where the Taloids are heading," West said. "It's a pretty big city in the mechanized area on the other side of the desert. It looks as if they're on their way to the palace or whatever of the king who runs that whole area. It seems that Lancelot and the others work for the king, but we're not sure yet exactly how Galileo fits in."

"You don't get three guesses," Thelma said to Fellburg.

"Huh?"

"Karl's called the king Arthur."

Fellburg groaned.

"What else did you expect?" West asked. "Anyhow, the bunch that the army wiped out was from some country over the mountains that's at war with Arthur for some reason, or something like that. But if these Taloids we've ended up talking to are Arthur's knights or whatever, then maybe we've gotten ourselves an introduction."

"So what are our people aiming at—a landing somewhere near that city you mentioned if Arthur agrees to it?" Fellburg asked.

West nodded. "You've got it."

"How long would we need to wait before Lancelot and his guys get there? Do we know that?"

"Nobody's figured out how they reckon time yet." West nodded toward the screen. "But if Karl gets his way, it won't matter too much anyway. He's trying to sell the Taloids on the idea of letting us airlift them the rest of the way. And you know something, Joe, I've got a feeling they just might buy the idea."

18

A LOW ROAR SOUNDED DISTANTLY FROM BEHIND JUST as the riders reached the crest of the saddle at the valley head, beyond which the land dropped again toward the river that marked the Carthogian border. They stopped and looked back to watch as the sky-dragon that had carried them high over the world rose, slowly at first, with violet heat-wind streaming from its underside, and then turned its head upward as it gained speed and soared higher to shrink rapidly to a pinpoint and eventually vanish. Dornvald had needed all of his powers of argument to talk the rest of the outlaws into allowing themselves to be flown the remaining distance to Carthogia in one of the Skybeings' dragons. Accepting a roof as shelter out in the desert was one thing, but being enclosed on all sides as if in a trap was another. And after watching the Skybeings entering and emerging from their dragon furnaces unscathed, how could one be sure they appreciated the limits that the mere steel and titanium casings of robeings could withstand?

"Those are strange dragon-tamers indeed, who reduce the King's soldiers to scrap in a trice, and then request Kleippur's pleasure," Geynor said as the riders resumed moving. "If they wish to meet with Kleippur, why do they not simply fly to the city of Menassim and command him forth? It seems to me they hold a considerable advantage in persuasiveness, which would assure a rapid reversal of any inclination he might choose toward recalcitrance."

"It appears to be their desire to give opportunity for the citizens of Menassim to be forewarned," Dornvald replied.

Geynor shook his head in amazement. "From such unassailable strength they speak, yet they would invite our agreement? Is this not true nobility of spirit? Horazzorgio could have spared himself his not inconsiderable inconvenience by attending more to his manners and yielding less to his impetuousness, it seems."

"And yet, who knows what subtleties and unsuspected protocols might constitute the chivalry code of Skybeings?" Dornvald asked. "Did their request in fact confer the freedom of answer that might be supposed, or was it no more than a command couched in such form merely through rules of foreign custom which we know not?"

Geynor pondered the question for a while, and eventually answered, "If the latter, then our refusal might have been construed as no less ill-mannered than the assault by the King's soldiers. As penalty for such error of judgment, we could have found ourselves strewn across the desert in like fashion."

"Aha!" Dornvald exclaimed. "Now, at last, I think you see my reasoning, for your words echo my own conclusion."

"Let us hope that Kleippur is compelled by the same logic," Geynor said.

"You need have no fear," Dornvald assured him.

Beside them, Thirg was unusually quiet. It was significant, he thought, that the outlaws were referring to the mysterious domeheaded visitors as Skybeings now, which seemed to indicate that they, like Thirg, no longer thought of them as servants. The Domeheads didn't act like servants. They seemed to come and go, and act freely. The two dragons, by contrast, had just sat docilely throughout the negotiations in the desert, and after a while had given the impression of serving no other function than of being bearers of the Domeheads and the strange creatures that carried them around like living chariots and attended their every need. Presumably, therefore, flying creatures existed in the world beyond the sky that the Domeheads were from, and the Domeheads had learned to tame them just as robeings had learned to tame steeds, power generators, load-lifters, and foodmaking machines. But what form of being was it that was not a machine yet was attended by machines, and at whose bidding magic creatures saw through mountains, reported distant events, and destroyed without hesitation any who aroused their masters' displeasure? Thirg brooded over the question and said little as the band descended into the valleyhead beyond the saddle and crossed the slopes below to pick up a track leading in the direction of the river.

Lower down, the slopes leveled out into flat banks covered by pipe-fronded chemical processing towers, storage tanks, and picturesque groves of transmission lines and distribution transformers, beyond which the track joined a wider road that crossed a stretch of open ground to a bridge. The party had just emerged onto the road when a group of horsemen wearing the uniforms of Carthogian soldiers appeared ahead, approaching at full gallop from the bridge. Thirg braced himself for the brutalized fanatics that Kroaxian teachings had led him to expect; then he saw that Dornvald had eased his mount to a halt and was sitting relaxed and at ease with a broad grin on his face while the column drew up behind. "Major Vergallet, unless I'm much mistaken," Dornvald murmured to Geynor, who was shading his imagers next to him.

"It is," Geynor confirmed. He glanced at Thirg and explained, "From the Carthogian border fort across the bridge."

Thirg nodded and turned his head back to look. The Carthogians were smartly attired, alert, and well disciplined, and their leader was at that moment smiling in a way that was anything but brutally fanatical. He drew up before Dornvald and saluted crisply. "It's good to see you back again, sir. I trust your mission was successful." Thirg blinked his imager shades, jerked his head round toward Geynor for a moment, and then stared back at Dornvald. *Sir?*

"Very much so, thank you, Major," Dornvald replied. He turned and indicated Thirg with a gesture. "This is Thirg, an inquirer, who has wearied of Kroaxia's stifling ways and comes to enjoy fresher air among our thinkers and artificers in Carthogia. Thirg, meet Major Vergallet."

"We are honored to have the general's companion as our guest," Vergallet said.

General? Thirg blinked again and shook his head. "The honor is surely mine to be admitted into such league," he replied lamely as the column began to move again and the soldiers formed up on both sides.

Dornvald laughed at Thirg's bemusement. "You will find Kleippur's officers in the most unexpected places and the strangest garbs," he said. "A small nation such as ours has to live by its wits and its ability to know more about its enemies than they know about each other."

"And more by the skills and knowledge of its armorers than by the size of its army," Geynor added as he saw Thirg looking curiously at one of the strange elongated steel tubular devices which the Carthogian soldiers were carrying slung across their backs. "And that of course, Question-Answerer, is one of the reasons why you are here."

The party rested and refreshed themselves at the border fort, and by the end of even that brief stay Thirg had already dismissed most of what he had heard about the Carthogians as ignorant superstition at best, and at worst as a campaign of misinformation and lies waged deliberately by the more orthodox ruling elites of other nations to protect themselves from the threat that Kleippur's social experiment represented. "The servility and obedience that the Kroaxian priests teach as a duty heretical even to question serve the nobles and princes in ways that are clear enough," Dornvald remarked as he and Thirg talked over their meal. "But why the whims and fancies of mere mortals should be of such concern to an all-powerful Lifemaker is far more difficult to conceive. And does it not seem strange that eternal salvation for the many, in a hereafter which they are asked to accept on mere assurances, should be attainable in no other way than by their enduring hardships gratefully and laboring their lives in wretchedness for the further enrichment of a pious few who exhibit a suspiciously unholy interest in the quality of their own herenow?" Neither Dornvald nor his companions mentioned the Skybeings, and Thirg followed their example.

When the party left to continue its journey, the garrison commander assigned a detachment of troops to escort it to the city of Menassim, apparently because the Waskorians had been causing trouble again in an area that the road passed through. The Waskorians, Dornvald explained to Thirg, were an alliance of extremist sects who denounced as sinful and decadent the liberties that had come with Kleippur's rule and were committed to bringing down the regime in order to return the land to its old ways. The rulers of Kroaxia and Serethgin had been quick to exploit the resentments of the Waskorians, and supplied them with weapons and fomented uprisings. The freedom to earn their salvation in their own way if they thought they needed to be saved from something wasn't sufficient for the sects, it seemed; everyone else, willingly or otherwise, had to be saved their way too.

The remainder of the journey passed without incident, however, possibly because of the escorts. Slowly the rugged border country fell behind and was replaced by hills of thin pipeline, power cable, and latticework scrub, giving way to open slopes of bare ice higher up. After leaving the hills, the riders passed through many miles of dense forest, and the first edge of dark was showing low in the sky before signs of robeing habitation began increasing noticeably. At first isolated homes and then villages appeared; at the same time the landscape took on a tidier appearance with lubricant-fractionation columns standing in well-kept rows, neatly cultivated nut, bolt, and bearing orchards, and rich fields of electrolytic precipitation baths.

Dornvald advised Thirg that they were approaching the outskirts of Menassim.

It no longer came as any surprise to Thirg to see that the reactions of the populace showed no signs of the fear and hatred manifested by downtrodden slaves encountering their oppressors; on the contrary, the soldiers were greeted with smiles and friendly waves, and children in the villages ran to the roadside to watch them pass. The adults seemed healthy and well plated; they were neatly and adequately dressed; and their houses were trim and in good repair. It was a strange kind of "living in perpetual terror" that produced such results, he thought to himself.

The city too, though bustling and crowded, was clean and seemed prosperous: The shops and stalls of the merchants were amply stocked, and the wares were of good quality; the streets were paved and cleared of rubbish; and the taverns and eating houses were noisy and busy. Other things that Thirg, who had tended to avoid cities as much as possible in Kroaxia, would have considered inseparable from the urban scene were conspicuous by their absence. There were no beggars or derelicts to be seen pleading or picking a living from the gutters, and neither did priests or nobles in tall headgear ride haughtily in six-legged carriages behind burly servants wielding bludgeons to clear the way. There were no burned or partly dissolved corpses on public display as a warning to others against blasphemy and heresy; no lesser offenders being exhibited and tormented by mobs in the marketplace; no penitents in emery cloth and carbon black confessing their sins to the world from street corners; no ascetic monks shackled to pillars for the length of a bright—no signs at all, in fact, of the holy and the devout dreaming up what had always struck Thirg as ever more absurd ways to degrade and debase themselves in order to prove themselves worthy creations of an all-wise and all-benevolent Lifemaker whose judgment and disposition were supposed to be capable of being influenced by such antics.

Nearer the center of the city the buildings became larger and taller, with organically grown structures giving way to fabrications of welded blocks of cut ice. Building with ice was not unknown in Kroaxia, but the scale and ingenuity of the Carthogian architecture made everything that Thirg had seen previously appear crude by comparison. Such advanced art was made possible, he learned, by the discovery of new methods for actually synthesizing artificial lifting and cutting devices from metals and other materials, which could mimic many of the functions of natural, living machines. Such discoveries also accounted for the extraordinary proficiency of the Carthogian army. The strange tubes that the soldiers carried on their backs, for example, were actually weapons that used explosive gases to hurl a projectile capable of shattering a slab of ice a finger's-breadth thick at over a hundred paces.

Thirg was astounded. To exercise his intellect he had often speculated on the possibility of creating artificial machines, but he had never expected to see anything actually come of it. He remembered a friend who long ago had entertained preposterous notions of creating a device to harness vaporized methane for turning wheels. The friend had vanished abruptly after escaping arrest on sorcery and heresy charges issued by the High Council of Pergassos, and Thirg had almost forgotten their interminable arguments. On impulse he asked the Carthogians if they knew of his friend's whereabouts. The friend was alive and well, he was told, and in fact lived not far away on the outskirts of Menassim. He was trying to improve a device he had constructed which used vaporized methane to turn wheels.

The news of Dornvald's arrival had gone ahead, and a messenger met the party to advise that Kleippur would receive them at his official residence, which turned out to be an elegant but not over-ostentatious ice-block building inside a walled courtyard, situated not far from the former royal palace, which now served as government offices. On arrival the riders were conducted to guests' quarters and invited to bathe and change into clean clothes, after which, refreshed and considerably more presentable, Thirg was taken to the warm, brightly furnished and cheerfully decorated Council Chamber on the ground floor, overlooking the courtyard across a wide terrace. Inside, Kleippur, flanked by two aides, was sitting at the far end of the large table that took up most of the room; Dornvald, Geynor, and Fenyig were also present, now wearing the uniforms of officers of the Carthogian army, and another figure was sitting with its back to the door. By the wall on one side of the room, one of Lofbayel's maps was fastened to an easel, and more were stacked on the table in front of it.

Then Lofbayel himself turned in his seat, grinned delightedly at the amazement on Thirg's face, and stood up to pump his hand vigorously. "Welcome to Carthogia, Thirg! I'm pleased to see you here safely. Have no doubts—you will find your true home here. I guarantee it."

"You h-here?" Thirg stammered. "What of Kersenia and the family? Are they—"

"All here at Menassim, and well. Indeed, we would have you as our guest again if it pleases you."

"But how? I thought you were watched constantly."

"Another escapade of Dornvald's, of which you will no doubt hear in good time. But come forward and meet Kleippur, and let us obstruct the more important business no longer."

Kleippur, who was younger than Thirg had imagined, and wore a tunic of gleaming plate gold with a short cloak of royal blue ceramic links, began by welcoming Thirg to Carthogia a second time. It had been a somewhat irregular way of extending an invitation, he said, but he hoped Thirg would understand the occasional necessity for such measures. Though not of exceptionally tall or heavy build, Kleippur carried himself with an unhurried dignity that Thirg found impressive, and commanded an authority that stemmed more from an instinctive respect displayed by his followers than from any overt exhibition of rank or assertion of status. He spoke with a soldier's directness and singleness of purpose, yet with an air of detachment and a disinclination to passion that marked him as a thinker.

He introduced his two colleagues as Lyokanor, a senior officer from a part of the Carthogian army that Kleippur described as "Intelligence," and Pellimiades, a director of military constructions and inventions.

Thirg said he was glad to be in Carthogia; there was no need for apologies. He had been treated well and courteously despite the difficult circumstances, and on top of that had enjoyed stimulating and thought-provoking company. "It had become a mystery to me even before the high pass above Xerxeon," he said in conclusion. "For what kind of outlaw was this who rode my philosophical challenges as skillfully as he did his steed?"

Dornvald laughed. "I'm surprised that you could have been so easily deceived. For most of the time it was all I could do to cling with my philosophical fingers to avoid falling off."

The preliminaries over with, Kleippur turned and gestured toward the maps. "I don't have to explain how valuable this kind of information is to us," he said. "Lofbayel has told me that you too believe the world to be a sphere, Thirg—a strange notion, and one which I admit causes me more perplexity than comfort... but nevertheless I will concede the possibility and grant that you have considered the evidence at greater length than I. So can this claim be tested? If so, how? If it is within my power to furnish the prerequisites, it shall be done, for I would sooner know the world as it is than place misguided trust in false appearances."

The utterance was so unlike anything that Thirg was used to hearing from those in authority that for a second or two he just stared in disbelief. Then he recovered quickly and remarked, "It would appear that heretics have little to walk in fear of in this land."

"Facts cannot be changed by convictions," Kleippur answered. "He who is willing to change his convictions to suit new facts cannot be a heretic, while he who persists in holding convictions that deny the facts is not a heretic but a fool—as would I be for fearing him. Therefore the term has no meaning to me."

"So is this the new faith of the nation that you would build?" Thirg asked.

"A philosophy, not a faith," Kleippur replied. "Since it acknowledges the existence of nothing unknowable to reason, it has no place for belief without reason. I could not build such a nation, but I would help it build itself."

"This is the land that Kroaxia has pledged to free from its chains and fetters?" Thirg said, sounding incredulous and allowing his eyes to come to rest finally on Lofbayel.

"Now you see which has the greater need to be freed," Lofbayel said.

Thirg looked mildly uneasy. "So does Carthogia now pledge itself to free Kroaxia?" he asked.

"The chains that bind the Kroaxians are in their minds," Kleippur replied, shaking his head. "Can a robeing be freed who asks it not, for is it not a self-contradiction to speak of imposing freedom? The Kroaxians must come to see truth as you have—each by his own way and in his own time. Only then can a mind be free and not merely have cast off one set of chains for another."

"A noble thought," Thirg agreed dubiously. "But let us not forget that my eyes were opened only after I was brought to this land forcibly."

"Not so," Dornvald said. "We merely brought your eyes to where they could behold the truth. You opened them yourself, a long time ago."

Thirg thought for a moment longer, and at last nodded, satisfied. "Then the building of your nation shall have the help of both of us," he told Kleippur. Kleippur nodded and seemed unsurprised. In that brief moment Thirg felt a touch of the compulsion that Kleippur was able to radiate as a leader. His simple and unassuming acceptance of Thirg's declaration had done more to cement a bond of mutual respect and trust than any kind of elaborate speechmaking ever could.

"And so to business," Kleippur said briskly. He looked at Dornvald. "Well, what tidings do you bring from Kroaxia? The Serethginians are reequipping and recruiting mercenaries as far afield as Corbellio in preparation for a new campaign against us, I am advised, but jealousies war within their camp which I have designs to turn to our advantage. What is new from beyond the Meracasine?"

A short silence fell. Dornvald's two lieutenants glanced at each other ominously. Eventually Dornvald said, "Serious though that matter may be, Kleippur, events have come to pass which render it insignificant. We do indeed bring tidings—strange tidings—not from beyond the Meracasine, but from within it."

Kleippur frowned from Lyokanor to Pellimiades, and then looked back at Dornvald. "Explain yourself, Dornvald," he said. "What new events?"

Dornvald nodded at Fenyig, who reached down and produced a flat package of what looked at first like more charts, and put it down on the table. When he removed the wrappings, however, the contents were seen to be not hand-produced drawings, but thick, glossy sheets carrying pictorial representations that contained incredible amounts of detail. Fenyig selected several sheets from the set and passed them to Kleippur, who leaned forward to pore over them while his aides peered down from beside him with equally mystified expressions on their faces. The pictures seemed to be of patterns of shapes distributed in rows and groups about an irregular network of lines. After watching in silence for a while, Dornvald stretched out an arm and traced a finger lightly along one of the lines on the sheet that Kleippur was holding. "Do you not recognize the Avenue of Emperors in our own city of Menassim?" he inquired casually. "And here... is that not your own residence, in which we are at this very moment gathered?"

Lyokanor gasped aloud suddenly. "It is Menassim! See, here is the course of the river, and the bridges. And there the palace... with the Courts of Justice behind. Every street and house is here!"

"What manner of artist drew this?" Pellimiades asked

in an awed voice. He looked across at Thirg. "Is this an example of the mapmaker's trade that I have not come across before?"

"Not of any art or trade of mine," Thirg said. "Indeed I have never set eyes on Menassim before this bright."

Kleippur looked up slowly. "Where did these come from?"

Dornvald's expression became serious. "Has there been other news of late, Kleippur?" he asked. "Reports of strange happenings in the sky, perhaps?"

Kleippur returned a strange, puzzled look. "Yes..."

"Reports of flying creatures descending, as was supposed to have happened twelve twelve-brights ago?"

"Yes," Kleippur said again, and frowned. "How do you know about them? Have you seen one too? What do they have to do with..." His voice trailed away as the connection suddenly became clear. He looked down at the picture of Menassim again, then disbelievingly back up at Dornvald.

Dornvald nodded gravely. He drew another picture from the stack but kept it facedown on the table. "The creatures exist, Kleippur. We encountered them in the Wilderness of the Meracasine. They are from another world that lies beyond the sky. They carry Skybeings whom they serve, that are stranger still—of the form of robeings, but not robeings... nor even machines. The Skybeings have mastered arts unknown to us by which they are able to preserve images and likenesses." Dornvald gestured at the picture in Kleippur's hand. "That is not an artist's or a mapmaker's creation. It is a preservation of a likeness of the city as was actually seen through the eyes of a creature that crossed the sky high above Carthogia. And the likenesses can be viewed in an instant from afar, even though the eyes that see them might be flying over distant lands, or even beyond the oceans."

Kleippur was staring at Dornvald dazedly. He shook his head as if to clear it and raised a hand to massage the shading vanes above his eyes. "Other worlds?... Creatures that serve beings who are not machines?... What talk is this? If it were not you telling me this, Dornvald, one of my most trusted officers..."

"It is as Dornvald says," Thirg confirmed. "I too was present. We flew in one of the creatures—all of us—to the hills that lie east of Carthogia's border."

"It's true," Fenyig said. Geynor nodded but remained silent. Still staring disbelievingly, Kleippur brought his gaze back to Dornvald.

Dornvald flipped over the picture that he had been keeping as final proof. Kleippur and his two aides stared down at it speechlessly. It showed Dornvald, Thirg, Geynor, and several other robeings standing with a group of ungainly, tubby-looking, domeheaded figures in front of what looked like a huge, smooth-skinned beast of some kind with stiff, tapered limbs. Fenyig passed more pictures. One showed Thirg and a Domehead with their arms draped jovially around each other's shoulders and the Domehead making a curious gesture in the air with an extended thumb; another showed a Domehead perched precariously on Thirg's steed, and Rex watching suspiciously in the background.

"We were being pursued by Kroaxian Royal Guards," Dornvald said. "The Skybeings destroyed them. They talked to us through signs and brought us here. They are friends, and wish to come here to Menassim to meet its ruler. That is the message that they asked us to convey. They will be watching from the sky for signs laid out on the ground as your answer."

As Thirg looked again at the pictures of the Skybeings and the strange animals and other life forms that served them, he thought back to the Carthogian projectile-hurling weapon and the devices constructed by the Carthogian builders. All were examples of the simple beginnings of new arts that mimicked the processes of Life itself. Was it possible that the weapons of the Skybeings and the vehicles that the Skybeings were carried in could be products of the same arts taken to a far more advanced stage of perfection?

Products?

Could the Skybeings have created the weapons and the dragons? But the weapons and the dragons were machines. The first machine must have been constructed by something that was not a machine. So could the Skybeings be the Lifemaker? No, surely not. Surely the thought was preposterous.

And then Thirg remembered that the idea of turning wheels with vaporized methane had once seemed preposterous too.

19

"OH, NO QUESTION OF IT, I'M SURE," PENELOPE Ramelson said over the breakfast table. "Burton would be happy to talk to him." She turned her head to look across at her husband. "When do you think would be a convenient time, dear?" Penelope's cousin, Valerie, who was from Massachusetts and staying for a long weekend, smiled expectantly.

Burton Ramelson realized that he had been allowing his mind to wander back to the storm of protest that the announcement the major Western powers had made of their intention to claim Titan unilaterally had provoked inside the UN. "Er . . . what?" he said, blinking as he dabbed his mouth with a napkin. "I do beg your pardon—I don't think I can be quite awake yet."

Penelope sighed. "Valerie was talking about Jeremy," she said, referring to the elder of Valerie's two sons. "Now that he and Gillian will be starting a family, he feels he needs a job to . . . well, you know—it's psychological more than anything, I suppose—to feel he's doing something to provide for them . . . something through his own efforts, as it were."

"I was hoping that perhaps GSEC might have something suitable that it could offer him," Valerie said, coming more directly to the point.

Ramelson frowned as he sipped the coffee that he was taking with the ladies before joining Buhl and some others for a business breakfast later. "Hmm, I see...So what would you consider 'suitable'? What can he do? I mean, it is true that he and Gillian have been spending all their time gallivanting around the Far East and the Riviera practically since they got married...and he didn't do much more than sail his sloop before that, did he?"

"Oh, don't be such a crusty old gripe, Burton, even if it is first thing in the morning," Penelope chided. "They're young, and they're making the best of it. What's wrong with that? You're always telling us how short you are of capable managers these days. Well, Jeremy has always struck me as very talented and highly capable. I'd have thought there'd be plenty of room to fit him in somewhere like that...After all, it wouldn't have to be a terribly responsible position to begin with, or anything like that."

"I could use a couple of good engineering project managers and program directors," Ramelson said, not quite able to keep a sharp edge out of his voice. "Could Jeremy handle a structural dynamicist ten years older than him and with twenty year's experience? What does he know about Doppler radar or orbital mechanics? Those are the people I need."

"Now you're being pompous. All I—"

"Oh, I didn't want to suggest anything like that," Valerie interrupted hastily. "But maybe something less demanding—possibly more in the administrative area, but not too humdrum..." She treated Ramelson to a smile of sweet, wide-eyed reasonableness. "Something with some life and glamor to it would suit his temperament—marketing, maybe, or advertising...Isn't there a place like that where he could do some good? There must be, surely, Burton."

Ramelson finished his coffee and made a face to himself behind the cup. He and Penelope would be able to talk about it much more freely on their own later, without his being rushed into committing to anything prematurely. And besides that, with the meeting probably waiting for him already, he didn't want to go into all the whys and wherefores. "I'll talk to Greg Buhl about it today," he promised. He put down his cup and sat back with an air of finality that said the matter was finished for the time being. Penelope glanced at Valerie and nodded almost imperceptibly. "So what do you two have planned for today?" Ramelson asked. "Anything wild and exciting?"

"We thought we'd take the shuttle up to New York and go shopping," Penelope said. "I called Jenny and Paul, and they invited us to dinner with them."

"Uh-huh. Sounds like a late night back," Ramelson said.

"Probably."

"Why not stay over and get a flight back tomorrow?"

"We could, I suppose . . . Yes, why not? I'll give you a call and let you know if that's what we decide to do."

Ramelson looked at Valerie. "You seem to be enjoying your stay. Glad to see it." He glanced at his watch, folded his napkin and placed it in front of him, and stood up. "Well, the others will be waiting for me, so I'm afraid I must ask you to excuse me, ladies. Have a pleasant trip to New York, and do give my regards to Jenny and Paul."

"Of course," Penelope said as Ramelson turned to leave. "Oh, and you will remember to talk to Greg about Jeremy, won't you?"

"I'll remember," Ramelson sighed.

He had forgotten less than thirty seconds later as he crossed the hall outside the breakfast room, and his mind returned to the Titan situation. The rest of the world, especially the Soviets, had been outraged when the true purpose of the *Orion* mission was finally admitted after the months of speculations, accusations, and denials that had followed Zambendorf's revelation at the mission's departure. But that event was no longer viewed so widely as the major catastrophe that it had seemed at the time, since at least it had half prepared the world for the true story when it finally emerged—as it had to eventually—and had thus partly defused what would otherwise have been a bombshell of immense proportions. The reactions had been expected, of course, but apart from making a lot of noise and threats, what could the Soviets do? True, they could have started a war, the Western leaders had conceded among themselves; but the Pentagon's strategic analysts had concluded that they wouldn't—for the same reason that nobody had dared risk anything serious since 1945 . . . or at least, very probably they wouldn't; better than 92.4 percent probability, the computers had calculated.

On the other hand, depending on exactly what Titan turned up, exclusive access to advanced alien technology might provide the means for solving all of the West's problems once and for all—with the Soviets militarily, and with the rest of the world commercially. So the West had taken the gamble, and so far it seemed to have paid off. About the only casualty that Ramelson had seen so far was Caspar Lang, who in his last videogram from Titan had still seemed to be smarting from the thought of a major security breach's having taken place right under his nose. But better to have a realistic measure of Zambendorf now, rather than later when things start getting serious, Ramelson thought to himself as he trotted briskly down the four shallow steps outside the entrance to the library. And Caspar would get over things in time.

Inside, Gregory Buhl and two other GSEC executives, along with Julius Gorsche of the State Department and Kevin Whaley, a presidential aide, were waiting to begin the meeting. The first item was a summary presented by Gorsche of Daniel Leaherney's latest report from the *Orion*. The dialogue with the Taloids had continued to progress since the Terran landing at the city of "Genoa," Gorsche said. First impressions of the Taloid culture had suggested it was a collection of autonomously interacting, sometimes warring, sometimes loosely allied, social-political entities vaguely reminiscent of the Italian principalities and city-states of the Middle Ages, which the names that the Terrans had given them reflected. No further violent incidents of the kind necessitated against the "Paduans" had occurred, and that affair did not appear to have jeopardized the further development of constructive relationships with the Genoese. A permanent base had been established outside Genoa, and Terrans moved about openly inside the city itself; although apprehension and a tendency toward avoidance were still observable among some of the inhabitants, the Terrans were succeeding generally in gaining acceptance.

"At least our main concern has proved baseless," Ramelson said when Gorsche had finished. "We haven't found ourselves confronting an advanced alien race with an ability to threaten the mission or Earth itself." He looked over at Buhl. "So where does that leave us, Greg? There's a whole world of unconventional but highly sophisticated technology out there. Is it a potential resource that we could use? Does it look as if we might be able to get enough of it working for us somehow to justify the effort? If so, how much might we stand to benefit?"

"One thing at a time, Burton," Buhl muttered, taking a moment to glance over his notes. "The scientists there are pretty well wiped out. They're working round the clock, but the sheer volume of what they're starting to uncover is staggering enough, never mind the complexity of it. The various specialists will be reporting separately in due course, but I'm trying to get a preliminary summary put together for sometime in the next few days. Okay?"

"Fine," Ramelson said.

Buhl went on, "The answer to the main question is yes—there are technologies and processes up and running on Titan that could be centuries ahead of anything comparable on Earth, and some of the things there are completely new conceptually. We've already identified bulk nuclear transformation of elements; total fusion-based materials processing; molecular electronics; self-improving learning systems; intelligent, optronic, holoprocessing brains . . . and there's no doubt all kinds of other things yet that we've never even dreamed of." He threw up a hand. "The best guess seems to be that it all began as some kind of alien, self-replicating industrial scheme that screwed up, possibly millions of years ago. But whether that turns out to be the correct explanation or not, there's little doubt that the entire system was conceived and originated as a high-intensity extraction, processing, and manufacturing facility dedicated to the mass-production of industrial materials and products, and despite what's happened to it since, it still operates to fulfill that primary underlying purpose."

"In other words, if you could unscramble the glitches and get things working on a more organized basis, you could supply just about all of Earth's needs for centuries from a setup like that," Richard Snell, one of the GSEC executives, said.

Whaley looked intrigued. "You mean it could give us a decent competitive edge again . . . and maybe a respectable strategic margin?"

Snell smiled humorlessly. "That could qualify as the understatement of the year, Kev." He shrugged. "Anyone who gets to control the Titan operation doesn't have any competitors, or any strategic opposition. Those problems all go away—permanently."

A short silence ensued while the full meaning sank in. Then Whaley asked, "What about the Taloids? Is there likely to be a problem over . . . 'ownership rights,' or anything like that? I mean, is all this capacity something that they need too, or is it all pretty valueless as far as they're concerned?"

"Hopefully we'll be able to work out a basis for joint development," Buhl replied. "Their experience and knowledge of the environment would constitute a valuable asset in any case, which makes a cooperative approach the most desirable goal to aim at."

Frederick Methers, the other man from GSEC, commented, "Despite their physical form, the Taloids' own culture is actually pretty primitive. They don't have the conceptual abilities to utilize more than a tiny fraction of the potential they're surrounded by. But with us giving direction and them providing the working skills, it should be possible to get the act together and run it for mutual benefit."

Whaley looked at him curiously for a second or two. "I can see our angle," he said. "What's in it for the Taloids?"

Methers spread his hands. "What every backward race wants when it meets a more advanced culture—access to greater wealth and power, security, knowledge... whatever."

"That's true of the Taloids too?" Whaley sounded surprised.

"I wouldn't mind betting on it, anyhow," Methers said.

Gorsche nodded. "Genoa is also a fairly small state that's constantly being attacked by larger enemies, and Padua is one of them. I'd have thought there's a good chance that the Genoese would be extremely appreciative of any help we might give them for defending themselves. And that incident with the Paduans will have provided a very convenient demonstration of the kinds of things we could offer."

Ramelson looked from side to side. All the faces were watching him expectantly, waiting for his endorsement of the policy being proposed. He sat back and drummed his fingertips absently on the arms of his chair while he thought over what had been said. At last he nodded. "It's certainly worth exploring further, anyway. Do I take it that the other people you've put this to are in agreement also?"

Gorsche nodded. "It's more or less Dan Leaherney's own recommendations, and the president has approved," he said.

Ramelson looked satisfied and turned to Buhl. "Then let's get a confidential policy memorandum off to Caspar, confirming our position," he said. "The sooner he knows where he stands, the sooner we'll start seeing some results."

"That's what I wanted to discuss next," Buhl said, reaching for some papers in his briefcase. "In fact I've got a draft here for you to look at. Maybe we can go through it while we're all here together."

On the other side of Washington, D.C., Walter Conlon and Patrick Whittaker were having breakfast at a Howard Johnson's. "I imagine Gerry Massey must be pretty pissed," Whittaker said. "After the job that he and Vernon did all through the voyage out... I mean, they've collected enough proof to debunk just about everything that Zambendorf has said and done since the mission left."

"That's right," Conlon agreed over a plate of scrambled eggs and hash-browns, but without sounding especially perturbed.

Whittaker looked puzzled. "But hasn't it all been a waste of time?"

"Why?"

"Well... who cares anymore?" Whittaker shrugged. "Compared to what's happened on Titan now, all that's trivial, isn't it? Anyone who tried to make a big thing now out of whether or not Zambendorf had pulled a few tricks would just be making an ass of himself, and Massey's smart enough to know it. I assumed that was why Massey and Vernon haven't been announcing any great revelations."

Conlon shook his head. "They probably watched Zambendorf just to help pass the time during the voyage," he said. "Massey's also smart enough to have figured out that I wouldn't have sent him all that way just to expose a stage psychic... not after he learned where the mission was really bound for and why, anyway."

Whittaker frowned. "You mean his job never was to blow Zambendorf out of the water?"

"Not unless he wanted to, anyhow," Conlon said, without looking up from his meal. "No—GSEC and the rest had their cover story, so I had to have mine. Massey figured that out a long time ago. Before the mission left I arranged with one of the ship's senior communications officers for Massey to have access to a private channel direct into my section of NASO at Washington, free from any restrictions or censoring... purely as a precaution. Massey wasn't told about it until they were well into the voyage."

"So what's he really there for?" Whittaker asked, intrigued.

"I don't know," Conlon said. Whittaker looked totally bemused. Conlon explained, "I'm not absolutely certain why GSEC sent Zambendorf there, but it wasn't to entertain at parties in the officers' mess. I suspect they intend to use his ability to influence public opinion as an aid to pushing the government in a direction that suits their interests."

Whittaker looked horrified. "You're joking, Walt."

"Uh-uh." Conlon shook his head. "His antics could become a significant factor in the formulation of major international policy."

"But what, specifically?" Whittaker asked. "What exactly do they intend doing with him?"

"They couldn't have had any definite plans until they found out what exactly the situation was on Titan," Conlon said. "But they've learned a lot by now that they didn't know then. I've got a feeling that someone should be passing more specific orders to Zambendorf very soon now. And when Zambendorf finds out what he's really there for, that's when Massey will know what his job is."

20

GRAHAM SPEARMAN PEERED INTO THE WINDOW OF THE cold chamber in one of *Orion*'s biological laboratories, where an automatic manipulator assembly was slicing test specimens from a sample of brownish, rubbery substance recovered from the wreckage of the bizarre walking wagons destroyed in the encounter with the Paduan Taloids. The cold chamber was a necessity since most Taloid pseudo-organic materials tended to decompose into evil-smelling liquids at room temperature. In the work area around Spearman, the displays and data presentations were showing some of the findings from electron and proton microscopes, gas and liquid chromatographs, electrophoretic analyzers, isotopic imagers, x-ray imagers, ultrasonic imagers, and just about every kind of spectrometer ever invented. Spearman had already described the incendiary chemical thrown by the catapults mounted on several of the Paduan war vehicles; it had turned out to be a substance rich in complex oxygen–carbon compounds that would be highly inflammable in Titan's reducing atmosphere once ignition temperature had been attained by the reaction of a fast-acting outer acid layer upon a metallic target surface. The catapults themselves had been shown by video replays also to be organic, and suggested enormous, finely sculptured vegetables that ejected their missiles either by releasing stored mechanical strain-energy or by compressed gas accumulated internally.

In his late thirties, with thick-rimmed spectacles and a droopy mustache, and wearing a tartan shirt with jeans, Spearman was the easygoing kind of person that Thelma could find interesting without running the risk of ending up being used as an ideological dumping ground if she spent time talking to him. The problem with many scientists, she found, especially the younger ones, was that their successful intellectual accomplishment in one field could sometimes lead them to overestimate the value of their views on anything and everything, which tended to make conversation a survival skill by turning every topic into a minefield. Spearman provided a refreshing contrast by holding no political opinions, having no pet economic theory for solving all the world's problems at a stroke, and no burning conviction about how other people should conduct their lives to make it a better place.

"I've never seen anything quite like this," he said, turning back and waving an arm to indicate the sample behind the window. "It's capable of growing under the direction of large, complex director molecules, sure enough, but you couldn't say it's alive. It's kind of halfway in between.... It has a primitive biochemistry, but nothing approaching life at the level of cellular metabolism. You see, there aren't any cells."

Thelma looked intrigued as she swiveled herself slowly from side to side in the operator's chair in front of the microscopy console, while Dave Crookes listened from where he was leaning just inside the doorway. "Then what's it made of?" Thelma asked. "How does it grow without cells?"

Spearman sighed. "A comprehensive answer will probably take years to unravel, but for the moment think of it as something like an organic crystal, but more complicated... with variations in structure that you don't get in crystals." He gestured at the sample in the cold chamber. "That's a part of one of the legs. It does have a rudimentary vascular system to transport nutrients for renewing itself, an arrangement of contractile tissues that enable it to move, and a network of conductive fibers that transmit electrical discharges in response to applied mechanical force. And that's about all. What it suggests is that the complete structure could respond by moving itself if something pulled it—a kind of passive friction-reducer."

"An organic wheel," Thelma said.

Spearman grinned. "Sure—that's just about what it is."

"But it couldn't do anything else, like reproduce itself or something like that?" Crookes asked.

Spearman shook his head. "No way. As I said, it can move and regenerate its form—parts of it anyway. But there's no way you could say it's alive."

Thelma frowned to herself. "So how could something like that ever have evolved in the first place if it can't reproduce itself?" she asked.

"It couldn't have," Spearman replied simply.

"So where did it come from?"

"The only thing we can suggest is that the Taloids created it."

Thelma and Crookes exchanged puzzled glances. "But how could they have?" Crookes protested. "I mean, their technology is back in the Middle Ages. You're talking about something that might be crude compared to the living cells we know, but surely it's still a pretty impressive feat of bioengineering."

"Astonishing," Spearman confirmed. "In fact I don't think any genetic engineering of ours could touch it—not without naturally occurring macromolecules already available to work with, anyhow."

"Well, that's the point," Thelma said. "How could the Taloids have done it?"

Spearman moved a few paces across the lab, then turned and spread his hands. "We've already found plenty of examples of quite complex hydrocarbons and nitrogenous compounds in the soil, very much like the molecules believed to have been precursors of life on Earth. But apparently they never progressed much further on Titan, probably because of the low temperature and absence of strong ionizing radiation and other mutagenic stimulants. Well, our best guess is that the Taloids somehow learned to manipulate such raw materials, and over a period of time developed techniques for manufacturing the kind of thing you see here." He waved toward the cold chamber again. "And I mean manufacturing. That stuff didn't grow naturally. It accounts for their peculiar houses too, as well as a lot of other things we've seen."

John Webster, an English genetic engineering consultant from the Cambridge Institute for Molecular Biology, nodded from a stool in front of a cluttered workbench jammed into a corner among shelves of bottles and racks of electronic equipment. "That's the way it looks. It's our culture turned upside down. We grow our food and our offspring, and make artifacts out of metals that we extract from rocks; the Taloids' food and offspring are produced on assembly lines, while they grow artifacts—developed from organic substances which they discovered in their rocks and soils. That explains all those 'plantations' that we've been wondering about: They're Taloid factories."

"That's right—they did the same as we did, but the other way around," Spearman said. "Man learned to make mechanical devices to mimic the actions of living organisms in his familiar environment—to lift weights and move loads, and so on. The Taloids found they could manufacture artificial devices too—organic ones—to mimic the only form of life they knew."

"It's a good way of looking at it," Crookes agreed. "But that still doesn't explain how the Taloids could engineer processes at the molecular level when their culture is centuries behind ours." He gestured to indicate the banks of instrumentation and equipment all around them. "We had to invent all this before we even knew what a protein was, never mind how to splice genes into plasmids. The Taloids couldn't make anything even remotely comparable to all this stuff."

"They never needed to," Spearman said. "They're surrounded by it already."

It took Thelma a moment to grasp what he was saying. "You're kidding," she said incredulously.

Spearman shook his head. "Man learned how to use enzymes and bacteria to make wine and cheese thousands of years ago without having to know anything about the chemistry involved. Who's to say that the Taloids couldn't have learned to domesticate the life forms that they found all around them too? We take wool off sheep to make overcoats; they take wire from wire-drawing machines." He shrugged. "It's the same difference."

"Everything about them is us the other way around, and taken back three or four centuries," Webster said. "We were practical artisans first, and from those beginnings we developed engineering and the physical sciences. Biochemistry came later. The Taloids developed applied biology first, but without any real comprehension of biological science, and now they're only just beginning to dabble in the physical sciences."

"That seems strange," Crookes commented. "You'd think that all the advanced hardware down there would have given them an intuitive comprehension of it from early on."

"Why should it have?" Spearman asked. "Human beings are advanced biological systems, but that doesn't give them an intuitive understanding of how their brains and their bodies work. That knowledge could only come later, when suitable instruments became available . . . and it's still far from complete. Human consciousness operates at a level way above that of the neural hardware that supports our mental software, and the world of raw sensory data which that hardware reacts to. We don't perceive the world as consisting of pressure waves, photons, forces, and so on, but as people, places, and things. Our awareness arises from the interaction of abstract symbols that are far removed from the original physical stimuli—shut off, as it were, from any direct knowledge of its own underlying neurological and physiological processes. So we can think about the things that matter without knowing anything about what the trillions of nerve cells in our brains are doing, or even being aware that we have any."

Crookes frowned for a moment. "So what are you saying—that the Taloids are advanced electronic systems, but that doesn't give them any intuitive understanding of how they work either? Their awareness operates at a higher, abstract level in the same way?"

"Just that," Spearman replied.

Thelma nodded as the implications became clearer. "So just because the Taloids are computers, it doesn't mean necessarily that they think with machine precision and possess total information recall, does it? They might not be able to remember a conversation from yesterday word for word, or behave the same way in the same situation every time . . . just like us."

"That's what Graham's getting at," Webster said. "At its basic hardware level, the human brain is every bit as mechanical and predictable as an electronic computer chip: A neuron either fires or doesn't fire in response to a given set of inputs. It doesn't go through agonies of indecision trying to make up some microscopic mind about what to do. At that level, there isn't any mind to make up. 'Mind' emerges as a property of organization that becomes manifest only at the higher level. . . . In the same kind of way, a single molecule doesn't possess a property of 'elephantness'; a sufficiently large number of them, however, organized in the correct way, do. Taloid minds are almost certainly a result of complexity transcending their underlying hardware in the same way."

Spearman moved back to the cold chamber, stooped to look at what was going on inside, and entered a command into the control panel below the window. "If you showed a Taloid a piece of holoptronics from the inside of a computer processor, I think it'd be about as mystified as someone in the Middle Ages trying to make sense of a rabbit brain," he said over his shoulder. "We understand machines because we were able to begin with the simple and progress through to the more complicated—from pulleys and levers, through dynamos and steam engines, to computers, nuclear plants, and spaceships. Hence we can explain every detail of our creations and its purpose, right down to the last nut and bolt of something like the *Orion*. But an understanding of biologial processes didn't come so easily because, instead of being able to start with the simple, we found ourselves confronted by the most complex—the end-products of billions of years of evolution. With no comprehension of DNA, protein transcription, cell differentiation, and the like, it's not easy to explain the totality of a rabbit or account for how it came together in the first place." Spearman entered another command, waited to check its effect, and turned back to face the others once more. "The Taloids had the same problem. They were confronted by the end-products of a long history of alien technology, plus probably millions of years of evolution after that, without any of the benefit of attending the schools and technical colleges that the alien engineers went to. So the physical sciences remained a mystery. But dabbling with biological techniques was something they could figure out for themselves, using the resources they had."

Thelma reflected for a few seconds. "You mean for a long time they never even experimented with simple tools as we know them?... They'd have had enough raw materials lying around down there. It seems... oh, strange somehow."

Spearman smiled faintly. "The reason's pretty obvious when you think about it," he said.

"What?" Thelma asked.

"Tools as we know them are made out of refined materials like metals, glass, plastics, and so on," Spearman said. "In other words, the same kinds of substances that are produced naturally all over the place on Titan. They wouldn't last very long. Neither would anything you tried to make with them."

Crookes gave a puzzled frown. "How come?"

Webster spread his hands. "Anything like that would probably turn out to be 'food' for something or other. And besides... who'd dream of making tools, ornaments, and houses out of candy bars and pizza?"

* * *

The crew mess hall inside the larger of the two prefabricated domes that constituted Genoa Base One was warm, stuffy, and crowded. At the serving window, Massey picked up a mug of hot coffee and a donut and walked away from the short line of bulky figures in extravehicular suits waiting to snatch a last-minute snack before another expedition into the city. Since he had come down from the *Orion* thirty-six hours or so previously and just awakened from a rest period, it was really breakfast, he supposed. The Taloids remained continuously active for a period of a little over ten terrestrial days, centered around the time of maximum total illumination that resulted from direct solar radiation and reflection from Saturn as Titan progressed through its sixteen-day orbit. Since Titan kept one hemisphere permanently toward Saturn, one side of Titan experienced changes in both direct radiation and reflection while the other side experienced the direct component only, the areas in between receiving a mixture of both in varying proportions; thus the light-dark cycle was a complicated function of orbital motion, and on top of that, varied from place to place.

"And how is the rationalist today?" a jovial voice inquired from behind him. "It's not a good time of year for the debunking business, I hear."

Massey had recognized Zambendorf even before looking round. Although many of the mission's scientists had shown some signs of disdain and aloofness toward Zambendorf and his team three months previously at the time of leaving Earth, things had changed noticeably in the course of the voyage. Now Zambendorf, Abaquaan, Thelma, and the rest were simply accepted as a normal part of the day-to-day life of the *Orion*'s community. Whether this was a psychological effect of everyone's sharing the same, tiny, man-made environment hundreds of millions of miles from Earth, Massey didn't know; but in his conversations he had detected a not-uncommon attitude among the scientists of amused respect toward Zambendorf and his crew for at least being indisputable masters of their chosen profession; the scientists' contempt was reserved more for those who chose to adulate Zambendorf's team.

Massey turned to find Zambendorf grinning at him over the metal-ring helmet-seating of his EV suit. "It looks as if you might last a few more days yet," he conceded gruffly.

"I should hope so too," Zambendorf said. "Surely it must be obvious by now, even to you, Gerry, that there is more important work to be done than wasting time with trivia that belong where we should have left them—a billion miles away, back on Earth."

Massey looked at him curiously. Zambendorf and his team *had* been showing a genuine interest in the mission's serious business—and surprising some of the scientists with how much they knew. Was it possible that Zambendorf could be undergoing a change of heart? "What's the matter, Karl?" he asked. "Are you developing a guilt complex now that you're seeing some real science for once?"

"Don't be ridiculous," Zambendorf scoffed. "And besides, even if it were true, do you think I'd tell you? You're the psychologist. You should be telling me."

In other words Massey could take Zambendorf's attitude either way. He was still the same old Zambendorf—forever confusing, and always a jump ahead of the game. "You re doing something worthwhile for once," Massey said "You've got a knack for getting through to the Taloids, and they trust you. That has to be a better feeling than ripping people off all the time, so why not admit it?"

"It's not the same thing," Zambendorf replied. "I'll help anyone who makes the effort to help himself. The Taloids might have some way to go yet, but they value knowledge and skill. They want to learn. They're willing to work at it. But people? Pah! They grow up surrounded by libraries, universities, teachers who could show them the accumulated discoveries and wisdom of millennia and they're not interested. They'd rather live junk-lives. How can you steal anything from someone who has already thrown everything away?"

"Perhaps people simply need to be shown how to think," Massey suggested.

Zambendorf shook his head. "It's like leading horses to water. When people are ready to think, they will think. Trying to rush them is futile. All you can do is show them where the water is and wait for them to get thirsty." He gestured over Massey's shoulder at Osmond Periera and Malcom Wade, who were standing by the doorway, debating in loud voices a speculation of Periera's that the antimatter spaceship responsible for creating the North Polar Sea might have come from Titan. "Listen to those two idiots," Zambendorf murmured in a lower voice. "You could spend a year of your life preparing a detailed refutation that might succeed in convincing them that what they're talking about is nonsense. Do you think they'd learn anything from the experience? Not a bit of it. Within a week they'd be off into something else equally preposterous. So you could have saved your time for something profitable. I'll save mine for the Taloids."

"Careful, Karl," Massey cautioned. "You're beginning to sound as if you're admitting you're a fraud again."

"Don't be ridiculous," Zambendorf said. "But even if it were true, do you think people would learn anything from the experience if you proved it?" He shook his head. "Not a bit of that either. Within a week they would have found something else too . . . just like friend Osmond and that other character behind you."

At that moment a loudspeaker announced that the personnel carrier that would be taking the party into the city was waiting at the vehicle-access transfer lock. "The problem with you is that you really are a scientist at heart," Massey said as they began moving in the direction of the doorway. "But you think it would be beneath your dignity to admit it."

Half an hour later they were among the passengers watching parts of the outskirts of Genoa slide through the headlamp beams of the carrier and its escort of two military scout cars fifty yards ahead and behind. All along the way, Taloids came to stand by the roadside to watch the procession of strange creatures that bore within them beings from another world. Some ran forward to bathe themselves in the light, which they apparently believed to possess miraculous and curative properties; a few shrank back as the vehicles passed, or fled into the alleys and sidestreets.

One—a mounted figure wrapped in a heavy riding cloak, its face concealed in a deep hood—watched inconspicuously from the shadows of a gateway near the city wall, absorbing every detail. When the Terran vehicles had passed, the rider reemerged and moved away along the side of the road in the opposite direction to resume the journey that would take it out of the city, beyond the borders of Carthogia, and across the Wilderness of Meracasine. Skerilliane, Spy-with-a-Thousand-Eyes, would have much to report when he returned to his royal master Eskenderom, the King of Kroaxia.

21

"CAN YOU IMAGINE A DISTANCE TWELVE TIMES greater than the greatest breadth of Carthogia?" Thirg asked Lofbayel's son, Morayak, who was sitting with his back to the large table strewn with charts and sheets of calculations, in the room that Lofbayel had given Thirg to use as a study while Thirg was residing with the family.

"I think so, though I have never journeyed but a fraction of such a distance," Morayak said. "Why, it must be greater even than the size of the strange, spherical world of which you and my father speak!"

"Not so, Young-Questioner-Who-Will-Become-Wise-by-Questioning," Thirg said. He picked up the Skybeings' globe that the Wearer-of-the-Arm-Vegetable had presented to him as a gift, and looked at it briefly. "In fact such a distance would be a little less than half the diameter of our world, of which I am assured this is a faithful representation." He put the globe down and looked back at Morayak. "And what of a distance yet twelve times that again—enough to span six worlds side by side? Can your mind grasp that?"

Morayak frowned and stared at the globe while he concentrated. "I'm not sure. To visualize the breadth of Carthogia requires but a simple extension of faculties that are familiar to me, but where is the experience to guide my intuition in attempting to judge a distance through a world rather than across it? But even taxing my mind to that degree does not satisfy you enough, it seems, for now you would have me grapple with conceiving six of them."

"Then instead of worlds whose surfaces curve in space, let us take as our model, time, which involves no complications from multiplicity of direction," Thirg suggested. "If the breadth of Carthogia be represented by a single bright, then the distance to which I refer, being twelve times twelve, equates to one Carthogia for every bright contained in the duration of twelve twelve-brights. Now—can you visualize that?"

It took Morayak a few seconds to grasp, but in the end he nodded, at the same time frowning intently. "That is vastness indeed, but it is not completely unimaginable now you have described it thus. My mind is stretched, but I think it can conceive of such a distance."

"And what of twelve times that, yet again?"

Morayak stared at Thirg with a strained look on his face, then grinned hopelessly and shook his head. "Impossible!"

Thirg paced across the room, swung around, and threw his hands wide. "Then what of twelve times even that, and twelve times that yet again still, and then even twelve times—"

"Stop, Thirg!" Morayak protested. "What purpose is served by uttering repetitions of words that have ceased to carry any meaning?"

"But they do carry meaning," Thirg said. He moved forward and raised his arm to point. Morayak turned in his seat to look at the large chart on the wall above the table, which Lofbayel had drawn from Thirg's records of conversations with the Skybeings. In the center it showed the huge furnace in the sky—large enough to consume the whole world in an instant, the Skybeings said—and around it the paths of the nine worlds that circled it endlessly, some of them accompanied by their own attendant worlds, which in turn circled them. It had come as something of a shock to learn that Robia, as Kleippur had named the robeing world, was not even a member of the nine, but just one—although, true, the largest—of a retinue of seventeen servants following at the heels of a giant. Dornvald had remarked that the giant was surely the king of worlds, because of his ringlike crown. But Thirg was pointing not at the giant, but at the third world out from the furnace—a humble little world, seemingly, with just a single page in attendance—which Lofbayel had labeled Lumia, since its sky shone with the heat light that accompanied the Skybeings, or Lumians, as they were now more properly called, wherever they went. Thirg swept a finger slowly across the chart. "That is the distance which separates our world from the world of Lumians, Morayak—the distance they have traveled to come to Robia."

Morayak stared at him incredulously. "It cannot be!" Thirg nodded. Morayak looked at the chart again, then back at Thirg. "But such a journey would surely require many twelves of twelves of lifetimes."

"One twelve-bright was sufficient, we are assured. The large dragon that circles beyond the sky is swifter, seemingly, than even the smaller ones which cross above the city in moments." Thirg studied Morayak's face for a few seconds and gave a satisfied nod. "Now, methinks, you understand better the wondrousness of the beings you are soon to meet," he said.

Morayak stared back at Thirg for a moment longer as if unsure of whether or not to take his words seriously, and then looked slowly back at the chart, this time with a new respect. Thirg and Lofbayel were due to leave shortly for Kleippur's residence to join the Carthogian leaders in more discussions with the Lumians, and Morayak had eventually succeeded in pestering his father into allowing him to go along too. He had been to see the strange growths that the Lumians lived in just outside the city, of course—his father said that the Lumians had created them—and he had caught glimpses from a distance of the cumbersome, domeheaded figures, which apparently weren't the Lumians at all but an outer casing that they had to wear on Robia because they needed to be bathed in hot, highly corrosive gas all the time; but that wasn't the same—he wouldn't be able to boast to his friends about that. "I wonder what kind of a world it is," he murmured distantly, still staring at the chart.

"Amazing beyond your wildest dreams," Thirg replied. "Its sky is filled with worlds too numerous to count, extending away as far as it is possible to see, for there is no permanent cover of cloud above Lumia to limit vision. It is so hot that the surface is covered by oceans of liquid ice. Methane can exist only as a vapor. Your body would be much heavier than it is on Robia."

"What of the countryside?" Morayak asked. "Does it have mountains and forests? Do the Lumians keep herds of bearing-bush formers, and hunt plate-melters out on the flatlands? Do they have children who go gasket-collecting among the head-assembly transfer lines, or baiting traps with copper wire to catch coil-winders?"

Thirg frowned, not knowing quite how to explain the differences. "The children there are assembled in miniature form," he said. "They grow larger by taking in substances which are distributed internally as liquid solutions."

Morayak stared at him in astonishment. "But how could the substances know where to be deposited?" he objected. "All form would surely be lost."

"The process is beyond my understanding," Thirg admitted. "Perhaps that is why the Lumians exist as jelly and must remain inside outer casings to preserve their shape. But natural assembly is impossible on Lumia because there aren't any machines . . . save for a few which aren't alive, but were created by the Lumians."

"It's true then—the Lumians really can make artificial machines?"

"Oh yes—those are the only machines they know. They do have animals and forests, but they're not machines. They're made of, well . . . the best way I can find to describe it is 'naturally occurring organics'—very like the Lumians themselves."

Morayak looked perplexed. "But artisans must exist to create organics. How can there be 'natural organics'?"

"I too am learning," Thirg reminded him. "We both have many questions that will tax our patience for a while yet."

"But organic forests and animals . . . a whole world full of such unsightliness?" Morayak made a face. "It sounds so ugly, so unnatural . . . How could anyone live there? Is that why they have come to Robia—to escape? But how—"

Lofbayel's wife, Kersenia, came in. "Ah, I thought I'd find you two here," she said. "Lofbayel has hitched up the cart and is waiting before the house for you now." Morayak got up, and followed with Thirg behind as Kersenia went back to the hallway inside the front door. "And remember, don't go getting in the way or making a nuisance of yourself," she said as Morayak put on his coat. "You are a very lucky and privileged young robeing to be invited to the residence of Kleippur. Don't let your father down, now."

"I won't," Morayak promised.

"I'm sure you have no cause to worry," Thirg said.

Thirg and Morayak left the house and climbed up beside Lofbayel, and Kersenia stood in the doorway to see them off as the cart turned onto the roadway in the direction of the city. It was good, Thirg thought to himself, to see the family living free and without fear, with Lofbayel pursuing his studies openly and able to teach at last in the way he had always wanted. He wondered if what he was seeing could be an omen of things to come on a larger scale for the whole robeing race. For the Lumians seemed to respect freedom and knowledge, and to share generally the values that Thirg felt Kleippur and his vision for Carthogia symbolized. Could the Lumians be offering a new future of opportunity for all robeings, just as Carthogia offered a new future of opportunity for Thirg, and for Lofbayel and his family? Would the old ways of the whole world of Robia now fade into the past and be forgotten, just as Kroaxia was already fading into their personal pasts and being forgotten?

So possibly the priests and the Scribings had been right

after all in a way, Thirg thought to himself. If the Lumians were indeed the Lifemaker, then perhaps the Lifemaker did offer salvation from the toil and drudgery of worldly life . . . not in some hereafter world, however, but in this one—simply by taking the toil and the drudgery out of it. That would seem the eminently sensible and simple way of accomplishing such an objective, after all. Why would a Lifemaker—especially one as intelligent and all-powerful as the priests were always depicting—choose to do things the difficult way?

But Thirg had learned from long and bitter experience not to let his hopes run too high about anything. There was always too much that could go wrong, and usually it found a way of managing to. He wondered if lifemaking Skybeings had the same problem.

"What he's doing is not compatible with the policy objectives that have been confirmed from Earth," Daniel Leaherney said to Casper Lang, on the *Orion*. "Also I've been getting complaints that his style is interfering with the ability of the personnel who are properly empowered to handle our relationships with the aliens to discharge their duties in an effective manner. Can I leave it to you to straighten the situation out?"

"What you mean is that Giraud's developing an inferiority complex because the Taloids take more notice of Zambendorf than they do of him, Seltzman doesn't feel he's getting all the glory he should be getting, and someone stuffy among the scientific chiefs—probably Weinerbaum—is getting jealous and thinks his dignity's being threatened," Lang said. He was getting just a little bit tired of having to stay up in the ship all the time, taking care of everyone else's problems.

Leaherney exhaled a long breath and snapped, "Look, that psychic is getting in everyone's hair and taking over the show down there as if this whole mission had been put together for no other reason than to boost his act. Your corporation sent him here, Caspar, and it's your responsibility to keep him under control. So read it any way you like, but I want something done about it."

An hour later Lang, feeling even more incensed after Leaherney's uncharacteristic outburst, was looking grim-faced across his desk at Osmond Periera. "Where's the schedule of the experiments you were supposed to be carrying out with Zambendorf?" he demanded.

Periera looked flummoxed. "What? Why, er . . . I thought that was just part of the Mars cover story. I thought—"

"The corporation isn't paying you to think; it's paying you to know," Lang fumed. "Have you any idea how much it's cost to bring you people this distance? My understanding was that you are here to investigate a serious scientific phenomenon."

"Well, there's no question of that, but—"

"Then how much longer do I have to wait before I see something happening?" Lang asked. "You're supposed to be responsible for organizing the experimental program, okay? Well, it's about time you started organizing something. You don't expect me to do it for you, do you?"

"No, of course not, but I . . . I, that is . . . He's down at Genoa Base One."

"Well, get him back up from Genoa Base One!" Lang yelled. "I agreed to his going down on one trip to see the surface. Okay—he's seen it. Now get him back up here and make a start on the job you were brought here to do. And nobody—repeat, nobody—from that outfit goes down there again until we start seeing some results. Understood?"

Periera gulped and nodded rapidly. "Yes, yes, of course."

"Good." Lang reached over to call his secretary on his terminal screen. "Get this update on personnel authorizations into the system right away, Kathy. Karl Zambendorf is recalled to the ship forthwith, and approval for surface descent is denied him and his party until further notice."

22

ESKENDEROM, KING OF KROAXIA AND DIVINELY ORdained Protector of the Lifemaker's True Faith, rested an elbow on an arm of his throne and glowered down over his hand while he listened. Bowed over one knee at the foot of the steps before him, Skerilliane, the spy, made a flourish in the air with his arm. "In tame dragons as long as the palace is wide, they fly—many twelves of them at a time. In strange, wheeled beasts the size of houses, through the streets of Menassim, they ride. They conspire in secret league with Kleippur, and outside the city they conduct rituals among the machines of the forest with the tame creatures and magic vegetables. They are formed from burning fluids contained in soft casings, and they share thoughts without impediment of distance, though they utter no sound."

Eskenderom brooded while he absorbed the information, then lifted his head and turned to look questioningly at Horazzorgio, who was standing to one side of the steps. One of Horazzorgio's imaging matrixes was covered by a plastic cap, and a welded plate blanked off the hole left by his missing arm. "The beings and the creatures that serve them, I have seen not," Horazzorgio said. "But the dragons are the same as those of the Meracasine, and the smaller spy-dragons are the ones that swooped upon us, spitting lightning bolts and hurling fire. The violet radiance too is the same."

"What is the substance of the discourse that beings such as these would enter into with Kleippur?" Frennelech inquired from the High Priest's seat, a level below the throne and to the right.

"My informants have overheard much talk among Carthogia's counselors and officers of forbidden arts and the unholy powers that are sought by heretics and accursed ones," Skerilliane replied. "Carthogia places itself at the Dark Master's disposal as a sanctuary for his servants and the base from which he would enslave the world. Many worshipers of evil who have forsaken enlightenment to serve him through his worldly lieutenant, Kleippur, are being conscripted to the task—Maker-of-Maps Lofbayel and Asker-of-Forbidden-Questions Thirg being among just the most recent additions." Horazzorgio's remaining imager glowed angrily at the mention of the names. "And now, it seems, the Dark Master has provided Kleippur with further aid as compensation for Carthogia's limited size and means," Skerilliane concluded.

The King looked at Frennelech. "So—Kleippur's Dark Master sends dragons from the sky to aid him. I see much energy expended on pomp and pageantry by the priests of Kroaxia, Serethgin, and the other nations of the Sacred Alliance; I hear endless praying, chanting, and supplication. Where, then, are your Lifemaker's dragons?"

"In the face of adversity, faith shall overcome," Frennelech quoted in reply. "It is a test sent to try us. We must not waver."

"Does the faith of the Waskorians help them to overcome in their struggle to throw off Kleippur's yoke? I equipped them generously and sent our best combat officers to instruct them, but in their last encounter with Kleippur's soldiers they were decimated. The new Carthogian weapon that can hurl a pellet of steel from thrice the range attainable by the strongest dartsman would appear more efficacious than a mountain of dreary books or an eternity of incantations."

"Dragon-beings' weapons," Horazzorgio muttered, fingering his shoulder unconsciously. "I know well of those too."

Frennelech looked uncomfortable, but before he could reply, Mormorel, the King's Senior Counselor, who had been pacing slowly to and fro as he listened, turned suddenly and moved to the center of the open floor below the throne and raised his hands to draw attention. Skerilliane straightened up and moved respectfully back while the others turned their heads curiously.

"It is possible that our alarm is premature," Mormorel said. "For what, precisely, is it that substantiates the assumption—which none of us has questioned—that these dragons are indeed emissaries of the Dark Master? That they bear beings possessed of skills unfamiliar to us, we know; that they are from regions unreported by our farthest-ranging travelers and explorers, we know. But more of whence they come and why, we suppose much and know nothing. Is it not possible that, rather than having been sent from some supernatural realm for the advancement of sinister designs upon the world, they too could be explorers, who find it expedient to enter into bargain with Kleippur for rendering that which is of value to him in return for that which they in turn have traveled far to seek?"

A silence descended around the throne room while the others digested the implications of Mormorel's observations. "The news that Kleippur was receiving powerful foreign aid could prove a strong source of inspiration and resolve for our people," Horazzorgio mused. "They have long been mystified by the inability of the Alliance armies to conquer tiny, stubborn Carthogia."

"What would beings such as these seek in lands such as ours?" Eskenderom asked doubtfully.

"No amount of speculation will tell us that," Mormorel replied. "But whatever the answer, can Carthogia offer anything that cannot be obtained in greater abundance from Kroaxia's vaster territories or produced more cheaply by our more numerous slaves and laborers? Thus we can better not only whatever bargain Kleippur has made with these dragon-beings, but also any improvement that lies within his power to offer."

"Mmm..." Eskenderom sat back and rubbed his chin thoughtfully. A gleam slowly suffused his imagers. "If the dragon-beings' aid can make such a difference to puny Carthogia, it would make a nation like Kroaxia..."

"Invincible," Frennelech completed in a distant voice.

Mormorel saw that he had made his point. He gave a slow, satisfied nod, and looked from one to another of the faces around him. "Invincible not only against Carthogia... but, should the occasion arise, against Serethgin, Corbellio, Munaxios—all of them."

Another short silence fell. Then Frennelech pronounced in a voice that was suddenly more sure of itself, "It is divinely ordained! The Lifemaker has sent the dragon-beings from beyond the Barrier as His instrument to carry the True Faith to all corners of the robeing world. We are the chosen bearers of that instrument, which the Dark Master, through Kleippur, is attempting to misdirect. The quest we are set is to initiate contact with the dragon-beings and discover what the Lifemaker has directed them to seek. Thus has He chosen to reveal to us His will."

Eskenderom looked at Skerilliane. "Has anything that you saw or heard provided indication of what the dragon-beings seek from Kleippur?" he asked.

"Nothing. But it was not my purpose to look for such."

"Then it shall be your purpose now," Eskenderom declared. "Your assignment is to return to Carthogia immediately and discover what the dragon-beings wish in return for their aid. You are empowered to speak on behalf of the Kroaxian Crown to express its desire for a direct dialogue, and to make appropriate offers as guided by your own discretion to secure the attainment of that end."

"I shall begin preparations at once," Skerilliane said.

"One of your officers is to go too," Eskenderom told Horazzorgio. "Skerilliane may have need of a soldier's expertise. Also, I would like to hear the opinion of a military professional who has observed these dragon-beings firsthand."

"I request the King's permission to accompany him myself," Horazzorgio replied at once. Eskenderom frowned, reluctant to make an issue of his captain's condition. Horazzorgio saw the King's gaze travel from his eye to his arm. "If I can return alone from the Meracasine, on foot and wounded, then surely I can survive it accompanied, mounted, and recovered. Neither will Skerilliane's mission be jeopardized, for my personal interests in this matter will more than make up spiritually for what has been lost physically."

Eskenderom looked at him for a moment, and then at Skerilliane. "You shall be the judge, for yours is the casing that will be at risk, not mine. Would you have confidence in Horazzorgio as your companion? Speak truly, spy. This is not a time to permit fear of personal insult to affect judgment and prudence."

"The spy should be never seen and never heard," Skerilliane answered. "Of what importance is the appearance of he who exists not? Indeed, such business is more often hampered than assisted by a penchant for deeds of recklessness and daring, which Horazzorgio has ample reason to avoid. I have every confidence in the prospect of our association."

The King looked at them for a moment longer, then nodded. "So be it." He stood up from the throne and descended the steps before it, then stopped as an afterthought struck him, and looked back at the High Priest. "I suppose you'd better pray for their success," he said, and with that turned and strode away.

23

IT WAS LIKE BEING IN A TOMB, CASPAR LANG THOUGHT to himself, or an ice cave inside a glacier that was too deep for light to penetrate.

With more room available on Giraud's diplomatic delegation now that Zambendorf and his team had been restricted to the ship, and with activities in and around Genoa becoming more organized, Lang had taken the opportunity to come down to the surface and involve himself more directly in the proceedings. He had seen the incredible tangles of cluttered machinery and derelict structures that surrounded the base and stretched away beyond the searchlight beams playing from the sentry posts around the perimeter; the ghostly shapes of the city's peculiar, cultivated houses and larger buildings of ice along the route to Arthur's residence—which had been named Camelot, of course; and the strange, clothed, bipedal robots and other machines that gathered to watch from the shadows at the fringes of the vehicles' headlamp beams. Now he was sitting awkwardly in a large ice chamber inside Camelot, which even had a sizeable table, although not a round one. Looking like gigantic upright insects in the weak circle of light from the two low-power lamps that the NASO engineers had installed, Arthur and several other Taloids were sitting opposite, while to the sides Giraud, Seltzman, and the remaining Terrans looked just as eerie and grotesque in their jointed, smooth-surfaced, machinelike garb. Most of the furnishings were of odd, Taloid pseudovegetable shapes, and the walls, indistinct and shadowy in the background, were covered by thick woven-wire hangings and weird designs worked in plastic and metal. The talks had been going on for some hours.

"Tell them they've got it wrong, Konrad," Giraud's voice said in Lang's helmet, coming through on local frequency. "We are not planning to exploit their people or set the value of their labor too cheaply. Anyone who desires economic prosperity has to work for it, just as we had to work for it back on Earth. There aren't any free rides."

Seltzman flipped a switch to direct his words into another audio channel, which was wire-connected through to the electronics box on the table in front of him. "Sorry," he said. "You still misunderstand. Earthmen do not wish to exploit Taloid labor. Titan must work for prosperity, just as Earth had to work for prosperity."

A couple of seconds went by while the control microprocessor inside the box conferred with a larger computer located in the communications center at Genoa Base One. Then the display on the screen in front of Seltzman changed to read:

NO MATCH FOR "EXPLOIT TALOID LABOR." EQUIVALENT PHRASE?

Seltzman thought for a second. "Benefit from Taloid work that is not paid for," he said.

"PROSPERITY = WEALTH in this context?" the machine inquired.

"Wealth for all Taloids," Seltzman replied.

The display changed:

SORRY. YOU STILL MISUNDERSTAND. EARTHMEN DO NOT WISH TO BENEFIT FROM TALOID WORK THAT IS NOT PAID FOR. TITAN MUST WORK FOR WEALTH FOR

ALL TALOIDS JUST AS EARTH HAD TO WORK FOR WEALTH FOR ALL TALOIDS.

Seltzman sighed. "Delete last word. Insert Earthmen." The machine complied. "Okay," he pronounced.

The "transmogrifier" that Dave Crookes, Leon Keyhoe, and some of the other signals engineers and pattern-recognition specialists had assembled and were still improving did not so much translate languages as enable the two parties in a dialogue—whose native languages were not only mutually unintelligible but also completely inaudible—to tell the machine, in effect, to note what was said and remember its meaning. It did this by matching recognizable sequences of human voice patterns against a collection of Taloid pulse-code profiles stored in a computerized library that was continually being enlarged. Upon finding a Taloid equivalent to an identified piece of speech input, it synthesized the corresponding ultrasonic Taloid pulse-stream, thus performing both the band-shift and time-compression needed to transfer information from one domain of intelligibility to the other. Also it performed the complete inverse process. The matches were determined not by sophisticated rules of grammar or elaborate programing, but simply by mutual agreement through trial and error between the parties involved. The system was thus very much an evolutionary one, and had developed from extremely crude beginnings.

"Bad-sad," the talking vegetable said. "Lumians no want good from *buzz-buzz clug-zzzzzipp* robeing slave for free. *Bakka-bakka* Robia workum hard get plenty finegood thing for robeings *wheeee chirrrp* like Lumia workum hard get plenty finegood thing for *chikka-walla-chug-chug-chog* Lumians."

Thirg frowned as he concentrated. "Methinks they have misunderstood," he said. "They believe that we fear they have come here to enslave us."

"It seems their vegetable exaggerates our concern," Kleippur commented. "My objection is not that they would make us slaves, for clearly it is within their power to have accomplished that end already if such was their desire, but their implication that our people's lives are my property to sell or barter as I would, instead of their own to direct as they choose freely."

"What are these 'good things' which they would have us work to acquire in our world as they have in theirs?" Lofbayel asked.

"Presumably the weapons and other devices of destruction which they have emphasized at such great expenditure of time and zealousness," Dornvald replied.

Kleippur shook his head. "The protection of Carthogia is important to me, 'tis true, but these merchants of havoc would credit my mind with no aspiration higher than an obsession for conquest and a hunger to possess the whole of Robia. Indeed these are Lumians of a disturbingly different breed from the Wearer and his companions." He looked at Thirg. "Advise the Lumians that the sharing of their lifemaking arts would be of far greater value to us, for with such knowledge we could divide our industriousness among protecting our people, providing for them, and educating them, in proportions of our own deciding. If the Lumians wish to enlist our help in taming the forests to expand their lifemaking abilities further, are we not justified in asking their help in turn to expand our comprehension of that which they would have us tame?"

Thirg reached out and touched the button that opened the talking vegetable's ears. The small light that showed when the vegetable was listening came on. "Knowledge of the lifemaking arts of the Lumians would be more valuable than quantities of weapons beyond those needed to ensure Carthogia's protection," he said. "If the Lumians wish robeings to help them tame the forests, robeings wish Lumians to help them comprehend the forests."

The transmogrifier turned the pulse-stream into numbers and flashed them to the base computer, which broke the numbers into groups and compared them to stored samples at the rate of a million per second. Where possible alternative matches were indicated, a decision-tree operating on selected, weighted attributes kept track of the best-fit score. An instant later the computer transmitted to the transmogrifier.

"Unclear *buzz-buzz gubba-gubba* what-mean 'lifemaking arts,'" the vegetable squawked. "Want-say *wheeee-phooom*alternative."

Thirg thought for a while, but couldn't bring one to mind. "Obtain new word," he said. The vegetable had learned that this was his instruction for it to get the Lumians' own term for something from the Lumians. Inside the transmogrifier's control processor, the pulse-sequence triggered a branch to a library-update routine.

EQUIVALENT ENGLISH WORD-FORM BEING REQUESTED, the screen before Seltzman reported.

"Okay," Seltzman acknowledged.

"Pray describe," the vegetable invited Thirg.

"Knowledge, art, skill, power," Thirg told it. "Creating, inventing—making of machines. Comprehension of how machines operate. Understanding origin of first machine. How could a first machine be possible?"

The screen responded:

FUNCTION	SUBJECT	ADDITIONAL DATA
Knowledge	Machines	First Machine
Ingenuity	Operation/Opera-	—source of?
Expertise	ting Principles?	Machine origins?
Understanding	Design/	Impossible?
(Domination?)	Manufacture	

Seltzman studied the display for a few seconds and replied, "Science and technology." He wasn't going to go into the metaphysics of the second part, he decided.

"*Buzz-wheee* Lumian word *wowumpokkapokka* get-good," the vegetable advised Thirg. "Need simplify other better *whoosh wow*."

Thirg thought back to what he had said, and replied, "Knowledge of lifemaking skills is worth more to Carthogians than too many weapons is worth."

"Now try maybe-read *buzz-buzz bakka-bakka* speak," the vegetable advised.

Seltzman read on the screen:

SCIENCE AND TECHNOLOGY KNOW-HOW BETTER DEAL FOR GENOESE THAN WEAPONS TOO MANY/TOO MUCH/ OVERKILL(?). IF TERRANS WANT TALOID AID FOR MANAGE MACHINE COMPLEX, THEN TALOIDS WANT TERRAN AID FOR KNOW-HOW MACHINE COMPLEX.

"We're back to the same stalemate," Lang said. "I don't think we're going to get much further for now. At least the translations are starting to make more sense, so it's not as if we had nothing to show for it. I vote we call it a day."

"Me too," another voice said on the circuit. "Let's get back to base and out of these things. I'm about ready for dinner."

Giraud sighed. "Okay, we'll wrap the session up there," he agreed. "Tell them we understand their position, but it involves a lot of complications that we'll have to go away and think about. And they have a lot of things to think over too—without adequate defense there won't be any Genoa, so they have to get their priorities right. Finish up with the usual thanks and courtesies."

When the laborious exchange was completed and the Taloids had added their closing respects, everyone rose and exchanged hand-touchings in the manner that had been adopted as combining aspects of both Terran and Taloid forms of customary goodwill salutation. As the party left, technicians collected the electronics equipment and switched off the lamps until the next session, and the French paratroopers who had been stationed outside the conference room formed up with an honorary complement of Arthur's guards to escort the Terrans and their Taloid hosts back to the vehicles. After a final round of parting formalities the Terrans departed for their base.

"The only way to exert pressure on the population as a whole is through its leaders," Giraud said, gratefully free of his helmet inside the cabin of the personnel carrier as the party drove back through the outskirts of Genoa. "But how do you do it when the leader thinks he can step into the twenty-first century overnight and become civilized instantly? I mean, their culture is still barbaric—centuries away, at least, from being able to grasp technology. But how can you make them understand that and persuade them they have to be patient without jeopardizing everything you stand to gain? It's a problem, Caspar."

"It's all a result of delusions of grandeur that they developed through talking to Zambendorf and his crazies," Caspar Lang said sourly. "We should never have let him near them at all."

"I agree, but it can't be undone," Giraud replied. "At least he's out of it all now. I hope you're keeping him busy until we need him—enough to prevent his getting into any more mischief."

"All taken care of," Lang said. "Osmond Periera and that wacky Canadian psychologist have got him tied up full-time. It's a wonder he gets a minute to eat and sleep."

"There's no chance of his interfering in our business with Arthur, then?" Giraud asked, just to be sure.

"No chance. Even if he had the time, how could he do anything? If he found a way of getting down from the ship, he'd never be let through the base."

"Well I'm glad to hear that, at least, Caspar," Giraud said. "The situation's difficult enough as it is."

"Don't worry about it," Lang said confidently.

At Kleippur's residence, Kleippur and the others returned to the Council Chamber and took from its place of concealment inside a cabinet the seeing vegitable that the Wearer had left as a gift before returning to the large dragon beyond the sky. Dornvald relit the violet Lumian lantern that enabled the vegetable to see, and Thirg pressed the button that would open another eye within the dragon. All in the room waited, their eyes fixed expectantly on the magic window.

In a cabin up in the *Orion*, Osmond Periera and Malcom Wade sat surrounded by notes and papers, concentrating intently on the sentences appearing on the computer screen in front of them and making occasional responses via keyboard. The screen was showing the attempts of Zambendorf, who was elsewhere in a sealed room with no means of communication to the outside apart from a non-switchable, hard-wired terminal, to divine the contents of closed envelopes selected blind by Periera, guess random sequences of numbers and ESP cards, and describe drawings made on the spur of the moment by both the testers. The use of only a narrow set of predefined mnemonic codes to communicate, would, Periera and Wade had agreed, effectively eliminate the possibility of their giving hints and clues unwittingly.

Actually it made no difference because Joe Fellburg had bugged their cabin, which they hadn't thought to check, and they both talked too much. They also hadn't thought to check whether the sealed room had been unsealed and occupied by someone pretending to be Zambendorf... such as Thelma and Clarissa taking turns to operate the terminal while the other stayed around for company. Any question of cheating was, after all, unthinkable; why would Zambendorf need to cheat if he was genuine?

Although progress had been painfully slow, the results that Periera and Wade had been getting were tantalizingly encouraging—enough, in fact, to have kept them shut away for the best part of several days. But that, of course, was the whole idea.

In the team's day suite, Zambendorf was pacing restlessly back and forth while Otto Abaquaan and Joe Fellburg pored over the latest Terran–Taloid transcripts from the duplicate transmogrifier concealed in Arthur's meeting room. The device Zambendorf had donated to the

Taloids before returning to the *Orion* was a joint effort—constructed by Joe Fellburg with the aid of assembly diagrams and programs donated by Leon Keyhoe, parts supplied by Dave Crookes, and a terminal assembly stolen by Abaquaan from the *Orion*'s electronics stores. It not only provided printouts of the screens that had been presented to Giraud's linguists, but also a complete audio record of the comments exchanged between the Terran politicans by radio.

"The main problem with today's high-technology society is that we allow politicians to run it instead of people equipped with the wherewithal to understand it," Zambendorf muttered irritably. "Their mentalities are still in the nineteenth century. How can they hope to manage complex economies when they're not competent to run a yard-sale. What can they do that requires even a smattering of knowledge or intellect?"

Drew West shrugged from a corner. "People let them get away with it," he said. "If people are gonna elect turkeys to tell them what to do, then the people are gonna have problems. You can't blame the turkeys. The Constitution never guaranteed smart government; it guaranteed representative government. And it works—that's what we've got."

"The trouble with the damn system is that it selects for the skills needed to get elected, and nothing else . . . which requires only an ability to fool a sufficient number of people for just long enough to get the votes," Zambendorf grumbled. "Unfortunately the personal qualities necessary for attaining office are practically the opposite of those demanded by the office itself. A test that you can only pass by cheating can't possibly select honest people, can it? You'd think that would be obvious enough, Drew, and yet—"

"Call coming in from Camelot now," Abaquaan said over his shoulder as Fellburg reached out to the touch-panel of the communications terminal beside them.

"It's Galileo, with Arthur and a few of the others," Fellburg said. Zambendorf stopped speaking and moved forward to see, while behind him West stood and crossed the room.

Thirg had become accustomed to the sight of Lumians without their outer casings by now. How they stayed together at all and kept their shape was mystery enough, never mind how they managed to move around. Apparently they contained a second, "internal casing" of some kind, though how a casing could be inside that which it encased, Thirg had no idea. Perhaps it was like the strengthening bars that builders and other artisans fashioned into their organic creations. Dark-Headed-One was looking into the magic eye, with the Wearer and Smooth-Faced-One visible a short distance behind. After a short exchange of greetings, Thirg began the tedious process of communicating the questions and concerns that the latest meeting with the Merchant-Lumians had prompted.

Zambendorf's mood became somber while he listened to Abaquaan's commentary as the message slowly emerged. "They did as we told them and didn't make any concessions," Abaquaan announced. "It's looking very much the way we figured—Giraud and his people are trying to talk them into getting lots of organized production going down there for Earth's benefit. They're trying to set up a colony, Karl. GSEC and the government must be in on it too. Galileo says Arthur's asking for a confirmation that he's doing the right thing and that we'll make sure everything turns out okay."

"They're saying they still think we're straight, but I guess they need reassuring," Fellburg said.

Zambendorf stared at the outlandish metal faces peering back at him from inside an ice vault thousands of miles away. Was it just his imagination, or could he read the trust and the pleading not to be let down that was written across those strange, immobile countenances? For some reason his determination not to let them down was stronger than had ever been evoked by people. He sensed too that the others in the team felt the same way. Though none of them had mentioned it directly because there was no need to, they all sensed it. Whatever it was that had brought such an odd assortment of individuals together had responded as a common chord in all of them.

"All I can say for now is to tell them to have faith and believe in us," Zambendorf said. "The time is not ripe yet for us to do anything." Exactly what he could do, he had no idea; for once in his life he was at a loss to come up with anything more constructive.

Fellburg talked to the terminal and juggled with the screen for a while. "Galileo thinks you sound too much like a priest," Abaquaan told Zambendorf.

Zambendorf smiled faintly. If the Taloids could crack jokes, they'd be okay. "Tell them they are not second-class citizens, Joe," he said. "They should be proud of what they are, believe in themselves, and trade with Terrans only as equal partners."

"Galileo's asking who's kidding who," Fellburg said, looking at the screen. "They want to know how they're supposed to come across as the equals of guys who can work miracles."

"We are not gods. They must have confidence that they can learn," Zambendorf told him.

"We can teach them to work miracles too?" Fellburg interpreted as the screen delivered the reply.

"There isn't any such thing as a miracle," Zambendorf said. "When you know how to work a miracle, it ceases to be one. Miracles exist only in the minds of those who believe in them."

"Galileo wants to know how the hell you know."

"Oh," Zambendorf said. "You can assure him that I'm an expert on miracles."

24

THE POLICY DIRECTIVE FROM EARTH STATED IN EFFECT that the Genoese were asking for a welfare aid program to be initiated and sustained from a distance of nearly a billion miles away, which would bankrupt the Western world even if it were acceptable on principle. The suggestion was completely impractical as well as being unthinkable ideologically. Giraud and Lang returned to their negotiations and spent several more long, arduous sessions explaining to Arthur and his colleagues that the Taloids would have to start thinking from the outset in terms of paying their way and earning the benefits they hoped to get.

Kleippur's understanding was that if the robeings cooperated, followed Lumian orders, and worked hard at taming the forests to produce the kinds of things that were evidently valued highly on Lumia, eventually they would acquire understanding. But, naturally, the benefits to the robeings could not be expected to materialize instantly—the Lumians had taken a long time to reach their current state of knowledge from a level comparable to Robia's. To Kleippur, the promise of salvation in the hereafter in return for patience, obedience, diligence, and sacrifice in the herenow sounded suspiciously familiar. Little further progress was made, and Kleippur began to feel that the Lumians were growing impatient.

Then Lyokanor, the chief of Carthogian intelligence,

reported that Skerilliane, the Kroaxian spy, had reentered Carthogia in the company of a one-armed robeing tentatively identified as Horazzorgio, previously presumed killed in the Meracasine. Curious as to Kroaxian intentions, Kleippur ordered the pair to be watched but left unmolested. Unfortunately, the small group of soldiers shadowing them from the border lost contact when it was attacked by Waskorians. Later, Skerilliane was seen in the outskirts of Menassim not far from the Lumian dragon-camp, and again a short while afterward with a party of Lumians out in the forest. Before the Carthogians could do anything to prevent it, the two Kroaxians were seen being brought back to the camp by Lumian vehicles and admitted inside. The breakdown in surveillance over the spies at such a critical moment was galling, but nothing could be done about it. In an effort to keep himself aware as much as possible of what was taking place, Kleippur informed the Wearer of what had happened, at the same time describing the differences between Kroaxia and Carthogia, and explaining the recent history of the two states.

Zambendorf wondered why nothing was being said officially about the contact that had been made with the two Taloids—dubbed James Bond and Lord Nelson by the Terrans, the team discovered—who had appeared from Genoa's enemy state, Padua. Then Joe Fellburg learned from Dave Crookes that their aid was being enlisted at Genoa Base to program the transmogrifier to respond to the Paduan version of Taloid speech as well as Genoese. A junior clerk on Giraud's staff confided to Abaquaan that plans were being made to suspend the discussions in Genoa, and that the political deputation was to descend to another part of the surface. The clerk didn't know the exact location of the proposed landing site, but Thelma found out from her dashing NASO captain that Bond and Nelson were to be flown secretly to somewhere near another Taloid city just under three hundred miles across the desert from Genoa, and sent to alert their rulers to the Terran presence. Arthur and Leonardo, who seemed to be the Genoese mapmaking and geographic expert, confirmed via Zambendorf's private line to Camelot that the city was Padua. Presumably, therefore, whatever had transpired between Giraud & Co. and the two Paduans had proved sufficiently interesting for Giraud to break off his negotiations with Arthur and begin again elsewhere.

Giraud and the diplomats made three visits to Padua, landing each time at a remote spot to which the Paduan leaders traveled overland, presumably to keep the fact of the meetings secret from the general Paduan populace. At the same time no public announcement of these developments was made aboard the *Orion*; the bulletins and news updates continued to focus on the activities of the scientific teams in and around Genoa, who were left to carry on their work with no indication being given that the political leadership had, at least temporarily, pulled out.

Zambendorf honored his promise to keep Arthur fully informed despite the further misgivings that the news he reported was bound to arouse among the Genoese. He wondered if he did it in a subconscious attempt to compensate for his inability to do anything else. Zambendorf was discovering that it was important to him to be able to show the Taloids something that might reassure them that their hopes and expectations of him were not misplaced. For the first time in his life he felt concerned that the powers which others attributed to him didn't exist; and what was so ironic was that, for the first time, those powers should be neither supernatural nor superhuman. Though he continued to display confidence and staunch optimism in the presence of the team, inwardly he had never felt so helpless and frustrated.

Then he received a summons to meet with Leaherney, Giraud, and Caspar Lang in Globe I. His cooperation in treating the subject as confidential would be appreciated, the message said—evidently Lang was learning at last that ordering Zambendorf to do anything wasn't the best way to get results. Accordingly, Zambendorf reciprocated by keeping the matter to himself.

* * *

"We've decided to fill you in on some developments that happened only recently," Daniel Leaherney said, stirring his coffee while seated in the private lounge adjoining the executive offices. "The fact is we found the Genoese to be obstinate and uncooperative, and suspended negotiations with them some time ago. We're exploring an alternative relationship with the Paduans, which is showing more promise."

"Hmm. I see . . ." Zambendorf grunted noncommittally on the opposite side of the table, not seeing at all. He sipped from his own cup and looked up at Leaherney's solid, heavy-jowled face topped by steely gray, straight-combed hair. Since liftout from Earth orbit Leaherney had tended to avoid Zambendorf, leaving it to his subordinates, usually Caspar Lang, to handle communications; his sudden call for a face-to-face meeting, especially over a subject considered too sensitive to be made public knowledge, could only mean that he needed Zambendorf for something. None of the possibilities that had occurred to Zambendorf as to what that something might be had left him feeling particularly convinced, and his responses so far had been guarded but curious.

"The Paduan outlook is more practical and takes better account of immediate realities," Leaherney said in answer to the unvoiced question written across Zambendorf's face. "The problem with the Genoese is that they insist on clinging to a totally unrealistic ideology which not only impedes their own chances of making any meaningful progress in the long term, but also is incompatible with our own policies and interests."

In other words the Paduans might be persuaded to accept the deal that he had told Arthur to reject, Zambendorf thought to himself. He already knew from his conversations with Arthur and Galileo that the Terran goal was to recruit Taloid assistance in bringing portions of Titan's phenomenal industrial potential under directed control, and turning the moon into an organized mass-production facility capable of supplying Earth's needs on a scale that would dwarf the existing capacity of all its nations put together. Needless to say, whoever controlled such an operation would be worth billions and might well come to command incontestable political power on a truly global scale for the first time in history. But Zambendorf still couldn't see where *he* fitted into it all. He shifted his eyes to Giraud, who had been the spokesman in the recent talks with the Paduans, as he had been earlier with Arthur and the Genoese.

Giraud, fair-skinned, with a high, rounded forehead, wide blue-gray eyes, and hair that was receding in the center and thinning on top, glanced at Leaherney for a moment, then said, "Paduan society seems to be dominated by religious dogma and beliefs to a far greater degree than the Genoese. At least, that's the way it looks right now."

"By mystical notions of some kind, anyway," Zambendorf suggested. He had formed a similar impression of the Paduans from his conversations with Galileo. "Any interpretations we make at this stage are bound to contain a strong subjective element."

"Well, whatever," Giraud said. "But using the analogy for now, power within the Paduan state seems to be divided between the clergy and a secular nobility. Our contact has been with the leading figure of the latter group—the king, if you will. We've named him Henry. He'd give a lot to be able to ditch the priests and run the state his own way."

Zambendorf nodded slowly to himself as the first of the pieces fit together. Henry no doubt commanded large segments of the Taloid labor force that the Terrans wanted access to. "But the priests aren't going to go away so easily," Zambendorf guessed.

Giraud nodded. "They have a strong traditional hold over the population and can mobilize widespread support by playing on insecurities, fears, superstitions—all the usual things. They're not a force to be trifled with."

"So what's the plan—to help Henry rid himself of the priests in return for plenty of Taloids to work the plantations?" Zambendorf asked, stopping just short of injecting an open sneer into his voice. Giraud hesitated. Zambendorf shifted his gaze back to Leaherney.

Leaherney ran the tip of his tongue along his upper lip and frowned for a moment. "Shall we say, to assist in bringing about the replacement of the existing form of priesthood by an alternative system that Henry would have greater control over," he replied. "It would probably be a mistake to demolish the clergy completely. After all, it does have considerable merit as an established instrument of social control."

"Er, I think Dan means as a temporary mechanism to preserve social order during the transition period to a more modern form of state," Giraud interjected hastily.

"Of course," Leaherney said.

Now Zambendorf was beginning to see where somebody like himself would fit in. "Does Henry have anyone in particular in mind to head up this new, tame priesthood that he wants to install?" he inquired.

Giraud nodded. "But not anyone we've met. We haven't talked to any of the priests—only to Henry and some of his guys."

"Hmm . . . It wouldn't be the present High Priest, Bishop, Magician, or whatever's equivalent," Zambendorf said. "If someone like that stands to get demoted in a big way, the last thing Henry would want is to leave him with any power to do something about the grudge. Henry's best bet would be to get rid of him completely and replace him with someone from the lower ranks—someone who'd feel insecure after a big promotion and would always be Henry's man. But Henry sounds enough of a Machiavelli to know about things like that."

"That's Henry's problem," Giraud said. "All we know is that he's got someone lined up. We call him Rasputin."

Zambendorf leaned back in his chair, steepled his fingers below his chin, and moved his eyes slowly from one to another of the three faces around him. "And of course, this Rasputin would have to pull off some pretty spectacular stunts to stand a chance of discrediting the present chief miracle-worker and taking over the job, wouldn't he," he said, making his voice casual. "He'd have to be convincing enough not only to impress the average Taloid-in-the-street, but also to convert enough of the priests over to his side too. Now, I wonder who'd be a good person to ask if you wanted to help someone work a few of the kinds of miracles that might do all that."

Caspar Lang, who had been listening silently for some time, fidgeted in his chair and looked impatient. He was tiring of Zambendorf's roundabout way of talking, a method Zambendorf employed to give himself time to think. Now Zambendorf was going to launch into more of it by asking why he should be interested and what was in it for him. Then Giraud would get into his negotiating stride and start to spell out all the angles and benefits. Lang could see it coming. He didn't want to hear it all.

"Look," he said, raising his face toward Zambendorf. "You're a good deceptionist and a top con artist—maybe the best in the business..." He lifted a hand to forestall any objection that Zambendorf might have been about to make. "Let's not go off into any of that stuff about whether you're genuine or not. What we're talking about now is serious, okay..." Lang paused for a second, then continued. "Ever since you first appeared in Europe, you've been moving in one direction—upward, toward becoming the biggest of the big-time operators ever—bigger sensations, bigger crowds, bigger fame, bigger money. That's always been the ambition." Lang spread his hands briefly. "You're smart enough to have figured out for yourself that this whole business at Titan could mean—if it's handled properly—the end of the Soviet empire and a return of Western industry and commerce to a position of undisputed worldwide leadership, which means a lot of people would stand to get very rich. What's in it for you, Zambendorf, is that you can reserve yourself a place in the club—a very special club. Whatever you were aiming at before in life doesn't matter anymore. This is it—the bonanza; the real big time."

"And how about the rest of the Taloids?" Zambendorf asked. "What happens to them in all this?"

Giraud frowned and looked surprised. "Their situation would be no different from what it's always been . . ."

"Exploited by their own leaders," Zambendorf supplied. "Serfs in a feudal order that gives them no opportunity for development. Kept in ignorance deliberately and fed superstition because education would be incompatible with unquestioning obedience and the domination by fear upon which the system depends. Is that what you wish to perpetuate?"

"What kind of talk is this?" Leaherney asked, sounding irritable suddenly. "Hell, they're only machines after all. You're making them sound almost human."

Zambendorf stared down at his cup for a long time. That was the whole point—the Taloids were human. He didn't quite know how, but he could sense it every time he talked with them. The phrases that appeared on the transmogrifier screen might have been crude and semicoherent, but that was a reflection of a restricted communications medium, not of the beings at whom the communications were directed. The clumsy strings of words did not, and could not, convey the richness and depth of qualities, meanings, feelings, and perceptions which Zambendorf somehow knew formed the Taloid world as seen through Taloid eyes any more than they could the human world as seen through human eyes. Both worlds were illusions created from the raw material of photons, pressure waves, and other forms of primary sensory stimuli, which were processed into abstract symbols and assembled via two forms of nervous system, one biochemical, the other holotronic, into consciously experienced interactions of people, places, and things. As external realities, the people, the places, and the things existed only as bare frameworks onto which minds projected covering, form, warmth, color, and other attributes which the minds themselves created; thus each mind manufactured its own illusory world upon a minimum of shared reality to conform to its own set of culturally defined expectations, and in such a way as to appear satisfyingly real in total to its creator. Zambendorf, the illusionist, could understand it all clearly. But, he could see just as clearly, he would never be able to convey what he understood to the three men sitting with him in the executive lounge of the *Orion*. "Suppose I decide I don't want to get involved with it," he said at last, looking up at them. "Then what?"

"Is that a decision?" Leaherney asked him.

"No. I'm just curious."

Lang answered. "We'd manage anyhow, either with your cooperation or without it. But from your point of view it wouldn't be too smart. The people who sent you all this way at considerable expense would be pretty upset about it. And they do have a lot of influence with the media..." Lang shook his head slowly and clicked his tongue. "You could find it's the end of the road for you, old buddy. And that'd be a shame, wouldn't it?"

25

GOYDEROOCH, HEADROBEING OF THE VILLAGE OF Xerxeon, stood with Casquedin, the village prayer and beseecher, in front of a huddle of elders and watched apprehensively as the column of royal cavalry filed slowly into the square. The soldiers and their mounts were covered with dust and looked as if they had ridden from Pergassos without stopping, which indicated that their mission was urgent. The colors carried by the pennant-bearer were those of the captain, Horazzorgio, who had passed through Xerxeon over five brights previously in pursuit of Dornvald the outlaw, Bringer-of-Sky-Dragons. Horazzorgio was missing an arm and had one eye covered, Goyderooch saw as the lead riders crossed the square and drew up before him. His synchronizing oscillator missed a pulse. Perhaps Dornvald's small band had been the bait to lure the King's soldiers into ambush by a larger force out in the Meracasine. If so, had Horazzorgio interpreted Goyderooch's readiness to indicate the direction taken by the outlaws as proof of the village's complicity in the plot and returned now to deliver his retribution? The fear that Goyderooch sensed from behind told him that the thoughts were not his alone.

"May the Lifemaker protect the King," Horazzorgio pronounced.

"Let it be so," the villagers returned dutifully.

"We are truly honored to welcome the King's Guards

to our humble village," Goyderooch said, extending his arms palms-upward. "Whatever services it is within our power to render shall be thine. Thou hast but to name thy need and utter thy request."

Horazzorgio cast his eye over them with contempt. "Yes," he said menacingly. "You would do well to remember me with respect, farmers. With great pleasure would I repay the debt that I owe the village of Xerxeon."

"A twelvefold curse upon Dornvald, the betrayer!" Goyderooch exclaimed, trembling. "Truly were we deceived by his cunning. Oh, had we but known of the fate that awaited thee! Believest thou not that we would have warned thee?"

"Pah! Enough sniveling," Horazzorgio snorted. "Do you dream for one moment that Dornvald's rabble of tinplate riveters would be match for a King's troop? These afflictions that you see were not the work of any mere robeing."

"Then what manner of—"

"The sky demons that appeared over Xerxeon," Horazzorgio said. "They are congregating in Carthogia, whither they come to aid Kleippur, servant of the Dark Master." Eskenderom, the Kroaxian King, did not want it made known to his people that he was treating with the luminous liquid creatures who had come from beyond the sky. It was important that the mystic whom Eskenderom intended to install as High Priest in place of Frennelech—and whom the soldiers had been sent to Xerxeon to find and take back to Pergassos—should be accepted unquestioningly as being possessed of genuinely wondrous powers.

"Thou hast not come hither to wreak thy vengeance upon helpless villagers?" Goyderooch inquired cautiously.

"We are here by the direct bidding of the King," Horazzorgio told him. "'Tis well for you that I heed first my loyalty to His Majesty, and second my private inclinations. There is one, a holy man from Pergassos, who was also at this place five brights since—the brother of Thirg, Asker-of-Questions."

"Thou speakest of Groork, the hearer, who came hither to commune with the Great Wilderness and prepare himself spiritually for the time of great works which is written as his destiny to perform for the greater glory of the Lifemaker," Casquedin said from beside Goyderooch.

"The same," Horazzorgio said. "His destiny has arrived, it appears. We are to conduct him back to Kroaxia, to the palace of Eskenderom, where omens have been witnessed of great things that shall come to pass."

Goyderooch dispatched Casquedin with the news to the house of Meerkulla, Tamer-of-Endcase-Drillers, on the edge of the village, where Groork was lodging. Casquedin returned alone a few minutes later. "Meerkulla asks forgiveness, but says that the hearer is locked in his cell and attending to his sacred devotions," he reported. "To intrude would constitute sinfulness of the gravest kind."

"But this is the King's command!" Goyderooch blustered. "Return at once to Meerkulla and tell him that—"

Horazzorgio raised a hand wearily. "Our need for haste is not so pressing as that, Headrobeing, for we have ridden without respite from Pergassos. We shall not depart until we have rested a while and partaken of refreshment and charge. So prepare a repast of your finest lube and filter stations, and leave the hearer to complete his meditations."

In the room that he had been given for his own use at the rear of Meerkulla's house, Groork was frantically bundling his belongings into the frame-backed sack that he used when traveling. Horazzorgio could have come for only two reasons: Either Eskenderom had not forgotten his scheme for removing Frennelech, the High Priest, and establishing a new priesthood under Groork, or Horazzorgio wished to settle a personal score over Groork's having warned Thirg when the writ had been issued for the latter's arrest. Either way Groork wasn't interested in staying around to talk about it, and had received a sudden revelation that the Lifemaker's plans required him to be the chosen instrument of other designs destined to unfold at another place to which the greater powers would in due course guide him.

After checking the room a last time to make sure he hadn't missed anything, he pushed open the window, poked his head out, and looked first one way, then the other. No one was in sight. He heaved his pack over the ledge, picked up his staff, and climbed outside. One of Meerkulla's steeds was tethered at the rear of the house, grazing on slow charge from a domesticated forest transformer and not yet unsaddled. Groork looked at it thoughtfully as he lifted his pack onto his back, and then glanced from side to side and back over his shoulder. Had the animal been left as a temptation to test his honesty at a time of stress, or was it a gift from the Lifemaker to ensure Groork's preservation for greater things? And then, as he stood waiting for inspiration, he heard in his head the first whisperings of a message from the voices that had begun speaking from the sky of late.

In a control room inside the *Orion*, a computer display changed to read:

> ORBITER FOUR MAPPING RADAR—COARSE SCAN 23-B37 COMPLETE ON SECTOR 19H. COMMENCING HIGH RESOLUTION SCAN, SUBSECTORS 19–22 THROUGH 19–38. MODE 7. FRAME 5. SWEEP PARAMETERS: 03, 12, 08, 23, 00, 00, 42.

Groork turned his face upward and gazed rapturously at the heavens as the meaning of the voices became plain in his mind. "Thy work in Kroaxia is ended, Groork," they sang. "Take thee forth from this place now, for thy path lies across the Wilderness and unto the lands of Carthogia.

"Am I, then, to find the Waskorians and join them in their struggle to preserve the true faith in the face of the barbarism wrought upon Carthogia by Kleippur, who serves the Dark Master?" Groork asked himself. "Indeed the ways of the Lifemaker are truly wise and all-seeing, for in that way also shall I find again my lost brother and return his soul yet to the way of righteousness." He looked again at Meerkulla's mount. "Could a mere robeing such as I presume to argue with the will of Him who sends thee as His gift to carry me across the Meracasine?" He unplugged the animals' cord and swung himself up onto the creature's back. "The Lifemaker gave, and the Lifemaker has taken away," he told the back of Meerkulla's house as he began moving off. Then he stopped and stared uncomfortably for a few seconds at the dwelling of the one who had given him shelter and hospitality. Slowly and deliberately he raised his arm and made the motions in the air which would confer blessings upon Meerkulla, his family, his descendants, his crops, and his animals for many twelve-brights to come. "There, my friend, now thou hast more than just compensation." Groork murmured. Feeling better, he turned his mount about again and slipped quietly out of the village.

26

"YOU CAN'T DO IT," MASSEY SAID, SHAKING HIS HEAD as he turned restlessly on his feet between the bunks in his cabin in Globe II. He sounded as near to angry as Zambendorf had ever heard him. "The Taloids aren't some race of natural inferiors put there to do all the work for free. It's taken us centuries to get over the consequences of trying to treat groups of our own kind that way back on Earth. Those days are over now. We can't go back to them. It would be a catastrophe."

"Any forms of life that have evolved intelligence and begun lifting themselves above the animal level possess something in common that makes accidental differences in biological hardware trivial by comparison," Vernon Price said earnestly from the edge of one of the lower bunks. "The word *human* has a broader definition now. It describes a whole evolutionary phase, not just one species that happens to have entered it."

They had the cabin to themselves as Graham Spearman was busy in one of the labs, and Malcom Wade, its fourth occupant, was busy running elaborate statistical analyses and cross-correlations on reams of worthless data that he and Periera had been avidly collecting from faked ESP tests. Zambendorf, who was sitting on a fold-out chair in the narrow space by the door, looked from Massey to Price and back again in bewilderment. Somehow they had gotten the idea into their heads that he had not only allowed himself to be brought into the plot to turn the Taloids into serfs, but that he had done so with enthusiasm, and they were very distressed about it. So was Zambendorf—to find himself accused of being a willing accomplice in the very thing that had been causing him so much concern.

"Okay, I know how you feel about a lot of today's people," Massey said, tossing out his hands. "They've grown up in the twenty-first century, surrounded by better opportunities for learning and education than anybody else in history, and if they're too dumb to take advantage of what they've got, it's not your problem. They had their choice. I might not share your view, but I can see your point." He waved a hand in front of his face. "But keeping the Taloids in a state of deliberately imposed backwardness is different. They never had any opportunity to know better. They don't have the same choice. That's all I'm saying."

Zambendorf blinked up at him and shook his head. "But—" he began.

"You must see that it's the beginning of the same line that's been used to keep wealthy minorities in power and the people in their place all down through the ages," Vernon Price said. "Real knowledge is strictly for the elites; the masses are fobbed off with superstition, nonsense, and hopes for a better tomorrow. New technologies and anything that might lead toward genuine mass education and prosperity are to be opposed. I know how you've made your living up until now, but as Gerry says, at least those suckers had a choice and should have known better. But with the Taloids it would be pure exploitation. You can't do it."

"FOR CHRIST'S SAKE!" Zambendorf exploded suddenly. The cabin became instantly quiet. He gave a satisfied nod. "Thank you. Look, doesn't it occur to either of you that I just mightn't have the faintest idea what in hell you're talking about?"

"Oh, come on, don't give us that," Massey said impatiently. "It's the real reason you were sent all the way to Titan. Who do you think you're trying to fool now? It's obvious."

"What *is* the real reason I was sent all the way to Titan?" Zambendorf asked, more baffled than ever but genuinely curious.

"Because a big-name cult leader like you can influence a lot of public thinking," Price said. "You're GSEC's lever into the congressional policymaking machine." Zambendorf shook his head and looked back at Massey.

Massey frowned down at him but seemed less sure of himself. "That's why our society tolerates so many zany cults and crackpot religions, isn't it," he said.

"Why?" Zambendorf asked.

"A politician can net a lot of votes for a small amount of effort by saying nice things about a guru who's got ten thousand disciples so brainwashed that they'll do anything he tells them," Massey said. "Or at least, if he's smart he doesn't say anything that might get them upset about him. So the guys who run the cults continue to get away with murder, and nobody bothers them very much. The business they're really in is selling blocks of controlled votes and molded public opinion in return for political favors and protection." He gave Zambendorf a long, penetrating look, as if to say that none of this should need spelling out, and then moved around the end of the bunks to pour himself coffee from the pot by the sink.

Vernon Price completed what Massey had been saying. "To a lot of very influential people, the political and economic implications of Titan's being up for grabs must add up to a crucial situation, which they knew long before the mission left Earth . . ." He spread his hands briefly. "And we all know that such people can make very attractive offers when it suits them."

"You think that I knew what the mission's purpose was all along?" Zambendorf said.

"You certainly seemed to know about Titan long before most of us did," Massey said. He stared down over the rim of his cup. "What was the deal—unlimited media hype and complete suppression of all competent reporting to make you the superstar of the century?" His voice conveyed disappointment rather than contempt. "Or was it the other way round—threats . . . everything over for you if you refused to go along with them? But that was a long time ago now, from a much narrower perspective—before we left Earth and before anyone knew what we all know now. All I'm asking you to do is see the big picture and think about the real implications."

Zambendorf brought his hand up to his face and stared down at the floor in silence for a while. Then at last he emitted a long, weary sigh and looked up between his fingers. "Look," he said. "I've got a feeling I'm wasting my breath saying this, but I didn't know any more about where this ship was going than you did, until after we embarked in orbit. What I did find out, I found out myself by my own methods. When I agreed to come on this mission, I thought we were going to Mars. I accepted the usual kind of publicity deal, sure, but as far as I was concerned it was to do with the kind of stunt GSEC had been talking about sponsoring on Mars—not anything serious. I didn't know anything about any aliens, or any of the things you've been talking about." He stood up and moved past Massey to help himself to coffee.

Massey glanced questioningly back at Price while Zambendorf was filling his cup. Price could only return a helpless shrug. "It's strange," Massey said to Zambendorf. He paused and tilted his head curiously to one side. "For once I get the feeling that you're telling the truth. Either you're the most accomplished liar I've ever met—and I've met more than a few—or there's something very screwy going on. I'd like to believe what you just told us."

Zambendorf tired suddenly of the feeling of being scrutinized under a microscope. "Well, why won't you believe it, then?" he demanded loudly, turning away and sounding annoyed. "What reason would I have to lie about something like this? If you must know, I was offered such a deal only recently. I turned it down. There, does that satisfy you?"

"You turned it down," Massey repeated, not quite able

to prevent a trace of mockery from creeping into his voice.

Zambendorf wheeled back again. "I turned it down." He forced the words out slowly and deliberately, thrusting out his beard to within an inch of Massey's face.

"Very likely the best offer you've ever had in your life, and maybe the best you'll ever get," Price drawled sarcastically from behind them. "With everything going for it, and all the right people lined up on your side . . . and you turned it down. Now, why would you want to do a thing like that?"

"My reasons are my reasons," Zambendorf said. "What damn business is it of either of you?"

"When you're helping people who are trying to condemn a whole race to second-class status to further their own interests and claiming that they're acting in my name, it is my business," Massey retorted.

Zambendorf colored visibly. "For God's sake, I haven't done anything to help them!" he shouted. "I turned their offer down. How many times do I have to say it? What's the matter with the pair of you?"

"Why would you turn it down?" Massey asked again.

"What is this? I refuse to be cross-examined in this fashion."

"Bah! . . . just as I thought," Massey snorted.

"He's copping out," Price murmured. "He has to. He's in with them up to his neck."

"Doesn't it occur to you that you may not have a monopoly on all this touching humanitarian concern for your brother beings?" Zambendorf raged. "If you must know, I turned it down for the simple reason that I care what happens to the Taloids just as much as you do . . . even more, possibly. Do you understand that? Is it plain enough to get through your thick skulls?" He glowered at Massey defiantly, then shifted his gaze to Price for a moment. When he resumed speaking, his voice quivered with emotion. "I probably know them better than any other person on this mission. Wasn't it I who exchanged the first meaningful information with them? Didn't they continue to come to me for confirmation even after they'd been told repeatedly that Giraud and those walking procedure manuals that he calls aides were the mission's official spokesmen? . . . Don't ask me how, but I can sense the Taloid world that lies behind the words we see on screens, and those unmoving metal faces."

Zambendorf's manner calmed a little. "There is a world there, you know—not a world that we are able to experience directly, or even one that we're capable of conceiving, maybe . . . but it's there—as warm, and as rich, and as colorful when perceived through Taloid senses as Earth is to us. I can feel it when I talk to them." The other two listened silently as he went on, now in a distant voice, "The Taloids know I can too. That's why they trust me. They trust me to teach them about the worlds that exist beyond their sky, and the new worlds of mind that exist beyond the clouds obscuring their present horizons of knowledge. They trust me to show them the ways of discovery that will enable them to explore all those worlds. That's more than all those fools back on Earth ever asked for, or understood that I could have done for them." His expression became contemptuous. "And you think I would have traded *that* for anything a bunch of deadhead executives and bureaucrats might have to offer—people who've never in their lives had an inspired thought or a vision of what could be?" Zambendorf focused his gaze back on Massey and Price, and shook his head. "No, don't you go preaching at me about the meaning of the word *human*, the insignificance of accidental differences in biological hardware, or any of that crap. Because I could give both of you a whole lesson on it."

The cabin remained very quiet for what seemed a long time. Massey drank the last of his coffee, then looked across at Price with his eyebrows raised questioningly. Price looked uncomfortable and said nothing. "I, er . . . I guess we owe you an apology," Massey murmured.

Zambendorf nodded curtly and left it at that. He looked at Massey curiously. "You still haven't explained what made you think I'd accepted a deal," he said.

Massey looked over at Price again. Price made a face

and shrugged. "I guess he's got a right to know," he said. Zambendorf frowned uncomprehendingly.

Massey drew a long breath, held it for a second or two, then exhaled abruptly and nodded his agreement. "Set it up, Vernon." Massey turned to Zambendorf. "Obviously what you're about to see is not intended to become public knowledge. I don't know if you're aware that the news from Earth is censored before it's broadcast around the *Orion*. In particular, a lot of what goes out across the Earth newsgrid is omitted from what's shown here. However, that was anticipated before we left Earth and arrangements were made for me to have a private channel direct into NASO."

Zambendorf watched as Price unlocked a storage locker in the wall and took out a small metal strongbox which in turn yielded a collection of video cartridges. Price selected one of the cartridges and walked over to the cabin's terminal to insert it, at the same time switching the terminal to off-line local mode. Whatever was stored in the cartridges evidently was too sensitive to be entrusted to the ship's databank. Zambendorf gave Massey a puzzled look. "If you were told we were going to Mars too, why would anyone give you a private information line?" he asked. "Why would you be supposed to need one?"

Massey smiled faintly. "I didn't know I had one until a timelocked message from the databank told me about it after we'd left Earth. I guess you weren't the only one who didn't find out what he was really here for until a while after you'd signed up."

"You mean you weren't sent to monitor the ESP experiments on Mars?" Zambendorf said, surprised.

"No more than you were sent to conduct them."

"So . . . what were you sent for?"

"I very much suspect that we're just beginning to find out."

The terminal screen came to life to show a man with a red, gnomish face topped by a mat of white, close-cropped hair saying something that was inaudible since the sound was still turned down. Zambendorf stared hard for a moment, then said, "Isn't that Conlon from NASO?"

Massey raised an eyebrow in surprise. "You know him?"

"I know his face."

"How come?"

"I make it my business to know lots of things."

The view on the screen changed to a picture of Saturn with the words TITAN MISSION superposed in large letters along with the GCN logo; then followed a shot of the *Orion* in orbit against a background of part of Titan's disk. Evidently the footage was a replay of a routine newscast from Earth. A woman's voice faded in as Price turned up the sound, and the picture changed again, this time to a view of an area of cluttered machinery and scrap piled just outside Genoa Base.

". . . said that there might be a possibility of salvaging something useful from the remnants of the defunct alien civilization discovered on Titan, but most of it must be considered a total write-off. In any case, the cost of attempting a full-scale cleanup operation from Earth would more than offset any benefits that could conceivably be obtained." A good-looking, auburn-haired, smartly dressed woman, probably in her midforties appeared, sitting at a desk facing the camera. She smiled out at the viewers as she turned a sheet of paper in front of her. "A disappointment, I'm afraid, for those people who have been hoping for a new Industrial Revolution that would change the lives of all of us here on Earth. But it's still the biggest junkpile in the known universe, I'm told. So who knows—it could turn out to be good news yet for all you scrap-metal dealers. Better start submitting your bids. You'll probably have to add a reserve tank to your pickup though."

Zambendorf turned a stunned face toward Massey and shook his head disbelievingly. Massey nodded for him to keep watching.

The newscaster looked down and scanned quickly over the next sheet. "More news about the Taloids—the man-size, walking maintenance robots that have been catching a lot of people's imagination. They see a composite image made up of electronically intensified optical wavelengths—in other words ordinary visible light highly amplified—and infrared wavelengths, or heat, according to an MIT professor who has been studying reports from the *Orion*. The pit-viper and boid families of terrestrial snakes employ a similar system, apparently, but nothing as sensitive as the Taloid version. We'll be talking to Professor Morton Glassner to hear more about that in just a few minutes. . . .

"Another question that a lot of people have been asking is, Can the Taloids think?" The woman's face vanished and was replaced by a shot of two U.S. soldiers in EV suits facing a Taloid. Although the shot was from Genoa Base, nothing of the city was visible in the background; only a jumble of derelict machines was visible. The view gave the impression that the Taloid had just emerged from some habitat in a kind of jungle. One of the soldiers was offering something, then pulling it away as the Taloid reached for it—as if teasing a big metal bear—while the second soldier could be seen grinning through his faceplate. Zambendorf wondered how many hours of recordings this particular sequence had been selected from.

"Well, there's no getting away from the fact that they are extraordinary machines," the voiceover continued. "But then, wouldn't we expect to find at least a few cute tricks in machines left behind by an alien civilization that most of our scientists are convinced must have achieved interstellar travel? It all depends what you mean by think, says well-known philosopher and social scientist, Johnathan Goodmay, in an article in this month's issue of *Plato*. If you mean the ability to accept and process information, and manufacture self-improving rules for problem-solving based on that information, then the answer is yes, the Taloids can do that—but so can any of the so-called smart machine tools in a modern automobile factory, an editor–transcriber computer, or any reasonably proficient chess-playing program that learns. The difference is merely one of degree, according to Dr. Goodmay, and not anything fundamental. But if by think you mean the ability to imagine, create, aspire to greater things, see the world through emotion-tinted glasses, and all the other things we take for granted when we apply the word to people, then the answer is no way. People can externalize aspects of their own thinking and project them into Taloids in much the same way as children can convince themselves that the computers they talk to at home are really alive and understand what the kids are saying."

Before Zambendorf could recover from the shock of what he was hearing, the picture changed to show himself with Osmond Periera, walking along a corridor inside the *Orion* and disappearing through a doorway. He couldn't remember when the shot had been taken—it could have been from any time in the voyage. The commentary resumed, "Another person who's spending a lot of time looking for answers to the same question is Karl Zambendorf, seen here with Dr. Osmond Periera, the *Orion*'s principal investigator of the parapsychological sciences." Zambendorf choked over the mouthful of coffee he had been about to swallow; the screen showed him apparently discussing experimental procedures and nodding at Periera, who was holding a clipboard in front of panels of flashing lights and a computer console. The voice went on, "After the encouraging results of the experiments performed during the voyage and after arrival at Titan to assess the effectiveness of extrasensory communications away from the terrestrial environment, the Austrian psychic and other experts with the mission have been examining the possibility of probing whatever emergent Taloid psyche might exist by means of what are called psychodynamic sympathetic resonances, or what amounts to the same thing, mind reading." Now Zambendorf was being shown with a set of wires and electrodes taped around his forehead and temples, staring, with an expression of deep concentration, at a wall of equipment racks. That was an old shot from the early part of the voyage. It was a stunt he had pulled to demonstrate how he could alter the readings of a mass spectrometer by changing its magnetic field profile through mind power; in fact Thelma had simply kicked the leg of the table supporting the chart recorder and produced an abnormal trace at a moment when everybody's attention had been on Zambendorf. The view switched to one of a Taloid surrounded by electronics equipment and recorders, which Zambendorf recognized as part of Dave Crookes' setup for capturing Taloid speech and facial patterns at the first meeting in the desert. The two shots had been taken months apart, but the continuity of the TV presentation suggested they were closely connected parts of a single process.

"This is insane!" Zambendorf protested. "I don't know anything about this. I've never tried any mind reading of Taloids."

The commentary went on: "Preliminary results were negative, however. Zambendorf was unable to detect any trace of the energy patterns that characterize intelligent mental activity, a certain degree of which, he says, he has no trouble picking up even from higher animals such as primates, whales, and some species of monkeys, dogs, and cats."

"Lies! Lies! Lies!" Zambendorf shouted. "I said no such thing. They're more intelligent than that stupid woman!"

"But the scientists out at Titan are not about to give up yet. According to Dr. Periera, a whole new technique might have to be developed for tuning into holoptronic minds. In any case, even if everything does turn out to be the way it looks at present and there aren't any minds on Titan to tune into, nevertheless, Zambendorf thinks it might be possible to link human minds into Taloid sensory systems and use them as free-moving vehicles for remote perception." The newscaster lowered the sheet and concluded with another smile from the screen, "There, wouldn't that be great—send your own Taloid wherever you'd like to go, and see the world through its eyes. Maybe one day that will turn out to be the regular way of exploring the surface of Titan—without any need for a spacesuit . . . and maybe other places too. Who knows?

Whatever happens, I'm sure we're in for more exciting developments."

She set the paper aside. "And now, returning from Titan, we move to Sydney, Australia, where a young man by the name of Clive Drummond is planning to—" Price stopped the recording.

"There's more," Massey said. "But I think you get the gist of it."

Zambendorf was nonplussed as he stared at the blank screen. "How long has this kind of thing been happening?" he whispered.

"About three weeks," Massey told him. "Before that, the media hadn't started systematically developing any particular thematic image of the Taloids."

"So there's no question it's deliberate?"

"None."

"What about that man Conlon back at NASO, and whoever else he's working with?" Zambendorf asked. "If you've got a direct line, they must know that what the public is being told is garbage. You must have told them. . . . Can't they do anything?"

"They're trying," Massey said. He shrugged. "But you know how it is."

Zambendorf shook his head. "Leaherney, Lang, all of them . . . they knew. Even while they were talking about offers, they knew these distortions were being made. And even though there was no question that I'd have to find out sooner or later."

"Perhaps they were certain they'd be able to swing you round if they simply cranked their offer high enough," Price said. "That is pretty much the way they operate."

"It fits with the way they think," Massey agreed.

Zambendorf walked slowly between the two tiers of bunks and turned when he reached the far wall. "So what does all this mean?" he asked. "What's behind it all? Have you any theories about that?"

"Well, I don't know that it's anything especially new," Massey replied. "But the first step toward reducing a nation to colonial status in order to exploit it has always been to dehumanize its inhabitants in the eyes of your own people and—"

The call tone from Zambendorf's personal communicator interrupted. "Excuse me," he said, taking the unit from his pocket and activating it. The miniature screen showed the features of Otto Abaquaan, calling from the team's quarters. "Yes, Otto?" Zambendorf acknowledged. His choice of phrase indicated to Abaquaan that Zambendorf had company.

"Have you got a moment?" Abaquaan asked.

"Go ahead."

"Um, do you know where Joe is? Need to talk to him."

"I'm afraid not."

"Got any idea where he went?"

"Sorry."

"Oh, hell. Too bad, huh? Send him back if you see him. We need to talk to him. Is that okay?"

"I will if I see him."

"Okay."

Zambendorf frowned for a second. Abaquaan wasn't interested in locating Joe Fellburg. His utterances had been structured according to a magician's code in which the mood of each phrase—interrogative or indicative—along with its initial letter, conveyed an alphabetical character. What Zambendorf had read from it was CMLT URGNT, which he interpreted as "Camelot. Urgent." Abaquaan was telling him that something had come in over the line from Arthur, and it couldn't wait. Massey and Price were looking at each other suspiciously. They were magicians too.

Zambendorf stared from one to the other and bit his lip uncertainly. Were Massey and he on the same side now? Now that Massey had taken Zambendorf into his confidence, did he owe it to Massey to do likewise? His instincts were to cement the alliance, but a lifetime's experience urged caution.

And he saw that the same question was written across Massey's face. Their differences were trivial compared to the things they now knew they shared. Zambendorf had to give some tangible sign that he felt the same way. Zambendorf looked down at the screen of the communicator in his hand. "I'm with Gerry Massey and Vernon Price," he said. "A lot has happened that would make too long a story to go into now. But you can speak plainly, Otto. The team has just acquired two more members."

The surprise on Abaquaan's face lasted for just a fraction of a second. He was used to adapting to new situations quickly without having to ask questions. "We've had a call from Arthur and Galileo," he said. "It's bad news—real bad news."

Massey gasped disbelievingly. "Arthur—the Taloid? But how? Where did you—"

"Oh, we also have a private communication line that you don't know about," Zambendorf told him. He looked back at Abaquaan. "What's happened, Otto?"

"Those fundamentalist fanatics out in the hills—the ones that Arthur's soldiers are always having trouble with," Abaquaan said.

"The Druids. Yes, what about them?"

"They wiped out a whole Genoese patrol and then massacred a larger force that was sent after them," Abaquaan said. "Putting it mildly, Arthur's pretty upset."

Zambendorf looked puzzled. "That's terrible, Otto, and of course I sympathize . . . but why is it such serious news? How does it affect us?"

"Because of how they did it," Abaquaan replied. "They did it with Terran weapons. Someone has started shipping Terran weapons down to Henry and the Paduans, and the Paduans are passing them on to the Druids to stir up trouble in Genoa. Arthur says he's had enough of promises and words. He wants something he can defend himself with. If we can't deliver, he'll take the deal that Giraud's bunch has been pushing."

27

THE FEATURELESS RED-BROWN BALL OF TITAN GREW larger and flattened out into what looked like a solid desert surface from the twelve-man flyer *Hornet* skimming above the aerosol layer, where it had leveled out after its descent from orbit. Zambendorf, clad in a helmetless EV suit, was sitting in the rear cabin, brooding silently to himself over the latest events, while opposite him Vernon Price gazed spellbound through one of the side ports at the rainbow-banded orb of Saturn beyond Titan's rim, seemingly floating half-submerged in the immense plane of its ring system viewed almost edge-on.

Sgt. Michael O'Flynn had reacted with a singular display of imperturbability and composure when Zambendorf asked for his advice on the best way to go about stealing a vehicle to get down to the surface. "Now, they're not exactly the kind of thing you'd expect people to just walk away from and leave lying around for anyone to help themselves to," O'Flynn had said. "And besides, even if you did get your hands on one, there's nothing you could do with it. A surface lander needs a minimum crew of four, all highly trained, and it couldn't take off without a preflight preparation routine by a regular ground team."

"I'm not talking about a full-blown orbital shuttle, for God's sake," Zambendorf had replied. "But what about a medium-haul personnel flyer—one of the small ones?

Couldn't you pull one of those out of service and list it as being withdrawn for maintenance or something?"

"But those are just surface flyers. They don't make descents from orbit."

"They could here, at a pinch," Zambendorf had insisted. "With Titan's low gravity you could use one as a miniature lander . . . if you were to ignore certain sections of NASO flight regulations and allowed the International Space Transportation Regulatory Commission's safety margins for wing loading and thermal stress to slip a little."

"Hmm . . . you seem to know what you're talking about, I see. Now, where would somebody like you have found out about things like that, I'm sitting here asking meself."

"Never mind. The question is, can you do it, Mike?"

"Well, maybe I can, and then again, maybe I can't . . . But supposing for the moment that I could, it would have to be for the hardware only, you understand. I'm not in the headhunting business. You'd have to find your own pilot."

"I think I can take care of that."

O'Flynn had sounded surprised. "Oh, who . . . and with what qualifications?"

"Former combat maneuver instructor with the Air Force Suborbital Bomb Wing; two years specializing in high-altitude attack and evasion tactics. Is that good enough?"

"Begorrah, you're kidding! Someone on your team?"

"Yes."

"Let me see now . . . it would have to be Joe, the big black fella. Is that who it is?"

"No."

"Who, then?"

"Don't worry about it," Zambendorf replied, his eyes twinkling. "Anyway, you wouldn't believe me if I told you. You'd be surprised at some of the talent we've got between us in our little outfit."

It had taken little imagination to see that supplying Terran weapons to the inherently belligerent Paduans would completely destabilize the situation between Padua and its neighboring states, and before very much longer the more distant ones too. Other Taloid nations would seek similar weapons to secure themselves against the threat of Paduan aggression—as indeed Genoa desired to do already—and then others would feel threatened as those that hadn't reequipped their forces found themselves being intimidated by the ones that had. Eventually all the Taloid states would be forced to follow suit, and in the process they would be progressively reduced to a condition of vassal-dependency on Earth, which would thus be able to negotiate separately with each on terms of its own choosing. It was an old, familiar pattern, which earlier centuries on Earth had seen repeated many times over.

Massey had composed a message summarizing the main points and had it transmitted to Conlon via his private NASO channel. Eight hours later a reply stated that Conlon had confronted some of the senior NASO officials with the allegations, but their version of the facts, as advised from GSEC's political liaison office in Washington, was very different. It said, in effect, that Padua was a peaceful nation whose leaders aspired toward Western democratic ideals, and that the limited aid being given by the mission had been requested by the Paduan authorities to combat incursions upon their territory from Genoa—an illegally imposed rebel regime—and to relieve Paduan religious minorities who were being persecuted within the Genoese borders. The decision to grant the request was seen as a goodwill gesture that would help establish cordial and cooperative future relationships. The situation back on Earth was still confused, apparently, and would take a long time to resolve itself, especially in view of the long turnaround of communications to Saturn. Zambendorf had not been prepared to wait. "We're not going to get any sense out of them for days," he had told Massey. "You'd better stay on the line here and keep in touch as things develop. I'm going down to Titan to talk to Arthur."

"What do you think you're going to do, even if you manage to find some way of getting down there?" Massey had asked.

"I have no idea, Gerry, but there's no way I'm going to sit up here with this kind of thing going on."

Zambendorf's thoughts were interrupted by Clarissa Eidstadt's summons over the intercom from the forward compartment. "Karl, can you get up here a minute? We've got problems."

Price turned away from the port and watched uneasily as Zambendorf stood up, stepped carefully round the team's recently completed second transmogrifier box, and moved forward to the open doorway at the front of the cabin. Clarissa glanced back at him from the captain's seat, while in the copilot's position Otto Abaquaan was flipping switches frantically in front of an array of data displays and readouts that were obviously unfamiliar to him. "It's no good," Abaquaan said, shaking his head. "I can't get the midrange to scale, and the monitor recall has aborted. This isn't making any sense."

"What's wrong?" Zambendorf asked.

"We're losing it," Clarissa said. There was a problem in fixing the flyer's position from the electronic navigation grid transmitted from the satellites that the *Orion* had deployed shortly after arriving at Titan. Clarissa had warned that it might happen without an experienced co-pilot-navigator to calibrate the on-board reference system to the shifting satellite pattern as the flyer descended. "We know we're somewhere near where we need to go down through the muck, but we don't have a fine-tuned fix."

"No go?" Zambendorf asked, looking at Abaquaan.

"Abaquaan spread his hands. "Sorry, Karl. I thought I had it down okay when we went through the routine up on the ship, but I guess it needs more practice."

"It was worth a try," Clarissa murmured.

"It's not your fault there wasn't more time, Otto," Zambendorf said and turned to Clarissa. "How serious is it? Can you take care of it?"

"Sure, but not while I'm flying this thing too. The easiest thing to do would be to put down someplace and reinitiate the full sequence on the ground, without the added complication of having to compensate for being on a moving platform. Once we're locked into the grid at a fixed point, I can update the inertial system so that it will supply the drift offsets automatically."

"How long would you need?"

"To get everything right and double-checked, aw . . . say, an hour. But we need to land now, while we still know we're roughly in the right place. If we leave it much longer, we could wind up coming through the blanket anywhere over Titan, in the dark, without a ground datum. Then the way to Genoa would be anybody's guess."

"You'd better take us down, then," Zambendorf agreed.

"Okay. Go back, sit down, and buckle up."

Zambendorf ducked back into the rear cabin and lowered himself into the seat opposite Price. "We're going down."

"Trouble?"

"An unscheduled stop to synch the on-board nav system with the satellite grid."

The red-brown desert outside began rising to meet them, and as it came nearer it was transformed slowly from smooth, rounded hummocks into jagged peaks of muddy cloud, bottomless canyons of darkness falling away between. Cliffs and precipices of vapor reared up ahead, then were towering above on either side and flashing past at greater and greater speed . . . and then the stars vanished from the overhead ports as the flyer plunged into darkness. Zambendorf felt the seat pressing against him as Clarissa flattened the craft against Titan's thickening atmosphere to shed velocity. The structure vibrated and pounded in protest as the stresses climbed above the limits it had been built to endure.

"Wing sensors reading nine-twelve, to ten-three, with orange-two on six," Abaquaan's voice shouted through the open door up front. "Belly and underwing skin temperatures rising fast."

"Forward retros, five degrees out and down sixteen both, ramp to three thousand and sustain," Clarissa snapped. Zambendorf was thrown forward against his seat harness; loud juddering noises came from somewhere under the floor. Across the aisle, Price was tight-lipped and saying nothing.

"In at ten, ramp factor five," Abaquaan's voice reported. "Coming up to eleven over glide."

"Gimme plus-three on dive—easy."

"Dive brake increased three degrees."

"Are we going to make it?" Zambendorf called out.

"What a question!" Clarissa shouted back. "You have to learn not to put up with any nonsense from these machines. If those guys up there can get a flying eggbeater all the way to Titan, I can sure-as-hell get this thing the rest of the way to the surface."

Then they were losing height rapidly again, and the flyer banked as Clarissa put it into a long, sustained turn that would slow them down without altering their general position. They were now well below the aerosol layer, and the view outside was black in every direction, with a few ghostly streaks of methane cloud showing faint white below. "See if you can get a ground radar profile," Clarissa said to Abaquaan. "I don't want to go too low in that mess on visual. Try and find us somewhere high and flat—a plateau or something." Abaquaan fiddled with a console to one side of him, muttered a few profanities beneath his breath, and tried something else. "Set the HG centerline to blue zero," Clarissa said, glancing sideways. "Then use the coarse control to lock the scan-base and select your profile analysis from the menu on S-three."

"What?...Oh yeah, okay...Got it." Abaquaan took in the information that appeared on one of his screens. "Looks like we're at altitude thirty-five thousand meters, ground speed three-zero-eight-five kilometers per hour, reducing at twenty-eight meters per second per second. Mountainous terrain with highest peaks approximately eight hundred meters above mean surface level."

"Any flat summits?" Clarissa asked.

"The higher ones all seem pretty grim. There are some below five hundred that look better."

"Gimme a slave of your scope on screen two."

"You've got it."

The flyer's circling became tighter as it continued to slow and lose altitude. "Okay, prime a couple of seventy-FV-three flares and set them for proximity-triggered air-bursts at fifty meters. Then activate the underbelly searchlight and give me a vertical optical scan on screen one," Clarissa instructed after studying the display for a few seconds. "I'm going to have a look at that big flat-topped guy between the two thinner ones. See which one I mean?"

"I see it," Abaquaan said, looking at his own screen. "Flares primed for proximity bursts at five-zero and five-zero meters; belly light activated; vertical optical scan selected and routed to pilot's screen one."

The flyer slowed to hover motionless in the gloom, and a few seconds later two brilliant white lights blossomed a short distance below it revealing the squat hilltop that its radar fingers had probed invisibly. The summit was reasonably smooth, free of cracks and fissures, and uncluttered by boulders or loose debris. The searchlight came on to pick out a landing spot and hold it in steady illumination, and then the flyer began to sink slowly downward once more to complete the final few hundred feet of its descent.

"What manner of omen is this?" Groork whispered fearfully to himself as he sat petrified, staring up at two radiant orbs of purest violet that had appeared in the sky above the mountaintop moments after the voices had gone quiet. "By the Lifemaker!" he gasped. A flying creature, similar to the one he had seen over Xerxeon but glowing with blinding light, and much larger, was floating over the mountain, above the orbs. It was sinking slowly toward the ground, balanced on a column of violet radiance. The orbs were descending steadily too, all the time keeping ahead of the creature as if to clear its way—harbingers of light sent on before the heavenly beast to conduct it from its sacred realm beyond the sky. The creature descended out of sight, and shortly afterward a halo of violet light appeared and continued to glow softly among the rocks at the summit.

What did it mean? Was it a sign for Groork to ascend the mountain or a warning for him to turn back? Would he risk being smitten for presumptuous arrogance if he went forward, or smitten for self-serving disobedience and cowardice if he went back? For a fleeting moment he wished his brother Thirg were present; blasphemer or not, Thirg's unholy methods of argument could prove useful in situations like this. And then Groork remembered the message he had been given at the time of his being commanded to leave Xerxeon: Soon he would be told of the path that it was the Lifemaker's will for him to follow. The ways of the Lifemaker were sometimes mysterious and devious, but they were never misleading or capricious.

So now, it seemed, the moment had come.

With a mixture of wonder, trepidation, and excitement rising within him at every step, Groork urged his mount off the trail he had been following and began to pick his way upward. When the smoother terrain gave way to steeper ice crags and broken rock, he dismounted near some mountain scrub growing by a stream, tethered his animal to a bar of a conduit-support trellis beside a clump of tubing winders, and climbed on foot toward the mystical light beckoning to him from the summit.

"So what does Gerry think he can do about it?" Zambendorf asked.

Vernon Price shrugged in his seat across the cabin. "He's not sure yet. What can you do? Try and get the message across to as many Taloids as you can about what's behind it all and why, maybe . . . Then perhaps enough of them will wise up sufficiently to throw out the leaders who'd go along with Giraud's deal. In a word, you educate them, I guess."

Zambendorf shook his head. "It's no good, Vernon. It won't work."

Price shuffled his feet awkwardly, as if deep down he

already knew that. "How come?" he asked anyway.

"Because the Taloids are too much like people—they believe what they want to believe and close their eyes to what they don't want to believe. They need to think the world is the way they'd like it to be because having to face up to the reality that it isn't would be too uncomfortable. So they carry on pretending because it makes them feel better."

Price frowned for a second. "I'm not sure I see the connection."

"When you look around at the leaders people follow and take orders from unquestioningly, what do you see? For the most part, you can't say that the leaders are where they are because of any particular talent or ability, can you—most of them aren't really very bright when all's said and done. In many cases their only claim to exceptionality is their abnormal gullibility and extraordinary capacity for self-delusion. But the people don't see it. The leader-image that exists in the minds of the followers is something quite different. The person that the followers follow is a fantasy that they manufacture in their own imaginations, which they can project onto anyone who'll stand up and play the role. All that a leader needs is the gall to stand up and tell them he's got what they're looking for. They'll believe it because they need to."

"They need to believe they're in capable hands," Price said, taking the point. "Truth isn't the important thing. The important thing is to be certain." It didn't sound as if he was hearing it for the first time.

"To have the illusion of certainty, anyway," Zambendorf agreed. "If they just know their place and do as they're told, life will be very cosy and uncomplicated. To feel secure they need their authority figures. They'd be lost without them—hopelessly, helplessly, and traumatically. They talk about being free, but the thought of real freedom terrifies them. They couldn't handle it . . . not until they learn how in their own time, anyhow." He raised his head to look at Price. "And that's why trying to tell them they're being taken doesn't do any good. Even if they do get rid of whoever is selling them up the river today, tomorrow they'll be flocking after somebody else who's just as bad, and quite likely worse. They wouldn't have learned a thing."

A few seconds of silence passed, broken only by the voices of Clarissa and Abaquaan reciting numbers to each other in the nose compartment. "So what do you do?" Price asked at last. "About the Taloids, I mean. We can't just wash our hands of the whole business and do nothing."

Zambendorf frowned down at the floor and sighed. "First we have to accept reality as it is," he replied slowly. "And the facts are that you can't turn people whose beliefs are based on ignorance and superstition into rational, objective thinkers overnight. You'd be wasting your time. They don't have the concepts. The only way they'll get rid of corrupt leaders is when they stop listening to them, not because of any slogans that you or I might have taught them to memorize, but because of reasons they've worked out for themselves and understand. You're right—the answer is education, but unfortunately there isn't any instant brand of it that you can get by adding water."

Price thought for a moment. "Well, if they're going to go on being irrational for a while anyway, maybe the best thing you can do is give them some kind of harmless substitute to get them by in the meantime," he said. "You should know what I'm talking about. It's what you've been doing for years, isn't it."

"Well, it took you long enough to figure that out," Zambendorf grunted.

Price worried at a tooth with his thumbnail and eyed Zambendorf dubiously for a second or two longer, then looked away and stared at the far wall. Suddenly he got up and crossed the cabin to peer through one of the ports. "What is it?" Zambendorf asked, turning in his seat.

"I thought I saw something moving just outside the light out there . . . Maybe not. I don't know."

Zambendorf rose to his feet and moved over to the port to look for himself. After a few seconds he called in the direction of the forward cabin door, "Can you turn on an outside flood, Clarissa?—port-side forward?"

"Why?"

"We think there might be something moving out there."

A moment later a cone of light stabbed from the craft and etched the figure of the Taloid clearly against the darkness. It was motionless on its knees, its hands clasped upon its chest and its head bowed in humble reverence.

28

"ARRGH!"

Groork raised his arms to shield his eyes as the shining creature's side opened and more blinding violet light poured from within. Clearly this appointment had been preordained and marked the moment that the Lifemaker had chosen to make known to Groork the purpose for which the whole of his life so far had been the preparation. A chorus of voices sang thunderously from a bulge on the creature's back, rising to a crescendo as if to announce the arrival of some great presence, and then faded. Groork moved his fingers from an eye to look . . . then gasped, and raised his head hesitantly in awe and terror. A figure had appeared, barely visible in silhouette against the glare from the shining creature's interior. Its outline took on form and substance as it emerged—a broad, round-headed angel with a face that shone as fire, wreathed in glowing vapors—sent down from the celestial realm as the Lifemaker's personal emissary to Groork.

"Oh, get up off your knees, you fool," Zambendorf said irritably.

The screen of the transmogrifier that he was holding displayed REMOVE UP FROM YOUR KNEES. YOU ARE JOKING.

"Delete," Zambendorf told it with a sigh. "Substitute: Rise up."

"Arise," the angel boomed, and advanced slowly a few paces. It held a frond from some strange tree that Groork didn't recognize. A second angel had appeared behind it, standing in the opening in the shining creature's side.

"There, Vernon," Zambendorf said into his helmet mike. "Your first Taloid at close quarters." The Taloid was wearing a tunic of woven wire, a thick cloaklike garment, and a dark cap of some rubbery-looking material. As it climbed slowly to its feet, it picked up a staff of metal tubing that it had laid by its side.

"It's . . . amazing," Price's voice replied haltingly. "It's so different from watching recordings up in the ship." There was a second or two of silence. "What do you think it's doing up here?"

"I've no idea . . . attracted by our lights and the flyer's thermal radiation, probably. From some of the things Galileo said, I wouldn't be surprised if it thinks we're gods or something."

"It's uncanny," Price said, staring.

"I am Zambendorf," Zambendorf said, activating the transmogrifier again and pointing to himself; then he instructed the instrument: "Get name."

"I am the Wearer," the angel announced as the computers returned the Taloid pulse-sequence that had been equated to "Zambendorf"—the Wearer of the sacred Symbol of Life, Groork decided. Then the angel asked, "What is your name?"

"Groork, known as Hearer-of-Voices, son of Methgark and Coorskeria, and brother of Thirg," Groork answered. He was surprised that the angel didn't know.

"No, too long. Shorter please," the angel said.

The celestial voices were rising and falling in the background again. They seemed to be saying, "Light and awe. Light and awe . . ." Or was it "Send light and awe"? Groork frowned as he tried to make sense of it. The angel was still standing and waiting. Why wouldn't the angel accept his name? What were the voices trying to say?

And then Groork understood. This was his moment of spiritual rebirth, which would be symbolized by his being rebaptized with a new name. The angel wished him to repeat the name by which the Lifemaker wanted him to be known from now on, and which the voices were telling him. "Enlightener!" he exclaimed as the inspiration struck. "I am called the Enlightener!"

NAME OBTAINED, the transmogrifier screen reported. ENGLISH MATCH REQUIRED.

Zambendorf thought for a moment, and then said, "Moses. Spell M-O-S-E-S."

Moses? the screen repeated.

"Okay."

"I shall go forth from this place as the Lifemaker commands and enlighten the world," the Enlightener declared, his voice rising in fervor. "I shall destroy the blasphemers and smite down the unbelievers who bow themselves not before the holy words that I shall bring unto them. I shall—"

"Stop! Thou jabberest. Makest not sense any. More simple. Shorter please."

It wasn't the angel that spoke, but the frond that the angel was holding, the Enlightener realized with a start—the angel was teaching the frond to speak. He stared in wonder. Then he realized that it was a miracle to show that the angel was truly a messenger from the Lifemaker. That explained its questions: The frond was like a child, and obviously couldn't be expected to comprehend all the complexities of speech in an instant. "My task now," he said to it, making his phrases short and simple. "Talk to world. Kill all Lifemaker's enemies."

"Talk to world means talk to robeings?" the frond asked.

"Yes," the Enlightener answered.

MOSES' JOB AT PRESENT—TALKING TO TALOIDS; KILLING HERETICS, the screen informed Zambendorf.

Zambendorf shook his head. "No! No! Killing each other is not the way. You have to understand that!"

The screen offered NOT KILLING EACH OTHER IS NOT A GOOD METHOD. HIGHLY PROBABLE THAT YOU UNDERSTAND.

"Damn," Zambendorf muttered beneath his breath.

"Delete. Substitute: Do not kill each other. Imperative that you understand."

(Phrase 1) DO NOT KILL.
(Phrase 2) IMPERATIVE THAT = command?

"Oh hell . . . Delete phrase two," Zambendorf ordered.

And the frond said, "Thou shall not kill."

"Clarissa," Zambendorf called into his radio. "How are you doing in there?"

"Nearly through. Why?"

"Is there any chance Otto can come out here? He's more used to this damn transmogrifier thing than I am."

"I'm done. I'll be out as soon as I get a helmet on," Abaquaan's voice said.

Meanwhile the Enlightener was standing transfixed in wonderment. He had heard the divine command. But what new wisdom was the Lifemaker revealing? Was His power so strong and invincible that His faithful need have no fear of enemies? Were heretics, blasphemers, and unbelievers not to be punished? The Enlightener stared at the frond in the angel's hand and puzzled over what the utterance meant. And then, slowly, his inner eye was opened. What did killing another robeing signify, apart from brutality and ignorance, and an inability to persuade by other means? It required no learning or schooling, no discipline and development of self, no comprehension of worth, or any aspiration to higher things. The lowest savages in the farthest reaches of the swamplands south of Serethgin were capable of that. They knew of no other way to settle their differences.

Truly this was a sacred moment that would be recorded in the Scribings, and this spot a holy place that would be visited by pilgrims and penitents for all the twelve-brights that were left to come until the world ended. The moment should be symbolized by an act that would immortalize it, the Enlightener thought, and the spot marked as the selected place of the angels' coming. He looked around him and saw a smooth, flat rock, obviously placed there to serve his purpose. He moved over to it, and with the tip of his staff inscribed slowly and solemnly near the top of the slab the words:

THOU SHALT NOT KILL.

When he had finished he looked up, and saw that a third angel had appeared. "What more of me does the Lifemaker command?" he asked meekly.

Abaquaan took the transmogrifier from Zambendorf. "He seems pretty impressed by the message," he said. "Maybe it's a new idea to these guys. He wants to know if you've got any more of 'em."

"They mustn't believe anyone who tries to tell them they're worthless or inferior," Zambendorf said. "But neither must they believe they are superior to any of the neighboring nations. All the nations must accept each other as equal partners and learn to cooperate in building a better future for all." After some exchanges with the transmogrifier, Abaquaan had reduced this to something the machine could accept.

And the frond spoke once more. The Enlightener listened, then added the numeral 1 before his previous inscription and wrote underneath it:

2. THOU ART THY NEIGHBOR'S EQUAL. HELP THY NEIGHBOR, AND THY NEIGHBOR SHALL HELP THEE.

The Enlightener was being enlightened, as he would bring enlightenment to others. With just a few simple words, the Lifemaker had opened up a vision of a whole new world that could come to be, a world in which all robeings everywhere would prosper and help one another grow strong in a spirit of compassion, cooperation, tolerance, and understanding. All would be brothers, like Thirg. A new era would come to pass, in which killing and violence would be renounced and universal love among robeings would prevail—a stronger, deeper, and more enduring force to shape the world than anything ever conceived previously.

"What's he doing?" Price asked as the Taloid finished scratching a second row below the marks that it had made on a large ice slab with its staff.

"Looks like he doesn't carry a notebook," Abaquaan replied. "I guess we must be saying the right things."

Price stared at the Taloid for a few seconds longer. "I'll be back out in a second," he said, and disappeared into the open outer door of the flyer's airlock.

"I'm all through," Clarissa's voice informed them. "How's it with Rin-Tin-Tin out there?"

"We need a few more minutes," Zambendorf said. He switched back to local to address Abaquaan. "They shouldn't blindly accept anything that others tell them to believe. Facts are the only guide to what is true, and facts can't be changed by wishing them to be otherwise."

The Enlightener wrote finally:

> 3. BEWARE THE TONGUES OF DECEIVERS. LET THY WORDS BE KEEN HEEDERS OF TRUTH, FOR TRUTH IS NO HEEDER OF WORDS.

It went on until the Taloid had written several more rows, and then Price reappeared carrying a video camera-copier and a light-duty general-purpose plasma torch from the flyer's tool locker. "What are you doing?" Zambendorf asked.

"Saving him the trouble of having to come all the way back up here if he forgets any of it," Price replied. "Also I'm collecting samples of Taloid handscript." He used the camera to transmit several shots of the slab into the flyer's computer storage system, and then, satisfied that a record of the original script had been preserved, carefully traced over the markings with the torch to melt a deeper, clearer impression into the ice. After taking several shots of this too, he directed one of them to the recorder's local hard-copier, and a few seconds later a sheet of Titan-duty plastic was ejected into his guantlet and quickly rigidified in the low-temperature surroundings.

"You know, Vernon, sometimes I get the impression you're too sentimental," Abaquaan remarked.

"Maybe," Price agreed cheerfully. He looked around, picked up one of the smaller ice flakes that lay all over the summit, and used the torch in fan-mode to melt its top surface all over. Then he pressed the plastic down onto it and waited a few seconds for the flake to refreeze, welding the ice and the plastic inseparably together. Finally, as an afterthought he melted some extra slivers of ice and allowed the water to flow over the face of the tablet, sealing the plastic beneath a thin protective layer of glasslike ice. The result was quite pleasing. He held it out toward the Taloid. "Here you are, Moses, old buddy—something for you to hang on the wall when you get home."

"We'd better wrap this up," Abaquaan said. "Time's getting on."

"Otto's right," Zambendorf agreed. "Happy now, Vernon?"

"I guess so. It just seemed . . . oh, like a nice thing to do."

The Enlightener gazed down in wonder at the holy Tablet lying in his arms, still glowing faintly—the Lifemaker's commandments entrusted to him, the Enlightener, as the Lifemaker's messenger chosen to carry the sacred Word to the robeing race. There was nothing he could say. The emotions surging within him were too violent and confusing for him to be able even to think coherently.

"Farewell, Enlightener," the frond said. "Our work awaits. Do not remain here now. Good fortune to thee." The Enlightener looked up and saw the frond-bearing angel turn away and return into the shining creature. Then the second angel—the one that had caused the living plant to bring forth the Tablet written in fire and sealed inside the solid rock—followed. Finally the angel that had appeared first of all backed slowly to the glowing opening, raised an arm in salutation, and was swallowed up by the light. Moments later the opening closed, and the cone of radiance that the shining creature had been emitting from a point just above vanished suddenly.

"Take thee hence from this place, Enlightener," the creature roared, "or thou wilt surely be burned." As if in a trance, clutching the Tablet securely under one arm and taking his staff in the other, the Enlightener retreated from the summit.

Only when the creature was lost to view behind the intervening rocks did his faculties begin functioning again. Still in a daze he retraced his steps downward to the stream. "Indeed thou wert meant to bring me to this place," he murmured to his steed as he untethered it and remounted. "Now may we rest easy in our minds that Meerkulla has received many blessings in return for his sacrifice." He turned the horse round and descended the slopes below. Only when he was almost at the trail did he see Captain Horazzorgio and the company of Kroaxian Royal Guard waiting for him.

According to Clarissa, they were between Padua and Genoa, at a point almost at the edge of the desert in which the first Terran–Taloid meeting had occurred—in fact not that far at all from the very spot at which it had taken place. Therefore the cruising time to Genoa would only be about fifteen minutes. Things hadn't worked out too badly at all, Zambendorf thought to himself as he stood in the cockpit doorway and watched the takeoff routine.

"Any sign of Moses down there?" Price asked curiously from the cabin behind.

Abaquaan brought up a series of infrared views on the copilot's scanner screen until one showed a bright dot on the lower part of a broad slope some distance below the summit on the side of the mountain down which Moses had disappeared. He switched in the telescopic viewer and produced a large, clear image. "He's got a horse," Abaquaan said. "Must have left it lower down someplace."

"He's riding a horse back down the mountain, with the

slab you gave him under his arm," Zambendorf said over his shoulder. "Want to come and see?"

Price moved forward beside Zambendorf and studied the screen for a few seconds. Moses had stopped and seemed to be staring down the hill at something. Abaquaan switched back to a low-resolution image, which showed more dots clustered together not far away below. A close-up revealed them to be more Taloids, also mounted. "I wonder who they are," Price murmured. "Do you think Moses might be in some kind of trouble down there?"

"I don't know," Zambendorf replied slowly. He sounded concerned. After a second or two he turned his head toward Clarissa and said, "Take it down lower. Let's have a closer look at what's going on."

"I have no fear of thee now, Horazzorgio, Defender-of-False-Faith," the Enlightener called down the hillside, his voice loud and firm and his eyes glinting brightly. "For verily have I climbed the mountain and seen the angels, and I return now to be known henceforth as the Enlightener, who has been chosen to carry the Lifemaker's true Word to all corners of the world and bring a new faith of love and brothership to all robeings. Heed my words well, Horazzorgio, for they are indeed His, the Lifemaker's." He held high a slab of ice that he was carrying. "Swear your allegiance now to the true faith of which I speak, and renounce thy false creeds, and thy transgressions shall be forgiven thee. Dost thou so swear, Horazzorgio?"

Uncertain if he could believe his ears, Horazzorgio was still too astonished to reply when he saw the sky-dragon rising from the mountaintop in the background. His imagers dulled in cold fear, and his body trembled. Twice now he had come to Xerxeon in pursuit of one or the other of this pair of accursed brothers, and twice they had eluded him. And now, just as before, the dragons of the sky-beings were appearing in the sky to protect them. He wasn't about to mess with dragons a second time, he decided. No way was he going through that again . . . not for anything or anybody.

Horazzorgio jumped down from his saddle and fell to his knees. "I swear, O Enlightener!" he shouted. "Horazzorgio has found the true faith! I believe! I believe! Truly thou speakest the Lifemaker's Word. What is thy wish, Chosen One? Thy servant awaits thy command."

The troopers behind were looking at each other in amazement and murmuring among themselves. "What sorcery has this hearer worked?"

"Horazzorgio on his knees? This is surely a miracle."

"What wondrous faith is this of which the hearer speaks?"

"I see no miracle."

Then the flier swooped down low over the riders, released two flares, turned on its searchlight, and circled slowly to observe the scene. All around Horazzorgio, metal figures were hurling themselves to the ground and adding to a rising chorus of terrified voices.

"We believe! We believe!"

"Behold the Enlightener, the Chosen One!"

"Spare us sinners, O Dragon. We repent! We repent!"

Even the Enlightener was astounded by the efficacy of his own words. "All this, and with such economy of effort?" he murmured to his horse as he stared disbelievingly. "I must truly be inspired."

"What's going on down there?" Clarissa demanded, totally bemused. "Karl, what in hell did you say to that guy?"

Price was looking worried. "Why are they all falling off their horses?" he asked. "Are they okay. What's happening to them?"

"They look as if they're worshipping Moses," Abaquaan said incredulously. "He's waving that videocopy you gave him."

Zambendorf had gone very quiet. His eyes narrowed thoughtfully as he continued staring at the screen. At last he said in a faraway voice, "They're all dressed very similarly, which suggests they're soldiers. And this is a part of Padua, isn't it."

"So?" Clarissa asked.

"Galileo says that the Paduan horse-guards are among the most zealous and fanatical soldiers anywhere on this part of Titan," Zambendorf replied. "Yet we've just demolished a whole squadron of them . . . and without a single one of the weapons that Arthur is yelling that he has to have—which we'd have a hard job getting our hands on anyway, even if we thought it was the right way for him to go."

Silence fell for a few seconds while the others absorbed what he had said. At last Price asked him, "Are you thinking what I'm thinking?"

Zambendorf frowned, rubbed his beard, and looked back at the screen. "Believe it or not, but I've absolutely no idea, Vernon," he replied candidly. "I do have a strange feeling, however, that we might just have stumbled on the answer to Arthur's problem with the Druids."

29

AT ONE END OF A SPECIALLY CLEARED AREA THAT stretched the full length of the walled grounds behind Kleippur's residence, the Carthogian infantry sergeant lay prone with a captured Waskorian projectile hurler fitted snugly against his shoulder and one arm partly extended to support its length. He sighted along its top tube at the first of the red disks along the far wall, aimed carefully, and squeezed the small firing lever with a finger of his other hand. The hurler barked and kicked vigorously, and in the same instant most of the red disk at the far end of the grounds disappeared. The sergeant repeated the process rapidly while Kleippur and Dornvald watched grimly with a small group of Carthogian officers and military advisers. In short order, a small ice boulder exploded; a piece of outer wall cut from an organic building disintegrated into pulp; and two sets of standard-issue Carthogian body armor mounted on full-size dummies at the end of the line were reduced to shreds. Dornvald signaled to the far end of the grounds, and soldiers who had been standing well back from the line of fire moved forward to collect the target plates.

"There can be no protection against this," Lofbayel whispered to Thirg, who was looking on numbly. "Those soldiers were doomed from the moment they set out to pursue the Waskorians. The outcome was a foregone conclusion."

"Truly," Thirg agreed. "Just as Horazzorgio and the Kroaxians were doomed from the moment they chose to set foot in the Meracasine. And now the whole of Carthogia is surely doomed."

Lumian weapons such as these which a Carthogian raiding party led by Dornvald had seized deep inside Waskorian territory, had been the cause of the disasters that had befallen the Carthogians recently in rapid succession. A routine border patrol had failed to return, and the force sent to look for it had been almost annihilated in a Waskorian ambush. Then the Waskorians had attacked a border fort which fell after putting up a stiff fight. A small band of survivors escaped and managed to join up with a relief column advancing from Menassim under the command of a General Yemblayen. Kleippur had ordered Yemblayen to halt and avoid further engagements until the reason for the sudden Waskorian invincibility was better understood.

The most worrisome aspect of the unexpected Waskorian successes was that the Lumian weapons must have come from the Kroaxians, with whom the Lumians were known to have made contact. If the Waskorians were taking over the border zone as preparation for an all-out invasion from Kroaxia, and if the whole of the regular Kroaxian army had been equipped with firepower as devastating as that being demonstrated behind Kleippur's residence, then Carthogia wouldn't last another bright. Kleippur's social experiment would be over; night would fall over an Age of Reason that had barely begun to dawn; and everything that Thirg and Lofbayel had sought to escape would ensnare them once again.

"What is your opinion, Pellimiades?" Kleippur asked the technical advisor, who was examining another sample of Waskorian weaponry with an artisan's keen eye.

Pellimiades shook his head dubiously. "Such detail and precision are only to be found growing naturally upon this world," he replied. "No work of any craftsman that I have seen, nor any of which I have heard tell, could remotely approach it. If this is Lumian workmanship, then the Lumians could well be lifemakers indeed."

"You can offer no imitation, however crude, nor any other means by which our soldiers might hope to compete on equal terms?" Dornvald asked.

Pellimiades shook his head again. "None, General."

Two soldiers arrived at a run from the far end of the grounds and presented four target plates. The first had the center of its red disk completely blown away; the second was torn into a tight cluster of overlapping holes offset to one side of the disk; the third was peppered with a pattern of more widely scattered holes; and the fourth was much like the first. Kleippur drew a long, heavy intake over his coolant vanes and shook his head gravely. "We have no choice," he said. "Our only chance is to accept the terms which the Merchant-Lumians offered us originally. If we cannot supply comparable armaments of our own, then we must obtain theirs; and if taming forests for Lumians is the price we must pay, then so be it. This has become a matter of survival." He turned to Lyokanor, the army's senior intelligence officer. "Assemble the Cabinet to agree what shall be the form of our message. We will convey it to the Lumian merchant princes by way of the inquirers who still occupy the Lumian camp."

"At once, sir," Lyokanor replied and hurried away.

"We will proceed to the Council Chamber and await the others there," Kleippur said. "Our first task must be to arm every able-bodied citizen as best we can in case the Kroaxians invade, and to agree on tactics for holding out until we begin receiving Lumian aid. The times ahead will be hard ones, I fear."

Thirg felt dejected as he and Lofbayel followed the rest of the party across the rear courtyard toward the house. Kleippur, with his usual pragmatic acceptance, was devoting his efforts to making the best of the situation as it existed and not wasting time and energy on futile accusations or complaints. But it was Thirg who had persuaded him that the Wearer was sincere, and who had talked him into heeding the Wearer's treacherous words. It was clear now that the whole episode involving the Wearer had been a Lumian ploy to keep Carthogia unsuspecting and inactive while negotiations were concluded with Kroaxia, the start of a process that would eventually bring all the robeing nations under the Lumian heel. The Lumian strategy to attain that goal had been cold, calculated, ruthless, and efficient, and its implementation seemed so practiced that Kleippur suspected the whole technique to have been perfected long ago—used, perhaps, for the enslavement of dozens, or even dozen-dozens, of worlds. But whatever the truth of that, there could be no stopping the process now. Better a slave state than no state at all—the main task now was to ensure the survival of Carthogia.

Worst of all, Thirg had placed all his personal trust in the Wearer and had no alternative now but to admit that he had been betrayed cruelly. That bewildered him the most. He had never been more sure of anything in his life than of the special relationship which he had thought he and the Wearer shared—a relationship based on a mutual understanding of the power of mind and reason that transcended differences in language, race, form, and even world of origin. Each had recognized a common quality in the other that reduced all their differences, striking as they seemed at first glance, to no more than trifling superficialities, indicating—or so Thirg had hoped—the existence of a bond that could unite all the unknown forms of life and mind that existed across the countless worlds above the sky. Truly inquiring minds everywhere had more in common than divided them, and could work together regardless of what they were or where they came from, just as the true inquirers from Kroaxia and Carthogia could work together without cognizance of the borders between their nations. Lumian ways would spread across Robia and bring an end to the reign of ignorance, superstition, and fear; no longer would beliefs be imposed by dictate or intimidation . . . and instead, knowledge and reason would prevail.

Or so Thirg had believed.

But the Wearer had deceived him and taken advantage of his trust. All of the promises and reassurances had been as devious and as self-serving as the practiced rhetoric of a trained prosecutor in the court of the High Council of Kroaxia. It seemed, then, that the appeal of reason was not so universal after all; possibly it was as rare among the worlds beyond the sky as was Kleippur among Robia's rulers, and the domain of reason as small a portion of the universe as Carthogia was of Robia. Thirg had to concede that he knew of no law of nature which said it had to be otherwise. Therefore, he told himself, partly in consolation, perhaps it was a mistake to feel he had been wronged, for the concept of "wrongness" was surely subjective—an expression of the limits that the majority of robeings placed upon desirable behavior, within robeing society, as judged through robeing eyes, on the basis of robeing teaching and experience. No valid basis could exist for extrapolating identical, or even comparable, ethical codes to beings from other worlds. So no compelling evidence could lead Thirg to conclude that the Wearer had deliberately "wronged" him—Thirg's behavior might simply have been considered hopelessly naive and infantile by Lumian standards. But the thought didn't make him feel very much better. He was still bitterly disappointed.

They climbed some shallow steps to the rear terrace of the main building and were about to enter the hallway outside the Council Chamber when the sentries at one of the courtyard's side entrances opened the gate to admit a mounted messenger. The messenger's steed crossed the yard at a gallop and halted below the terrace. Kleippur, who had been about to enter the door, looked back over his shoulder then turned and strode to the head of the steps, followed by Dornvald, while the entourage parted to let them through. "Speak," Kleippur said to the messenger. "What is your news?"

"Tidings from General Yemblayen," the messenger replied, his words coming fast with urgency. "The Waskorians have crossed our lines and are heading toward Menassim."

Alarmed murmurs broke out among the others on the terrace. "How many and how armed?" Dornvald snapped. "Was there a battle? Where, and what were our losses? What is the condition of Yemblayen's force?"

The messenger shook his head. "Your pardon, sir, but you misunderstand. There has been no battle. General Yemblayen opened his lines to allow the Waskorians free passage. They have agreed willingly to travel under Carthogian escort and are approaching Menassim peacefully, led by their prophet, Ezimbial."

"Ezimbial . . . leading them peacefully?" Kleippur stared in disbelief. "Have you been imbibing uranium salts, messenger?"

"'Tis true, 'tis true," the messenger insisted. "They are seized by a new faith that renounces all war and killings. They speak of Carthogians as brothers and are proceeding to the Lumian camp to return the Lumian weapons, which the Waskorians say they no longer have use for."

A frown darkened Dornvald's face. "They are heading toward Menassim with their Lumian weapons? It is a trick! What madness could have possessed Yemblayen?"

"The Waskorians have entrusted the weapons to their escorts and bear no other arms."

Kleippur stared for a few seconds longer, then shook his head helplessly. "New faith? . . . Renouncing war? Where did this come from. Do you know anything more?"

"The Waskorians speak of a Divine One whom they call Enlightener, who was brought down into their land by shining angels from the sky to preach the Lifemaker's commandments to the world," the messenger answered. "He came with disciples, some of them former Kroaxian cavalry troopers; others are from Xerxeon, where all the villagers have been converted. Chief among the disciples is a baptizer called the Renamer, who was previously Captain Horazzorgio of the Kroaxian Royal Guard."

Dornvald gasped. "Horazzorgio, a baptizer? What kind

of miracle-worker is this Enlightener?"

"Indeed the Waskorians tell of wondrous miracles that accompanied the Enlightener's coming," the messenger said. "Of fires that burned in the sky, rocks that melted, streams that boiled, objects that levitated, and holy dragons bearing shining angels from above."

Dornvald's eyes twinkled suddenly at the mention of dragons. "And what of our forward scouts and observers?" he asked. "What have they had to say about all these miracles and dragons?"

The messenger remained expressionless. "Nothing, sir. But many reports were received of what sounds like the same Lumian flying vehicle being very active in the areas where the miracles were supposed to have occurred, and at about the same times."

"I see," Dornvald said. He stepped back from the balustrade and turned to catch Kleippur's eye. Kleippur was smiling, as were the others behind him. Then Dornvald too started grinning.

And Thirg too smiled—at first faintly and disbelievingly, then broadly, and finally he clapped Lofbayel heartily on the back and laughed out loud. Who the Enlightener might have been, he had no idea... but he thought he knew well whose the flying vehicle had been, and who the real miracle-worker was at the back of the whole business.

Up in the *Orion*, Gerold Massey walked angrily out of an elevator in Globe II and turned to follow the corridor leading to the day quarters used by Zambendorf's team. He had talked to a number of the mission's scientists and other professionals about the situation and had managed to galvanize some of them into crackling, dynamic action sufficient to lodge a formal protest with Leaherney. And that was it. The protest had been rebuffed amid a tangle of expertly contrived obstructions, denials, technicalities, and bureaucratic obfuscations, and a demand for unrestricted access to the Earth communications link politely but firmly refused. Having thus done all they could, the protesters had expressed their regrets to Massey—all in a very decent and civilized way, naturally—and returned to their various interests and duties. Even more galling was the thought that while he, Massey, was the professional psychologist, everything had happened exactly as Zambendorf had predicted. "We both understand what makes people tick, Gerry," Zambendorf had said. "The difference is that I accept it but you won't."

Massey reached the door of the suite, knocked, and waited while Thelma checked on a viewer inside to see who it was before letting him in. "No good," he told her, tossing out his hands as he stamped inside. "Leaherney was expecting it. He was all set up. Anyway, apart from Dave Crookes and Leon Keyhoe, Graham Spearman, Webster, and a couple of others who do seem genuinely concerned, they weren't that interested. Nothing about all this affects anything that's really close to them."

Thelma seemed unsurprised. "You had to give it a try though," she said. "Forget it for a minute and come take a look at this." She led him into the suite and sat in front of the screen she had been watching when he arrived.

Massey moved behind the chair to look over her shoulder. The screen looked down on a procession of Taloids dressed in flowing white robes and wearing garlands of some kind—probably pieces of metal strung on wire—around their necks. Some of them were carrying banners that bore Taloid inscriptions, and others were beating on or blowing into what looked like musical instruments while the rest swayed rhythmically as they marched. Flanking both sides of the procession were uniformed cavalrymen that Massey recognized as Genoese, moving at a slow walk and leading pack animals loaded with bundles of Terran rifles and submachine guns, ammunition boxes, and grenade packs. Behind the files of cavalry, other Taloids were gathered along the roadside to watch. "Is this a view from Karl's flyer?" Massey asked.

Thelma nodded. "Uh-huh. It's coming in live."

"What's happening? Where's it from?"

"The road to Genoa," Thelma told him. "It's all over

with the Druids. They're on their way to Genoa Base to give all the hardware back. Moses went over real big."

Massey shook his head slowly as he watched, and found that he was smiling. "I don't know . . . I've never heard of anything so crazy," he muttered. "I wouldn't have given it a snowball's chance in hell."

"Arthur and Galileo called a little while ago," Thelma said. "They seem pretty pleased with it all too."

"Have you got a line to the flyer?" Massey asked her.

Thelma nodded and touched a button below the screen. "Hello, *Hornet*. Anybody down there?" she said.

"What's new?" Clarissa's voice replied.

"Oh, Gerry Massey's just arrived. I think he wants to offer his congratulations," Thelma said.

"I wouldn't have believed it," Massey called over her shoulder.

"That's why we've always given you problems," Clarissa answered. "You underestimate your opposition."

"Maybe I do. Anyhow, is Karl there?"

"Hang on."

A few seconds of silence went by. Then Zambendorf's voice said, "Hello, Gerry. Well, what do you think of our little show down here?"

"I'm impressed. I gather Arthur and Galileo are more than satisfied with the service they're getting too."

"We always try to give our customers their money's worth," Zambendorf replied. "How did things go with Leaherney?"

"No good—pretty much the way you predicted."

"Mmm . . . a pity," Zambendorf murmured. Then his voice perked up. "Anyway, never mind. I think we've proved our secret weapon sufficiently to move on to the next phase."

"What next phase? I thought this was it. The Druids won't be causing any more trouble, and Arthur's happy with the outcome. What else do you want?"

"All very satisfying, I agree, but I still have a large personal score to settle with friend Caspar, Dan Leaherney, and the good people back on Earth who thought I was just another puppet they could buy," Zambendorf said. "What you've seen has been just the dress rehearsal, Gerry. The real performance is about to begin."

"Karl." A note of suspicious dread crept into Massey's voice. "What are you talking about?"

"This is the most devastating thing since the H-bomb," Zambendorf's voice said, sounding exuberant. "First Moses, then a squadron of Paduan cavalry, after that an entire Taloid village... and now a whole tribe. It's snowballing down here like nothing you've ever seen."

"So?..."

"Next we bag the whole Paduan army, which is on the march toward Genoa right now, and then we import the complete operation right into Padua and dump it in Henry's backyard!" Zambendorf exclaimed, chortling. "Imagine if the whole Paduan nation told Leaherney where to stuff his military aid... and later on, maybe, the whole of Titan. What a way to screw GSEC, Ramelson, the politicians—all of them!"

"But... but you don't have enough people to do something like that," Massey objected.

"What do you mean, not enough people? We've got Moses, and Lord Nelson with his cavaliers down here, plus a lot more from the village... and now I don't know how many thousand Druids from this latest addition. I told you, Gerry—the whole thing's snowballing."

"Yes, I know, but what I meant is you've only got a twelve-man Hornet flyer down here. You don't have the transportation capacity to move enough bodies into Padua fast enough to trigger a real revolution. See what I mean? You need the right critical mass. Otherwise it'll all just fizzle out."

"Oh, that's all under control," Zambendorf said breezily. "Just as soon as we—"

Thelma cut him off. "Karl, don't go into all that right now. Gerry doesn't know about it yet. I haven't had a chance to—"

"Know about what?" Massey demanded. A cold, creeping feeling deep down inside somewhere told him that his worst fears were about to come true.

"You wouldn't want to know about it," Thelma told him. "Now, why don't you just—"

"I *want* to know about it. What's going on? What is it that you haven't had a chance to tell me about yet? . . ."

"Tango Baker Two to Control, launch sequence completion confirmed and BQ checking at zero-three-five. I have fourteen on beta-seven and a clear six-six. Transferring to local."

"Roger, Tango Baker Two. BQ vector confirmed and delta repeater reading green. *Orion* Control standing down. Have a good trip."

"Roger. Out." Andy Schwartz, captain of the surface lander that had just begun its descent from the *Orion*, checked his instruments once more and settled back in his seat. Course was set on automatic to a reentry window that would bring them down onto a shallow descent from seventy degrees east, direct into the ground base at Padua, and trim was adjusted for the heavy-load cargo of materials and machinery. No passengers were aboard this trip—apart from the two Special Forces troopers who had missed their flight through an admin foul-up and were hitching a ride down to rejoin their unit.

Most of the soldiers that Schwartz and his crew had flown to the surface lately had been instructors being sent to train Paduans in weapons-handling. The "base" at Padua was just a couple of pads and some landers parked at an isolated location among some hills well away from the city, apparently because its existance had not been revealed to the general Paduan population by their leaders—not at all like the situation at Genoa. Not even the Paduan army had been let in on the secret; the rank and file received their weaponry training from a small, select corps of Paduan instructors who were the only ones who ever actually met Terrans. Schwartz didn't know what to make of it all.

"Have they shipped any girls down to Padua Base yet?" the copilot asked casually from the seat next to him.

"No chance, Clancy."

"Maybe you could use the break, Clancy," Mike Glautzen, the flight engineer, suggested from his station behind them. "I read somewhere that occasional abstinence is good for your health."

"Baker needs to try something that's good for his health," Hank Frazer muttered as he tapped commands into a touchboard below the displays at the Communications Officer's position across the aisle from Glautzen.

"I read somewhere that too much health's bad for you," Baker said.

"Causes cancer, huh?" Schwartz murmured.

"Doesn't too much of anything always cause something?"

"How about too much moderation?" Frazer said.

"It causes excess-deficiency," Baker said. "That's real bad."

Glautzen sniggered. "Gonna have to get used to that for a while, Clancy. No parties when we get to Padua—just work, man."

Baker frowned down at his instrument for a second. "Say, I've had a great idea, guys," he said, turning his head to look back over the seat. "How about the latest swingers' with-it thing, straight from Southern California?"

"What's that?" Glautzen asked.

"An inflatable-doll-swapping party! It's all the rage with—" Baker broke off as he saw the large, black soldier, clad in Special Forces camouflage combat dress—one of the lander's two illicit passengers—entering through the door at the rear. "Hey, you're not supposed to be up front here, pardner," he warned. "You're supposed to stay back in your seat, belted down till we're on the pad."

"Get outta here, willya," Schwartz said, glancing back. "If you wanna see the flight deck, that's fine—but not until after we touch down, okay?"

Joe Fellburg eased himself fully inside the door and

leveled his machine carbine. His teeth shone pearly white against his skin as he flashed an amiable grin. A moment later Drew West, also wearing combat dress and holding a .45 automatic, entered behind him and moved away from the door to cover the crew from a different angle. "Now let's all be friendly and sensible about this," Fellburg suggested. "Just do like we say, and you'll all be fine. Now switch the H-twenty-seven to F range and lock onto a surface transmission that you'll pick up at twenty-eight point-three megahertz. Then reprogram the descent profile and follow the beam down to where it takes us, okay?"

30

PRIVATE SALLAKAR OF THE KROAXIAN INFANTRY INhaled deeply from the effort of climbing the rise and coughed as his coolant system switched over to reverse-flow to eject the intake of dust raised by the foot soldiers ahead of him. Mumbling profanities and curses at the dust, the desert, the army, and the seemingly endless distance to Carthogia, he moved to one side and stopped to look back at the long column of infantry and cavalry regiments, fireball throwers, war chariots, and supply wagons snaking its way back and out of sight among the rounded dunes and low scarps of the Meracasine. It was going to be the real thing this time, he reflected glumly. He had tangled before with the Carthogians in border skirmishes, and the experience hadn't left him restless with impatience and wild with enthusiasm to meet them again. Oh yes, the officers had sounded very confident, as usual, and been full of assurances that the new weapons would make short work of the Carthogians; but Sallakar had heard too much of that kind of talk before. It was easy to tell everyone not to worry when you knew you'd have a fast mount underneath you to get you out of trouble if it all went wrong. Oh, yes indeed, it was fine for them to talk. But—according to the barracks gossip, anyway—the cavalry captain, Horazzorgio, hadn't been doing so much talking since he'd chased after a Carthogian undercover unit and come back minus his whole company, and an arm and an eye to boot. Oh no! Now that didn't sound like opposition likely to allow itself be made short work of.

He moved a hand to feel the cold, hard lines of the newly introduced projectile hurler that was slung across his back—the product, so he and the others had been told, of many twelve-brights of labor carried out in secret by some of the best artisans and craftsmen in Kroaxia. Oh yes, it was a nice-looking piece of workmanship, and yes, it had seemed effective enough in the hurriedly improvised training sessions that they had been rushed through, with everything left until the last minute as usual—probably for security reasons—but what did that prove? Only that somebody had discovered how to make better weapons. The Carthogians had good artisans too. If the Kroaxians could do it, why couldn't the Carthogians? No reason at all. In fact, from what Sallakar had seen in the past, the Carthogians were more than likely to have done it first. And that would be something the officers wouldn't tell us about, he thought to himself. Oh no, they'd never tell the troops about something like that.

"Sallakar, what the 'ell d'yer think yer a-doin' of? 'Avin' a nice nap there, are yer?" the voice of Sergeant Bergolod bellowed from farther back down the line. "Get fell back in."

"Go fornicate with yourself," Sallakar muttered as he hitched his pack into a more comfortable position and rejoined the column at a gap next to Moxeff.

"You must find your delight in serving extra watch-duty, Sallakar," Moxeff murmured. "Is it the tranquillity of contemplating the desert in solitude at early bright that attracts you so? And to think, I had no idea you were of such poetic disposition."

"A plague of rusts and poxes upon this desert!" Sallakar spat. "Thrice have I crossed it now, and each time its breadth doubles."

"More likely the quality of thy temper halves."

"Your constitution is unaffected by this heat, no doubt," Sallakar said.

"Pleasantly dry and refreshing after Kroaxia's debilitatingly humid air," Moxeff agreed.

"Zounds! Your own admission disqualifies the sole excuse left you for your insufferable temperament."

"You should save such peevishness to vent upon the Carthogians," Moxeff advised.

"In truth I do believe you welcome combat as you relish the desert heat. And do you thrive also on breathing this carborundum powder, and conserving one bucket of methane per bright to top up your solutions and wash off the grime extruded from your joints?"

"Ah, as always you bitch too much, Sallakar."

"And the likes of you bitch not enough. Would any bondslave tolerate abuse such as this? Oh no! But it is I who bitch too much. Oh yes! Do you have no desire to assert your freeman's rights?"

"Must I remind you that the army is our law, Sallakar? Who ever heard of foot soldiers demanding rights?"

"And why not?" Sallakar asked. "In Carthogia, so 'tis said, authority is conferred by majority agreement among the citizens, and owes naught to any force of arms nor nobility of birth—a most commendable precedent. Why not, then, I say, in the army also?"

"You're kidding!"

"Not so. This matter has occupied my thoughts now for many brights. We will form ourselves a union, Moxeff, to match rank with collective strength, and bargain our services and loyalty only in return for fair and reasonable conditions that shall be contractually underwritten. To fight, we would require favorable numerical odds of two-to-one or better, at least moderately clement weather, and a minimum-compensation guarantee against worthless plunder. Rest periods would be fixed at mid- and quarter-bright, one bright in every six declared combat-free, and a peace-tax levied from the populace to maintain our remuneration in times of unemployment."

"Oh, that the foot soldier's life should bring such bliss! And have you the intention of reading this, thy proclamation, to our King, Eskenderom, and his Court personally? Well, may good luck go with you, Sallakar. Doubtless we shall all speak of you with fondest sentiments and remembrances."

"Shame on you who can speak thus contemptibly without embarrassment. Would you partake your share of the betterments we might secure? Oh yes—unquestionably! But to pledge in return your share of allegiance to our cause? Oh no—unthinkable! Is it not . . ." Sallakar stopped speaking and turned his head away to look as a commotion broke out somewhere up ahead. A moment later the column halted. "What the forn—"

"The desert heaves!" Moxeff exclaimed.

"Is't a storm?" someone ahead shouted.

"No storm appears thus," another cried.

"Is this some Carthogian trickery?"

"The ground ahead boils! It is on fire!"

"And around us also—we are trapped!"

A wall of smoke and flame had erupted across the line of march and was climbing higher by the second to blot out the sky ahead, while above, on the overlooking slopes to left and right, curtains of shimmering violet light had appeared, hemming in the front of the column. "I AM THE ENLIGHTENER, WHOM THE LIFEMAKER HAS SENT AMONG YOU," a voice boomed, seemingly from everywhere at once, and echoing among the surrounding hills. "SOLDIERS OF KROAXIA, LAY DOWN YOUR ARMS, FOR HE HATH COMMANDED, 'THOU SHALT NOT KILL.'"

"Deploy for ambush! Scatter the column!" a mounted officer shouted as he galloped back down the line. "Infantry under cover. Cavalry to the flanks. Close up the wagons."

"A Company to those rocks. B Comapny, string out along the gully. C Company, follow me," Sergeant Bergolod called out. Officers in front and in the rear began to shout orders, and in moments the column had disintegrated into bodies running in all directions. Sallakar found himself crouched with Moxeff and a couple of others behind some rocks. He peered up over the rock and saw that figures dressed in white had appeared amid the wall of swirling radiance higher up—elusive, dancing, etheric figures, apparently devoid of physical substance. They seemed to be approaching, down the slope.

A soldier nearby raised his hurler loosely to his shoulder and fired, knocking himself over backward with the recoil. A ragged volley came from another group behind, and in seconds firing had broken out all along the column. Gripped by the fear that had seized everyone, Sallakar sighted at a pair of white-robed figures, held the hurler hard and firm against his shoulder as he had been taught, and squeezed the finger-lever. The hurler juddered . . . but had no effect, even though Sallakar was aiming straight at the advancing figures. He swept the weapon desperately from side to side and up and down to cover every inch of them, but they kept on coming.

Inside the flyer hovering just at the edge of the smoke clouds boiling upward from the napalm tanks and explosives planted ahead of the Taloids, Zambendorf was watching the scene in close-up. It was as well that they had allowed for the possibility of the Paduans' panicking, he reflected, and decided not to expose any of the Taloids on their own side prematurely. Stretching away from the lurid glow immediately below the flyer, two streaks of whiteness flickered eerily where recorded Taloid images were being projected onto internally illuminated smokescreens from lanterns concealed several hours earlier on the rock-strewn slopes overlooking the obvious route through the valley. "Let's see if we can put a stop to that shooting," he said to Clarissa.

"Plan C?" she said.

"Yes—a low-level bomb run at those ice crags, accompanied by some pyrotechnics."

In the copilot's seat, Abaquaan prepared to repeat another recording of a pretransmogrified message from Moses over the flyer's bullhorns, suitably modified for high frequency, and from the ultrasonic amplifiers positioned to command the area.

"*Ayee!*" One of the soldiers dropped his weapon and

stood up, pointing in terror at the sky above the wall of fire. "A dragon decends! We have brought the Lifemaker's wrath down upon us!" A sleek, slender-limbed creature, unlike any that Sallakar had ever seen before, was swooping down at them. Instinctively he turned and aimed his hurler upward in its direction, then realized the futility of that and lowered it again.

"We are doomed," Moxeff moaned next to him. Several nearby infantry robeings dropped their weapons and began running blindly back the way they had come. Then a series of brilliant lights and clouds of violet radiance blossomed overhead, and simultaneously more lights streaked down from the dragon and destroyed a formation of rock outcrops and large boulders in a fury of deafening concussions. Sallakar cringed and covered his ears . . . but he was still alive.

"DESIST, SOLDIERS," the voice that had called itself Enlightener thundered again from above. "THE COMMANDMENT IS, 'THOU SHALT NOT KILL'!"

And then a much larger dragon emerged from the fiery wall before them, flying slowly and majestically right above their heads with fire blasting from beneath it. "Angels!" Moxeff gasped, straightening up and pointing. "Angels are descending from the skies!"

"See how they shine!" another soldier shouted. "Truly this is a time of miracles." On every side, soldiers were running from cover and standing with their faces raised to watch. Some had thrown away their weapons already and were clasping their hands together, and some had fallen to their knees. Even the officers were sitting motionless, awed and cowed by what was happening. Above, more heavenly figures, each borne on white, frilly wings, were floating serenely downward behind the dragon.

"PREPARE TO MEET THE ENLIGHTENER," the voice boomed. "I COME TO THEE IN PEACE, BRINGING GOODWILL TO ALL ROBEINGS."

Inside the cargo bay of the NASO surface lander making a low pass at just above stalling speed, Joe Fellburg checked Moses' harness one last time, gave a satisfied nod, and motioned the Taloid to the edge of the deck by the open loading-doors. Moses leaned forward a fraction and peered down apprehensively. "Tell him he'll be okay if he makes sure to jump hard and clear, and counts five before he pulls the ring," Fellburg shouted to West, who was standing by them, holding the transmogrifier. "And look at the others who've just jumped—they're doing fine." West spoke into the microphone, verified the interpretation that appeared on the screen, and the machine passed the message on to Moses. Moses nodded trustingly.

"Great stuff, guy," Fellburg said. He stooped to ignite the fireworks lying on the floor and attached to Moses' pack by wires long enough to ensure they would hang a safe distance below him, then stood up again, stepped back a pace, and patted the top of the robot's head. "Geronimo!" he yelled as the assemblage of sputtering flares and white-robed robot launched itself out into space. A searchlight from the flyer, which was circling nearby, picked out the figure as its parachute opened and it began to descend slowly through Titan's dense atmosphere.

A gasp of wonder went up from the soldiers as at last the Master appeared, descending in a luminous halo and bathed in a beam of heavenly brilliance. Sallakar didn't know what to believe, but in his own mind he had already come to a profound realization of immense theological significance: Rejecting the Enlightener's creed would mean having to fight the Carthogians; conversion to it, however, would not. "Hallelujah!" he shouted, throwing his weapon aside and climbing up on the rock to stand with both arms extended. "I am saved! This sinner has seen the light! Hail to thee, Enlightener!"

Most of the Kroaxian army, it seemed, was only just behind him in reaching the same conclusion. All along the column, figures were standing up, coming out from cover, and throwing their weapons to the ground. The air rang with hundreds of voices rejoicing:

"I see the light! I see the light!"

"The Enlightener cometh!"

"Praise the Enlightener!"

"We are saved! We are saved!"

"No more killing! No more war!"

"All are my brothers. I shall not kill!"

For many hours the Enlightener preached great words of love and wisdom from a hilltop to the soldiers assembled on the slopes below. When he had finished, they abandoned their weapons in the desert and turned back to return to Kroaxia. The Enlightener was lifted again into the sky to be borne ahead by the angels. He promised he would await his converts at the city of Pergassos, where they would join him to begin together the founding of the new world.

"It's amazing! I simply don't believe this," Massey said to Zambendorf over the link from the *Orion* as the departing flyer climbed higher and transmitted a view of the shambles that had been the Paduan army.

"Just the last phase left now, Gerry," Zambendorf told him confidently. "Next stop—Padua. We've rehearsed the cast, tested all the props, perfected our technique, and everything works just fine. What could possibly go wrong?"

An hour later, a military reconnaissance aircraft flew over the deserts between Padua and Genoa, and sent a series of views up to the *Orion* showing the entire Paduan army streaming back the way it had come. Caspar Lang was given the report shortly after receiving confirmation that a surface lander had disappeared on a routine descent to Padua. No signal had been received from any of the ship's automatic fault-monitoring devices, and the crew had been highly rated for reliability and stability; the NASO experts who investigated were unanimous in concluding that the vessel had been hijacked.

Lang arranged with the military commander at Padua base for James Bond, the spy employed by the Paduan king, Henry, to be airlifted ahead of the retreating army in order to intercept it and learn what had happened. Afterward, Bond rode off into the hills to a rendezvous with the Terrans and was flown back to Padua Base to make his report.

The news was that the planned Paduan invasion of Genoa was off. The entire Paduan army was out of its officers' control and was returning home to build a new society after encountering a messiah in the desert who had converted all of them to a new religion of tolerance and nonviolence. The messiah had descended from the sky accompanied by flying dragons, winged angels, heavenly voices, and all kinds of miracle-workings.

Lang's suspicions were immediately aroused. "Check Zambendorf out," he instructed his chief administrative assistant. "He's been too quiet for too long. I want to know where he is, and every move he's made in the last forty-eight hours."

Neither Zambendorf nor practically anyone on his team were anywhere to be found.

"You were supposed to have been keeping him busy and under observation at all times!" Lang screamed at a white-faced Osmond Periera in the Globe I executive offices fifteen minutes after Lang received the news. "Well, he isn't anywhere in the ship; he's not down at Genoa Base, and nobody's seen him for two days. Where is he?"

"I, er, I thought he was with Malcom Wade," Periera replied shakily. "But apparently Wade thought he was with me. I can't imagine how the mix-up was possible. Thelma seems to have garbled all our instructions somehow . . . but then, she is only the secretary. I'm afraid we must have overestimated her abilities."

"And I'm damn sure I overestimated yours!" Lang seethed. "Never mind all those excuses—just find him, understand? I want him found!"

A half hour later, Periera was confronting Thelma in the team's quarters in Globe II. "I'm sorry if we confused you, but it has now become imperative that the situation be resolved as speedily as possible. We have to know where he is. Now listen to me very carefully, Thelma, and concentrate hard on what I'm saying. Now, do-you-know-where-Karl-is?"

Thelma stared back at him wide-eyed. "On Earth, I think."

"Oh, come now, that's quite absurd. Please try to be sensible. How could he have gone back to Earth?"

"He teleports there," Thelma's face was deadly serious, and her eyes burned earnestly. "Didn't you know? He's been working at it for months now."

"Don't be silly."

"Really."

Periera looked at her uncertainly. "Really? You're not joking?"

"Now, would I joke about something as serious as that—especially to you, Osmond?"

So Periera reported back to Lang that he was pretty sure Zambendorf had mastered teleportation and returned to Earth.

When Lang blew up, Periera decided it was because business executives were unimaginative, inflexible, and didn't understand science.

31

UNLIKE POPULAR IMAGES OF THE HIGH-RANKING CORporation Executive, Caspar Lang was not consumed with a passion to accumulate wealth, and he harbored no particular lust for power over other men. GSEC's rewards for his services, and the authority that he commanded within the corporate hierarchy—second only to that of Gregory Buhl—left him with no reason to feel financially vulnerable, psychologically or emotionally insecure, or especially apprehensive about his future. This general situation resulted in his being relatively unbribable by competing organizations, incorruptible by opposing ideologies, and fully motivated to the preservation of personal interests that coincided with those of the corporation, whose policy was to insure that he remained feeling that way. In short, the quality that the corporation valued above all else in its senior management, and did its best to foster in every possible way, was loyalty. Since Zambendorf was deliberately attempting to prevent the corporation's achieving the goals toward which it had elected to direct itself, Zambendorf was now the corporation's self-declared enemy, which automatically meant Lang's enemy too. Personal feelings didn't enter the equation—not that Lang's feelings toward Zambendorf had ever been more than lukewarm; Lang's duty was to stop Zambendorf by any means available to him within the bounds of acceptable cost—and with the ramifications of the situation as they were, the limit of cost acceptability was high by any standard.

"As best we can reconstruct it, the whole thing was a circus act involving low passes by the lander, parachuting Taloids, tricks with optical images and acoustics, and lots of fireworks," Lang said to Massey across the table in the conference cabin of Leaherney's suite in the *Orion*. Opposite Massey, Leaherney stared grimly at his knuckles, clasped in front of him, while across from Lang, Charles Giraud was listening with lips pursed and steepled fingers propping the bridge of his nose. Lang went on, "The Paduan army has disintegrated and is on its way back to Padua. The officers that James Bond talked to said they were going home to meet this messiah and begin building the New Era. We figure that means Zambendorf's planning a repeat performance in Padua city itself."

Massey rubbed his nose and frowned down at the table. He still wasn't sure why he had been summoned. "Well, my feelings on the whole business of supplying weapons to the Paduans and fomenting trouble between them and the Genoese were plain enough before this happened. I can't pretend to be sympathetic now that your plan's fallen through. In fact, as far as Zambendorf's concerned, this one time I have to say good luck to him."

"Whatever personal opinions you might hold concerning the objectives set for this mission and the policies of its directing institutions on Earth are irrelevant to the purpose of this meeting," Leaherney said. His voice was uncharacteristically sharp. Massey shrugged but said nothing. Leaherney glanced at Lang and nodded for him to continue.

"We have no way of locating where they're hiding the lander down there," Lang said. "It could be anywhere in an area of hundreds of thousands of square kilometers. So we have to assume that the next time we see Zambendorf will be when he decides to make his appearance at Padua and wheel in this messiah he's manufactured.

We won't get an opportunity to confront him again until then."

"What we'd like is your professional opinion as one of the mission's senior psychologists on Zambendorf's probable reaction to the course of action that we have in mind," Giraud said.

There would have been no point in Massey's feigning disinterest. He raised his head and thrust out his chin inquiringly, but remained silent. Lang waited for a moment, and then resumed in a strange, curiously ominous voice, "As I'm sure we all know, modern infantry-launched homing missiles for use against armor and low-flying aircraft are pretty devastating weapons. They carry smart electronics for target identification and tracking, and are designed to be very simple to use—without requiring specially trained personnel. The Taloids could learn to fire them very quickly." Lang tossed out his hands in a brief motion and let his meaning hang for just a second. "If, ah . . . if anything like that just happened to have been included in the weapons that we shipped down to Henry, it could be real bad news for anyone who tried a slow-speed, low-level run over the city in a surface lander, couldn't it?"

Massey's eyes were blazing even before Lang had finished, and his beard quivered with indignation. "What are you saying? That would be murder! You can't—"

Lang held up a hand protectively. "Hey, take it easy, Gerry. Just . . . take it easy. I was talking hypothetically. But suppose that Zambendorf believed that the Paduans really did have weapons like that. . . . You see my point—he's got his own people down there with him, plus the crew of the shuttle they hijacked. . . . What would he do? Would he back off and forget this whole damnfool thing about going for Padua, or would he risk it, and to hell with the others down there? Or would he do something else? What do you think?"

A short silence went by. "Are you asking me to make a prediction?" Massey asked guardedly.

Lang shook his head. "No—only an opinion. As Charles said, we're interested in what you think in your professional capacity as one of the mission's psychologists. We've some important decisions to make and not much time to make them in. We just want to be sure that we don't overlook anything that might be relevant."

Massey stared down at the table again, now very thoughtful. If his opinion was being sought and respected, perhaps he had judged the situation too hastily. "Why should Zambendorf believe anything like that?" he asked, looking up.

"We call the lander via the comnet and tell him," Lang replied simply.

"They wouldn't reply," Massey objected. "You'd be able to pinpoint their location."

"Not necessarily," Giraud said. "They could route their transmission through a surface relay dropped anywhere on Titan—or maybe several of them. We could locate the relays if we wanted, but it wouldn't help us get a fix on the lander."

Massey nodded distantly as his mind raced to absorb the implications of what was being said. Surely there was some way he could turn this situation to advantage, he told himself. Lang and the others would have deduced a long time ago NASO's real purpose in sending him with the mission, which would give them no reason for supposing that he and Zambendorf should since have discovered any common interests. All of their plans would be based on the assumption—now false—that he and Zambendorf would have nothing to communicate. The possibilities were intriguing.

After another long silence, Lang said, "Obviously the thought could cross his mind that we might be bluffing—in fact with a guy like Zambendorf, it's probably the first thing he'd think of. But on the other hand, the international political and commercial implications of the situation are big—very big, as Zambendorf is only too well aware. Who's to say what we might do when the chips are down? Would he risk it with all those other people down there? You're supposed to think the same way he does—that's why NASO sent you here, right? Okay—I want to know what you think."

Would Zambendorf risk it? Not if he were uncertain whether or not the warning was a bluff, Massey was sure. But now of course, with the seemingly impossible alliance between Zambendorf and Massey having so recently come about, and over an issue that the mission's directors were apparently incapable of comprehending, Zambendorf would not be left in any uncertainty on the matter. Therefore any conclusions based upon his presumed ignorance of the true state of affairs concerning the Taloid weapons would be invalidated. If Lang was basing his strategy on a bluff, Massey had an opportunity to undermine its entire foundation.

Massey looked up and ran his eyes slowly over the three faces waiting across the table for his reply. "Maybe Zambendorf is a rogue and a scoundrel in some ways, and maybe his concept of ethics doesn't exactly measure up to society's ideal, but basically his values are just and humane. If he has any real doubts, he won't gamble."

"You're sure?" Leaherney asked, sounding uneasy.

"No, it's just my opinion. That is what you asked for, and it's all I can offer."

"But you are reasonably confident," Giraud persisted.

Massey frowned and bunched his lips for a moment, then exhaled suddenly and nodded. "Reasonably," he conceded, quite truthfully.

Leaherney looked from Giraud to Lang, then back again, and finally at Massey. "Then if no one has anything more to add, we need detain you no longer. Thanks for your time."

"Thank you," Massey said, just a trifle stiffly. He remained expressionless as he rose to leave, but inwardly he was smiling broadly.

After Massey left, Leaherney emitted a long sigh, slumped back in his chair, and took a cigar from the box in the center of the table. He rolled the cigar beneath his nose and eyed Lang curiously while he savored the aroma of the tobacco. "Okay, Caspar," he said. "And now would you mind telling us exactly what that whole stunt was supposed to mean?"

"Sorry about the melodramatics, but I didn't want to tell you the latest until after we'd talked to Massey," Lang replied. "Your reactions needed to be genuine." He paused for a second to survey the other two briefly, and then informed them, "Our military-intelligence people are pretty certain that, improbable as it may seem, Massey and Zambendorf are now working together."

A puzzled frown crossed Giraud's face. "But if that's so and we send Zambendorf a warning, Massey will tell him it's just a bluff."

"As he's supposed to," Lang agreed.

Giraud's expression became even more perplexed. "So . . . what good will it do?" he asked.

"It will conflict with other information that will reach Zambendorf through the other two channels that we've identified," Lang replied. "That NASO captain—Campbell—has been leaking classified information to Thelma like a sieve ever since we left Earth, and a number of the scientists are sympathetic to Zambendorf's humanitarian ideals concerning the Taloids. I intend to plant information that will find its way to Zambendorf from both those sources, indicating that the bluff story we fed Massey was intended simply to put us on record as having tried to warn Zambendorf off—thereby exonerating us from any blame for his actions—and that really the Paduans do have smart missiles."

"Zambendorf won't know what to believe," Leaherney said. He stopped to think for a second and shook his head bemusedly. "In fact I'm not even sure I know myself."

"And I agree completely with Massey's prediction that Zambendorf won't gamble if he's in any doubt as to the true situation," Lang said. He smiled humorlessly, braced his hands on the edge of the table in preparation to rise, and looked at Giraud. "The next thing we have to do is arrange a descent to Padua for another meeting with Henry. No doubt he'll be pretty mad when James Bond tells him what happened to his invasion, but if all goes well and Zambendorf backs down, I don't think we'll have too much trouble persuading Henry that the whole thing was just a temporary setback. A week from now we'll all be back on track."

32

THE FLYER SPED LOW OVER THE SURFACE OF TITAN, guided through the darkness by forward-scanning radars that felt the landscape with their electronic fingers and translated its contours into binary number-streams that the flight-control computers could understand. In the right-hand side of the cockpit, his thick mustache transformed into a gaping slash across a face thrown into eerie reverse-relief by the subdued glow from the instrument panel, Otto Abaquaan stared silently out at the blackness, absorbed in his own thoughts.

Over twenty years had passed since the serendipitous courses that he and Zambendorf had been following through life happened to collide in Frankfurt, West Germany. Abaquaan had been working a stocks-and-bonds swindle at the time. Overconfident and careless after a three-month run of easy pickings from wealthy dowagers along the French Riviera, he hadn't bothered to check up on Zambendorf thoroughly enough before selling him a portfolio of phony certificates, and it wasn't until his contact-man was arrested and Abaquaan was forced to flee the country hours ahead of the police that he discovered Zambendorf had paid for them with phony money. Soon afterward, Zambendorf had managed to track him down again—apparently without too much difficulty—not to moralize or crow over the lesson Abaquaan had been taught, but to express interest in the scheme and compliment Abaquaan on his style. A partnership had developed, and the rest of the team had appeared one by one in various circumstances over the years since.

During those years with Zambendorf he had wound up in some unexpected places, been mixed up with some strange people, and found himself involved in all kinds of bizarre affairs, including being paid a quarter of a million dollars by a Chinese industrialist for communicating with several generations of honorable ancestors; setting up an ESP-based military espionage system for a West African government; selling information from an almanac to a fashionable Italian horoscope writer at exorbitant rates; and prospecting for strategic metals over the estates of a Brazilian landowner. And now to top it all, they were on one of Saturn's moons, of all places, stage-managing a mechanical Jesus Christ and starting a new religion among a race of intelligent robots. And what was strange was that nothing about the situation really struck Abaquaan as being so strange at all. He was a long time past that. Nothing that involved Zambendorf was capable of seeming strange anymore.

After consulting with Joe Fellburg and Andy Schwartz, the captain of the surface lander on unofficial loan from NASO, Zambendorf had accepted that parachuting down over the built-up area of Padua would be a risky enough business for anyone, let alone untrained Taloids, and had therefore abandoned his original plan to repeat the performance that had played so successfully before Henry's army in the desert. Instead, Clarissa and Abaquaan had flown Moses to a point just outside the city, from which he would make his way into the metropolis on foot and begin to preach the Revelation during the busiest trading period in the central marketplace. On receipt of a radio signal from Moses' transmitter, the lander would make a dramatic descent into the heart of the city, accompanied by lights, voices, and special effects, and disembark a specially rehearsed celestial troupe consisting of Lord Nelson and a supporting act of Druids. The result would be instant conversions of Paduans by the drove, Zambendorf had predicted confidently; Henry would be deposed; Genoa would be saved; the Taloids' future would be assured; and the war against unscrupulous Terran business tycoons and politicians would be won. It was one of Zambendorf's strengths as a leader—and a source of some of the biggest problems that came from working with him—that he always made everything sound too easy.

The most recent developments, however, were causing Abaquaan misgivings. First, twenty-four hours or so before, Massey had called from the *Orion* to advise that Caspar Lang would probably use a ruse to warn Zambendorf off from any intention he might have of reproducing his desert spectacular over Padua city.

Sure enough Lang had come through a couple of hours later and issued a solemnly worded warning containing all the points that Massey had predicted. Zambendorf had put on an impressive act of trying desparately but not quite successfully to hide his dismay as he listened, and mumbled about needing time to rethink the whole situation. Then, roaring with laughter after Lang was off the line, he had told the team jubilantly, "This has to mean we're over the last hurdle! Thanks to Massey we've bluffed the bluffers with their own bluff. Lang and the rest of them will just be sitting up there in the *Orion*, waiting for us to call back while we're going in over the city. They won't expect a thing!"

Zambendorf's enthusiasm had infected the lander's NASO crew, who were gradually being won over by a combination of his magnetism and his explanations about the *Orion* mission and its real purpose. The team had effectively acquired another four members and was all set to launch the final phase of the operation that would make its task complete. The situation could hardly have been more favorable. In fact it was too favorable. Everything was going too well, Abaquaan felt. Buried somewhere deep down in the whole intricate pattern was something that didn't quite fit—something still too subtle for him to raise to the level of conscious awareness, but his instincts had detected it. Twenty years earlier Abaquaan had learned the dangers of overconfidence; a premonition kept telling him that at long last Zambendorf's turn had arrived to learn the same lesson.

An annunciator on the instrument panel bleeped suddenly, and a symbol on a display screen began to flash on and off. In the seat next to him, Clarissa glanced down, flipped a switch to reset the audio warning, punched commands into the pilot's touchpanel, and took in the data that appeared on another display. "We've just triggered the outer approach marker," she murmured as she throttled back on power and banked the flyer round to line up for landing. "Open up a channel to ground, and let's have a profile check."

Abaquaan selected an infrared view of the terrain ahead and used another screen to conjure up images of a series of flight instruments. "Steepen to one-eight-zero, rate five-four, reduce speed to four-twenty, and come round onto two-five-nine," he instructed. "Autoland lock-on programed at ten seconds into phase three of glidepath."

"Descent monitor and systems?" Clarissa queried.

"Green one, green two, and ah . . . all positive function."

The flyer came round an invisible mountaintop and straightened out onto its final approach and descent into the narrow, sheer-sided valley where the surface lander was hidden. The valley floor was a sprawling mess of alien industrial constructions, tangled machinery, and derelict plants, and would blur any radar echos to overflying reconnaissance satellites sufficiently to conceal the outline of the lander, which as an extra precaution had been copiously draped with aluminum foil and metalized plastic. The site was showing no lights, and electronic transmissions were being restricted to low-power local communications and ground beams aimed at satlink relays. Abaquaan pressed a button and spoke into the microphone projecting from his headset. "*Hornet* to Big Bird. Do you read? Over."

The voice of Hank Frazer, the lander's Communications Officer, replied a few seconds later: "Reading you okay, *Hornet*. The landing area is clear here. How'd it all go?"

"Hi, Hank. Mission accomplished," Abaquaan replied. "Moses is on his way. No hitches. How have things been back there?"

The flyer slowed to hover in the darkness, and Clarissa quickly scanned graphics displays presented by the flight computers. Moments later the vehicle began sinking vertically. "I think we may have problems," Frazer's voice answered. "Dave Crookes called down from the ship. It seems like he overheard a couple of army officers up there talking about infantry missiles being issued to the Paduans specifically for use against the lander if Zambendorf tried any more tricks with it. Crookes didn't know what to make of the conversation, but it sounded serious and he figured we ought to know. In other words it looks as if Henry may really have those weapons after all."

In the semidarkness of the flyer's cockpit, Clarissa and Abaquaan exchanged ominous glances. "Have they talked to Massey about it?" Clarissa murmured, tight-lipped. Outside, the tops of fractionating towers and steel pylons, indistinct and ghostly in Titan's feeble light, were drifting slowly into view from below. The flyer's engine note rose as the computers increased thrust to absorb the last remaining momentum of its descent.

"Has Karl talked to Massey about it?" Abaquaan asked.

"He couldn't locate him, but he's trying again right now," Frazer answered.

"Does Karl still think Lang was bluffing?"

"He doesn't know what to think."

The flyer gave a final lurch on its shock absorbers, and something deep down in Abaquaan's stomach lurched with it. The engines fell to idling speed, and the computer displays switched to a series of postflight test routines. "We're down," Abaquaan said. "We'll be over in a few minutes. Talk to you then. Out."

Clarissa leaned forward to scan the ground ahead of the nose, and a few seconds later a light appeared from among the shadows. The figure of Joe Fellburg, clad in an EV suit and carrying a flashlamp, an M37 automatic infantry assault cannon slung across his shoulder, moved forward and guided the vehicle out of the open and into its parking area beneath the girder-lattice roof supports of what had once been a building of some kind. More forms took shape in the gloom behind him as some of Moses' followers from the Taloid encampment nearby came closer to watch.

"What do you think?" Abaquaan asked, reaching for his helmet as Clarissa cut the engine.

"I don't know what to think either," she said as she proceeded quickly through the systems shutdown sequence. "It doesn't sound too good."

Abaquaan unbuckled his harness, hoisted himself from his seat, and moved into the forward cabin to put on his helmet. Clarissa followed, and they exited through the main lock. Fellburg was waiting for them outside. "Good flight?"

"It went fine," Abaquaan said. "Moses is on his way into the city."

"It's a pity we can't bring him back. There might be problems."

"Yeah—you mean about what Dave Crookes heard. Hank told us."

"Drew thinks we'll have to call off the whole operation."

"What about Moses?" Clarissa's voice asked, sounding clipped.

Fellburg threw out a heavily gauntleted hand. "It's tough, but what can you do?"

Just then, something scurried furtively in the shadows below one of the flyer's wings. Fellburg snapped on the flashlamp, and the beam caught a silvery, insectlike machine, about the size of a kitchen chair, with an elongated, tapering head, a body covered by sliding, overlapping plates, and six slender, segmented legs, in the act of stretching one of its sensory appendages to investigate the flyer's extended landing pad. A piece of metal hurtled from the darkness and bounced off the creature's flank, and a moment later two Taloids rushed forward waving their arms wildly to chase it away; the creature had fled before Fellburg's gun was even half unslung. As they resumed walking toward the black silhouette of the lander, Fellburg swung the lamp from side to side to pick out the bullet-riddled remains of a half dozen or so similar machines. Another flashlamp shone briefly some distance ahead of them where Clancy Baker was patrolling on the far side of the lander. "Looks like some of these overgrown tin bugs are partial to NASO-specification alloy," Fellburg grunted. "But they're learning pretty quick that getting too close ain't all that healthy."

Inside the lander, Zambendorf and Drew West were standing in front of one of the screen consoles on the flight deck, with Andy Schwartz sitting to one side. Across the aisle, Mike Glautzen sat in the flight engineer's seat, which was reversed to face them. Hank Frazer and Vernon were watching from in front of the doorway leading aft into the main cabin. "We managed to get hold of Massey a few minutes ago," Frazer murmured as Clarissa and Abaquaan arrived from the midships lock.

"I'm not sure what to believe, Gerry," Zambendorf was saying to the screen. "Do you think that what Dave Crookes overheard could have been deliberate—a plant intended to scare us off?"

"Who knows? It's possible," Massey replied.

"But how could Lang have known that Crookes would pass the information on?" Glautzen queried from behind.

"Easily," Zambendorf said over his shoulder. "He was one of the few among the scientists who were solidly behind Gerry in protesting the mission's policies. Also Dave is a communications specialist."

"The other possibility is that it could have been you who was fed wrong information," Drew West said to Massey. "Perhaps the Paduans *have* been given smart missiles. The story that it's a bluff might really be a double bluff aimed at persuading us to persuade ourselves that there isn't any risk."

"Yes, that's also possible," Massey admitted. He sounded far from happy.

Andy Schwartz shook his head and tossed his hands up helplessly. "I'm confused," he protested. "What is all this? The management doesn't want us doing the same thing at Padua that we did to Henry's army—right? If that's so, they'd want us to believe what Lang said, wouldn't they—whether the Paduans really possess any missiles or not. So why would they set Gerry up to tell us Lang was bluffing? Either way it makes no sense."

Drew West bit his lip for a moment, then said, "Unless they wanted us to get shot down." The cabin became very still as everyone tried to tell himself West hadn't meant what they knew he'd meant. After a pause West went on, "It would get rid of their number-one problem permanently. No Terrans need be directly involved since the Paduans would have done everything necessary through a contrived accident... And Leaherney's people would have gone on record as having tried to do the civilized thing and warn us, even after we hijacked their lander." He shrugged. "So how would it look to an investigating committee afterward? A bunch of hotheads insisted on flying an illegally acquired vessel into the home territory of heavily armed aliens of known warlike disposition despite attempts to warn them, and got themselves killed—a clear verdict of death by misadventure. All parties in authority get exonerated. Some recommendations would be filed for tightening up security precautions against similar seizures in future. And that would be it. Case closed." West turned from the screen and moved away to stand staring moodily down at the empty captain's couch.

Hank Frazer was shaking his head and looking appalled. "You're kidding!" he gasped. "Are you saying they'd deliberately set us up to be shot down? But they're our own people!... All over some lousy robot religion? I don't believe it. The whole thing's insane."

"This operation might be worth millions to them—billions, probably," West said without turning his head. "And on top of that it could be curtains for the Soviets. With stakes like that, who knows what they might do?"

"I have to agree with Drew," Abaquaan told Zambendorf from the cabin doorway. He knew now what had been bothering him: After Massey's attempt at organizing a formal protest, Lang wouldn't have confided in him over something like this. The leak had been planned.

"They wouldn't think twice about it," Clarissa declared flatly. "I've seen 'em waste more people over peanuts. It just depends on how much somebody decides he wants the peanuts."

"They're right," Andy Schwartz agreed morosely.

A heavy silence descended once again. Zambendorf brought a hand up to his brow, emitted a long, weary sigh, and moved a couple of paces toward the door. There was nothing more that any of the others could add. Zambendorf was going through the motions of tussling with a difficult decision, but Abaquaan, West, and Clarissa, who had worked with him for a long time, knew already that there was no decision for him to make; as bitter as it would be for him to have to concede defeat—and to cap it all, defeat in the final round after winning every round that had gone before—he would never ask them to risk their lives for any cause, and wouldn't for a moment consider risking the crew, even if they were to volunteer. It had been a good fight, but it was over. All that Zambendorf was really looking for now was a way to climb down gracefully. The lander's crew could sense it too, and while they sympathized with his predicament, none of them was particularly disposed to help make it any easier. After all, being hijacked to help a worthy cause was one thing; going on suicide missions was something else. They remained silent and avoided one another's eyes uncomfortably.

Then Massey turned his head suddenly to look somewhere offscreen. "There's somebody at the door here," he said. "Just a second while I see who it is." He leaned away and vanished from sight for a few seconds, then reappeared once more and announced, "It's Thelma. I've let her in. She said something about having important news."

Zambendorf frowned and moved up to the screen. Drew West came back from the forward end of the flight deck to stand next to him. In front of them, Massey moved to one side to make room for Thelma. She looked worried. "Have you sent Moses into Padua yet?" she asked without preliminaries.

Zambendorf nodded. "Yes—as scheduled. Why? What's happened?"

Thelma groaned. "You can't go through with it. Larry Campbell got me a copy of the cargo manifest for the latest arms shipment down to Henry. Those missiles are there, Karl. The list includes twenty-four Banshee Mark Fours, half with training warheads and the rest of them live. They could blow you out of the sky from up to eleven kilometers away. There's no chance that going in there could achieve anything now except get everyone down there killed. You have to call the whole thing off."

For a long time nobody moved and nobody spoke. Schwartz and Glautzen stared down at the floor, while on the screen Thelma waited pale-faced and Massey kept his eyes averted woodenly. At last, Zambendorf gave a single curt nod, turned away, and stumbled unsteadily forward between the pilots' stations. He sank down heavily into the captain's seat and sat staring out through the windshield with unseeing eyes, his frame hunched and his shoulders sagging as if he had just aged twenty years.

Drew West moved round to bring himself full-face to the image of Massey and Thelma. "I think Karl sees the way it is," he told them quietly. "Look, you've done all you can for now. It'd probably be best if you left things with us for a while. We'll talk to you later, okay?"

Thelma was about to say something more, but Massey checked her with a warning touch on the shoulder and shook his head. "Okay, Drew," he murmured. "I guess it was a good try, huh?" The screen went blank.

Abaquaan looked from one to another of the subdued

faces around him. "What about Nelson and the Druids outside?" he asked in a low voice. "They're all ready for the grand entry into Padua. What do we tell them?"

Nobody had any answers, or seemed to care all that much. At length West said, "Well, perhaps that's something we ought to talk about." As the others looked at him, he motioned with his head to indicate the direction of the door. Andy Schwartz got the message and nodded silently; he got up from his seat, waved a hand for Glautzen to do likewise, and followed Abaquaan, Clarissa, and the others near the doorway through into the main cabin. Glautzen and West came next, closing the door quietly behind them to leave Zambendorf alone and unmoving, staring out into Titan's perpetual night.

33

FRENNELECH, THE HIGH PRIEST OF KROAXIA, SAT alone in his private chambers in the Palace of the High Holy One at Pergassos, brooding over the latest reports from his spies. He smelt a conspiracy in the air, and the evidence pointed to Eskenderom, the King, as being very much mixed up in it.

Eskenderom's ambition had long been to sweep the other nations of the Sacred Alliance aside and establish Kroaxia at the head of a mighty empire that would stretch to the Peripheral Barrier, with himself as its leader. His preparatory plans had involved political intrigues and subterfuges aimed at undermining the kings and rulers of neighboring states and weakening their holds over their realms; but in the case of Serethgin, the very destabilization that Eskenderom had brought about had given Kleippur opportunity to seize control over the province of Carthogia, and the resulting state of affairs had proved a hindrance to the further development of Eskenderom's scheme ever since.

Kroaxia's acquisition of weapons from the Lumians, however, suddenly put everything in a new light. If the reports of decisive Waskorian successes against Kleippur's forces were accurate—as the invasion of Carthogia was intended in part to test—the invasion would be completed swiftly and devastatingly, and Kleippur would cease to be a problem. Then Eskenderom would have to make his move against the other Alliance nations just as quickly and with total surprise, while his advantage was overwhelming—before the Lumians could restore a balance by arming Eskenderom's rivals in like fashion, as was doubtless their longer-term intent. For a long time, however, Eskenderom had been growing increasingly impatient over the traditional division of the powers of state between its secular and ecclesiastical authorities; if the King were now to find himself commanding powers potent enough to build an empire that would stretch to the ends of the world, Frennelech was under no illusion that his better nature would lead him to share such powers graciously with the clergy to serve the founding of a universal Church as well.

As Eskenderom would already have concluded, the prospect of such a dramatic decline of clerical power would put Frennelech squarely among his potential opposition—the kind of opposition, moreover, that Eskenderom would doubtless prefer to do without while he was dealing with the Alliance nations. The most probable explanation for Eskenderom's taking such a secretive interest in a laughable pipsqueak like Groork, therefore, and dispatching the loyal captain Horazzorgio to retrieve Groork from Xerxeon, was that Eskenderom intended replacing Frennelech with a tame puppet appointed by the Crown as its obedient caretaker of all matters spiritual. As far as Frennelech's sources had been able to ascertain, Horazzorgio still hadn't returned although he was long overdue by even the most conservative estimates. That was worrisome because it suggested that perhaps even more might be going on than Frennelech knew about.

Frennelech knew that Eskenderom frequently visited Gornod, the desolate spot in the mountains east of Pergassos where the Lumian flying vehicles landed, to meet treacherously with the Lumians behind Frennelech's back, even when Eskenderom's servants assured him that the King was somewhere else. He also knew from his own private rendezvouses with the Lumians in the dense forests to the west of Pergassos that Eskenderom was trying to enlist the aid of Lumian magic to present Groork to the Kroaxian population as a genuine miracle-worker and revealer of Divine Will—because the Lumians had admitted it. True, the Lumians had steadfastly denied that they had agreed to any such request, but how could Frennelech rely on the words of those who had already betrayed Kleippur's trust? Their only interest seemed to be their obsessive desire to tame the forests, and they would reward with wealth, power, and protection any robeing in a position of authority or influence who was prepared to cooperate with them in achieving that end. Eskenderom commanded the Kroaxian army, but Frennelech controlled the minds of the Kroaxian people. Which process would deliver a greater quantity of willing robeing labor to the Lumians—force or persuasion? Both Eskenderom and Frennelech were pressing their cases to the Lumians, and no doubt both were hearing reassuring responses. But ultimately, which would the Lumians elect to go with?

He gathered the sheets of foil together and locked them in a concealed compartment in his desk, then stood up and walked through into the outer chamber where his secretary, Archdeacon Jaskillion, was copying columns of numbers into an enormous, plate-bound ledger. "Over eight twelves of dozens of six-crowns received in penitents' dues and eternity prepayments last bright, and less than two dozen twelve-brights' remission of Reduction Furnace time paid out," Jaskillion said, sitting back and looking up. "Gross margin up a twelfth and a half. The Lifemaker should be well pleased."

"Then let the Lifemaker's business be kept private to the Lifemaker, lest Eskenderom should commence levying a tax on it," Frennelech advised.

Jaskillion looked shocked. "But to tax the sacred revenues would be tantamount to disputing the Lifemaker's judgment of His needs and interfering in the prosecution of His works," he protested. "What sacrilege would the King be committing thus!"

"Then it is our holy duty to avoid exposing him to the temptation," Frennelech said.

The archdeacon studied Frennelech's face for a few seconds. "But thou didst not come to banter such matters, I see. What troubles thee?"

"The Lumians," Frennelech said. "I cannot trust their assurances, but neither am I able to order their casings seared with flame and acid for the truthfulness of their words to be assessed by Inquisitors. And yet we dare not allow this business to be decided by the whims of these unworldly aliens whose motives and whose notions of truth are as unknown to us as the sky's far side of which they speak."

Jaskillion's mood became more serious. "The question has been occupying my thoughts too," he agreed.

"And what answers have thy thoughts supplied?"

Jaskillion paused for a moment to collect his words. "When a king becomes too strong, it is usually time for the Lifemaker's divine, immutable plan to be revised," he said at last. "It would be an error to permit Carthogia to be sacrificed just yet."

"A force aligned against Eskenderom at this time is not one to to be squandered—I agree. But our invasion has been dispatched, and Kleippur's army is about to be scattered and smashed. What shall save Carthogia then?"

"The Waskorians lie interposed between our army and Kleippur, and they too are equipped with Lumian arms," Jaskillion pointed out. "Were they, upon our secret instruction, to ally themselves with Carthogia, the resulting combined strength would perhaps be sufficient to hold out while Serethgin mobilizes against Kroaxia."

"What relief could Serethgin's horde bring against Lumian devilment, which confounds even Kleippur's trained regiments?" Frennelech asked scoffingly.

"Much, if the Serethginians too were issued Lumian arms," Jaskillion replied.

"Is this some foolish jest? We cannot confide in Serethgin's leaders and admit them into our dialogue with the Lumians."

"Of course not."

"But who else would supply them with Lumian arms?"

"We would . . . discretely. And after Eskenderom's defeat and removal, would not Serethgin's gratitude lead it to support a claim by thee in turn to assume the Supreme Archprelacy within the new unified state that Kroaxia and Serethgin would become?"

"Mmm . . ." Frennelech looked suddenly more interested. "And Carthogia also, after Serethgin regains the territory that rightfully belongs to it," he mused.

"Exactly . . . And if we could arrange by some means for all direct dealings with the Lumians to be conducted through ourselves exclusively, the king of Serethgin would have far more inducement than Eskenderom to agree to a reasonable compromise on the sharing of power in any empire that might ensue."

Frennelech smiled faintly. "Certainly our claim to being intermediaries between a higher form of mind and the world of mortal robeings would be indisputable," he murmured.

"Indeed so."

Frennelech became more businesslike once again. "But could Serethgin be equipped and mobilized in time?"

"How long did Kroaxia need to be equipped and mobilized?"

"What reason could the king of Serethgin offer to his people for taking arms against Kroaxia?" Frennelech asked.

"To defend their Waskorian brothers, whose faith Eskenderom is sending his armies illegally into Carthogia to persecute," Jaskillion suggested.

"Hmmm—an appeal that would be rendered all the more persuasive after the Waskorians had gone over to Kleippur's side."

"Precisely so. And Kleippur's insistence on freedom of worship for all is well known."

"Would Kleippur accept Waskorian aid?"

"He has been deserted by the Lumians; his soldiers have been defeated by rabble for lack of the weapons that the Waskorians possess; and now the survival of his entire nation is threatened. He will accept."

Just then, hurried footsteps sounded outside, and muffled voices sounded of a sentry at the door challenging and someone blurting a reply. A sharp rap sounded on the door. "Who knocks?" Frennelech called out.

"Kelessbayne, O Illustrious One, sent by Chroschanor to convey urgent tidings of events in the city."

"Allow him entry," Frennelech called to the guards. Kelessbayne entered and closed the door behind him. He looked flustered. "Well?" Frennelech demanded.

"Groork, the hearer, has appeared again," Kelessbayne gabbled. "He calls himself Enlightener, and has entered the city riding on a steam-donkey, preaching words of faith that he says are the Lifemaker's. A multitude that grows larger by the moment, bringing its sick, its blind, and its lame, is following him toward the Central Square, where he says great revelations will be made known and wondrous miracles come to pass."

Jaskillion was on his feet, his face tense with alarm. "What else has happened?" he snapped. "Have there been signs of dragons in the sky?" Kelessbayne was not among the few who knew the true nature of the Lumian vessels.

"Not in Pergassos. But Groork speaks of awesome happenings in the Meracasine—of the whole Kroaxian army renouncing the ways of war, abandoning its weapons in the desert, and returning hither to spread a new, nonviolent faith of universal brotherhood."

Frennelech groaned inwardly. It could only mean that the Lumians had chosen to back Eskenderom and were carrying out his plan to pass Groork off as a miracle-worker. "Is the army at the city also?" he asked weakly.

Kelessbayne shook his head. "It is still an eighth-bright's march from the gates, if Groork speaks truly."

"Was Groork present at these events that took place in the Meracasine?"

"Such is his assertion."

"Then how came he to the city so far ahead of any soldiers?"

"He claims that to prepare the way he was borne ahead

by shining angels who ride in creatures that fly beyond the sky."

That was as conclusive as anything could be—the Lumians had brought Groork to Pergassos. There could no longer be any doubt but that they were in league with Eskenderom. "Is the King still away?" he asked Jaskillion.

"He is," Jaskillion replied. Eskenderom was at Gornod, talking to the Lumians again; Jaskillion wouldn't mention the place in Kelessbayne's presence.

Frennelech thought desperately. With Groork's arrival at Pergassos an eighth of a bright ahead of the army, and Eskenderom still away, was it possible that the Lumians could have miscalculated somewhere in their timing? If so, perhaps Frennelech could do something yet to make their victory a little more costly. From what he had seen of the Lumians' powers he could probably do nothing to change the final outcome if they had made up their minds . . . but, if he was going down anyway, he would go down fighting.

"Collect as many of the Palace Guard as you can scrape together and send them immediately to the Central Square," he instructed Jaskillion. "Also, have my carriage brought to the side entrance and inform the guard commander that he will be under direct orders from me." He went back into his inner chamber to don his outdoor cloak.

"What is thy design?" Jaskillion called after him.

"I have a suspicion that Groork's behind-the-scenes miracle-makers might not be as prepared at this moment as they ought to be," Frennelech's voice replied. "If that should indeed turn out to be the case, I fear for him that this performance may well prove to be his last."

The crowd filled the Central Square of Pergassos and had started to overflow into the surrounding streets as word spread around the city and onlookers continued to arrive. Trading in the market had virtually ceased as stallholders covered their wares and closed down, either to protect their stock or to give undivided attention to what was happening. At the focus of it all, the Enlightener, who had mounted the steps of the platform and speaker's rostrum built in the center of the square, was holding a tablet of ice above his head and sounding forth in a voice that rang with fervor and conviction. "I have climbed the mountain and seen the angels. I have flown in the skies and seen persecutors turned into baptizers. I have seen armies crumble at His command, for now it has been written, 'Thou shalt not kill.'"

"Hear the Word that the Enlightener bringeth," one of the followers cried.

"Hail to the Enlightener!"

"We shall not kill!"

"Let he who disobeys be cast into the slave pits," another shouted.

"No!" the Enlightener's voice boomed around the square. "I say to thee that henceforth no robeing shall be a slave, one to another, for the Lifemaker's commandment is written, 'Thou art thy neighbor's equal.' Thou shalt not bow thy head nor bend thy knee before any that would proclaim thy inferiority to his worth, or demand the fruits of thy labors as thy duty to his station."

"How, then, shall we accept the Carthogians, Master?" another asked.

"Accept them as the soldiers of Kroaxia, once their sworn enemies unto death, have already accepted them—as comrades and brothers. No more shall robeing murder robeing, but all shall work together to gain wisdom and understanding until they are worthy to lift themselves into the skies and soar with the angels that appeared over the Meracasine."

"What sayest thou, Master—that we too shall fly?"

"Yes! Yes! All who have faith and believe in His Word shall fly with the shining angels, just as I have flown with them. This I promise you." The Enlightener could feel the mood of the crowd, its desire to believe, willing that it should be so. His eyes blazed, his skin shone in the light of the mid-bright sky, and the expression burning from his face radiated the ecstasy that he felt as the Lifemaker's force surged through every chip and channel of his being. He extended his arms to stand with his cloak spread wide above the crowd, and the crowd roared as the waves of rapture flowed outward from the center to break against the surrounding walls like methane breakers in a storm, crashing against ice cliffs at the ocean's edge.

"All are equal. We shall not be slaves!"

"We will work with our neighbors! We shall not kill!"

"When will we see the angels?"

The crowd's emotions were at a peak. The Enlightener sensed his optimum moment approaching. "I shall summon angels, and then every robeing will know I speak truly," he told them.

That was more than any mystic had ever offered before. "Show us the angels!" they shouted back. "Summon the angels!"

"I shall command miracles that you may know I speak truly?"

"Show us miracles! Then we will know!"

"THEN BEHOLD YE HIS POWER!" the Enlightener thundered, and with a flourish drew the praying-box from his pouch and held it high over his head. The whole square erupted in shouts of wonder, and then quietened expectantly. The Enlightener pressed the sacred button, and stabbing his finger upward, threw back his head. "IN THE NAME OF THE LIFEMAKER, I COMMAND THE SKIES—OPEN AND DELIVER THY WONDERS!"

Every face in the square tilted upward to peer at the heavens. Some of those present were screaming. Some had collapsed into unconsciousness. The Enlightener stood poised, waiting, still pointing at the sky. The crowd could see the irresistible compulsion burning in his eyes, and feel the cosmic force streaming from his outstretched finger. The moment was crushing, terrifying, overpowering. They were inextricably a part of it now, and being swept along helplessly in a flood tide of rising, swirling, passion and emotion. They watched, and waited. They howled. They shouted.

And then, very suddenly, a silence descended and spread to cover the square from one side to the other as completely as had the excitement only moments before. All at once, seemingly, everyone had noticed that nothing was happening. All the heads tilted back down and looked at each other quizzically. The Enlightener's image evaporated, and all that was left where he had stood was a foolish-looking mystic holding a peculiar vegetable in the air. He lowered the vegetable and jabbed at it frantically, still looking upward with a pleading expression on his face. He shook his head in disbelief and tried again.

"Well?" a voice asked from somewhere.

"He's just a fake," someone else murmured, sounding disgusted.

"He was lying. Nothing but a fraud."

"He speaks for no Lifemaker."

"Blasphemer!" another voice shouted, sounding angrier now.

"Where art thy angels, O Enlightener?" someone called out mockingly.

"They are walking here like us, for are not all beings equal?" a voice answered, and another laughed. More laughter began to rise up from all sides. A blob of thick, black grease flew out of the crowd and *squelched* on the Enlightener's cloak. A piece of partly decomposed fuel cell followed, then a lump of organic goo from one of the stalls, and within seconds the Enlightener was being pelted down from the platform while the air filled with hoots, boos, and shouts of derision.

"Here—give this to thy angels!"

"Did Kleippur send thee to make mockery of Kroaxia's soldiers?"

"Carthogian agent! Spy!"

"Why do thy angels not rescue thee?"

"He has seen no angels!"

"I'll believe it when I see our soldiers at the city gates."

"Yes—and proclaiming that the Carthogians are their brothers!"

"Blasphemer! Profaner! Execute him!"

The sound of heavy footsteps crashing in unison came from the rear, and the crowd parted to make way for a detachment of the Palace Guard, led by a major wearing the red sash of Frennelech's handpicked household elite. The outer files fanned out to form a cordon in front of the crowd, and the remainder followed the major through to where the Enlightener was standing, stained and disheveled with a stunned expression on his face. "You are under arrest on charges of blasphemy, heresy, incitement to riot, sedition, and high treason," the major announced. He turned his head to address the captain at the head of the squad behind. "Seize him!"

Angry murmurs broke out and rose to a roar as the Enlightener was hustled away, too bewildered to hear any of the words. At the end of the street that led into the square from the direction of the Holy Palace, he found himself looking suddenly into the face of Frennelech, who had been watching from the window of his carriage. The High Priest shook his head reproachfully. "Tch! Tch! You really should have given yourself more time to get the hang of it," he said. "And now we'll have to drop you into an acid vat to prove to everyone that my Lifemaker is more powerful than your Lifemaker. In some ways it's such a shame because I do believe you really were sincere. It just goes to show, my friend—you can't trust every angel that you meet." He nodded to the guard commander, and the Enlightener was led away.

"I've been thinking," Jaskillion said from the seat next to Frennelech.

The High Priest turned his head away from the window curiously. "Oh, really? What?"

"Perhaps we're being unduly pessimistic about this whole matter of the Lumians' disposition. That mystic has clearly been deceived and betrayed. Could not the Lumians' act of delivering Eskenderom's intended replacement for thee into our hands in this fashion be meant as a signal to convey their decision? Our previous conclusion could well have been mistaken."

"What an attractive notion," Frennelech agreed. "We

will investigate it further . . . But first, let us avail ourselves of the opportunity that Eskenderom's absence presents to ensure a permanent end to all further problems from this scheme of his. Summon Rekashoba, the Prosecutor, as soon as we get back to the palace, and let us get rid of this 'Enlightener' now, once and for all, while we still have the chance to do so without interference."

In the lander parked in the steep-sided valley to the north of Padua city, the indicator lamp on the Communications Officer's console had stopped signaling. First it had blinked once; then, after a pause of several seconds, it had flashed on and off in a frantic burst which had seemed to shriek the desperation of the robot pressing the transmit button just over two hundred miles away. After that there had been another pause, then two or three shorter sequences of flashes. Since then, nothing.

Hank Frazer reached out a hand and flipped a switch to turn off the panel. "I guess that's about it," he said in a dull voice.

Nobody else said a word. After a long stillness, Zambendorf got up from his seat and walked slowly into the main cabin.

34

DANIEL LEAHERNEY SPOKE FROM A SCREEN IN THE aft communications cabin of the surface lander parked at Padua Base, which was located in a bare, ice-covered valley among the hills east of the city. "I hope I didn't interrupt at an inconvenient time, Caspar, but we have some good news that I wanted to give you personally."

"That's okay," Lang said, standing before the console in a helmetless EV suit. "I was due for a coffee break anyway. What's the news?"

"Latest from the reconnaissance drones over Padua city: Zambendorf's messiah showed up in the middle of town about two hours ago."

"Two hours ago!"

"Yes—we had a slight communications hitch up here. The message fell down a crack on its way to me. I called you as soon as I found out."

Lang nodded. "Okay. So . . . what happened?"

"He drew a big crowd, but there were no miracles."

"Zambendorf didn't show?"

"Uh-uh."

"And?"

"Flopso—even better than we hoped. The troops arrived and hauled his messiah away. I guess our main problem just got solved."

Lang was beginning to grin as the full meaning sank in

completely. "Yeah . . . yeah, I guess it just did, Dan. Well, how about that! I guess Zambendorf really went for the missile story, huh?"

"It sure looks like it. I don't mind telling you now though, Caspar, I thought it was a long shot—but I have to hand it to you: You had every one of them figured. Maybe we should retire Gerry Massey and make you the psychologist."

"They don't get paid enough," Lang said.

Leaherney grinned briefly, and then his expression became serious again. "So how are things going with Henry down there?"

"Pretty much as we expected," Lang replied. "He's still sore about what happened to his invasion, but I don't think we'll have too much trouble straightening that out now. As I said, a week from now we'll be back on the right track."

"Well, I hope you're right. I'll let you get on, then, I guess. Sorry to drag you away, but as I said, I just wanted to tell you the news personally—especially after the delay."

"That's okay, Dan. Thanks for the thought. I'll talk to you later."

Inside the cavern of the Lumian flying vehicle, Eskenderom paced irascibly over to the huge, opened door, and stopped for a moment to glower out at the other two vehicles and the temporary Lumian shelters huddled together against a background of barren hills and stark rock. Then he turned and stamped back to where Mōrmorel, the royal counselor, was standing a short distance away from the table at which General Streyfoch and the three Lumians were sitting on opposite sides of the talking Lumian plant.

"Our whole army, disarmed and vanquished without a fight . . . babbling nonsense about being the Carthogians' *brothers* and returning to Kroaxia?" Eskenderom fumed. "What kind of bungling oafs of aliens are these? Within two brights of promising us invincibility, they have succeeded in rendering us impotent beyond Kleippur's wildest dreams. Are they in league with Carthogia, therefore, or afflicted with such crass incompetence that the only thing miraculous about them is that any of their flying constructions should ever leave the ground? Am I betrayed by deceivers or undone by fools?"

"It would be as much an error to assume a unity of purpose among all Lumians as among all robeings, it appears," Mormorel replied. "Our army was intercepted by a rogue band of Lumian criminals, whose actions were not sanctioned by the Lumian king. They have gone into hiding and are being hunted."

"One tiny band of criminals can confound a whole army? Are these aliens unable to maintain discipline among their own kind?"

"Perhaps their criminals have access to the same powers as their artisans," Mormorel suggested.

Eskenderom snorted, paced away a few steps, and then wheeled back again. "What of the identity of this so-called miracle-worker that they used?" he demanded. "Is there news of that?"

"Not as yet," Mormorel confessed. "But it appears he was brought from Carthogia, where similar events are reported to have taken place among the Waskorians."

"So now the truth begins to emerge," Eskenderom said darkly. "Kroaxia has not been favored by special considerations as we were led to believe. While one faction of Lumians brings aid to me, another is supporting Kleippur. What result can this bring but the destruction of both our realms? Is that the goal of the strategy which these incomprehensible Lumians are unfolding? If so we should unite all the nations of Robia against them and at least perish honorably."

"I think not," Mormorel said. "I believe them when they say that what happened in the Meracasine was as much a surprise to them as it was to us. I say we must trust them."

"I too," General Streyfoch advised from the table. "We cannot risk being deprived of Lumian weapons if there is a possibility that Kleippur has acquired them. We must hope Mormorel is right, and trust the Lumians."

Eskenderom scowled and moved back to the cavern door. He didn't know whom to believe or what to make of the situation. Kleippur had trusted in the Lumians, and as soon as they found it expedient, they had deserted him and commenced dealing with Kroaxia—or so Eskenderom had been told. But now that there could be no further concealing of the fact that some Lumians had continued to deal with Carthogia all along, the "official" Lumians were asking him to believe that the ones talking to Kleippur were nothing more than a band of criminals that nobody had known about. But the Lumians had eyes everywhere and knew everything. So had they been merely distracting Eskenderom while their king treated with Kleippur, and deliberately leading him on into launching the invasion so that his army could be lured out into the Meracasine and destroyed?

The other possiblity that Eskenderom had to consider was that the villain behind everything was not Kleippur at all, but Frennelech, who, as Eskenderom knew from his spies, had been meeting secretly and treacherously with Lumians in the forests west of Pergassos. It would not be to Frennelech's advantage to allow either Kleippur or Eskenderom to grow too strong by inflicting a crushing defeat upon the other, and his motives would be compatible both with his original endorsement of the decision to invade Carthogia—thus sustaining a state of tension between the two rulers—and with plotting subsequently to make sure the Kroaxian army was incapacitated to prevent its carrying out the task.

But what could Frennelech have offered the Lumians in return for their assistance? Presumably only the potential that his office gave him for inducing the robeing population to tame the forests—which seemed to be the Lumians' only objective. Surely, however, Eskenderom told himself, it would be the Lumian king who would want the forests tamed, not these alleged criminals, which again led him to the conclusion that no band of criminals existed and that the Lumians aiding his rival—in this case Frennelech—were therefore the Lumian king's official representatives.

So either way, it seemed to Eskenderom—whether the "Enlightener" was the product of Lumians working with Kleippur or with Frennelech—the aliens were committed to getting rid of him. He didn't know why, for he had agreed to everything they had asked. If he had been put to some test of weakness and failed, the verdict was unjust, for how could robeings be expected to abide by the intricate rules of conduct of a remote, incomprehensible, alien world that none of them had ever seen?

At the makeshift conference table that had been set up in the lander's open cargo bay, Sharon Beatty, the transmogrifier operator assigned from Leon Keyhoe's staff, was using the lull to tidy up her computer-file notes of the proceedings to the point where Lang had excused himself to take a call from Leaherney inside the ship. During the last couple of hours of Terran–Taloid exchanges, she had learned that Henry was furious because his army had been turned around and was returning to Padua instead of invading Genoa, and Giraud was denying official responsibility and blaming Zambendorf and his people, who for some reason or other were hiding out down on Titan with a stolen surface lander.

Sharon had never been sure why Zambendorf should have been included in the mission, and she found it disturbing that so many seemingly intelligent and rational people should have either the time or the inclination to take his antics seriously. After traveling one billion miles to Saturn in the largest spacecraft ever built and sharing the excitement of her fellow scientists at the staggering discoveries on Titan, she had had more interesting things to do than pay much attention to Gerold Massey's concerns about the sociological implications of the mission's purpose, or Dave Crookes' attempts to recruit her as a political activist. She had seen enough of crusades and causes while she was at college, and wasted too much of her time and energy on them. Now she had more worthwhile things to attend to. If more people only felt the same way, all the Zambendorfs would long ago have been put out of business.

"Miami Beach," Seltzman was saying to Giraud on one of the local frequencies. "Just imagine it, Charles—liquid water, all blue; a real, full-disk, golden sun; palm trees; and a hundred degrees in the shade, without an EV suit. What would you give for that?"

"Hmm, it sounds wonderful," Giraud's voice answered. "But if it's all the same to you, Konrad, I think I'd take Cannes or St. Tropez."

"Aw, okay. Who cares? From this distance it's all the same place anyhow."

"What do you think the Taloids would say to it?"

"Not much. Did you know that some parts of them are made from solid mercury? They'd melt in your refrigerator back home."

"No, I didn't. Would they really? That's amazing!"

Lang's voice added itself to the conversation suddenly. "Charles, this is Caspar. I'm inside the forward-bay lock now—be back out there in a few seconds. Has anything new been happening?"

"No. We decided to take a break too," Giraud answered. "What did Dan want?"

The outer door of the airlock at the front end of the bay slid open, and Lang emerged. Even in his bulky suit, his step seemed brisk and jubilant as he came over to the table. At the same time Henry, who had been standing at the cargo doors, staring out at whatever Taloids saw in the darkness, turned and came back to rejoin the group. "It's all over with Zambendorf!" Lang announced. "His messiah was arrested in Padua city about two hours ago. Zambendorf didn't appear anywhere." He grinned through the faceplate of his helmet. "Maybe something happened that made him nervous about flying all of a sudden."

"Well, that's just great, Caspar!" Seltzman said enthusiastically. "So you really did have it all figured, huh."

"Congratulations." Giraud sounded pleased. "Zambendorf bought the story, then."

"Looks like it," Lang agreed, lowering himself ponderously back onto the seat he had been occupying earlier. "So let's give Henry and the others the news. It should make things a lot easier all round."

"Ready to go again, Sharon?" Giraud asked, looking at her through his faceplate.

"Ready." She nodded and cleared the screen of the transmogrifier. Lang's news had obviously signified something to the others that was lost on her. Perhaps that was why she had been assigned this duty stint. If so, big deal.

"Can we resume, please?" Giraud said, switching his speech channel into the transmogrifier's input channel. Sharon verified the interpretation on her screen, and the machine produced its Taloid equivalent at the correct pitch and speed. The Taloids took up their previous positions opposite, with Henry in the middle; Giraud nodded at Lang to commence.

"My apologies for having to leave," Lang said. "I was called because we have received important news." He paused while Sharon monitored the conversion of his phrases into Taloid substitutions. Machiavelli, who seemed to be Henry's principal adviser at all the talks, indicated with a gesture that the Taloids had understood. Lang continued, "The pretender whom you seek has been found. We have delivered him to your city and placed him in the hands of your authorities to be dealt with by Taloid law." He paused again while Sharon restructured his words into shorter sentences. "Our criminals have not yet been located. When they are found, they will be taken to our city above the sky and dealt with by Terran law. So Taloid justice will have taken its course, and Terran justice will have taken its course. We trust that this action will be accepted as proof of our good faith."

"They have found him!" Streyfoch exclaimed as he listened to the Lumian plant's strangled utterances. "They have found the Enlightener, who tricked our soldiers."

"We shall see a public execution before this bright is through," Eskenderom promised grimly.

"He was handed over fairly and without protest to our own authorities," Mormorel observed. He looked at Eskenderom. "Perchance we have judged these aliens hastily, for deeds such as they have described would constitute a most unusual form of treachery."

A new light of hope had come into Eskenderom's eyes suddenly. If the Lumian king had handed the imposter over in Pergassos, then perhaps the rout of the Kroaxian army had been the work of Lumian criminals after all. If so, had they been working in league with Frennelech or with Kleippur?

"What manner of reception was this imposter accorded at the city?" Eskenderom asked. In his absence, the policy would have been decided by Frennelech. Mormorel pressed the button to activate the Lumian plant, and repeated the question. After a brief exchange of queries and answers, the plant responded that as far as the Lumian eyes in the sky had been able to ascertain, the imposter had been arrested. "Then does this not tell us that our culprit cannot be Frennelech?" Eskenderom said to Mormorel. "He would hardly welcome his own agent thus."

Mormorel considered the proposition dubiously for a few seconds. "An agent who has passed forever beyond the point of further usefulness," he pointed out. "Readily expendable, perhaps, if such a sacrifice would establish Frennelech's blamelessness in Kroaxia's eyes?"

"Hmm." Eskenderom sounded disappointed. "Observation of this imposter's treatment will therefore tell us nothing of Frennelech's complicity or otherwise," he concluded.

"Not necessarily," Mormorel agreed.

Eskenderom scowled to himself, and then slammed his open hand down on the table angrily. "Then by the Lifemaker I will have this Enlightener's head boiled in acid! Let both Frennelech and Kleippur read the warning, whichever of them was behind him . . . and anyone else who might be contemplating a compact with Lumian criminals to overthrow the Kroaxian Crown."

"Attention please. Colonel Wallis here for Ambassador Giraud," a voice said inside the Terrans' helmets.

"Yes, Colonel?" Giraud acknowledged.

"Number three perimeter guardpost has intercepted a mounted Taloid who indicates that he is known to the visitors. Our records show him listed as James Bond. Request identity confirmation and your further instructions, sir."

"One second, Colonel," Giraud said. Then, "Konrad, did you get that? Pass the message to Machiavelli, would you."

Seltzman talked to the transmogrifier, and the transmogrifier talked to the Taloids. Colonel Wallis sent a view of the new arrival through to a communications screen on one of the portable compacks beside the transmogrifier, and Henry verified that the Taloid was known and friendly. Giraud authorized Wallis to let Bond pass.

A few minutes later, Skerilliane was escorted into the cavern by two Lumian soldiers. He looked as if he had ridden hard all the way from Pergassos, where, he informed Eskenderom and the others, the Enlightener had shown himself and been arrested by Frennelech's Palace Guards.

"We know as much already from the Lumians," Eskenderom said. "But who is he? Can you tell us that?"

"Indeed, Majesty, for he is no stranger to the city," Skerilliane replied. "None other than thy chosen one Groork, the brother of Thirg, who departed Kroaxia to serve the Dark Master's wordly lieutenant, thine enemy Kleippur."

"Him?" Eskenderom roared, leaping to his feet. "The hearer that I offered to install in Frennelech's palace? . . . He has come back from Carthogia as Kleippur's henchman? *He* is the one who directed Lumian sorcery down upon my army?"

"The same, Majesty," Skerilliane replied.

Eskenderom kicked aside the chair upon which he had

been sitting and strode to the far wall and back again, all the time pounding his fist into his palm with rage and shouting. "The traitor! The deceiver! Is this the gratitude I am shown? Is this how I am rewarded for my generosity? Arghhh! The swamp-guzzler! Corruption and corrosion upon him! May the Reduction Furnace take him! I'll slow-melt his casing and leach his eyes! I'll hang him from high-voltage trees in the forest! I'll boil him in acid! Mormorel, find the servants and have them bring our horses at once. Indeed there will be a spectacle for the citizens of Pergassos to enjoy before this bright is through!"

"Frennelech has already proclaimed a public execution to take place one-twelfth of a bright from now," Skerilliane said.

"Then for once he and I have no quarrel," Eskenderom declared. "Let us repair at once, full haste to Pergassos, for this shall be entertainment that I would not wish to miss."

Giraud stared in astonishment at Henry's reaction to whatever Bond had said. Machiavelli and Caesar stood up, and Machiavelli went over to the doors and began waving toward where the rest of Henry's party were waiting with the mounts in one of the nearby ground-vehicle sheds. "What in hell's going on?" Lang demanded.

"It looks to me as if they're taking off," Seltzman said bemusedly. "I guess the meeting just adjourned."

"Sharon, find out what's happening," Giraud instructed.

Somehow Sharon managed to sustain a dialogue of sorts while the Taloids paced back and forth gesticulating wildly at one another, while mechanical steeds and more Taloids appeared outside the loading doors and Henry continued to show all the signs of throwing a fit. "They're going back to Padua," she said at last, shaking her head dazedly. "Something about a public execution that Henry doesn't want to miss."

"Execution of whom?" Seltzman asked.

"I'm not sure, but I think it's the messiah."

"Can we let that happen?" Giraud said, looking uneasily at Lang.

Lang's expression was stony behind his faceplate. "It's their business and their customs. Who are we to interfere?"

There was a short pause. "Are you sure you're not really aiming at Zambendorf?" Giraud asked uneasily.

"I've given you my decision," Lang said.

Konrad Seltzman met Giraud's eye for a split second, then shifted his gaze to Sharon. "Did they say exactly when?" he asked her.

Sharon glanced at the computer's conversion of the Taloid time measurement that had been mentioned. "About twenty hours from now."

35

THE OUTER DOOR OF THE MIDSHIPS AIRLOCK OPENED on the hijacked surface lander hidden in the valley two hundred miles north of Padua city, and the suited figures of Zambendorf and Andy Schwartz, the lander's captain, came out onto the extended stair-head platform and descended to join Drew West and Clarissa, who were already waiting on the ground. Then, walking two abreast and guided by hand-held flashlamps in the darkness, the melancholy little procession made its way through the labyrinth of steel and concrete shapes to the crude shanty-camp that the Taloids had made for themselves. Abaquaan, Fellburg, and Price, who had gone on ahead a while earlier, were waiting at the camp with Lord Nelson and Abraham, the leader of the Druids, and the rest of the Taloids gathered around on all sides. The time had come for Zambendorf to tell the cast officially that the show was wound up and they were being paid off, to wish them good luck, and send them back home.

"We've told them they won't be going to Padua," Abaquaan said. The team had agreed on the storyline that Moses, his main task of preventing the invasion of Genoa now successfully accomplished, had been called elsewhere to attend to other things. It was hardly a satisfying end to their venture, but nobody had been able to suggest anything better.

Zambendorf nodded inside his helmet. "How are they taking it?" he asked.

"Not as badly as we thought they might," Abaquaan replied. "They're disappointed all right, but not disillusioned. They seem to have rationalized some way of coming to terms with the situation in their own minds."

"I don't know . . . A true believer is a true believer anywhere, it seems," Zambendorf sighed. "Oh well, bring the transmogrifier here, would you, Otto. I'd like to say a few words to them before they go." The plan was that the surface lander crew, having ostensibly been released from forcible detainment, would fly to the Terran base at Genoa to return themselves and the vehicle to the authorities, and take the Taloid contingent home at the same time. As to what should happen after that, opinions were divided; Abaquaan, Fellburg, and Clarrissa felt that the team had no alternative but to follow in the flyer and turn itself in, whereas Zambendorf and Drew West wondered if there might be some way of extricating Moses from his predicament first.

Indeed this was modesty and graciousness of spirit that was truly worthy of noble beings, the Renamer—formerly Captain Horazzorgio—thought to himself as he listened to the enchanted plant speaking the Archangel's thoughts. So much had been accomplished in so little time—a new faith founded; a village saved; the whole sect of Waskorians at peace now with Carthogia; the Kroaxian tyrant checked and his army scattered—and yet here the Archangel was, expressing regret that the chosen ones who had descended over the desert on billowy wings would not be present to witness the Coming at Pergassos. For it was clear that the Enlightener had asked their assistance in the Meracasine merely as a precaution while he tested the powers that the Lifemaker had bestowed upon him. The powers had proved so awesome that he had elected to go on alone and complete the conversion of Pergassos single-handed, leaving his followers free to attend to other matters back in Carthogia.

"Wish them good luck, and tell them I'm sure we'll

meet again sometime, I hope in happier circumstances," Zambendorf said to Abaquaan.

"Hear how the Archangel promiseth that he will return!" Ezimbial, the Druid prophet, told the assembled followers. As a prophet Ezimbial had always been holy and therefore hadn't needed renaming. "And let it be written that the time will be one of great rejoicing. Thus hath it been prophesied."

"It has been a privilege to work with them. Their help will never be forgotten," Zambendorf said.

"This collaboration with angels hath brought great blessings. Our place in eternity is assured," Ezimbial interpreted.

"They must return to Genoa now, and help Arthur to found institutions of true learning. That is the way to acquire the knowledge that will allow them to fly beyond the sky. Then—who knows?—perhaps one day we'll be able to welcome them at our world."

"It is revealed that Carthogia is the Land promised in the Scribings. There shall the Enlightener's followers erect a Great Temple, and Kleippur shall direct them. And they who heed no false teachings before those that shall be preached in the Temple will be redeemed, and then will they arise and rejoin the angels in the shining land that floats beyond the sky."

"I guess that's it, Otto."

"And here endeth the lesson."

"Andy, you'd better stay here and work out a schedule with them for getting packed up and loaded aboard," Zambendorf said to Schwartz. "Otto will stay with you to handle the translating. We'll see you both back in the ship when you're through."

"Sure," Schwartz answered.

Vernon watched Zambendorf and the others turn to leave, and then wheeled himself around in his suit to look at Nelson and Abraham. "I'd like to stay back too," he said, ". . . for the last few minutes." He couldn't help feeling guilty about what had happened to Moses—he had started the whole thing with the ice slab he'd given Moses on the mountain. Now he instinctively put off what he felt subconsciously would amount to desertion of the remaining Taloids as well.

"As you wish," Zamdendorf said. "We'll see you later, Vernon." His party began to walk back to the ship, the probing, flitting beams of their flashlamps growing fainter and more distant in the darkness.

Schwartz turned back toward Abaquaan. "Tell them I'd like to be ready for takeoff not later than three hours from now, but it'd help a lot if they could get all their personal stuff loaded right away. We can take all the animals they brought with them, but they'll have to let go the ones they've been collecting since . . . the big rock-crushers with the caterpillar tracks, anyhow."

Abaquaan conveyed the message, and Abraham responded with a question that appeared on the screen as DESTINATION IN GENOA?

"The Terran base just outside the city," Abaquaan replied.

DRUIDS' ASSIGNMENT AFTER THAT? the screen asked.

And Abaquaan answered, "We have no specific instructions to give. You'll be on your own then. Talk to Arthur's scientists at Camelot. That's where the most useful work is being done."

Ezimbial puzzled over the plant's reply for a moment. "Kleippur's inquirers?" he said to the Renamer. "The Lifemaker will make known His wishes through them? But knowest thou which among them? Whom are we to approach?"

The Renamer stared thoughtfully at the trees in the background. "Perhaps," he answered slowly. "There is a one called Thirg, whose steps the Lifemaker directed out of Kroaxia to enter the service of Kleippur. The workings of the Lifemaker's plan are clearer to me now. It was I who in blindness would have frustrated the Maker's design, and for that it has been my penance to bear the afflictions that you see."

"How knowest thou it is this Thirg whom we should seek?" Ezimbial asked. "Does he carry some special qualification of eminence among Kleippur's inquirers that sets him apart as the object of our quest?"

"None less than that of being the Enlightener's brother," the Renamer replied.

"The Enlightener has a brother in Carthogia!" Ezimbial's eyes widened. "Indeed Kleippur's realm is the Promised Land of the Scribings, and artisans have been congregating thither from the corners of the world to build the Temple that was prophesied."

Just to be sure, the Renamer activated the enchanted plant and said into it, "Is it our quest to seek Thirg, Asker-of-Questions, who was born brother to the holy Enlightener?"

The plant replied, "Unlcear *hiss-buzz* what-mean 'brother.' Want-say alternative *hoo-whoo-bonk-bonk*. Else obtain new word."

The Renamer couldn't bring an alternative to mind immediately, and instructed, "Obtain new word."

"EQUIVALENT ENGLISH WORD-FORM BEING REQUESTED," the screen advised Abaquaan.

"Oh hell, can't we wrap this up?" Andy Schwartz said. "I've gotta get the ship up to flight readiness. There's a lot to do."

"Give them a few more minutes," Vernon said. "How often do you get a chance to talk to people like these."

Abaquaan eyed Vernon through his faceplate, nodded with a sigh, and instructed the transmogrifier, "Okay."

"Pray describe," the plant invited the Renamer.

"Male child born of common parenthood," the Renamer said after a few seconds' thought. "The relationship thereof to either another male child, or to a female child."

The screen presented:

FUNCTION	SUBJECT	ADDITIONAL DATA
Personal relationship	Male child, same parents	To another male/female child

Abaquaan told the machine simply, "Brother."

Back at the ship, the others had just arrived below the stair-head platform outside the midships lock. "I've got a hunch that Casper still doesn't realize we've got the flyer too," Zambendorf was saying. "Certainly there's no question that the lander would have been a sitting duck over Padua, but the flyer's a lot smaller and more maneuverable. When the lander's picked people on radar up flying back to Genoa, everyone will be off their guard and not expecting us to show up anywhere else. I think there's an excellent chance we'd be able to pull off a quick dash in and out at rooftop level in the flyer."

"I go along with Karl," Drew West said as he began climbing up to the platform. "We sent Moses in there. Trying to get him out again is the least we can do. It's worth a try."

"Sure, but it's not the sentiment I'm arguing with, it's the practicality." Clarissa answered. "It's all right to talk about excellent chances, but you've never tried dodging those missiles, and I have. I'm telling you it's not a piece of cake."

"We don't know what's happening in Padua—if anything is, or when, or even where Moses is," Joe Fellburg pointed out. "Exactly what would we be supposed to do—at what place, and at what time?"

"I don't know either, but we can find out," Zambendorf said. "There has to have been a lot of talking going on between Leaherney's people and Henry. There might be records of the dialogues stored in the files where Dave Crookes or somebody could get at them. Maybe we'd pick up some clues that way. Or possibly we could find out who the transmogrifier operators are at Padua. They might have heard something. I don't know—All I'm saying is that we should give it a try rather than just quit."

"Mmm, maybe . . ." Fellburg murmured. He didn't sound wildly enthusiastic. He'd had some experience with smart missiles too.

At that moment there was a click on the circuit as somebody switched through to a medium-range channel, and Vernon's voice came through excitedly from back at the Taloid camp. "Hey, Karl, everybody, don't go away—listen to this. We've just learned something from Nelson that maybe changes everything. He assumed we already knew about it because these guys think we know everything. Anyway . . . it seems that Moses is Galileo's brother!"

Fifteen minutes later, back inside the ship, Zambendorf called Thelma in the *Orion* and asked her to beam the call back down to the surface to connect to the communications set hidden in Arthur's conference room at Camelot. One of Arthur's knights answered, and went to fetch Arthur. Zambendorf transmitted some stills over the link from recordings showing Moses, but Arthur was unable either to confirm or deny that the figure shown was Galileo's brother. Galileo himself was elsewhere, but Arthur promised to send for him at once. Galileo called back over an hour later, after Arthur's staff eventually found him locked away in a workroom where he was constructing a model of the Saturnian system of planet, rings, and moons from information that Massey and Thelma had sent him several days previously. Zambendorf showed Galileo the pictures and asked if the Taloid shown in them was his brother.

Thirg, utterly bewildered at seeing for the first time the face of the fabulous Enlightener that the whole country was talking about—who had pacified the Waskorians, saved Carthogia from invasion, and now, allegedly, departed to put a permanent end to further Kroaxian mischief—confirmed to the Wearer that it was.

"He is the brother of whom you spoke?" Kleippur asked incredulously as Thirg gaped at the Lumian long-distance seeing device. "The hearer who came to warn you when the Kroaxian Council ordered your arrest?"

"It is he!" Dornvald exclaimed, having also just arrived. "Behold—the mystic we last saw praying to the skies with the villagers of Xerxeon."

"He was convinced that his voices had led him there to see the fulfillment of some momentous destiny," Thirg said weakly, still staring at the viewing window. "It appears his inspiration was more substantially founded than I had credited."

"How comes Thirg's brother, Groork, to this exalted station in which we now find him?" Kleippur inquired, pressing the button that would open the viewing vegetable's ears.

Several hundred miles away across darkened deserts of rock-strewn hydrocarbon sands and mountains of naked ice, Zambendorf read the words that appeared on the screen in front of him. "I'll explain it all later. We may not have a lot of time," he said gruffly, and cut the connection.

At one of the consoles across the aisle behind Zambendorf in the Lander's aft communications cabin, Hank Frazer was taking a return call from Dave Crookes. "I found out which operator had the most recent slot down there," Crookes said. "It was Sharon Beatty—one of our people from Leon Keyhoe's section. I talked to her about ten minutes ago. She said that the Taloids are staging a big public execution in Padua, and Henry got all excited and went galloping off to be sure not to miss it. All she knew apart from that, she said, was that it concerned a miracle-worker who's been causing Henry a lot of trouble lately. Is that enough for you to figure out the rest?"

"It sure is," Frazer said. "Oh, and Dave, one more thing—did she have any idea when this was supposed to happen? Did you ask her that?"

"Yes I did. She said about twenty hours from when Henry heard about it—that's something like ten hours from now."

Back at the Taloid camp, Zambendorf, Vernon, and Abaquaan told Nelson that they had received word from the sky that a public execution was being arranged in Padua city, and it was Moses' desire that the intended victim should be saved—which they felt safe in presuming to be the case. They didn't say who the intended victim was, and Nelson assumed they were referring to someone that Moses had learned about after his arrival at the city.

In response to their further questioning Nelson informed them that the customary place for conducting executions of major criminals and heretics was a high cliff located just outside the city. Here, before a natural public amphitheater, the victims were pushed from a wide rock ledge halfway up the face at the top of a long, ceremonial staircase, to fall two hundred feet into an open tank containing some kind of corrosive liquid. This was the usual method of executing heretics, Nelson explained, because the procedure also embodied the elements of a trial, permitting a higher justice the opportunity to intervene in the event of wrongful conviction: According to doctrine, any innocent cast from the ledge would be snatched from death by the Taloid god before completing the fall. Apparently nobody had ever been snatched yet, which the Taloid priests contended was proof that they'd never issued a wrong verdict.

Clarissa located the cliff on a series of reconnaissance pictures of Padua and its vicinity which she retrieved from the Orion's databank. It formed the end face of a ridge of craggy hills that descended almost to the city from a more distant range of higher mountains. Even more interesting was that the geography of the area seemed to make its own weather: Every set of pictures taken since the *Orion*'s arrival, along with the accompanying sets of meteorological data, had shown a formation of apparently permanent low-altitude methane clouds only a thousand feet or so above the clifftop. That changed Clarissa's assessment of the odds considerably. "We could come in low along the ridgeline from the mountains in the rear, and probably get up inside those clouds right over the cliff without even the Taloids knowing we were there," she said. "They'd obviously be restricted to visual sighting since they don't have anything like radar. If the chance presented itself, yeah—maybe we could pull a quick grab and be back up again before they could react. Okay, you've sold me, Karl. I'll give it a try."

"But no stunts or miracles, right?" Abaquaan said. "We just go straight down and straight up again."

"Too right," Clarissa agreed. Her tone left no room for dissent. "Just a quick grab—no tricks and no clowning."

"I agree, I agree," Zambendorf said, nodding. "All I'm interested in is getting Moses out if we can. I'm not asking for anything else to be changed. The operation is still scrubbed, and the lander goes back to Genoa with its crew and the Druids as agreed . . . except that we time it to coincide with our going in at Padua. Okay?" He cast his eyes anxiously over the faces around him.

"Okay, boss—I'll buy it," Fellburg said resignedly.

"I'm already in," Drew West reminded them.

Abaquaan nodded his assent. "Aw, what the hell . . . We've scraped through everything else so far. Okay, let's do it."

"Let's do it," Vernon repeated.

Zambendorf looked at Vernon uncertainly for a second. "You don't have to get involved, you know. There's still plenty of room in the lander going back to Genoa."

"I gave Moses his tablet, so it's my fault as much as anyone's that he's where he is." Vernon shook his head. "No, if there's a chance we might be able to get him out again, that's where I want to be."

Zambendorf, apparently having half expected it, nodded briefly, and left the matter at that. "Fine. So let's get our things moved into the flyer and let Andy and his crew get on with whatever needs doing in the lander. Then let's get together again one hour from now and have another look at the layout around that cliff. There won't be any chance for an actual rehearsal for this performance, I'm afraid, so we'll have to make do with the next best thing—a lot of imaginary ones."

36

WEARING A LONG, HOODED CLOAK THAT HE HAD BARtered from a peasant for his helmet and body armor, former private Sallakar pushed his handcart into the city's Central Square and selected a spot for himself in one of the normally busy corners of the market area, between a plating-salt vendor's stall and a wheelskin dealer. The square, however, was quiet for this time of late-bright, and many of the merchants had already closed down. Never mind, Sallakar thought—all the more business for those like himself who were still on the street to trade. And besides, his reason for hurrying to arrive ahead of the main body of the army was to enjoy a few hours of profitable monopoly before the competition appeared and drove down the prices. He threw back the cover of the cart to reveal a collection of rock and ice fragments, pieces of parachute silk, burned-out firework cannisters, and other oddments, and unfurled a sign which read:

GENUINE MERACASINE HOLY RELICS
GET YOUR ENLIGHTENER MIRACLE SOUVENIR HERE

"Genuine relics, direct from the scene of the Meracasine miracles," he shouted. "Here is a rock that was melted by the Enlightener's thunderbolts—only five duodecs. Own your own miracle rock. Miraculously preserved cuttings of discarded angels' wings, guaranteed to keep demons from the house—seven duodecs. Angel-light pots, complete with sacred inscriptions; lengths of holy cords; pieces of heavenly flying-vestments; stones from the sermon hill, and lots more. Every item guaranteed to have been brought direct from the scene of the Enlightener's coming."

A small group of unkempt, rough-looking idlers had stopped in front of the cart and was watching him curiously. Behind them a few people were looking on, apparently apprehensively, but most were continuing on their way, their eyes fixed solidly in front of them, or turning their backs to hurry away. Sallakar frowned. This wasn't at all the kind of reception that he'd anticipated. "Come on then, how about you, sir?" he said to the nearest of the ruffians in front of him—an ugly-looking character with a lot of unsmoothed, red-tinted facial plating, a soiled and torn jerkin, and a navigator's hat pushed jauntily to the back of his head. "A special price for this one only—three duodecs for this piece of Meracasine rock. An excellent talisman and warder-away of evil influences, oh yes. Brings good luck and protects your health. Do I hear an offer?"

"You're outta your mind," the sailor commented sourly.

"What are you trying to do—get yourself fizzed too?" one of the others asked.

"Better lay off that kind of talk and just be grateful there aren't any guards within earshot," another advised.

Sallakar gave them a puzzled look. "Didn't he show up here, then?" he asked them. "The whole city was supposed to have been converted by now."

"Who?" the sailor asked.

"The Enlightener. He was supposed to come here and call miracles down from the sky."

One of the band laughed. "Oh, he showed up all right, but the miracles didn't. The priests will be throwing him off the cliff before bright's end. Where else d'you think everybody's going?"

"Convicted as a blasphemer," another one said.

"And he might not be the only one, from the way you're

carrying on," a third commented. "But don't mind us—you go ahead. Two fizzings for the price of one would really make the day."

"And we'd better be on our way," the sailor said to the others. "Or we'll miss even the one."

Sallakar watched them walk away muttering and laughing among themselves, then turned round and hastily took down his sign and pulled the cover back over his cart. He stood thinking hard for a while and frowning perplexedly to himself. Then all of a sudden a glint came into his eyes. He took a piece of marking stick from inside his robe, turned the sign over, and slowly and deliberately wrote on the back in large letters:

BLASPHEMER SOUVENIRS AND RELICS
BROUGHT BACK BY THE ARMY HE TRIED TO CORRUPT
GET YOUR EXECUTION MOMENTO HERE

Nodding in satisfaction, he rolled the sign up again, tucked it beneath the cover, then grasped the handles of his cart and moved away to join the general drift of the crowd toward the southern outskirts of the city.

In a dungeon in the lowermost levels of the prison behind the Palace of the High Holy One, Groork sat on his rough bed of mill-swarf and lathe-turnings, staring forlornly at the bare ice floor. The nightmare, he had at last accepted fully and finally, was really happening. After dedicating his life unswervingly to upholding the Lifemaker's faith, denouncing its enemies, and taking scrupulous care never to permit an utterance that might be taken as contradicting the Church's teachings or denying its doctrines, this was the bitter end to which it had all brought him—convicted and condemned to die the death of a heretic and blasphemer.

The injustice of his reward for ceaseless vigilance and untiring devotion was causing him to question seriously the whole foundation of his belief-system for the first time ever. He had believed, and he had trusted; he had remained faithful in the face of adversity; he had never wavered. And now Frennelech, the High Holy One whom he had served selflessly as the Lifemaker's true worldly personification, had become the very instrument by which that service was repaid with betrayal and callousness. How, then, could such a Holy One personify an all-wise and all-knowing spirit, or be representative of such a being in any way whatever? Certainly in no way that Groork could see. And if he admitted that much doubt, what further credence could he give to any other facet of the whole system of credos and dogmas that was derived from the same suspect premises by means of the same dubious processes? None, obviously. But it was inconceivable that the Lifemaker's chosen method for communicating true knowledge could include suspect or dubious elements. Therefore it seemed to follow on principle that the Lifemaker's chosen method for making true knowledge available couldn't depend on inspired interpretations of sacred revelation by self-proclaimed diviners.

The mental processes that had brought Groork to these conclusions seemed uncomfortably like the methods of reason by which Thirg hypothesized and evaluated possible answers to his questions—a practice that Groork had always denounced as sinful. When Groork applied this newfound skepticism to the question of the Wearer and the angels, he found only two possible answers to explain their failure to materialize over Pergassos: Either they had been unable to, or they had chosen not to. If they had been unable to, then their powers were not infinite, and they could not have been sent by the Lifemaker; if they had chosen not to, then they had lied, and that alone was enough to force the same conclusion. Groork felt the first possibility to be the more likely since the philosophy of living that the Wearer had expounded would surely have been irreconcilable with any form of moral deficiency, but either way it meant that the angels hadn't come from any supernatural realm. Since they were clearly not of the known world, they could only be from some other, unknown one—a world where, admittedly, arts and skills that were perhaps not mistakenly described as miraculous seemed to be commonplace—which could exist only above the sky. So again one of Thirg's long-standing insistences and convictions appeared to have been vindicated. And if that were so, was not Groork obliged to concede also that the arts and skills that the angels exhibited were not the results of any magical abilities at all, but simply the consequences of applying knowledge gained by the universally accessible, comprehensible, nonmysterious methods of inquiry that Thirg had always propounded? He regretted particularly that he would not see Thirg again; he saw the world so differently now, and there would have been so much for them to talk about.

The muffled tramp of heavy footfalls penetrated from outside. They stopped just beyond the dungeon door. Groork could feel his coolant recirculator pounding, and a sudden tightness wrenched his insides. He rose to his feet as the heavy, organic-fibroid door curled itself aside, and the jailer entered, accompanied by a guard captain, two priests, Vormozel, the prison governor, and Poskattyn, Frennelech's Judicial Chancellor from the Holy Palace. An escort of Palace Guards remained outside in the passageway.

Poskattyn produced a scroll and read, "Groork, of the city of Pergassos, thou hast been tried and found guilty of the crimes of heresy, blasphemy, and high treason against the State, and sentenced to suffer death in the manner prescribed by ecclesiastical law. Hast thou any final words to speak before thou art taken to the place of execution?" Groork could only shake his head numbly. "Hast thou prepared thyself and made thy peace with the Lifemaker, may He have mercy on thy soul?" Groork made no reply. Poskattyn rerolled his scroll, stepped back, and looked at Vormozel. "Proceed, Governor." Vormozel nodded to the guard captain, and Groork was led into the passageway and placed between the two priests, with the captain in front, the governor and chancellor behind, and the guards forming a file on either side with torch-bearers at front and rear. Their footsteps echoed hollowly from the gaunt walls as the procession walked slowly toward the damp stone stairs at the far end of the passageway. Faces appeared and watched grimly from the windows of some of the other cell doors along the way, but none of them made a sound.

Groork's impressions were confused and fragmented—of drab, torchlit stairs; massive doors being opened and gratings being raised; and the priests on either side of him chanting monotonously as they ascended to ground level and came out into the prison yard. There a legged wagon pulled by two black-draped, wheeled tractors was waiting before a cordon of guards, while several carriages full of dignitaries were lined up with a mounted escort just inside the main gate. Still dazed, Groork climbed up into the wagon with the priests, the chancellor, two of the guards, and the guard captain, while the rest of the detail and the governor watched from behind. The cart moved away to form up with the other vehicles and the riders, the gates were opened, and the cavalcade emerged to be greeted by the roars of the crowd that had been waiting outside.

Past the Courts of the High Council they went, across Penitents' Square, and over the Bridge of Eskenderom-the-Elder to the Thieves' Quarter on the south side of the city, while the crowd closed and surged behind. Groork gripped the handrail in front of him and took in his last glimpses of the city he had lived in for most of his life. He was bewildered and unable to understand what he had done that could suddenly turn fellow citizens and old schoolfriends into a crazed mob whose only interest was to see him die. For the first time he saw the reality of the savage mindlessness that could be engendered in a people who had been conditioned to believe without questioning, to accept without understanding, and to hate upon command. He remembered the few times he had glimpsed the calm, dignified bearing of the citizens of Menassim, and in that moment he understood how the tolerance and wisdom of Kleippur's realm were products of the philosophy that Thirg stood for as inevitably as the ignorance and brutality seen in Kroaxia were of the repression that he himself, until so very recently, had helped to perpetuate. Indeed his conversion had come late, he reflected sadly.

The city's buildings fell behind, and now he could see the Cliff of Judgment looming ahead, above the Spectators' Hill, its face black and menacing against a setting of broken crags behind, sullen gray mountains in the more distant background, and unsettled storm clouds overhead. The grim procession followed the road around the hill, and on the far side the terraces facing the cliff were crowded to capacity, with many more figures standing on the open ground above. On a rock platform at the base of the cliff, the huge vat of acid fumed white wispy vapors and bubbled in cackling anticipation. Groork found himself trembling suddenly. He looked up, and high above, on the ledge at the top of the long, tapering stairway, he could see the scarlet-robed figures of High Council priests grouped before an unmoving line of Palace Guards, and in front of them all, dressed completely in black and hooded, the Executioner, standing with arms folded while he gazed impassively down over the scene below.

Both the King and the High Priest were present with their respective retinues in the raised, canopied enclosure occupying the center at the bottom of the amphitheater. Groork and those with him descended from the wagon and stood in front of the enclosure while the spokesmen of the Head of State and of the Head of Church delivered formal addresses. Groork was too petrified by the scene and the mood of the waiting crowd to hear the words. Had he really caused such turmoil that the nation's two most powerful holders of office should take such personal interest in the proceedings? Apparently so, but Groork couldn't think why. He was incapable of thinking anything anymore. Everything was disintegrating into a jumble of disconnected and incoherent sights and sounds, colors and noises, words and faces. What was the point in trying to understand any of it now? What difference would it make? A few minutes more, and nothing would make any difference to anything ever again. He thought of his brother, he thought of their parents, and he tried to compose a prayer to the Lifemaker. And then he realized that the group was moving again and had begun to ascend the broad steps below the stairway that led to the ledge high above. He could hear the crowd growing noisier and sense its rising excitement.

In the dignitaries' enclosure, Eskenderom was watching Frennelech intently from a distance. "Indeed, if this Enlightener is a product of the High Priest's working in league with the aliens to hinder my expansion, then Frennelech is displaying a most remarkable composure at his impending loss," he whispered to Mormorel. "I am tempted to conclude that the architect of the machinations whose consequences it has been our misfortune to suffer was none less than Kleippur as we suspected."

"I too," Mormorel replied. "And now Kleippur shall learn of the fate that awaits those who allow themselves to be enticed into conspiracy with alien criminals."

"Thus has the Lumian king chosen to demonstrate the folly of opposing his rule," Eskenderom said. "An illuminating lesson, the study of which will not be restricted to Kleippur, I trust, or confined within merely the boundaries of Carthogia."

"The news will be repeated rapidly far and wide," Mormorel assured him. "All nations shall know that the powers of the gods have aligned themselves with thee."

Groork's universe had narrowed to the silver-shod heels of the guards ascending the steps ahead of him and the incessant chanting of the priests on either side. He had lost all estimate of how high they had climbed or how far was still to go. He didn't dare look up. Endless steps; endless steps; endless steps . . .

"The King's disposition seems strangely agreeable if this Enlightener was indeed his chosen replacement for you," Jaskillion murmured in Frennelech's ear. "I must confess my expectation was that Eskenderom would intervene to protect his protégé when I heard of his return posthaste from Gornod."

"A protégé who has exhausted his potential usefulness," Frennelech replied. "And what surer way could Eskenderom find than this to conceal all trace of his involvement in the plot so recently frustrated and, at the same time, eliminate all risk of embarrassing indiscretions and exposures in the future? The smugness so evident upon the royal visage is not as deeply seated as it appears, I feel, for it was against Eskenderom's plan that the Lumians elected to direct their magic, not ours. If these aliens are indeed the god of which the Scribings speak, then I think we can feel safe in claiming that He is with us."

Groork and his escorts had reached the ledge. A line of trumpeters along the rear wall blasted a fanfare, and then everyone stood silently for what seemed an eternity while more speeches were delivered inaudibly far below—deliberately intended, Groork was certain, to prolong his anguish. A hush fell, and the Executioner advanced onto the narrow, tapering platform that projected outward from the ledge and held up a full-size effigy of a robeing. It was customary to commence the proceedings with a dummy to test the quality of the acids; it also added to the victims' terror and therefore helped excite the crowd. An expectant stillness descended over the sea of upturned faces on the hill opposite. Very slowly, the Executioner pushed the dummy forward to the edge of the platform, held it steady for a few seconds, and then allowed it to tumble forward into space. A thunderous roar came up from the spectators and sustained itself for a long time. From where Groork was standing, he was unable to see what happened. But he didn't have to; he'd seen executions before. After the dummy, a succession of sacrificial animals was led forward and dispatched, one by one, from the platform. With each the crowd grew wilder.

And then the last of the animals was gone. Groork stared in horror at the platform, and felt himself freeze. The priests had formed a solid wall immediately behind, and to the rear the line of guards was closing up and moving forward. The Executioner left the platform and removed his long lance from its stand beside an altar bearing fire, while behind Groork the line of priests drew into a semicircle that drove him outward toward the end of the tapering platform. Then he was standing on a tiny island of ice that seemed to float high in the air, nothingness yawned in front of him and on both sides. Groork's senses reeled. He recoiled instinctively from the drop, but something sharp prodded him in the back. He looked back desperately. The Executioner had leveled his lance, and behind him the stone-faced priests had closed ranks to the very edge of the platform. There was no way back.

Goaded by another jab with the lance, Groork tottered a step forward and for the first time found himself looking straight down the sheer cliff face. Far below, the acid vat was foaming and boiling, with the last of the animals still writhing and convulsing in their death agonies. Groork shook his head wildly in protest. This would serve no purpose. It would achieve nothing. There was no point, no reason. If he was going to die, he pleaded inwardly, let it not be for no reason. "*No!*" he shouted. "This is not the Lifemaker's will. This is savagery! This—"

"Know all ye here that in this way shall all heretics and blasphemers perish!" the Executioner shouted, and lunged hard with the lance. The landscape wheeled around him as Groork pitched forward into emptiness. Brilliant violet lights flared in the sky above, but Groork didn't see them. A roar of voices rose to meet him. He felt himself scream, but couldn't hear. Land and sky spun together.

And in the same instant, something pointed and streamlined swooped down from the clouds above the clifftop.

"Four-zero-zero on vertical boost. Gimme more flaps!"

"That's one through four at full. Take it down! Take it down!"

"Harder to starboard! Faster with that line, Joe!"

"It's at max now."

"You've got it. Easy, easy! Coming round fine. Hold that turn, Clarissa. Hold that turn!"

As the flyer dived out of the blackness and banked into

the full glare of the light from the flares, the net trailing on a line from its rear portside door swung out in a wide arc and scooped the tumbling figure of Moses from the air. The tangle of robot and net dipped low to swing past the base of the cliff, rose again like a pendulum, and then swung back in a wide, rising curve as the flyer began to lift again. The return trajectory carried back up to the ledge, where robots were running to and fro in confusion and waving things in the air, with a few—presumably the radiosensitive types that Dave Crookes had speculated about—writhing around on the floor under the close-range influence of the flyer's mapping radar. Lower down, visible at the edge of the glow being generated by the flares, the hillside opposite the cliff seemed to be alive with deranged figures waving, running hither and thither, and throwing themselves to the ground in all manner of agitation and commotion.

Then the swinging net caught on a construction of steel girders standing at one end of the ledge, and the line tightened. Joe Fellburg, who was with Drew West in the flyer's opened aft compartment—both of them suited up, as were all the flyer's occupants—crashed the winding mechanism into neutral, and the power winch whined in protest as it was jerked abruptly into reverse. "We're caught!" Fellburg yelled. "Level out and slacken it off for chrissakes!"

"Back it off, Clarissa!" West shouted, and Clarissa slammed into reverse thrust, throwing everyone violently forward against their restraining harnesses. The line went taut, yanking the winch off its mounting and trapping the line in a mess of crushed supports, buckled floorplates, and a seized winding drum. "The winch is wrecked!" Fellburg shouted. "Everything's screwed up!"

In the copilot's seat, Abaquaan increased vertical boost to provide lift while Clarissa slowed frantically and banked into a tight turn to take the strain off the line. "Christ, those missiles!" Abaguaan yelled. "We can't hang around here. You'll have to cut the line."

Zambendorf fought his way uphill across the tilted floor

and pulled himself into the aft compartment. "We can't give up now," he bellowed. "We've got him. Drew, give me the end of that auxiliary line and then reel me out. I'm going down there to attach a magnetic grab."

"You can't go down there, Karl," Fellburg protested.

"There isn't time to argue. Give me that line."

Fellburg clipped the auxiliary line to Zambendorf's harness, then took a rigger's tool belt from the doorway locker and attached it over his own suit. "You're crazy, but you'll still need some help," he said. "I'm coming too."

"Get right above the net and steady up, Clarissa," West called over the intercom. "Karl and Joe are going down with a magnet."

Below, the Kroaxian crowd was in pandemonium. All had seen the miracle of the heavenly beast descending to preserve the Enlightener as the Cliff of Judgment delivered its verdict, and the false priests who had condemned him being smitten to the ground by the Lifemaker's wrath. Once before had the Enlightener preached the true Word to the people in the marketplace, and the people had ridiculed him; but such was his wisdom and forebearance that in place of anger or retribution, he had chosen this way to open their eyes to the light, and to demonstrate the powerlessness of the priests before him. This time the people would listen and be grateful for the mercy that had been shown them.

"Indeed the Enlightener teaches the true Word of the Lifemaker!" they cried. "We shall not kill. We shall not enslave. We shall not be enslaved."

"Down with the false priests who teach hatred!"

"Down with the King and his ministers who wage war!"

The roaring of the voices was swollen even louder as the first contingent of the returning Kroaxian army came round the hill and joined in.

"We have returned to unseat the tyrant! We shall not kill!"

"All Carthogians are our brothers!"

"See, the Enlightener awaits us and has converted the

citizens of Pergassos as he promised! Praise the Enlightener!"

The citizens howled louder, and the crowd began closing in around the dignitaries' enclosure.

"Our soldiers have returned from the Meracasine. Indeed has the Enlightener spoken truly!"

"Out with Eskenderom!"

"Out with Frennelech!"

"No more shall we cringe beneath the heels of tyrants!"

"No more shall we tremble at the words of charlatans!"

"Out with them! Out with them!"

In the canopied enclosure, all was chaos as priests and courtiers, officials and dignitaries, counselors and ministers dashed backward, forward, and in circles shouting for guards to close ranks and for servants to fetch mounts. In the middle of the panic, Eskenderom and Frennelech collided. "Traitor!" Eskenderom screamed into the High Priest's face. "Thou holy vermin! Sump sludge! What bargain didst thou conclude with thy aliens that they should cheat me thus?"

"I?" Frennelech howled, outraged. "I?—thou royal emetic! Thou pox-blistered discharge vent! It is through thy contract with the sky-devils that they have defrauded *me!*"

"What sayest thou? Is this spectacle not thy final triumph that shall take away my crown and remove me from my realm?"

"Nay. What gibberish dost thou prattle? Is it not the fruitful consummation of *thy* design to promote this imposter, thy creation, before the people and thence to subordinate to royal command all authority hitherto invested in my office?"

Eskenderom shook his head. "Would I, by my orders to my handpicked agent, command the disintegration of my own army? What kind of priest's babbling is this?"

Eskenderom stared at Frennelech; Frennelech stared at Eskenderom. Both arrived at the same conclusion at the same instant.

"Zounds! Egad! Forsooth!" Eskenderom shrieked. "I

see it now—the aliens have outwitted us both! We have been betrayed!" He raised his fists high in the air. "Arghh! The leaching-tank scum! The drain-filter dregs! I'll have at them! I'll smear their jelly bodies across the valley of Gornod. Mormorel, rally the guard and let us ride now to the camp of the alien deceivers. All who value honor and dignity, follow me! And if we be blasted to rivets and strewn across the deserts, then at least it will be said that we were dismantled gloriously. To Gornod!"

"Have the equerry fetch the mounts," Frennelech called to Jaskillion. "Muster the Palace Guard and tell them we will ride with the King to the valley of Gornod to avenge this alien treachery. If the nation of Kroaxia is to be rent asunder by outworlders' stratagem, its final episode of glory shall not be Eskenderom's alone. To Gornod!"

Then the voices of the crowd rose to a crescendo. "Angels! See, angels are descending! Shining angels descend from the heavens!"

Above, two figures were lowering toward the Enlightener, who had returned to the execution ledge after casting himself forth and allowing his fall to be miraculously intercepted, and was now giving thanks at the sacred tree opposite the top of the stairway. The creature from heaven was watching down over them protectively, and at the far end of the ledge, the guard commander seemed to be trying to reorganize his cringing soldiers.

"How is he?" Zambendorf barked, struggling to maintain equilibrium on the wildly swinging line. The Taloids on the ledge had scattered from the falling cable when Drew West cut the line to the net from above, and seemed to be keeping their distance.

"Can't tell," Fellburg answered. "He seems out of it. The net's all caught up in this junk. We'll have to cut him out."

Zambendorf worked frantically to draw in the magnetic clamp on another line while Fellburg hacked into the net with a pair of long-handled cutters. "What's the score?" West's voice said over the intercom from the flyer.

"All a mess—Joe's cutting Moses out," Zambendorf

answered breathlessly. "Is the generator hooked up yet, Drew?"

"Ready when you are."

"Hurry it up down there," Abaquaan's voice said on the circuit.

"Watch out behind you," Clarissa warned.

Zambendorf looked round and saw that some of the Taloids seemed to have recovered and were coming across the ledge, brandishing objects that looked like weapons. "Get a move on, Joe," he shouted, and braced himself against the girders with his legs and one arm while helping to pull pieces of netting away with the other.

"That's it," Fellburg called.

"Hit the switch, Drew!" Zambendorf shouted. "Clarissa, take it up! Take it up!" Current flowed through the cable, and the flyer rose to take up the slack. At the same time Zambendorf and Fellburg were lifted away as West began to haul in the lines. Just as Moses swung clear of the girders, the other Taloids rushed forward and were instantly caught by the magnetic field to form a daisy-chain of six or seven figures joined head-to-toe, head-to-toe in a string extending to the ground. They hung convulsing helplessly as the field passing through their skins played havoc with their internal circuitry.

"Oh shit," Fellburg moaned miserably.

"Hold it, hold it!" Zambendorf shouted in his helmet. "They're stuck."

"I can't cut the current," West called down. "We'd lose Moses. Jeez, what a screw-up!"

"Let us down again, Drew, about ten feet," Zambendorf ordered. "Joe, we'll have to grab him and hope we can hold on."

They came back down, and a few seconds later Fellburg's voice said, "I've got one arm. Are you okay there on the other side, Karl?"

"Okay," Zambendorf yelled. "We've got him! Cut it now, Drew." West threw a switch to deactivate the magnet, and the chain of Taloids fell apart into bodies dropping all over the ledge among their terrified colleagues.

"We've got him!" Fellburg shouted. "Clarissa, let's get the hell outta here." As the flyer at last lifted away, a wrench that had almost been dislodged from a loop in Fellburg's tool belt fell away into the darkness beneath.

Far below, the crowd had seen the High Priest's Palace Guards snatched up into the air and scattered like playthings, and the Enlightener being borne away triumphantly by the angels. As he departed to join the Lifemaker, he sent something tumbling down to the multitude gathered at the bottom of the cliff. Figures rushed forward frenziedly to pick up the sacred symbol and hold it high for all the faithful to see. "A sign! A sign! We have been given a sign! Behold the form that has been given us to mark the Day of Miracles!"

"Behold the sign! Behold the sign!"

"We are saved! We are saved!"

From one side of the dignitaries' enclosure, most of which had by now been overrun, a ragged body of riders comprising the King, the High Priest, and a couple of hundred or so of their loyal followers and guards broke through the crowd and departed at full gallop amid jeers, catcalls, and a barrage of rocks and assorted other missiles.

Meanwhile, high above the craggy ridge rising behind the cliff, the flyer came out of the top of the cloudbank and streaked for the safety of the distant mountains.

37

A TENSE ATMOSPHERE HUNG OVER THE EMERGENCY meeting that had been called in the Directors' Conference Room on the top floor of the NASO Building in Washington, D.C. Samuel Dulaney, the NASO president, was sitting in the center on one side of the long, polished-mahogany table, with Walter Conlon and Warren Taylor from the North American Division on one side of him, and two European representatives on the other; facing them were Burton Ramelson and Gregory Buhl from GSEC, Robert Fairley—Ramelson's nephew from the GSEC affiliate New York Merchant Bank, and two of the consultants who had been involved in negotiating the funding for the *Orion* mission. Phillip Berness, the U.S. secretary of state and Julius Gorsche from his department were sitting clustered around one end of the table with Kevin Whaley, the presidential aide, and an advisor on international relations from the European Parliament.

Walter Conlon held up the sheet of paper that constituted one of his most damning pieces of evidence, copies of which he had already circulated, and stabbed at it with a finger of his other hand. It was a reproduction of a document that had been faked on instructions from Caspar Lang for Thelma's benefit; but Gerold Massey hadn't known it was a fake when he prepared an urgent communication for transmission from the *Orion*, and neither did Conlon. "It says right here in black and white, item five—'Antiaircraft missile, short-range, actively guided, infantry-launched. Model ILAAM-27 /F, Mark 4, "Banshee." Quantity: 24 . . .' And items six and seven call for twelve dummy warheads, normally used for training, and twelve *live* ones." Conlon lowered the paper and sent a challenging look round the table. "What could be clearer than that? Those weapons were shipped down to the Paduans at a time when it was known full well that Earth-people were at large in a purloined surface lander, and likely to show up in the very area where those weapons would be deployed. The implications don't have to be spelled out. This amounts to nothing less than attempted murder."

Buhl looked along the table at Berness. "Something like this couldn't have been agreed without Dan Leaherney knowing about it," he insisted. "What in God's name could have possessed him? I can't afford to see GSEC's name linked to this kind of thing if it ever becomes public knowledge." In other words, the mission was technically under political direction, and the corporation men were already preparing themselves fireproof boxes to jump into.

Berness shook his head. "I can't explain it, Greg. It goes beyond all the guidelines. I don't know what in hell's been going on out there."

"You, er . . . you still haven't told us how you come to have this document in your possession," Robert Fairley said, hoping to ease the strain by sidetracking.

"How I got it doesn't make any difference," Conlon replied tightly. "It's a reproduction of part of a loading manifest for one of the shuttles sent down to Padua base from the *Orion*. Why we should be shipping weapons down there to enable the Taloids to kill each other more effectively is a big enough question in itself, but the only purpose of the particular ones I've just indicated can be to kill *people*—our people."

Dulaney, the NASO chief, gnawed at his knuckle for a few seconds longer, straightened up in his chair, then pushed himself back, looked up at the others, and shook his head decisively. "I thought we were just giving token support to the ruler of a small country that's having insurgency problems." He shook his head again and pointed at the sheet of paper still in Conlon's hand. "But that?— That's enough to start a war! I mean, what in hell are our people there playing at? I can't let NASO even be suspected of condoning anything like that. Our involvement covers getting the *Orion* to Saturn and back, and the scientific research programs that we're committed to. We're not responsible for the mission's diplomatic and economic policies, and I can't promise to be supportive of them in any official capacity or public statement." What he meant was that if he didn't back Conlon on this one, Conlon would go straight to the media and to hell with the consequences.

One of the European NASO representatives next to Dulaney nodded. "That would have to be our position also."

"But what kind of policy are Leaherney's people trying to carry out?" another European asked from the far end. "From what Conlon said it sounded as if they were equipping a full-scale Taloid invasion. That's not token support. It's blatant power-politicking—meddling in alien affairs. Who sanctioned anything like that?"

"Does it matter?" Julius Gorsche asked. "It seems they managed to turn the whole thing into a fiasco anyway."

"It matters to me that the name of our government stands to be associated with whatever their next antic might be," the European replied coldly.

Berness spread his hands. "I don't know. Maybe the strain of being in charge of a mission that big, for that long a time, that far from Earth, is greater than anyone thought," he said. "But I can assure you, gentlemen, that the events that have been described are not compatible with any policy of the United States government. They must be a result either of some aberration involving the personnel delegated operational authority at Titan, or of a misinterpretation of our instructions. It goes without saying that further investigation of the matter will be initiated immediately."

Lies, Burton Ramelson thought to himself as he listened. You knew what the policies were, and you allowed your tacit approval to be understood, just like the rest of us. Typically, everyone was surreptitiously sharpening the hatchets in anticipation of a possible bloodletting, and at the same time trying their rubber gloves for size to show all clean hands afterward. But Ramelson hadn't yet been panicked into losing sight of the magnitude of what was at stake. He wondered if there might yet be a way of repairing the damage done and getting everything back on course. If so, it would best serve his purpose to see the *Orion*'s management exonerated and their reputability preserved, for despite whatever had gone wrong with the plan to assert Terran influence by aiding the Paduans—and Ramelson had suspicions that a lot more than met the eye could have been behind that—they were all loyal and capable, and would not be easily replaced. Ramelson needed more time to collect the facts on what had really happened at Titan, and was reluctant to commit himself to a hasty judgment. His response for now would therefore be neutral, he decided, but the circumstances would not allow any more bungling. One more miscalculation in the handling of the Paduan situation would be enough to lead him to conclude that Leaherney's team was beyond redemption, and to embark on whatever course of action would best protect his own interests and keep his reputation intact.

Having clarified his thoughts on the matter, he began, "I have to agree that on the face of it, these are alarming allegations. But they are, when all is said and done, just that and no more—allegations. Before we allow ourselves to be stampeded into a witch-hunt, I would like to propose that—" At that moment a tone sounded from the chairman's console recessed into the table before Dulaney.

"Excuse me, Burton," Dulaney said. "Calls aren't supposed to be put through unless extremely urgent. I'd better take this." He looked down and touched a button below the level of the table. "Yes, Bob?"

"Sorry to interrupt, Sam, but we've just had something through from Titan that I thought you'd want to hear about since it concerns the meeting. It came through from General Vantz about ten minutes ago, via his Communications Officer."

"What is it, Bob?" Dulaney asked. He turned a knob to increase the volume, and the others in the room sat forward in their chairs to listen.

"There's been some kind of god-awful commotion down in Padua city that culminated in Henry and a couple of hundred other Taloids' getting so screaming mad that they went galloping off to take out the Terran base there with their bare hands. Nobody on the ship ever saw anything like it before."

"Christ, that's terrible!" Dulaney exclaimed. "What happened to them?"

"Oh, they're okay," Bob's voice answered. "Our guys at the base saw them coming on the recce scopes and got the hell out. The base was evacuated—of personnel, anyhow—it seems they left a lot of equipment behind. Must have been a real panic."

"Who was in charge down there?" Dulaney asked, dismayed.

"Caspar Lang and Giraud. They got away in one of the military landers with the last of the garrison, but they hadn't arrived back at the *Orion* when the message was transmitted. Apparently they weren't being very communicative, so no one was too sure exactly what had happened. We're standing by for an update."

Dulaney frowned to himself for a second or two. "If they've been kicked out of Padua and we don't even have a base there anymore, it means the whole Paduan program just came apart at the seams."

"I know—that's why I thought you ought to hear about it," Bob said.

"Any more?" Dulaney asked.

"Not for now. Shall I call through there again when we get the next bulletin?"

"Yes, do that. Thanks, Bob. I'll talk to you later." Dulaney cut the call and looked up at the numb faces across the table. "Well, I guess you all heard that. It sounds as if they've really screwed up this time. Let's wait and see what comes through next . . ." His eyes came back to Ramelson. "Anyhow, in the meantime, where were we? You were just about to say something, I think, Burton."

Ramelson emitted a long, remorseful sigh. "I agree with Phil," he replied. "The most charitable view we can take is to attribute it all to psychological breakdown within the mission's directorate, caused by a combination of high stress, excessive demands of responsibility, and totally unforeseen effects of the remote extraterrestrial environment. It's imperative that the situation be remedied immediately, before we run into any further misadventures. My proposals are therefore as follows: . . ."

38

CAPTAIN MASON OF THE U.S. SPECIAL FORCES acknowledged the call on the monitor panel inside the guardroom of the main perimeter gatehouse at Genoa Base One.

"Taloid riders and vehicles approaching the gate, sir," the voice of Pfc. Caronetti reported from the searchlight post on the upper level. "Some of the passengers appear to be Terrans." At the same moment the screen in front of Mason came to life to show the view being picked up by a rooftop camera. A procession of walking wagons and mounted Taloids was approaching along the broad avenue between steel lattices, girderwork frames, and pipe-draped processing tanks that led from the city. The pace was slow and easy, giving no cause for alarm.

"I wonder what the hell this is," Mason muttered over his shoulder to Petrakoff, the guard sergeant.

"Five'll get you ten it's Zambendorf and his people showing up at last," Petrakoff said.

Mason stared at the screen for a few seconds longer, and then nodded. "Yeah . . . you're probably right, Jan. You'd better alert the Base Commander. Call three more of the guys out front and get them helmeted up on standby. I'm going outside to join Pierce and Macnally and find out what's happening."

In the first of the open carriages behind the advance guard of Genoese cavalry, Zambendorf was sitting between Abaquaan and Arthur, facing Galileo and Moses, who had their backs to the raised platform supporting the seats of the two Taloid coachmen. The rest of the team was in the second carriage with Leonardo, the Genoese mapmaker, and Lancelot, Arthur's knight who had brought Galileo out of Padua. Various aides and officials from Arthur's court followed in the train behind, which included Leonardo's family, Lord Nelson, and a representative contingent of Druids.

The advance guard emerged into the clear area in front of the main gate through the perimeter fence of Genoa Base, and moments later a searchlight beam swung round to illuminate the procession in brilliant white and transform the surrounding structures into ghostly skeletons of steel standing out vividly against the background darkness.

"I don't see Tango Baker Two anywhere," Abaquaan said, turning in his seat to scan the immense, squat, stubby-winged forms of the surface landers, parked amid floodlit clutters of service gantries, maintenance platforms, cargo hoists, and access ramps on the far side of the fence. "Andy and the boys must have gone back up to the ship already."

"Well, at least they should have come out of it all with their noses clean," Zambendorf answered."

"Let's hope so."

After snatching Moses from the cliff at Padua, Zambendorf had decided to fly directly to Camelot, Arthur's residence, to deliver Moses safely into the Genoese care and reunite him with his brother, Galileo, before the team gave itself up to the Terran authorities at Genoa Base. The Genoese had insisted, however, on making the occasion one for all kinds of elaborate farewell formalities which had involved seemingly half the Taloids in the country, and the team had remained there, resting and eating in the flyer, for fully twenty-four hours. To minimize the risk of the proceedings' being distastefully interrupted, the team had maintained a strict communications blackout, omitting even to contact Massey and Thelma, since a genuine ignorance of the team's whereabouts would be less likely to compromise their position in the face of questioning by Leaherney's people. Finally, to round everything off in style, Arthur had proposed a grand procession across the city to carry the team to the Terran base; not wishing to risk unwittingly giving any offense, Zambendorf had accepted the offer, leaving the flyer parked in Arthur's rear courtyard to be collected later by its rightful owners.

It had been a good try, Zambendorf thought to himself, and even if in the final part of it all they hadn't succeeded in rendering Padua completely harmless, at least the nation of Genoa had been kept intact for the time being. He could only hope that the team's gesture would attract enough attention to cause the mission's directors to have second thoughts about the whole question of Terran–Taloid relationships, and hopefully would stimulate a more enlightened outlook among the policymakers on Earth. And if it turned out that he had soured his backers and promoters sufficiently to permanently impair his career, then that was just too bad. He had stood by the principles that mattered on his own scale of values and had achieved something that he believed worthwhile. He had done as much as anyone could have, and the future could take its course. He had no regrets.

"See how brightly the violet halos shine around the Lumian flying-ships," Kleippur said from beside the Wearer. "Dost thou still see them as magic beasts sent from heaven, Groork?"

Groork shook his head. "Nor the Lumians as angels. What more dismal a prospect could be imagined than that all the universe's knowledge could be contained in one ancient book? Nothing new to discover? Nothing more to be learned? Never again the excitement of exploring the unknown? How pathetic is the future that some would wish upon themselves!"

"Your future, at least, promises to be a busy one," Thirg said. "The answers to the questions that I hear you asking now will not spin themselves into skeins of words as effortlessly as before, however, I fear."

"Maybe so, but thou shalt see that my energies are undiminished, and the mystic's passion is not quenched but merely redirected," Groork replied confidently.

"The application of this industriousness to the studies into which thou hast declared intent to launch thyself will show interesting results indeed, if my prognostications serve me well," Kleippur commented.

"I do not doubt it," Thirg said, sighing. He still hadn't recovered fully from the astonishment with which he had learned of Groork's escapades in the Meracasine and at Pergassos, and his even greater amazement at observing his brother transformed into a staunch advocate of the methods of impartial questioning and objective inquiry. Now that Groork had flown through the sky, his latest passion was to view firsthand the other worlds that Thirg had told him about, and he had been pestering the Wearer for an opportunity to go on one of the voyages that the Lumian flying-ships made to the Great Ship beyond the sky.

As for Carthogia, while the threat from the Kroaxians had been temporarily extinguished, the longer-term future was far less certain. The issuing to Eskenderom of weapons sufficiently potent to have deterred the Wearer from honoring his pledge to Groork seemed to confirm that the Lumian king was firmly committed to promoting rivalry among the Robian nations in order to obtain their dependency and ultimately their complete subjugation. It was unlikely, therefore, that Kleippur would see his realm free to determine its own destiny; the Lumian conditions for supplying the weapons that Carthogia needed would doubtless entail sacrifice of its independence just as surely as would conquest by a reconstituted Kroaxian army at some later date.

On the other hand, it seemed that despite their arts and their skills, the Lumians were as divided among themselves as the royal houses and the clergy of Kroaxia and

Serethgin. There were other, more powerful kings in Lumia than the king who ruled the Great Ship, the Wearer had said, and the Lumian system of government constrained the actions of its kings, making them very much subject to the approval of their citizens. The Wearer's many friends who held positions of high office in the trades guilds of Lumian town criers and heralds would spread the news far and wide of the Wearer's willingness to anger the Great Ship's king and face imprisonment in protest against Robia's treatment. That the Wearer and his followers had chosen to defy the Great Ship's king and were willing to face imprisonment upon their return was evidence that integrity and high moral principle were not unknown among Lumians, and that was grounds enough for hope. Kleippur, therefore, characteristically coming to the conclusion that all was not necessarily lost, had refused to allow his capacity for action to be weakened by an unduly pessimistic outlook and braced himself to face the future with fortitude and the resolve to make the best he could of such opportunities for bettering his situation as might present themselves. And a better example than that to model his own attitude on, he wouldn't find anywhere, Thirg had decided.

Three figures in Terran military suits walked forward from the gate as the procession drew up. "Well, I suppose this is it, Otto," Zambendorf said. "Thank Arthur and his people again for their hospitality and tell them it might be a while, but I'm sure we'll be back to see them again sometime." Abaquaan relayed the message via the transmogrifier, and Arthur responded in like vein. Clarissa, Vernon, West, and Fellburg came forward from the second carriage, and after a final round of handshakes and salutations, Zambendorf turned to face the three soldiers waiting patiently behind him. "Thank you for the courtesy, er . . . Captain, isn't it? Well, everyone's accounted for. We're all yours."

"Captain Mason, Special Forces," a voice replied. The figure wearing a captain's insignia peered at the nametag on Zambendorf's suit and at the tags of the two others nearest him. "You are Zambendorf and his people, I take it."

"Of course we are. Who else did you expect to come wandering in from the surface of Titan?"

"It's good to see you back. A lot of people were getting worried." Behind Mason, several soldiers left the guard-house to open the gate, and another group of figures was approaching from the base administration building.

"Well, aren't you supposed to arrest us or something?" Zambendorf said.

"No," Mason answered. "I guess you're maybe gonna have to answer a few questions about stealing that lander, but you probably had your reasons . . . I don't know. Any-how, we don't have any orders that say anything about arresting anybody. The Base Commander should be on his way here now. He'll know a lot more than I do."

Zambendorf blinked with surprise at the mildness of the reception. "This is amazing," he murmured, more to the others with him than to Mason. "I'd have thought Leaherney would have been more upset about what hap-pened to Henry's army. In a way I feel quite disap-pointed."

"Maybe we didn't achieve as much as we thought," Abaquaan said uneasily.

"Even Caspar Lang wasn't bothered? I figured he'd be apopleptic," Clarissa said.

Mason looked puzzled behind his faceplate. "What does it have to do with them?" he asked. "They're all out—finished. General Vantz is in charge of the mission now."

"Out?" Zambendorf repeated incredulously. "Who? When? How?"

"Leaherney, Giraud, Lang," Mason told them. "I guess a whole heap of crud finally hit the fan somewhere back home. A directive came through to the *Orion* about twelve, maybe fourteen hours ago, relieving them of command, effective immediately, and putting the mission under full NASO control. They upset the Taloids over at Padua somehow and got their asses kicked outta the base there—musta had something to do with that. Anyhow, here's Mackeson, the base chief, now."

The group from inside the base arrived and began to usher Zambendorf's party through the gate. "Harold Mackeson, NASO—Genoa Base Commander," the most prominent among them announced in an English accent. "Glad to see you're all safe. Welcome back again. When it started looking as if you might have had an accident, O'Flynn finally owned up about the flyer. Do you know, he'd been faking the log all the time and nobody missed it—extraordinary! We've been calling you nonstop, but heard no reply. Is the flyer okay?"

"Yes, and not far from here," Zambendorf said as they all began to walk toward the administration building. "I gather there have been some changes."

"Oh, you wouldn't believe the ruckus: Giraud and Lang getting thrown out of Padua; the base there being abandoned; Leaherney's whole team out on their ear... There's been more going on than in all the time the *Orion*'s been in orbit."

"What happened at Padua?" Zambendorf asked.

"Well, Henry's gone, with his chief priest and just about all the others that Giraud and Company were dealing with," Mackeson replied. "It seems the Paduan Taloids had some kind of revolution and got rid of the whole bunch. Vantz—he's in charge now—has sent down an exploratory team, who have managed to make contact with the new leaders that seem to be emerging from it all."

"What started this revolution, or whatever it was?" Abaquaan asked.

"I don't know if you heard about it, but some kind of new, nonviolent religion broke out suddenly among the Druids, then became all the rage in Henry's army and messed up his invasion plans... something to do with some Taloid messiah who appeared out of nowhere. Well, apparently this messiah and his religion finally found their way to Padua. Result—out with Henry, and out with our arms-dealers. To be honest with you, old boy, I can't say I'm all that sorry to hear it either."

Zambendorf stopped walking abruptly. Mackeson halted a split second later and looked back with a puzzled expression. "What was that again?" Zambendorf said. "What's happened with the Paduans?"

"A new religion is sweeping the whole country," Mackeson answered. "They say everybody's equal, they won't kill, they won't fight wars, and they've told us where to shove our weapons."

Zambendorf swallowed hard. The formula sounded very familiar. "If that's true, then the Paduans aren't very likely to try attacking Genoa again," he said.

Mackeson snorted. "Oh, from what I've heard, you can put any thoughts like that completely out of your head, old chap. The Genoese are their brothers now. Everyone's their brother. They aren't going to be attacking anybody."

Gasps of surprise were audible from the rest of Zambendorf's party. "My God! Do you know what this means?..." Zambendorf looked back toward the gate, where the Taloids were standing and watching, their hands lifted in a final salute. He looked back at Mackeson, waved his arms excitedly, and pointed. "That's Arthur and his advisors. The messiah's there too, with his brother. They don't know about any of this yet. We have to tell them!"

"What?" Mackeson sounded bemused. "That's absurd. How could a messiah cause all that fuss and not know about it? Be sensible old boy, please."

"It would take too long to explain now," Zambendorf said. "But we have to tell them. It's important. Come on, Otto." Without waiting for an answer, he turned and marched back in the direction of the gate. Abaquaan started after him with the transmogrifier.

"Wait," Mackeson called over the radio. They stopped and looked back. "Trying to communicate it all to the Taloids through just that box would be a hell of a tedious business," Mackeson said. He waved an arm to indicate an open extension built onto the end of the administration building just ahead. "That annex is our meeting room for Taloid talks, and communications equipment is installed there. We'd get along a lot faster if we brought Arthur and his friends inside where we can show them some pictures too."

"That sounds good," Zambendorf agreed. Abaquaan nodded, and they started walking back again.

Mackeson switched his suit radio to another channel. "Mackeson to Captain Mason at the gate. Bring the Taloids there inside, would you, and have them escorted to the admin block annex. Also put a call through to the duty controller and have the lights switched on in the annex and a couple of communications techs suited up and sent out. It looks as if we're going to have an impromptu conference."

Fifteen minutes later, Zambendorf was standing in the center of a mixed group of Terrans and Taloids inside the annex, staring wide-eyed and speechless at the scene being transmitted from a NASO reconnaissance drone hovering over Padua city. It was a telescopic view of an evidently wild procession that stretched from one end of the city to the other. Thousands of Taloids were involved, festively dressed, singing, dancing, waving pennants, bearing banners, and playing musical instruments. The ecstasy and rejoicing could be felt from the pictures.

But most astonishing was the shape that seemed to be the centerpiece of the whole celebration, which was being pulled along on a large, elaborately decorated and draped, mobile platform by several dozen Taloids fanned out ahead and hauling lines. As best Zambendorf could estimate from the size of the Taloids moving alongside, it stood about ten feet high and seemed to be fashioned from some metal that gave it a reddish hue. There could be no mistaking what it represented: It was a wrench—an immense, painstakingly rendered, replica of a standard toolbox wrench. And immediately behind the platform bearing the Sacred Wrench, a huge banner was being carried on which were written crudely but recognizably the mystic symbols U.S. GOVERNMENT.

"Good heavens! Did we do that?" Zambendorf said disbelievingly.

"Those are the guys that Arthur was so worried about?" Joe Fellburg asked in a weak voice. "He doesn't have any problems now. It's all over down there."

Abaquaan shook his head dazedly. "I'm not seeing this. Somebody tell me it isn't real."

"Well, Caspar Lang told Karl way back that he wanted him to sell Moses in Padua," Drew West reminded everybody. He shrugged and tossed out his hands. "So he got what he wanted—Moses went over real big. Is it our fault if Caspar miscalculated the effects?"

"That sure was some act, Karl," Vernon complimented. "You know, I don't think even Gerry could top that one."

Clarissa looked at the screen again and wrinkled her nose. "And before anyone tells the president, the answer's positively no," she told everybody. "There's no way I'm gonna try a repeat performance over Moscow—just no way!"

Thirg, Kleippur, and Groork exchanged awed looks. "Do I understand this news correctly?" Kleippur said. "The Wearer is not to be imprisoned? Already word of the injustices of the Great Ship's king have reached the mightier kings of Lumia, and they have sent orders by which he and his lieutenants have been dismissed?"

Thirg nodded slowly. "Now, methinks, we see the Wearer's plan unfolding in its entirety," he said. "Carthogia saved and free from further threat of molestation; Eskenderom and Frennelech undone; Kroaxia pacified and reduced to harmlessness within a single bright; . . . and now within the Lumian house itself, the would-be architects of havoc exposed and vanquished. Indeed these are powerful champions that good fortune hath appointed as our allies."

"Carthogia shall be free to pursue its quest for knowledge, and its borders shall be always open to true inquirers from all nations," Kleippur declared. "Thus shall the works of all be concerted, our resources directed to enterprises of constructiveness, and one day robeings shall, through their own diligence and inventiveness, find Lumia and the other shining worlds beyond the sky."

"And the nations like Kroaxia, whose collective understanding will require time yet before it is mature, have been provided with a harmless distraction which will predispose them meanwhile in thought and deed toward reasonableness and tolerance," Groork said. "We must be careful to ensure that our acquiring of Lumian knowledge is paralleled by the cultivation of a comparable measure of such Lumian wisdom."

"So it shall be," Kleippur assured him.

Eventually the two groups repeated their farewells, this time amid a lighter, more exuberant mood than had prevailed previously. The Terrans entered the airlock at the rear of the annex, and Zambendorf turned in the outer door to send a last wave back to the Taloids before passing through into the administration building proper, where the first thing everybody did was get out of their EV suits in the lock antechamber. Then, feeling reborn, they moved out through the far door to return to the wonderful world of bright, airy corridors, people in shirt-sleeves and slacks, the smell of canteen food and the clatter of cutlery, the sounds of shoes on metal stairways, and piped music in the restrooms.

"Just think of it," Abaquaan said to Zambendorf as they followed Mackeson and one of his officers to be officially checked into the base. "A hot bath, clean sheets, and as much uninterrupted sleep as you want. What more could anyone ask for? Who'd have ever thought we'd find a NASO base on Titan the last word in luxury? You know, Karl, I've got a feeling that the place at Malibu might never seem the same again."

Zambendorf blinked. "Malibu? Why, I can't even imagine it any more. In fact I can't imagine anything beyond getting back up to the *Orion*. That's the last word in luxury as far as I'm concerned, Otto, the *Orion*—pure, blissful, unashamed luxury."

Meanwhile Thirg was looking out of the presidential

carriage at the head of the stately cavalcade proceeding through the outskirts of Menassim along the picturesque and colorful Avenue of Independence. The crowds lining the way to watch the carriages and the soldiers pass seemed buoyant and joyful, as if they could somehow sense or read in the faces in the carriages the good tidings that would affect the whole land. Thirg had never seen the city looking quite so beautiful, with the fading light of bright's-end softening the hues of the trees along the avenue and painting a delicate blue haze over the rolling forests outside the city and the mountains rising distantly behind. Ahead, he could see the tall, clean lines of the new buildings of the central city rising proudly above the intervening suburbs as if in anticipation of the new era about to be born.

A gentle breeze was blowing from the east, carrying the fragrant scents of distilled tar-sands and furnace-gas ventings, and a family of dome-backed concrete-pourers was laying out filter beds on the far bank of the bend where the river flanked the avenue, downstream from the ingot-soaking pits. From somewhere off in the distance he could hear the muted strains of a power hammer thudding contentedly while nearer to the road a flock of raucous coilspring winders was playing counterpoint with the warbling of a high-pressure relief valve, and on all sides the undergrowth chirped happily with piezoelectric whines and whistles. He had a true brother now, a home again, and a patron, and the soldiers and priests of Kroaxia would trouble him no more.

Yes indeed, Thirg, Asker-of-Questions-No-Longer-Forbidden, thought to himself as he gazed out at the scene in contentment, it was a beautiful world.

Epilogue

GEROLD MASSEY STRETCHED HIMSELF BACK IN AN ARM-chair in one corner of the team's lounge in Globe II, finished his scotch and soda, and set the glass down on a utility ledge built into the side of the communications console at which Drew West was sitting with the chair reversed to face the room. Thelma was with Fellburg and Clarissa on a couch folded down from the opposite wall; Zambendorf was sprawled in another armchair near Vernon, who was perched on a stool with his back to the shelf being used as a bar; and Abaquaan was leaning by the door. They had been back aboard the *Orion* for almost a week.

"I don't think there can be much doubt that the Taloids' future is assured now," Massey said. "The rest of the Paduan alliance is falling apart. The Venetians threw their king out yesterday, and the last I heard the one in Milan had decided to climb down gracefully and sent Moses an invitation to visit the city. He's probably hoping to salvage what he can by proposing some system of joint management."

"So there's no chance of Titan's being turned into some kind of colony?" Vernon said.

Massey shook his head. "No way that I can see. Any possibility of that has been scuttled permanently. The Taloids will never accept second-class status now. They're the chosen ones. Their God has spoken to them and told them they're as good as anyone. Anybody who tries to tell them differently can go jump in a methlake. They'll trade with you, sure—their kind of know-how for your kind of know-how, but only as equal partners. If you've got any ideas of exploitation or screwing anyone on the deal, forget it."

Zambendorf swirled his sherry round in his glass and watched it for a second, then looked up and nodded. "And the Western world is going to have to play it that way because if it doesn't Asia will. And what's more, it won't be much longer before the Soviets arrive. Then everybody will be competing against everybody to give the Taloids a better deal."

The *Orion* would be leaving Titan in ten days since many of the mission personnel—Massey and Vernon, for example—had pressing affairs to attend to back home. All remaining material and equipment would be shipped to the surface and used to expand Genoa Base One into a permanent installation, where a skeleton crew of scientific researchers, Taloidologists, and other specialists would remain behind under the command of Vantz's deputy, Commander Craig, until the arrival of the Japanese ship in five month's time. They would probably rotate to Earth at some later date with the Japanese, by which time the *Orion* would be returning with more people and equipment. With the completion of the Soviet vessel and the others that would come after it, a regular two-way traffic would eventually evolve.

Massey picked up his glass again and passed it to Vernon for a refill. "I don't often say things like this, but I think we can all congratulate ourselves on a job that worked out pretty well," he said, looking about the room. "I have to say that I'll miss you all after we get back. It's strange how things sometimes work out, isn't it—I came aboard determined to run you out of business, and here I am coming out of it with a whole bunch of new friends."

"Well, I'll drink to a long continuation of it, Gerry," Vernon said. "I'm amazed at how everything turned out too."

Massey accepted his glass and cast an eye curiously round the cabin again at the others, who were being unusually quiet. "I guess what I'm trying to say is that I'll stay off your backs from now on," he told them. "I don't suppose we'll ever see quite eye to eye on some things, but I have to admit I've been forced to reevaluate a lot of what I thought I was sure of. So it's live and let live, huh?" Despite the gallant face that he was doing his best to maintain, there was an undertone of disappointment that he couldn't quite conceal. He spread his hands and concluded, with a grin and a sigh, "I just thought you'd like to know."

Nobody responded immediately. Zambendorf raised his head and looked from one to another of his colleagues. "You don't seem exactly overenthralled," he remarked. "We can speak freely in front of Gerry and Vernon now. Aren't you looking forward to going home again? Think of the TV spectaculars we'll be able to put together after this—with a much stronger science flavor than ever before, which will appeal to younger people . . . maybe a world tour. We could establish an Institute of Astral Parapsychology, possibly, with Osmond as the founder—there'll be other backers besides GSEC. We might even be able to straighten things out with Ramelson again. Who knows?"

The atmosphere remained wet-weekendish. "It's a living, I guess," Abaquaan agreed vapidly from the doorway. In his mind he was copiloting the flyer again, and comparing it to the prospect of hanging around hotel lobbies and theater foyers, collecting snippets of gossip about gullible, witless people who had nothing to offer him and who didn't interest him. He had several ideas on improving the transmogrifier that he would have liked to discuss with Dave Crookes, who would be among the party staying behind. But besides all that, he realized that he cared what happened to Arthur's Taloids; they were among the few people he'd met outside of Zambendorf's team whom he had not simply dismissed as suckers. They valued their minds and were willing to rely on themselves without need of magical powers or supernatural revelations as substitutes for thinking. In Abaquaan's book that made them worth the effort of seeing that the feeling was mutual.

Clarissa hadn't had so much fun for years and was feeling a little nostalgic. As the base at Genoa was expanded and more Terran installations began to appear across the surface, there would be more demand for pilots than pilots available to meet them, she reflected ruefully. She could think of more attractive propositions than having to deal with jerks like Herman Thoring again, who thought the world stopped revolving for five minutes every time he went to the bathroom. Publicity management, she had decided, was the manufacture of make-believe news out of trivia when nothing newsworthy was to be said. On Titan she had cultivated too much of an appetitie for the real thing to want any part of an imitation again. "How wonderful," she said in a flat voice. "Maybe we could make some extra bucks by doing TV commercials for psychic-proof spoons."

Drew West thought back to the world of booking fees and box-office takes, and then to the world of the Taloids, ice mountains, methane oceans, vegetable cities, and mechanical jungles. He had always had a penchant for enriching his life through frequent changes of scenery and atmosphere and spicing it with dashes of the unusual and the exciting whenever possible. That was what had drawn him out of the domain of more orthodox, humdrum, show-business affairs and resulted eventually in his gravitating into Zambendorf's team, where he had remained for far longer than had been the case with any of his previous positions. But his restlessness for something new had been making itself felt again for some time before leaving Earth, and he had contemplated moving on even before the sudden prospect of the *Orion* mission to Mars had caused him to postpone any decision. What had happened on Titan would make the old life seem that much more uninspiring. Although he had no firm plans or prospects, in principle the decision was made. He raised his glass, took a long sip of his drink, and said nothing.

"I guess for me it's been kinda like the old days," Joe Fellburg said. "You know what I mean—I feel like I was back in the service out of retirement, except on reflection maybe I'd retired too early in the first place." He frowned, as if not satisfied that the words conveyed what he had meant to say, then shook his head with a sigh and resigned himself to the fact that it didn't make much difference anyway. "I dunno . . . Anyhow, we'll get used to it again in the end, probably." He had enjoyed having military people around him again and the feeling of being involved in something that mattered again instead of just playing games. It was his rapport with the team that had held him, not the business the team was in. Now that he saw that clearly, he was far from certain that he would be able to make the relationship work again.

Thelma looked from side to side uncertainly, and then across at Zambendorf, who was watching curiously. She spread her hands and shook her head. "Well, I'm gonna say what I think everyone's feeling. Look, you know how it is with me—I'm a Ph.D. in physics and mathematics, but I've always protested a society that thinks more of performing adolescent Neanderthals than the people who design the amplifiers that they scream into. But with the Taloids I really feel we did something important for people who were worth it, and who genuinely appreciated it. And that was just a start. There's so much more to be done down there, and I think we could contribute a lot to that too. But I guess none of us is exactly crazy about the idea of . . ." Thelma broke off and gave Zambendorf a puzzled look as she realized that his eyes were twinkling roguishly. Her expression changed to one of suspicion. "Karl, you're up to something. What are you laughing at? You know something that you're not letting on about, don't you."

Clarissa looked up at him. "What is it, Zambendorf?" she demanded. Zambendorf smirked back at her and remained silent. "Come on, you're not handing out tablets on some mountaintop now. Give."

"Well, thanks to my power to divine the future by

supernatural—" Zambendorf began, but Abaquaan cut him off.

"Never mind all that crap. What do you know that you haven't told us?"

"I don't exactly 'know' anything for sure yet, Otto, which is why I didn't want to risk raising anyone's hopes too soon," Zambendorf replied. "But I had a pretty good idea of your attitudes—I feel the same way myself. So I took the liberty of presuming—" The call tone sounded from the console behind West. "Ah, this might even be the news I've been waiting for," Zambendorf said as West swiveled his chair round to accept.

"Is Karl Zambendorf there?" a NASO flight officer inquired from the screen a couple of seconds later. "This is Captain Matthews, calling on behalf of General Vantz."

"Here, Captain," Zambendorf said, putting down his drink and rising to face the screen.

"General Vantz would like to know if you and your people could be available in Globe I for an interview with him and Commander Craig immediately after the current shift—say at fifteen hundred hours. Would that be convenient for everyone?"

"Oh, I don't think we have any prior engagements," Zambendorf replied airily. "Yes, thank you, Captain Matthews—that would be most convenient."

"I'll put you down for then," Matthews confirmed. "Fifteen hundred hours, in the executive office suite, Globe I."

"Did Vantz say anything else?" Zambendorf asked curiously.

"Only that he didn't think there would be much of a problem," Matthews answered. "Commander Craig will need all the help he can get. I think you can take it there'll be a slot for anyone who wants one."

"Thank you, Captain. That tells me all I wanted to know. Thank you very much indeed!"

"Fine," Matthews said. "We'll see you later." The screen blanked out.

Thelma blinked her eyes several times, shook her head, and whispered disbelievingly, "Did I really hear that? We're going to stay here with Craig's group at Genoa Base and wait for the Japanese? Is that what he said?"

"Well, if you want to, anyway," Zambendorf said. "I mean, I didn't want to assume anything. I just thought—"

"You didn't want to assume!" Clarissa exclaimed accusingly. "Hey, what is it with this guy? How long have you known us, Karl? So what did you do—go talk to Vantz?"

"Yesterday," Zambendorf said. "He wanted to discuss it with Craig before committing himself. That was why—"

"Hey, guys—it's okay!" Fellburg shouted, swinging his head from side to side, looking up, and beaming. "It's okay. Everything's gonna be okay." He burst into loud laughter and clapped Clarissa heartily on the back, causing her to slop her drink.

"Hey, Kong—lay off of that, willya!"

Drew West started laughing too, and so did Thelma. Massey caught Vernon's eye, and his face split slowly into a broad grin. Suddenly the whole room was full of noisy, excited, laughing voices. Zambendorf stood up amid a barrage of backslapping and raised a hand to acknowledge the congratulations coming from every side. "Tonight we must throw a party for all our friends, especially the ones who will be staying on," he said raising his voice above the commotion. "But before that, we can have a private celebration. It's time to move this show along—to the Globe IV Recreation Deck and the bar, I say! The first round is mine."

Everyone began moving toward the door, and at that moment Osmond Periera burst in with Malcom Wade close behind. They seemed excited about something. "I've been studying the transcripts of some of the conversations with the Taloids down in Padua," Periera said, waving some papers. "All that business about the revolution and the new religion didn't just happen, you know, Karl. There were some good reasons—amazing things going on in the sky at the time, all well authenticated. I don't think we're the only beings who are watching developments down on Titan. There are aliens here too—alien UFOs around Titan!"

Zambendorf brought a hand up to his face and frowned down at the floor over his knuckle. If he was going into a new line of business, there was no better time to start, he supposed. He drew in a long breath and looked up at Periera, hesitating for a moment as he searched for the right words. And then he saw Massey smiling ruefully and shaking his head behind Periera's shoulder. Massey was right—there was no point. With even a million years to try and explain, there would have been no point.

Zambendorf sighed and draped an arm affectionately around Periera's shoulder as he turned him around and began walking him back toward the door. "Really, Osmond, my friend?" he said. "It sounds fascinating. We're just on our way to the bar. Why don't you and Malcom join us. You can tell us all about the UFOs there. It will be far more comfortable, and I'm sure you'd agree that we all owe ourselves some time to rest and relax a little, eh?"

the only beings who are watching over you [illegible] them. There are aliens here, too—alien! This [illegible]-rand!"

Commandant brought a hand up to his face and frowned down at the floor over his knuckle. If he was going into a new line of business, there was no better time to start, he supposed. He drew in a deep breath and looked up at Periera, hesitating for a moment as he searched for the right words. And then he saw Massey smiling ruefully and shaking his head behind Periera's shoulder. Massey was right—there was no point. With even a skilled [illegible] [illegible], there would have been no point.

Commandant sighed and [illegible] slipped an arm around Periera's shoulder as he turned him around and began walking him back toward the door. "Really, Desmond, my friend," he said. "It sounds fascinating. We're just on our way to the [illegible]. Why don't you [illegible] [illegible] [illegible] there? It will be far more comfortable, and I'm sure you'd agree that we all owe ourselves some time to rest and relax a little, eh?"

ABOUT THE AUTHOR

JAMES HOGAN WAS born in London in 1941 and educated at the Cardinal Vaughan Grammar School, Kensington. He studied general engineering at the Royal Aircraft Establishment, Farnborough, subsequently specializing in electronics and digital systems.

After spending a few years as a systems design engineer, he transferred into selling and later joined the computer industry as a salesman, working with ITT, Honeywell, and Digital Equipment Corporation. He also worked as a life insurance salesman for two years "... to have a break from the world of machines and to learn something more about people."

In mid-1977 he moved from England to the United States to become a Senior Sales Training Consultant, concentrating on the applications of minicomputers in science and research for DEC.

At the end of 1979, Hogan opted to write full-time. He is now living in northern California.